Children of the Mist

Nigel Tranter

CORONET BOOKS
Hodder and Stoughton

The right of Nigel Tranter to be identified as the author of this work has been asserted by him in accordance with the Copyright, Designs and Patents Act 1988.

British Library C.I.P.

Tranter, Nigel
Children of the Mist
I. Title
823.912[F]

ISBN 0 340 57099 7

Printed and bound in Great Britain for Hodder and Stoughton Paperbacks, a division of Hodder and Stoughton Limited, Mill Road, Dunton Green, Sevenoaks, Kent TN13 2YA (Editorial Office: 47 Bedford Square, London WC1B 3DP) by Clays Ltd, St Ives plc.

CHILDREN OF THE MIST

Patrick MacGregor of Balquhidder himself, a hot-eyed man of early middle years, came pushing up to mount the chancel-step. He did not join Alastair and Ewan but moved behind them on their stone-slab, to the altar itself. Thereon was draped a plaid of the clan tartan, part-covering it. This he reached out to twitch off, to a great shouting.

Underneath was a man's head, a dark-haired, crumpled-featured, twisted-mouthed head, horribly blackened at the neck – Drummond's, of Drummond-Earnoch.

Balquhidder placed a hand on that bloody trophy. "Before God, all here present, and Himself, MacGregor, I, Patrick, swear to defend and avow the deed done, to maintain the honour and repute of Clan Alpin, unto the death! This I do affirm," he cried.

To resounding applause there was a concerted surge forward to follow suit, by all present, hands outstretched to touch that ravaged head and swear, Alastair almost overwhelmed in the rush.

When all had made their vows, every eye was turned on their chief. For his part, that young man looked at Ewan. His uncle nodded and shrugged in one; but the nod was towards the altar.

"Himself! Himself! MacGregor!" the cry went up.

Principal Characters in order of appearance

Alastair MacGregor of Glenstrae: MacGregor Himself, Chief of Clan Alpin

Duncan Campbell of Glenorchy: Known as Black Duncan of the Cowl. Chieftain of a Campbell sept.

Robert Ban MacGregor: Illegitimate uncle of the Chief.

Ewan MacGregor of Larachan: Uncle and Tutor of Glenstrae.

John MacGregor of Dochard: Brother to Glenstrae.

Gregor MacGregor of Roro: Chieftain of a sept.

Lady Marie Gray: Wife of the Master of Gray, daughter of the Earl of Orkney.

Mary Gray: Illegitimate daughter of the Master of Gray, and mistress of the Duke of Lennox.

Ludovick, Duke of Lennox: Cousin of the King.

Master of Gray: Patrick, heir to Lord Gray, and renowned in Scottish politics.

King James the Sixth

Sir John Maitland: Chancellor of Scotland.

Sir John Campbell of Cawdor: Chieftain of another Campbell sept.

John Stewart, Earl of Atholl: Great noble.

Drummond of Drummond-Earnoch: Royal forester.

Anne of Denmark: Queen of James the Sixth.

Archibald, Earl of Argyll: MacCailean Mhor, Chief of Clan Campbell.

Alexander Menzies of that Ilk: Chief of Clan Menzies.

Thomas Duncanson: A Dumbarton lawyer.

Aulay MacAulay of Ardencaple: Dunbartonshire laird.

Campbell of Ardkinglas: Chieftain of another Campbell sept.

Sir John Murray of Tullibardine: Powerful Highland laird. Later Earl of Tullibardine.

Alastair MacGregor stood staring down Glen Strae from the terrace of the hillside on which stood his modest castle, youthful brows downdrawn. He was a friendly enough young man, and suitably neighbourly normally, but he was going to find it difficult to be neighbourly towards this visitor, he well knew. At least he had had warning; the Campbell had announced his arrival, by means of a panting, sweating gillie, in advance.

Down there, southwards, where the track wound its way through the valley to the gleaming waters of great Loch Awe, Alastair could see the party approaching, still almost a mile off. He could pick out three horsemen amongst what might be two score or so of running gillies. Duncan Campbell would not come alone, to be sure – but need he bring a tail of such proportions with him to make a private call? It seemed almost . . . vulgar.

What could the man be wanting? For wanting something he must be – Black Duncan of the Cowl would not make such a call lacking a purpose. None of the Campbells would, from Argyll himself downwards. What, then? He, MacGregor, could provide nothing which would appeal to the creature. Yet here he came.

Alastair rubbed his chin – and wondered whether perhaps he should have shaved it, this morning? As yet he did not have to shave so very often. Yet even a few hairs sprouting could look unsightly, especially red hairs – and like so many of his race, Alastair was a red-head. But, God be good, why should he shave for Black Duncan?

Red hair, unshaven or otherwise, Alastair was an adequately built and proportioned young man, presentable, with features strong rather than fine, a firm chin and ready smile – usually that is, if not today – only the intensely blue eyes hinting at something of a hot temper and a degree of determination. None in Glen Strae, and rather further afield than that, was unaware of that temper and determination – for, after all, he was MacGregor, *the* MacGregor, the only one who could call himself just that, just MacGregor, Chief of the Name and of Clan Alpin, the proudest if scarcely the richest, largest or most powerful of all the Highland clans, the Gregorach, the Children of the Mist, whose motto was "My Race is Royal", descended from Gregor mac Alpin, brother of the great Kenneth mac Alpin who had united Picts and Scots. No Campbell could claim such ancestry.

If Alastair's attitude towards a neighbour's visit was something less than heartily welcoming, perhaps he might be forgiven. For besides the general suspicion of all Campbells by the other clans, there was rather a special reason for a reservation about this one. For Duncan Campbell of Glenorchy's father, Sir Colin of the Seven Castles, Justiciar of Argyll, had personally beheaded Alastair's father, in the name of justice at Kenmore, before the Lord Justice Clerk of Scotland, the Earl of Atholl, in the year 1570, thereby winning a substantial slice of MacGregor territory. It was not the sort of thing that a warm-blooded youth was apt to forget, even though that was nearly nineteen years ago, when Alastair was almost two.

The approaching company came at a trot up the last quite steep incline to the castle's terrace – the three horses trotted, that is, while the gillies continued to lope with the typical untiring motion which they could keep up for hours on end. Quickly Alastair counted. Besides the half-dozen of his own men that he had sent down to escort the visitors up, easily distinguished by the ragged reddish tartans they wore, he made it thirty of the green-tartaned Campbells, in a tight formation around their masters. The said masters were differently clad, two in long, leathern, sleeveless waistcoats and silken shirts above their kilts, wearing bonnets, the third wholly in black, doublet, trews and high riding-boots, only the shirt and cravat white, and instead of bonnet a strange black turban-like cap with a long scarf or tail to it, less than any plaid or shawl, which hung over one shoulder, the cowl which earned him his by-name. He might have been a Southron by his garb.

2

As they came up, the smell of sweat from those running gillies, wafted on the south-west breeze, was throat-catching; after all, the Campbell ones would have been running for miles, whether they had come from Glen Orchy itself, or Kilchurn on Loch Awe or any of the other five castles Duncan had inherited from his acquisitive father. Hospitality being what it was in the Highland way of life, these would expect an ocean of the Glenstrae store of spirits to quench their legitimate thirsts. Campbells!

"Greetings, MacGregor!" Black Duncan called, as they drew rein a few yards from the standing youth. "Here is pleasure, whatever." At least the man's voice was Highland enough, softly sibilant, kindly on the ear, however at odds with his reputation.

"Glenorchy!" Alastair jerked, inclining his bare head stiffly. Too late it occurred to him that perhaps he should have worn his bonnet, with its three eagle's feathers, to which as a full chief he was entitled, whereas this Campbell was entitled only to two, as chieftain of a sept, however powerful a one – which was perhaps why he wore that cowl in preference to a bonnet. His two mounted companions, *duine-wassails*, lairds, sported but one each.

They dismounted. "The weather is good for the time of the year, and the snow all but gone from Cruachan," Duncan observed amiably, although the mention of Ben Cruachan, the greatest mountain of these parts, which soared so dominantly only four miles to the west of Glen Strae, frowning over all, was not calculated to please the younger man, for although it was now the Campbell war-cry, "Cruachan! Cruachan!" it had been a MacGregor mountain once, like all the rest hereabouts.

Alastair nodded, wordless. He was not normally a silent character – far from it. But this visit and visitor set him on his guard.

Black Duncan, a dozen years older, was no fearsome object, however strange his garb. Dark-haired, with a small pointed beard, sallow of complexion but with good features if perhaps an over-prominent nose, he was slenderly built. He did not trouble to introduce his companions.

Alastair had to say something. He would have to invite the

3

man into his house, of course, although he doubted whether ever before a Campbell would have been inside Glenstrae Castle. But he was not going to seem too eager.

"Have you come far?" he asked.

"This morning, only from Kilchurn," he was told. "Yesterday, a long day. From Balloch. And I go on to Barcaldine."

That reply was itself telling, however factual it might sound. For Balloch, at Kenmore, at the foot of Loch Tay, was the furthest east of Duncan's castles, fully fifty miles away, on the other side of what was known as Braid Alban, the central Highland watershed; and Barcaldine was the most westerly, in Lorn, almost as far in the other direction. That he could be travelling on Campbell land all that way, save for this brief incursion into Glen Strae of the MacGregors, was as significant as it was deplorable. It was to be wondered at that the man had not managed to introduce the names of the other castles he had inherited from that wretched father of his – Achallader, Loch Dochart, Edinample and Finlarig.

Alastair strove to keep his voice level, civil. "Then your gillies will need their drams. And yourself and friends some small refreshment. If you will honour my humble roof . . .?" His tone and manner were less humble than his words.

The other, however, waved a dismissive hand. "Not to trouble you, whatever, MacGregor," he said. "This is but a brief call, in passing, you understand. On a small matter. We shall not detain you."

If that was meant to reassure, it missed its mark. For it was almost unheard of, in the aforementioned Highland code of hospitality, to appear at a man's door and refuse to enter, if the call was well intentioned; and of course, once hospitality was provided and accepted, the salt eaten as it were, the code required friendly behaviour thereafter. So this refusal, however civilly put, could well imply that this unlooked-for visit meant trouble.

But Alastair MacGregor was concerned to play the gentleman, even if Black Duncan was not. He turned, to glance back at the archway under the little gatehouse which gave access to the courtyard of his castle, where stood a man of middle years, watching. This was Robert Ban – he had been very fair once, although now greying – the steward, actually an illegitimate uncle.

"Rob," he called, "drams for all the Campbells, if you please." That would demand a little producing, to be sure – but Rob would cope, he always did.

"No need . . ." the Campbell began, with a quick frown. Then shrugged. But he still made no move towards that gateway. "See you, if you have a moment to spare me, MacGregor, we can deal with our business here and now."

"Business?" That came out on a jerk.

"Yes, a small matter. Concerning Glen Lyon."

"Glen Lyon? What business could *I* have with Glen Lyon, sir?"

"You are chief of the name of MacGregor, are you not? And therefore concerned with MacGregor lands."

Alastair stared, those so blue eyes narrowing, as some faint inkling of what might be coming dawned. Glen Lyon, a dramatic long valley which lay well to the east over a score of miles, over the watershed of Braid Alban, indeed into the shire of Perth – where Pontius Pilate of all people had been born, son to the Roman governor who had tried to subdue the Picts there, and failed – was just north of Loch Tay and the Lawers range. It had been MacGregor land once also, but they had lost it to the Campbells long ago, over a century past. But not all of it. Midway along its twenty-mile length lay the small property of Roro; and the lairds of Roro, one of the minor septs of the Gregorach, had been tough indeed and somehow managed to hang on to their lands. MacGregor of Roro was still there.

"What concern have you with MacGregor lands in Glen Lyon?" he demanded.

"No little concern, my friend. Roro sits in the middle of my glen. And moreover astride the main drove-road from my people's shielings and summer grazings on the high ground of Lawers and Cairn Mairg."

"It always has done. Before ever a Campbell came to Glen Lyon!"

"Perhaps. But it is not . . . convenient. Especially when Roro charges toll on the herds passing through. As the herds must do, to reach the lower pastures. And the markets."

5

"That is one of the privileges of such baronies and lairdships. As here in Glen Strae. And on a score of Campbell lands, I swear!"

"No doubt. But it remains inconvenient. And expensive. I have sought to better the situation, and generously. I have offered a good price for Roro, and had it refused – "

"The Gregorach do not sell their land!" Alastair interrupted. And then added, "Save with their blood!" since they had in fact had to part with so much.

"I have offered Roro other land. In Glen Dochart or in Strathearn, or Lomondside. But, arrogant, he will not heed me. I could not have done more."

"You could have left him in peace! Do these tolls he charges mean so much to you? One beast in fifty, is it? That is usual. What we charge here. Although I have heard of Campbells who charge more! Is that too much for Glenorchy's purse?"

"It is more than the tolls, just. There is their behaviour, their prideful arrogance. There, in the midst of my glen. They net salmon in my river. They dam burns, to form lochans, depriving my lower ground of water. They have mills, grinding corn which should be ground in mine. They hunt the deer on *my* hills, beyond their own. It is not to be borne."

"It has been borne, has it not, since Campbells entered Glen Lyon?"

"No longer! I . . ." Duncan restrained himself with an obvious effort. "This of Roro is unsuitable and, and inappropriate. I have put up with it for overlong. So – I wish you to speak with Roro. Advise him for his good, for his people's good. He will heed you, I think."

Alastair drew a long, quivering breath, not trusting himself to speech.

"Tell him that he can have good land in the south. Below Tay. Better land than Roro. And some payment of moneys. He would be near to other MacGregor lands at either Dochart or Earn or Loch Lomond. I am not ungenerous . . ."

There was a pause, as the two men's eyes met in a long stare. The younger's features worked as though in preparation for a major statement; but when it came it was brevity indeed.

"No!" he said.

The other fingered his pointed beard. "You would be wise to think again, MacGregor," he said thinly. "To consider well."

"There is nothing to consider, I tell you."

"Oh, but there is, I assure you. Much. For yourself and for Roro both. Indeed, yes."

"You are not *threatening* me, Campbell?"

"Threaten, no. I but warn. In all goodwill. I am not prepared to thole this inconvenience longer. I have been patient for sufficiently long. And I think that I have means at my disposal to amend matters to my satisfaction . . . if Roro continues obdurate and will not respond to my generous offers."

"Means? Other than your Campbell money?"

"Means, yes. Which I do not wish to have to use. But will, if need be." The visitor shook his cowled head. "But this is folly," he said, in an evident effort to lessen the tension which had built up. "No cause for ill feelings between us, MacGregor. All over a small extent of rough territory in the midst of a twenty-mile glen. What matters it if Roro and his people move to another property? Better land and in lower ground, finer pasture and more fertile to till. They should thank me, I say . . ."

At this juncture Rob Ban and assistants emerged from the castle with jugs and flagons and beakers of *uisge-beatha*, or whisky, water of life. Courteously they brought the liquor over to Black Duncan and his companions first, but that man waved it away dismissively. When offered to his gillies, however, the reception was quite otherwise. There was much appreciation expressed.

"So I ask you to consider well," Glenorchy went on. "There are other MacGregor lands south of Tay. Balquhidder and Glen Gyle and on Lomondside. Thereabouts Roro and his people would be better placed. Near to their own folk. Not in the midst of Campbell land . . ."

"But in the midst of Colquhoun and Buchanan land!"

"Campbell could reach agreement with these small clans, I have no doubt. They will heed us."

"As MacGregor will *not*! We have held Roro since time was. And will continue to do so, if I have aught to do with it. Because you wish to extend your Campbell sway over every

7

foot of land in Mamlorn and Braid Alban, to make a Campbell kingdom! Think you we shall bow to that? Save us – it occurs to me that if you got Roro, the next you would want is this Glen Strae itself! It lies between the lands you have won from us in Cruachan and Glen Orchy. And with a pass, the Fionn Lairig, over to your Achallader and Loch Tulla. Will Glen Strae be the next for you, Campbell?"

The other eyed him hard for long moments on end. Then, wordless, he turned to mount his horse, with a peremptory wave towards his waiting gillies. Hastily his two lairds clambered into their own saddles, not having so much as opened their mouths. Black Duncan reined his beast around and, without a backward glance, kicked heels to flanks and set off down the glen.

In distinct disarray his company hurried after him.

Alastair stared after them, deliberately not turning to face Rob Ban and the others until he had mastered the all but trembling anger and emotion which had built up in him. It took him a little time. When he did turn, he was all too well aware of the eyes of them all, watching him. He was aware that here was testing, men weighing, assessing, however loyal and even fond of him they might be. Here, perhaps, was the first real challenge to him as chief of his name, MacGregor challenged before them all. Apart from the ominous threat and problem of it all, there was this other – how had he acquitted himself? At barely twenty years that was important. Being MacGregor Himself was no light responsibility.

He discerned no scorn, nor disappointment, nor pity, at least, only concern and anger to match his own.

"Campbells – they do not change, do they?" he got out, with a smile which was more of a grimace. "Their hearts even wryer than their mouths!" He was rather proud of dredging that up, despite the quiver in his voice. That was what the name was derived from, *cam* meaning crooked or wry and *beul* meaning mouth.

Rob Ban spat. "Scum!" he said simply.

There was a growl of hearty agreement from the gillies.

"Aye, but potent scum! Dangerous. They can match their words with deeds, as MacGregor has cause to know."

"*I* know it, whatever!" That was grim. After all, Rob Ban

had seen his half-brother Gregor actually beheaded by Black Duncan's father, and others of the clan with him, something Alastair had not seen; not a sight a man would forget. "Here, Alastair, a dram. You could do with it." And he proffered a beaker of the strong spirit.

"You have some left then? Despite all the Campbells!" That too he was pleased to be able to produce, in the circumstances.

They moved within, under the gatehouse archway and through the small courtyard to the square keep, thick-walled and stocky, no great fortalice like Kilchurn down at the lochside but sturdy enough, so long as cannon were not brought against it – and cannon would be difficult indeed to get up here within range. Plump, comfortable and comforting, Janet, Rob's wife, who had all but mothered Alastair these last many years and who no doubt would have been watching all from one of the upper windows, although not hearing what was said, came to him questioningly. But reaching out, he patted her arm and brushed past her, to mount the twisting, narrow turnpike stairway. He wanted to be alone for a little. In his own chamber, Alastair sat on his bed and gazed at the floor. What, now? What to do? For something would have to be done. Nothing surer, with Black Duncan making the running. Mere waiting on events would not serve, with that one. The Chief of MacGregor must act . . .

Alastair would have ridden his garron, but decided to walk. It was not all that far. And walking was good for the soul and the wits, or so his Uncle Ewan said. And he had a lot of respect and faith in Uncle Ewan. Hence this walk up Strae.

Larachan was only about three miles further up the valley but on the other side of the river, so that Alastair had to cross the ford. Fortunately, with this May weather, the water was not high and the stepping-stones uncovered and less slippery than sometimes. The young man leapt across easily.

He could see the house of Larachan now, round a bend in the glen, no large establishment for the Tutor of Glenstrae, on its shelf well above where the floodwaters could reach it. Evidently his approach likewise had been observed, for two figures were coming down to meet him, one thick-set, of middle years, the other slender, of Alastair's own age, father and son.

"What brings Himself to Fearnan's door this fine day?" the elder called. "Whatever, it is a pleasure for an old done man!"

That greeting was less than accurate in more ways than one, for the old done man was of but forty-five years, and sufficiently hale; and to call his door Fearnan's was what might be termed an anachronism. For although he had been MacGregor of Fearnan once, and still so called himself as a reminder of injustice done in the name of law, he was no longer owner thereof, Fearnan being in fact far off on the north shore of Loch Tay, beneath towering Ben Lawers, and now part of that Campbell barony, part of the price paid, along with his brother's head, as sentence by the Justiciar of Argyll, in the King's name. But at least Ewan MacGregor was still Tutor of Glenstrae, tutor being the style and title of the guardian and principal adviser of a young chief until he came of age, a sort of regent.

Not that Alastair did not consider himself to be of age already, at just twenty, and acted accordingly. Some stupid law said twenty-one, so his uncle, this legitimate one, could remain tutor.

"Pleasure, old done man!" Himself called back. "Wait you until you hear *why* I have come!"

His cousin Patrick grinned. "Bearer of ill tidings, are you? They must be ill indeed to have MacGregor *walk* to Larachan!"

"Sufficiently so, yes. And the walking has not cleared my mind for me, despite what your father says of it."

"What, Alastair?" the older man asked, in a different tone, noting his nephew's expression.

"It is the Campbell. Glenorchy. Black Duncan . . ." The whole story came pouring out.

They listened, without interruption, although once or twice the tutor gripped his son's arm to still urgent question or interjection.

When Alastair was finished his uncle was looking grave indeed. "This is . . . beyond all," he said. "Roro will never do it. Nor can you urge him to."

"I know it. But something I must do to aid him. If I can."

"Rally the clan," Patrick declared strongly. "Fire and sword! Rally. Show that the Gregorach are not to be mistreated. Make the Campbell think again . . ."

"Quiet, you!" his father ordered. "Wits we require in this, not loud belly belching! We are not facing some other clan, out for booty or flourish – MacLarens, Buchanans, Colquhouns, MacNabs, MacNaughtons and the like. We are facing the whole power of Campbell. And that is great. God knows! The power, not of broadswords and cold steel, although they can raise sworders in their thousands. But the power of the realm itself. For they have the law in their pockets, these Campbells. Always they have contrived to have that, proving parchment in the end stronger than any steel, ink more effective than blood. King Jamie they sway and use like any puppet, poor lad. With Argyll, young as he is, Lord Justice General, and Black Duncan wed to the daughter of Atholl, Lord High Chancellor. And himself Justiciar, as was his accursed father before him. We are not dealing with broadswords here."

"What, then? We cannot call on friends in high places," Alastair said. "We have none. But we cannot just bow to the Campbell's will – MacGregors."

"No-o-o. But this requires much thought, Alastair . . ."

"Surely the Campbell could not seek to use all this, the Chancellor, the Justice General and the rest, just to gain a few acres of Roro?" Patrick said. "Use a great hammer to crack an egg! Roro cannot mean so much to him as all that?"

"Do not be so sure, boy. Pride will come into this. Having made his demand to MacGregor, Black Duncan will not be thwarted and accept it. He will play every card he can to win his game, not only for Roro but for his pride's sake. Of that you may be sure."

"If I did muster the clan, it might at least give him pause . . .?"

"Give him excuse, rather. To declare MacGregor in arms against the King's law-abiding subjects! My guess is that he will seek to use first the law the Campbells are so clever at, on some pretext, against Roro. He will find something. Then, when Roro resists such move, he will claim him to be in rebellion against the law of the land, even have him declared outlaw. So that his lands could be forfeited. The Campbells have done that before. And if the clan is mustered to support Roro, then the Gregorach themselves could be outlawed . . ."

"And should we care?" Patrick exclaimed. "Let them call us outlaw if they like. What difference would that make to us, here in Glen Strae? Or in Glen Gyle. Or in Kilmanan and the rest. Is the Southron law so important to us? With a thousand broadswords to assert *our* law!"

"Spoken like a fool!" his father asserted. "Outlaws cannot sell or buy in a market. So who would buy our cattle at the autumn trysts? No paper they sign is lawful. Any dealing with them in any way, assisting them or trading with them, is guilty before the law also. Outlawry is no mere empty threat, boy."

Up at the house now, they stared at each other.

"I must do something!" Alastair repeated, banging fist down on fist. "Should I go and see Roro?"

"Yes. That would be wise. Tell him to do nothing which Glenorchy could claim was against the law – *his* law! Not that that will save him. But make it less easy for the Campbell to gain his ends." His uncle took a turn or two up and down. "I think, yes, I think that you will have to go higher, lad. Higher."

"Higher? What mean you? Who is higher than the Campbells, with their chancellors and justiciars and earldoms?"

"One is. The King's Grace."

"The King! Jamie? Me, go to the King? How could I do that? How could I get near to him? He would never see me. And even if he did, would he heed me against the powerful Campbells?"

"He might, just. I have heard it said that he does not greatly love his Campbells. He is a strange one, is James Stewart, and scarcely a strong King. But he can sometimes play the monarch."

"But . . . how could I win into his presence? And if I could, would he heed me?"

"He is *Ard Righ*, as well as King of Scots. His proud boast is that he comes of a long line of one hundred kings. None other in Christendom can boast such a thing. And most of that hundred were not just kings, but *Ard Righ nan Albannach*, High Kings of Alba, of the Picts. And it was, and is, the privilege of every chief of a clan to enter the presence of the *Ard Righ*, on request. Even this sixth James should know that, oddity as he is. You must claim it."

"If I get that far! To his palace in Edinburgh. Or Stirling Castle. Or – where is it he is ever at his hunting? Aye, Falkland, in Fife. These Lowland places where I have never been."

"*I* have – and I will come with you, Alastair. But . . . I have a notion, lad. How to win close to King Jamie. His cousin, Lennox. I have heard much good of Ludovick Stewart, Duke of Lennox, the late Esmé's son. James has innumerable kinsfolk, but all illegitimate, James the Fifth's bastard progeny. But only the one lawful close kin, this Ludovick of Lennox. And he is fond of him, all say. And Lennox your own age, just, as is James. All speak well of him. Forbye, his house is none so far off – Methven Castle in Strathearn, on the verge of our Highlands. If you could see Lennox he would, I think, bring you before the King."

"Would he? Why should he?"

"He would listen to you, at the least. And the Campbells, for all their power, are not loved. *Because* of their power, it may be, and how they use it. Strathearn verges on Campbell land. Much of Strathearn is indeed Black Duncan's, or his kin's – Aberuchill, Monzie, Edinample and the rest. The Campbells' neighbours seldom love them – as we have cause to know! Lennox may well lend you his sympathy. It is worth the trying, anyway. But, Roro first."

"Aye. So be it. Bless you, Uncle Ewan! Where would I be without you? Tell me that."

"Doing none so ill, I think – so long as you were not taking this Patrick's advice! Now, come away in, and see what your aunt can find to refresh a man . . ."

So, two days later, Alastair was again heading up Glen Strae, but this time not alone and not on foot. He would have to ride through a deal of Campbell land to reach Roro, so it was wise to go sufficiently well escorted. He would go by quiet ways and empty valleys, as far as possible, and not be provocative, as was equally wise in the circumstances. No use preaching circumspection to Roro and being challenging himself; although in fact, the route he was taking happened to be the most direct, if by no means the easiest.

He picked up Uncle Ewan at Larachan, to make a second horseman in the midst of a dozen running gillies. They could have brought along ten times that number, but why overdo it?

Glen Strae was a long and twisting valley rising high as they progressed northwards, becoming barren between lofty and rugged mountains. The lower reaches were quite populous, with many small farmeries and crofts, and two mills, the higher parts given over to summer grazings and shielings. But there was a major drove-road through it, for this was the way the herds came from all the Black Mount, Moor of Rannoch and Glen Coe area on their way to the markets of Taynuilt and the Oban, this a source of revenue for MacGregor, at one beast in fifty toll. The Highland glens and pastures would not support much more than the basic breeding-stock in the snowy winters, and so the surplus cattle had to be sold off at the autumn trysts and markets, beasts by the thousand, to fill Lowland bellies, such wealth as the Highlands produced.

Some eight miles up, the glen suddenly narrowed and changed character, the Strae becoming almost a continuous cataract, the incoming burns reaching it as waterfalls, the drove-road beginning to climb steeply between all but sheer craggy mountainsides. This would continue right up to the watershed, at nearly fifteen hundred feet, to the Fionn Lairig, the White Pass, so called because it was so frequently snow-filled.

At the summit of this, Alastair drew rein, not only to give the gillies a breather – which they would have pantingly denied was necessary, being MacGregors – but because always he did so here. For the vista in both directions, north and south, was stupendous, even though nothing was to be seen east and west but bare rock and heather close at hand. Ahead opened a vast prospect beyond the jaws of the approach glen: first the lovely wooded trough which embosomed Loch Tulla and behind that the almost limitless spread of the Moor of Rannoch's waterlogged immensity, backed, far off indeed, by the blue mountains of Mamore. Directly in front were the grandly savage peaks of Glen Coe, and half left the ranged, dark summits of the Black Mount; all in all one of the most magnificent scenes in a land where magnificence was next to normal.

Downhill now, as steeply, presently they came to a junction of valleys and waters, not far from the foot of Loch Tulla, on the right. Although that way lay their route, Alastair turned leftwards, up a narrow glen, this leading to a smaller loch, Dochard – not to be confused with the greater Loch Dochart near Strathfillan many miles to the south-east. Only a short way up this a few cot-houses clustered round a larger one, no castle this but strongly sited. Here, cutting scrub-birch to build extra fencing for cattle-enclosures, they found Alastair's brother, John MacGregor of Dochard, Iain Dhu in Gaelic, and his men. He held this northern entrance to the Fionn Lairig, and his was the duty of collecting the tolls from the drovers on their way to markets.

The brothers were not alike. John, although a year younger, was more burly, a little shorter and with heavier features, and dark-haired. But he had the same intense blue eyes, and an even hotter temper.

That temper, when he heard of the Roro threat and Alastair's present mission, was evidenced sufficiently strongly in an outburst of indignation, fury and demands for action, unmistakable MacGregor action. Alastair found himself aiding Uncle Ewan in playing down this urgency, however much he understood and all but shared it. This was a challenge to be met with wits rather than fists or swords, he emphasised.

They had to persuade John not to accompany them also, his place meantime being here at Glen Strae, with chief and tutor away. He accepted that with ill grace.

They left Dochard and turned back eastwards to the foot of Loch Tulla, that fair three miles of water flanked on both sides by ancient pine forest. They took the north side, advisedly, but little populated as it was. They were in Campbell country now, although most of the inhabitants would be of MacGregor blood, whatever they called themselves, for this too had been the clan's land once. Discretion was today's unlikely watchword for MacGregor.

Beyond the loch they had to be careful indeed. For not far from its head reared the new castle of Achallader, built by Glenorchy's father. It was unlikely that Black Duncan would be there – he had said that he was going on to Barcaldine, far to the west; but the place would have a keeper and strong garrison, no doubt, and was to be avoided. So they kept well to the north of it, on the other side of the Water of Tulla, heading for the high hills behind. Fortunately no would-be interceptors appeared.

Soon they were climbing again, this time up over long heather slopes, different terrain however high, no roads now, only deer-tracks. It was a long haul to reach the ridge of a shoulder of Meall Buidhe. But once thereon, they were rewarded. For immediately below them now opened a major, long, wide valley, so long that they could not see to the end of it, two lochs nestling only a mile or two beneath but fully fifteen hundred feet lower, Lochs Daimh and Lyon. For this was indeed Glen Lyon, a strange dead-end valley, twenty-five miles of it, ending thus abruptly against the wall of Meall Buidhe, one of the fairest and most secluded of all the Central Highland glens. Down they went into it. Thus far they had come some twenty miles. Another ten to go.

Although Glen Lyon was now one of the proudest jewels in the Campbell crown, the MacGregors were not troubled about traversing this west end of it, for the same reasons as at Loch Tulla. The folk herein were of Gregorach blood. When one clan took over another's land they must take

16

over the inhabitants with it – or else either exterminate them or resettle them elsewhere, a costly and difficult procedure. Much simpler, unless the people were rebellious or persistently hostile, just to leave them there and call them by the new clan's name. So a great many who were now ostensibly Campbells were in fact MacGregors, MacNabs, Menzies, MacNaughtons and the like, whose chiefs and tacksmen had been dispossessed.

Down this pleasant glen, then, fully half a mile wide, they went, past the lochs and the little communities there, where they were greeted warmly, if in surprise, past Gallin and Meggernie – this last a tacksman's house where, however, they were not challenged – from where, oddly enough, Alastair's own mother, long dead, had come, a so-called Campbell of MacGregor blood, and on to Milton of Eonan. This place was named for St Adamnan, an ancient Abbot of Iona, he who had written the renowned story of Columba, and who had presumably established a cell or little church here. That had been moved further east, to Innerwick, nearer Roro, for convenience, but the monastic mill was still functioning, to grind the local corn – one of Black Duncan's grievances, since it was a MacGregor mill, part of Roro still on the edge of their land, and could charge the miller's tithe. As well as the mill, there was a ford here of the River Lyon, for this was where that other drove-road came south from Loch Rannochside and Glen Garry, the Lairig Chalbhath, and crossed to climb over the shoulder of great Ben Lawers to Tayside – to the Campbells' resentment, for here toll had to be paid, and to Roro.

Now the glen became more populous, with many MacGregor tacksmen's houses and their farmeries, cottages and herders' cabins – Balgie, Kenrowmore, Innerwick itself and the rest, the source of Roro's manpower; for although a comparatively small estate, as clan lands went, it held a quite large and concentrated population, more so than Glen Strae for instance; hence the sept's ability to hang on to it all, when so much else was lost.

Roro itself occupied a distinct widening of the glen, where no fewer than four quite major side-valleys entered it, two from the north, two from the south, creating a sort of elliptical amphitheatre over a mile in length. These incoming valleys, with their waterfall-producing streams, because of all the rocks and debris they brought down off the mountainsides, had created a series of quite large islands in the main river, an unusual feature, very useful for the capture of salmon, with sluices formed and nets, one more of Black Duncan's complaints, for there were no similar facilities further down in the Campbell reaches of the glen. In a way, the usurper's envy was understandable.

Gregor MacGregor of Roro came to meet them well before they reached his house of Roromore, for their approach could have been observed for well over a mile. He was a huge, hearty bear of a man, all shaggy hair and beard much more vehemently red than Alastair's, his greeting bellowingly resounding and genial. Anything less resembling a man under threat would have been hard to imagine. His only complaint was why had not Himself let him know that he was coming and he would have prepared a feast suitable for the Chief of MacGregor. As it was, they would not starve, to be sure, and there was liquor in plenty; but not what might have been. It had been a year since Alastair had come to Roro.

It took some time, amidst all this welcoming and declaiming, with liquid hospitality all but poured into the travellers, the gillies at least deserving it with some thirty miles' running, before Alastair could get down to the subject and object of their visit – and even then Roro began to pooh-pooh it all as typical Campbell bluff and bluster. Almost old enough to be his chief's father, he was difficult to gainsay, until Uncle Ewan added his warnings and urgings.

"Heed us, Gregor," he intervened. "This is no mere clan feuding or grasping for lands. You will be up against the full might of the Campbells, not only Black Duncan, I think . . ."

"What is new in that?" the other demanded. "Always they have wanted Roro, to have the whole of Glen Lyon for themselves. I, and my father before me, have had attempts to buy us out, to have us out by force, to threaten us and cheat and cozen us. What is new?"

"Something is new, yes. Pride. Glenorchy has come to your chief. He has not done that before. Now all MacGregor is involved, not just Roro. He has appealed to Alastair to persuade you, or to command you, to get you out. And has been sent away, empty-handed. This will resound round all the clans – and Black Duncan's name and fame suffer. Pride, man! That one seeks power and station, as well as lands and moneys. He would be *the* Campbell, I say, rivalling even his own chief, if not replacing him. For Argyll is but a youth, but sixteen years or so. Glenorchy already owns almost as many castles and great lands as does MacCailean Mhor. Now he has been rebuffed by MacGregor in front of many. Think you he will accept that?"

"He can do no other, man. For he will not get Roro, whatever."

"Not by the sword, perhaps, nor by gold. But by using the law and the powers of governance he might well achieve his fell purpose. And to the great hurt of more than Roro."

"I have broken no laws, man. Even Campbell laws!"

"Are you so sure? Do you *know* all the laws, Gregor? All the lawmen's writings? All the wordings of charters, deeds, Acts of Parliament, Privy Council records, justiciars' court judgments? Do you? *I* do not!"

For once Roro was silenced.

"Black Duncan will know them – make it his business to know them. He is Justiciar, after all, as was his damnable father. The Campbells make sure to hold such offices. He will find some crack or cranny in the law to trip you, if he can."

"Let him!"

"And have you outlawed for transgressing the law? Your lands forfeited? And not only yours but MacGregor's, who supports you?"

Roro stamped up and down. "What, then?" he demanded hotly.

Alastair resumed. "We ask that you go carefully, Gregor. Very carefully meantime. Consider well whether aught that you, or your people, do could be twisted to seem less than lawful. Even a small matter. To give Duncan no shot-hole to fire through. Perhaps in the tolls you charge. In the deer your folk take. After all, Roro's marches with the Campbell land are not marked by dykes or cairns; so you could easily stray over and kill beasts on Duncan's land, your cattle feed on his pastures. Fly no hawks over Campbell territory . . ."

"God damn it – would you have me creep and crawl and hide like some mouse before the Campbell cat! Me, Roro!"

Even Alastair had to smile at such a simile. "Scarce that. But go warily for a while. To give us time to go seek some help."

"Help? Whose help can you seek in this? Save the fullest muster of MacGregor strength!"

"That will not help us fight the law. No, we must go high. Higher than Campbell. The tutor, here, suggests that we approach King James himself. As is my right, it seems."

"The King! God be good – how can you do that? You will never reach Jamie Stewart."

"There may be means. We can try, at the least. And quickly. So, do not give Campbell any opportunity meantime, Gregor, while we seek to clip his wings. Tell your people. No provocations, however hard to resist."

"As you will . . ."

Roro's hospitality thereafter was far from overshadowed by the Campbell menace and the steps advised to counter it, however distasteful to the Gregorach. Indeed, an all but uproarious evening was spent, with late bedding, and it was a somewhat bemused and heavy-eyed party which set off in the morning, back westwards up the glen, for home. But they did have Roro's promise as to discretion, although just what that word might mean to that man was doubtful.

Alastair wasted no time. Three days after the return to Glen Strae he was off on his much longer journey, to what was almost a foreign country to him. Not that he was heading for the Lowlands straight away; for he would visit Strathearn, as Uncle Ewan advised, where the young Duke of Lennox had his home.

To get from Glen Strae to Strathearn, some fifty miles to the south-east, it was scarcely possible not to pass through some Campbell country. So this required forethought. Black Duncan had said that he was going to Barcaldine, which was his furthest west castle, in Lorn, on the very edge of Argyll. But for how long? It seemed likely that he would go to see his chief, Argyll himself, to whom he acted almost as a tutor, while he was so near to Inveraray, especially if he wanted to involve him and his influence in this Roro matter. But they could not be sure that he was not back in these parts already. Not that the MacGregors could not travel through Campbell land without express permission – although they might have to pay toll here or there; but in the circumstances it could affect the size of tail, or escort, which Alastair felt he required for safety, not to mention dignity. Yet he did not want to attract too much attention to his mission, with a large body of retainers.

It was decided that a score of gillies would be best, and that the route taken should be indirect – for if the Campbell had them reported and followed, and guessed that they were heading for the Lowlands, he might well seek to take steps to thwart their purposes if he could. And he would have much more ready access to the royal court than would Alastair. So although south-east was their direction, they indeed went *north*-east again, up Glen Strae, picking up Uncle Ewan at Larachan, Alastair dressed in his best.

In fact they followed the same road, by Loch Tulla and past Achallader Castle, but instead of climbing the shoulder of Meall Buidhe, they followed the Water of Tulla up almost to its source, and so over the north-east corner of the vast tract of Rannoch Moor, where it was less waterlogged than elsewhere. Crossing the watershed there, they came down to Loch Rannoch itself, safely out of Campbell country now and into Robertson territory. By the loch-shore they camped for the night.

Ten miles down Loch Rannoch they turned southwards between it and Loch Tummel, under the shapely peak of Schiehallion, and on up Glen Goulandie to the Strath of Appin. The foot of this was admittedly very near to Campbell ground again, indeed close to the eastern end of Glen Lyon, but they were just within Clan Menzies land. They halted again at the ancient and historic Abthanrie of Dull, once a monastic college of the Celtic Columban Church, founded by the same Adamnan of Milton of Eonan.

In the morning they called in at Weem, to pay respects in passing to the Menzies chief. The neighbours of Campbells seldom loved them, so that the travellers did not anticipate any ill reception here. Indeed it was to be expected that Menzies would be quite flattered by a call from so royal a race as MacGregor for, although Highland now for almost four centuries, Menzies was not in origin a truly Celtic clan at all, but of Norman extraction, de Meyners having come to England with William the Conqueror and to Scotland with David the First, along with other Normans and Flemings, and had gained these lands by marriage, adopted the name of Menzies – whereas their relations in England had called themselves Manners. They were still somewhat concerned over their comparative newcomer status.

However, The Menzies was not at home, so the callers pressed on. Southwards from Aberfeldy they mounted Glen Cochill, and over and down the two glens of Almond, Upper and Lower; whereafter only a single belt of lofty ground separated them from mid-Strathearn. They reached Methven by nightfall.

Methven Castle, looking south over the wide, fertile vale, its back as it were turned to the Highlands, was very fine. It had been built about seventy years before by Henry Stewart, Lord Methven, a young man whom Queen Margaret Tudor, widow of James the Fourth who fell at Flodden, had wed as her third husband, she, Henry the Eighth's sister, being old enough to be Methven's mother. But at least she had enabled him to erect this handsome mansion; and her great-grandson, the present James the Sixth, had given it to his young cousin Ludovick, Duke of Lennox.

Sadly, Lennox was not at home either; indeed, according to the keeper of his castle – who eyed the MacGregors distinctly suspiciously – he was seldom at Methven, King James demanding his company at court more or less continuously. Although disappointed, in a way they had no complaint, for since it was the King that they wanted to see, the nearer the duke was to him, the better. Where, then, were King and court apt to be, at this present?

They were told that, although the royal seats were at Holyroodhouse, in Edinburgh, and the castle of Stirling, King James's favourite haunt was the palace of Falkland, in Fife. He had the craze for hunting deer, on horseback. This was his preferred way of spending his time, affairs of

22

state having to be fitted in, if possible, where they did not unduly interfere with his hunting. In season and out of season he rode deer-chasing; and Falkland was the chosen venue, where he had the Fife Lomond Hills and their woodlands for his sport, yet not too remote as to situation. In this fine late May weather, the chances were that he would be at Falkland, although it was of course the breeding season. And the duke with him.

Fife, to be sure, was easier to reach from Strathearn than was Edinburgh at least. The MacGregors spent the night in the stable-block premises – they were not invited into the castle itself – and in the morning were told to proceed on down Earn right to the river's joining with the Tay estuary, where they would be in north Fife. At Abernethy there they would be only some dozen miles from Falkland.

Out of the great hills now, their passage attracted a deal more attention than heretofore, two tartan-clad horsemen and a score of half-naked running gillies not being seen every day in the Lowlands. But however askance they were eyed, they were not interfered with, the reverse indeed, Highland barbarians tending to be looked upon as dangerous savages to be avoided at all costs.

They reached the Earn at Gask and turned eastwards along its banks, by Forteviot and Forgandenny, coming to its eventual junction with Tay, where the latter river was widening into a firth, in late afternoon. They could have gone further but, considering how best to time their arrival at Falkland, decided to camp near Abernethy meantime. It was an ancient Pictish capital, its curious, slender round tower still surviving, but the travellers viewed it from a distance, not sure of the kind of reception they would have in the town.

The journey down through Fife greatly interested Alastair MacGregor. Never had he seen so much cultivated land, so many villages and hamlets, castles and tower-houses, not to mention the great abbey of Lindores, still seeming to be a thriving place despite the Reformation of thirty-odd years earlier. As good, or goodish, Catholics, the MacGregors approved of this seeming survival, although Uncle Ewan declared that the revenues thereof would be going to one of King James's court favourites, to be sure, as a commendator-abbot. There were a lot of odd abbots these days, few indeed in holy orders and able to pronounce a blessing – however able at cursing.

They reached the Falkland vicinity by midday, and were quickly reassured as to the court's presence there by large numbers of folk hanging about, a large proportion of them overdressed. If the Highlanders had attracted stares before, now they were the object of pointings, exclamation, derision, hard to thole for proud men. But they must needs ignore it all in the interests of their mission.

The palace of Falkland stood within a little town at the northern foot of the East Lomond Hill, no great establishment in fact. All teemed like an ant-hill disturbed. Clearly all these people, so expensively clad, could not be lodged in the palace itself, so the town must be housing most of them. Alastair and his uncle left their gillies in an orchard on the outskirts, and proceeded into the town streets, seeking information. At a tavern would be best.

They had no difficulty in finding such, at any rate, for there were many. Inside one, ordering drams, and the target for all eyes, they found the place to be full. There were some guffaws and sniggers at their appearance – but when the Highlandmen gazed around them, hands on dirks, such quickly died away.

Alastair spoke into the sudden hush. "I am MacGregor," he said simply. "And I seek the Duke of Lennox. Does any here know of his whereabouts?"

None actually answered that, although there was some muttering.

"The duke," he repeated. "Surely some must know of him?"

"What want *you* wi'him, Hielantman?" somebody demanded.

"That is between himself and myself, sir. Where do I find him?"

"Whaur but at the King's side."

"No doubt. But to gain the King's presence? Is it difficult, here?"

"For siclike as you!" another voice suggested. That provoked laughter.

The two MacGregors looked at each other, shrugged, and

were on the point of leaving when a young woman serving ale spoke up.

"Sirs, gin ye were tae gang ower the wynd here, to yon hoose wi' the iron yett, and spier there, ye'd mebbe win some bruit o' it."

They eyed her doubtfully. Such Lowland speech was scarcely intelligible to them. But she sounded helpful.

"Your pardon – but would you be after telling us again? We are not well acquainted with your tongue."

That produced more mirth, and there followed some shouted interpretations, few more informative. The girl tried again, pointing.

"Yonder. Ower the wynd, just. Yon big hoose. Wi' the yett. Iron. Yon's whaur the Maister o' Gray bides. He's far ben wi' the duke. Leastways, his lassie is!" That seemed to be more mirth-provoking than ever. When she could be heard, she added, "He'll be awa' after the deer, wi' King Jamie the noo. But *she'll* no'. She'll tell ye, mebbe . . ."

They got enough of that to thank her, and move to the door.

Across the narrow street outside, a row of houses stood, of varying size. One had a quite massive iron gate, which was half open. Iron was one of the few words they had been sure of. Yett could mean gate.

They crossed to this and entered the small courtyard of what seemed no very grand establishment. A hand-bell at the doorway summoned an elderly servitor, who eyed their tartans with the usual distaste.

"Is this the house of the Master of Gray?" Ewan asked. That name was well known, even in the Highlands, as allegedly the handsomest man in Europe, and one of the cleverest, although not all trusted him.

"Aye."

"This is MacGregor. *The* MacGregor. He seeks speech with the Master."

"He's no' here, the noo."

"Are any of his household, then?"

"Weel, mebbe . . ."

"Then tell them that MacGregor and the Tutor of Glenstrae are here." That was authoritative.

Muttering, the man went off.

When he returned he had two ladies with him, and both remarkably good-looking, one perhaps in her early thirties, the other of no more than sixteen or seventeen years. They eyed the callers with interest, but more kindly than any had yet done since they crossed the Highland Line.

The callers bowed. "MacGregor," Alastair said.

"I am the Lady Marie, wife to the Master of Gray," the elder told them. "And this is Mary Gray."

The younger laughed – and she had a delightful laugh, gurgling, most friendly. Indeed the impression she gave was all delight, a lovely, personable young creature, but somehow nevertheless with more than just delight to her.

"Is it true?" she wondered. "A real Highland chief! Three feathers in your bonnet! Always I have wanted to see a real chief and never seen one. Save my lord of Argyll, that is. But – *he* is not a real chief, is he?"

Nothing could have more greatly commended that young woman to the visitors, needless to say.

"Oh, I think that you are wrong, my dear," the Mistress of Gray said, but she also smiled. "Do not they call him MacColin More or something such? Meaning son of the Great Colin Campbell. That surely makes him one of the great chiefs."

"You are knowledgeable, lady," Ewan said. "There are chiefs and chiefs!"

"No doubt. And you are the MacGregor?"

"Alastair here is. Glenstrae, Himself."

"Seeking my husband?"

"Seeking the Duke of Lennox, rather," Alastair amended. "We were told that here we might find one able to bring us to him."

The two women exchanged glances. "We are friendly with the duke, yes," the Lady Marie said, a little cautiously. "He is with the King."

"Why do you seek the duke?" her companion asked, interestedly.

"To bring us to the King's Grace," she was told, simply.

"It is the privilege of chiefs of clans to have audience with the *Ard Righ nan Alban*, the King," Ewan explained. "But it

26

is not always so easy to reach his presence. Hence . . ." He gestured.

"You have come all the way from your Highlands for this?"

"Yes. For the matter is . . . urgent."

"Then we must see that you gain the audience, sir," Mary Gray said, and she sounded quite decided on the matter. "How do we call you, sirs?"

"MacGregor, lady."

"Just MacGregor? Does not that sound . . . less than civil?"

"It is our Highland usage," Ewan explained. "Alastair here is the chief. Only he can call himself only MacGregor. I am Fearnan, Tutor of Glenstrae. Uncle to Alastair Himself."

"Alastair himself? I think that I like that. Alastair himself! Better than just MacGregor."

"*I* think, my dear, that whatever we call them, we had better have them within, and offer them some small hospitality, refreshment," the Lady Marie said. "Come, gentlemen."

They were led within and taken upstairs to no very handsome apartment for the great Master of Gray to occupy. The Lady Marie indeed apologised for the cramped quarters, explaining that Falkland was so full and the palace so small, that they were fortunate to have even these premises. Many of the court had to be content with much less, even had to lodge in the neighbouring village of Freuchie.

"You will have heard that it is King James's wont to say to those who displease him, 'Och, awa' to Freuchie wi' you!'" Mary Gray added, mimicking a distinctly thick and slobbery voice.

While they were regaled with wine, cheese, oatcakes and honey, the younger woman quite frankly enquired of them what was the mission that had brought them all the way from their Highlands to see the King at Falkland; she made it sound as though they had come from a very distant land. The Lady Marie gently reproved her for being unsuitably inquisitive, but was smilingly ignored. This lass was clearly something of a law unto herself, and favoured the straightforward approach.

Alastair was that way inclined himself. "It is the Campbells," he declared. "They would have our land. By fair means or

27

foul." He also ignored his older companion's frown. "Black Duncan of Glenorchy, that is."

"And you would have the King aid you against him, MacGregor?" That sounded just a little critical.

"If it was but swords, cold steel, fighting men, we could see them off, easily. But it is otherwise. The law. They use the law to fight with – paper, charters, courts, claims. They know it all – and use it. The Gregorach are no lawyers, 'fore God!"

"I would think not, no, Alastair himself! And you think that the King will aid you?"

"We can but put it to him, at the least. If we can but gain his presence."

"Vicky – that is the duke – he will see to that." She paused. "My Uncle Patrick – that is the Master of Gray – has a friend who is a Campbell. I have met him indeed. You know him, Marie. A tall, friendly man. Campbell of Cawdor, is it not?"

"John Campbell of Cawdor, yes. But he, I think, will not be of the Campbells these gentlemen will be concerned with. Cawdor is far north, in Moray, not the Campbell country at all, as I understand it."

"Ah, Cawdor, yes." Ewan nodded. "Never have I met Cawdor. But have heard that he is . . . different."

"How came the Campbells up in Moray?" Alastair wondered. "Hundreds of miles from Argyll and Lorn and Braid Alban."

Lady Marie wagged her fair head. "I do not know . . ."

"It is an old story. I wonder that you have not heard of it, Alastair. A son to Argyll, Archibald the second earl it would be, Sir John Campbell, for some reason travelled up to Moray, to Nairn. And there, at Cawdor Castle, he saw the ailing Laird of Cawdor, said to be a descendant of King MacBeth's brother. That king was Thane of Cawdor, and he left it to his brother. And this descendant had as heir only a red-haired lass, Muriella Cawdor, but fifteen years. He saw also that it was a great and fair property. So there and then he asked for her hand in marriage – although he was no young man. Indeed he had his seven sons with him, whatever was his purpose at Nairn. And when the laird refused him, that night he stole the girl and set off there and then for Argyll. With her . . ."

"Campbells!" Alastair exclaimed, eloquently.

"Aye, so! The Cawdor had them pursued by his illegitimate brothers and many men, all the way to Lorn. This Sir John was Campbell of Inverliver. Many were the fights, as the seven sons were left as rearguards. One by one these fell, but always Inverliver with the girl pressed on. She was not fit to ride this hard and far, and some asked what if she also sank and died of it. Campbell said then that Muriella Cawdor would never die, so long as there was a red-haired girl on either side of Loch Awe, he meaning as her substitute!"

"Campbells!" Alastair repeated.

"When, almost across all Scotland and the sea-lochs of Lorn in view, at the last fight before Cawdor's men had to turn back, the seventh son fell, Sir John, reproved even by his own folk, said that it was well worth it. For Cawdor. Or that is the story as I heard it." He shrugged. "So he married Muriella, and Cawdor has been Campbell's since."

"An ill story, indeed!" the Lady Marie commented, shaking her head.

"But not unlike the Campbells. In their greed for land," Alastair pointed out.

"Perhaps it is all but a fable," Mary Gray suggested. "Invented by enemies. It is too cruel, I think."

"It may be so. But – you do not know the Campbells as we do."

"And this John of Cawdor now? He is related?"

"He will be the grandson, I think. Grandson of this Muriella."

"He is a man of middle years . . ."

They were still discussing Campbells and their doings, the Lady Marie asserting that they were not all so black as they were painted, when a young man came running up the stairs to them, a youth, sturdily built, plain-faced and plainly clad, his clothing mud-spattered. Alastair, assuming him to be a horse-boy or something such, thought it strange that he should burst in on them so. But when he hurried over to Mary Gray, to take her arm, and then turned to stare in astonishment at the two Highlanders, it was clear that he was no servant nor groom.

"Here is Vicky – the Duke of Lennox," the girl informed.

29

"Vicky, here is MacGregor himself. And his uncle. From the Highlands."

"Eh . . .?" The youth blinked. "MacGregor . . .?"

"Yes. Himself!" She dimpled at that. "Come to see you." She gestured towards the bonnets on the table. "See – three feathers. Eagle's feathers, are they not?"

"My lord Duke!" Alastair made something like a bow. "I am MacGregor. This is the Tutor of Glenstrae."

"We called at Methven, my lord," Ewan added. "But learned that you were here, at Falkland."

The newcomer looked from them to Mary and back again. "You want to see *me*?" That sounded surprised indeed.

"To have you bring them into the King's presence, Vicky. You will do that, will you not?"

"Well . . ."

The Lady Marie, possibly feeling that all this was just too direct and abrupt altogether, spoke. "You are back early, Vicky. Is all well?"

"James's horse went lame on him. Leaping a fallen tree. I gave him mine – for, you know him, he will ride only the best beasts. I had had enough of the hunt, anyway. Have had enough, for days! We had killed thrice, as it was. But James presses on – you know him. So I came back on a borrowed mount, leading the lamed Barbary. I hope *my* beast survives!" He spoke jerkily, with the trace of a foreign accent – for Ludovick Stewart had been born in France, son of Esmé Stewart D'Aubigny, a cousin whom King James had created first Duke of Lennox. He seemed an unlikely duke and representative of that lofty and resplendent line, more like some honest burgher's son.

"Uncle Patrick is still hunting, then?" Mary Gray asked, making a face. "I wonder that he did not seize the opportunity before you did, to get away." She turned to Alastair. "Not all King James's court are as fond of hunting as their liege-lord."

"Not every day and all day!" the duke said.

"You hunt deer on horses?" Alastair wondered. "How is that done? We do it otherwise. Stalking them on foot, or on our bellies, more like, with bow and arrow. On our mountainsides."

30

"Aye, that I know. And much prefer. I have done it at Methven, in Upper Glen Almond. Much better sport. But James never walks; he has but poor legs. He is happiest on a horse." He paused. "You are from . . . Glen Strae, was it? I do not know Glen Strae."

Alastair stiffened a little – although he recognised that that was not meant to be any sort of insult. "All that we have left, my lord Duke, of the wide MacGregor lands. That, and a few patches – Roro, Glen Gyle, Balhaldies and the rest."

"And you are . . . the chief? Glenstrae?"

"MacGregor, yes."

"Himself!" the girl added, with one of her gurgles.

"Where is this glen?"

"Near to Loch Awe, in Braid Alban. Between Glen Orchy and Cruachan."

"Is that not Campbell country?"

There was a moment's silence.

"It was all MacGregor's once."

Lady Marie, ever the soul of tact, intervened again. "Vicky, you will be tired, thirsty, after all the hunting. These gentlemen have been having some refreshment. You will have something?"

"My thanks, yes, Marie." But he turned back to Alastair. "Glen Orchy, you said? Glen Orchy, I know – not the glen but the man. Dark. Able. Clever, they say. He comes to court at times."

"When he requires something, no doubt!" Ewan put in.

"As, as do you?"

"Yes," Alastair admitted. "Do you wish that we tell you of our mission?"

"Yes, do." That was the younger woman, almost eagerly.

Sighing, the Lady Marie turned to attend to the hospitality.

So the MacGregors settled down to recount their story and problems. And inevitably it took a long time. Their hearers were highly interested and by their interjections, questions and comments, sympathetic, the girl not attempting to hide it, and the young duke taking his tone from hers. The Lady Marie came to listen also, and although she was more restrained, was friendly in her remarks.

The MacGregors sought not to seem too greatly prejudiced against the Campbells, although that was difficult to maintain.

The recounting and discussion was still not finished when there was another interruption, the arrival this time of a notably different individual, a brilliantly handsome, elegant man in his late thirties, bearing himself with an easy, casual authority, his rich clothing somewhat travel-stained. Pausing in the doorway, his quick glance took in all the scene, but without change of a sort of wryly genial expression. He flourished a bow.

"We are fortunate enough to have visitors, I see!" he announced. "And from beyond the Highland Line, if I am not mistaken. Welcome to this poor house, my friends." The Master of Gray went to kiss his wife; and Mary Gray ran to his side.

The MacGregors could scarcely hide their stares, from the newcomer to the girl, so alike in features and even bearing were they.

Introductions followed and partial explanations, the Master listening interestedly but forbearing comment. It was noteworthy that Duke Ludovick was adopting a very pro-MacGregor stance, in line with the girl's.

When they had finished, the Master, sipping wine, asked, "And what do you expect King James to do?"

Alastair spread his hands. "Hear us, sir. Then, then perhaps use his royal powers to prevent Glenorchy from grasping Roro."

"And . . . should he? The King?"

"If he would see justice done in his realm, sir. Is that not part of his simple concern? Even duty?"

The other smiled. "James may have other notions as to that. He is a strange young man. Judging in clan feuds may not be his conception of his royal role."

"It was, for the *Ard Righ nan Alban*. From whom this James inherits his highest authority."

"Ha – the *Ard Righ*! It is long since I have heard that title mentioned. I doubt whether James Stewart has ever heard of the *Ard Righ nan Alban*. Although, he is learned in many ways – so he may have done."

"Without that descent, sir, he is no better than this Queen of England we heard of. Or the Kings of France or Spain," Alastair said simply.

Gray considered him thoughtfully. "That, now, is a consideration. Worth the mention to him when you see him. It might just appeal."

"You think that he will see us, then?"

"I shall ensure that he does." That was factually said. Then he recollected. "Vicky and I, both."

Mary Gray nodded her lovely head. "That is well," she said. "Tell me about this Ard Rye, is it? I know naught of it . . ."

"Then Brother Davy has neglected your education, my girl!" the Master declared. He turned back to the MacGregors. "But we cannot promise you a favourable hearing, see you. The King thinks highly of Glenorchy – although he does not greatly love him, I judge. For he is a most notable man, remarkable in many ways, I have heard. He drains the bogs. He plants trees, and has his people to do so also. He encloses fields. He improves the land . . ."

"For profit," Ewan put in. "Land stolen from the Gregorach."

"Perhaps. But the land benefits, if also does he. Few are so able at it as Glenorchy."

"As well!"

"I but warn you. James may not take your side."

"But you and Vicky will help, will you not, Uncle Patrick?" the girl said, nodding. "Now, tell me of this Ard Rye. Of Alban, is it? Was not your grandsire Duke of Albany, Vicky?"

"No. That was earlier. Not the Lennox line . . ."

"*Ard Righ nan Alban* was High King of Alba, of the Picts. Long before ever the Scots came across the sea from Ireland," Alastair told her, earnestly. "A hundred High Kings there were, before the brother of our ancestor Gregor, Kenneth mac Alpin, united Picts and Scots. That was seven hundred years ago . . ." There was no stopping him now. And the young man had appreciative listeners, as it happened.

33

3

In the end, then, winning into the presence of James, the Lord's Anointed, presented no difficulty at all, although the MacGregors had to wait until the end of next day's hunting for what could hardly be called an audience.

Filling in the day, Mary Gray escorted them around palace and town – for the duke and the Master were not available, the King insisting that those close to him joined in the chase, however unenthusiastic their hunting. For herself, the girl was particularly interested in the running gillies, still camped in the orchard whose owner was evidently much too alarmed by their warlike and dirk-bearing appearance to attempt to eject them. Mary assured him that the Duke of Lennox would compensate him for any damage done; and also arranged with an innkeeper to provide them with simple food and drink, again at ducal expense. Clearly this young woman was as practical as she was winsome – and had Ludovick of Lennox very much at her beck and call.

The visitors got their first glimpse of the monarch in late afternoon, when the hunt returned from the Lomond Hills, a straggling, weary company – for they had been out since sunrise – with led-horses bearing four dead and gralloched stags. At least, most of them looked weary, but whether the young man who rode immediately behind the carcasses was so would be hard to say. That this was the King was evident only because he rode there, at the front, and alone, with the duke immediately at his back and a group of great ones just behind, including the Master of Gray. For his appearance was anything but regal, indeed was almost ridiculous. He rode slumped in the saddle, ungainly as to posture, his clothing, much too rich for hunting but untidy and not over-clean, hanging about his person loosely, and he wore an extraordinary high hat, which must have been very difficult to keep in place when riding at any speed. He was about Alastair's own age, and far from handsome.

As he rode past, Mary waved and the MacGregors bowed. They saw the monarch glance at them from great liquid eyes, his best feature, but he made no acknowledgment.

After they had fed at the Gray lodging – James Stewart did not relish the unnecessary expense of feeding his court – the Master and the duke took the MacGregors over to the palace. There they perceived how difficult it would have been to gain entry, past relays of armed guards and officers, these however bowing their escort through respectfully. It was the same within. In present company the newcomers' passage was assured, however doubtfully their tartan garb was eyed by all.

Along corridors, and passing through sundry intercommunicating apartments, they came at length to an inner doorway where two halberdiers in the royal livery stood barring the way.

"Is His Grace alone?" Lennox asked.

"Alone, my lord Duke." The guards stood aside.

Ludovick rapped on the door, opened it without waiting, and went within, closing it behind him. He was the only one at court who could have done that.

They heard voices within, one sounding querulous. Then the door opened again and the duke beckoned.

It was in fact a bedchamber that they entered, untidy, littered with discarded clothing and containing a huge, canopied four-poster bed. On this, strewn with papers, the monarch sat, a quill pen in his ink-stained hand, and an ink-horn precariously balanced nearby, clad in a bed-robe over a nightshirt, and, scarcely to be believed, still wearing his high hat. He did not smile upon the visitors.

"Hielantmen!" he greeted. "I saw you, wi' yon Mary Gray. I kent you'd be wanting something, mind, or you'd no' have come out o' your Hielant wastes! But what-like a time to come and fash me, when I'm in my bed . . ."

"James, when else could they come?" Lennox asked. "You are risen and away by sun-up, hunting. You could not have them waiting on you before that? And on the hunt you could scarcely heed them – "

"I'm no' sure that I can heed them now, Vicky Stewart!" he was interrupted. "Can you no' see I'm right busy? Occupied, aye, occupied. I'm inditing a poem. A right profound poem. To my Annie beyont the seas. Poesy's no' easy, mind. And wi' a' these papers and charters and Acts to read and sign. Och, if I've got to see these Hielantmen, I'll see them some ither time."

"Sire," the Master of Gray put in, "they have come a long way to see you, and express their loyal regards and duty. And MacGregor here is also a poet."

"Eh? A poet? Him!" James stared, with various expressions chasing each other across those slack and sallow features – interest, disbelief almost, possibly even offence at the possibility. "No *true* poesy? Frae the Hielants!"

"True, yes, Sire. Or so *I* judge." Since the Master of Gray was, amongst his many other accomplishments, himself a notable poet, majesty could scarcely scoff.

"Och, weel – it'll no' be the poesy he's come to show me, I'm thinking! What is it, man? What's to do? No' at great length, mind, for I'm fell busy."

Alastair cleared his throat. "It is about Campbell of Glenorchy, Your Highness. Duncan Campbell. We seek your royal aid . . ."

"Glenorchy? Yon's the dark one – him who plants trees. And gars the hillsides tae bring forth crops, they do say."

"Other folk's hillsides, Sire," Ewan put in grimly.

"Eh? Who are *you*, then?"

"I am Tutor of Glenstrae, Highness. Uncle to Himself."

"So! You speak when you are spoken to, Tutor! I'm no' here to heed Hielantmen's ill words and complaints against each other. You're a' ay at feud. Guidsakes, we a' ken that. It's nay concern o' mine."

"But they say that it is, James," the duke averred. "They claim that you are indeed concerned. By your ancient role and duty."

"Eh? Duty!" The royal pen jabbed towards the MacGregors. "D'you tell me these, *these*, think to tell me, the Lord's Anointed, my duty!" James Stewart's tongue, too large for his mouth, could hardly get that out for slobbers of indignation.

"They mean no discourtesy, Sire," Gray assured. "They do not think to appeal to the Lord's Anointed, I believe, but to something much more ancient. The *Ard Righ*. If Your Grace knows of the title?"

"Eh, eh? *Ard Righ*? The *Ard Righ nan Alban*, is it? To be sure I ken o' the *Ard Righ*. Yon means High King. Of Alba. Alba was this land afore the Scots came."

"You are *Ard Righ* now, Sire. As well as King of Scots," Alastair pointed out.

"Aye. In a kind o' a way I am, to be sure. Nane other is, leastways."

"For a thousand years there were High Kings of Alba. Picts, the Romans called them . . ."

"I ken that, fine. Yon was because they hadna a written language, but used pictures, symbols. So the Romans called them Picti, frae *pictum*, picture. I'm no' ignorant, MacGregor!"

"No, Sire, that I well perceive. It is as *Ard Righ nan Alban* that I approach Your Highness now. As of right. For always chiefs of clans had the right to come into the presence of the *Ard Righ* if they had some serious complaint against another chief. To the Chief of Chiefs."

"Is that so?" James looked wary. He was not the one ever to admit that he did not know anything which conceivably he ought to have known. "I'll no' say you are wrong, mind. But . . . yon was lang syne. I'm no' sure that it applies to the King o' Scots today."

"But, Sire, do you not claim, as did your royal forefathers, to be the most ancient line of monarchs in all Christendom? That, not because you are Kings of Scots but because you are *Ard Righ*. The Emperor could claim to have older origins than the Kings of Scots, I think. But not than the High Kings of Alba."

"M'mmm." James laid down his pen and tapped his hat more firmly in place. "Aye, there is something in that," he admitted. "You are nane so ill read for a Hielantman, MacGregor." That might sound grudging, but it was a notable step forward.

"Not well read, Sire. Only . . . informed."

"Eh . . .?"

"I do not read, Sire. Like the Picts!" Alastair said.

His liege-lord all but gobbled. "You dinna *read*, man?

37

Guidsakes! Here's a right dumfouner! Hey – how do you write your poetry, then?"

"I do not write it, Highness. I speak it. Or sing it. It is not required that a Highland chief should write words on paper. We have clerks for that. But my uncle here reads and writes."

"Save us! D'ye hear that?" The King looked at the duke and the Master. "Hae ye ever heard the like? Clerks!"

Alastair perceived that he had perhaps been tactless. "It may be that we are foolish in this," he admitted. "Certainly where Black Duncan of the Cowl is concerned!"

Ewan took a breath to add something, but remembered that he was not to speak until spoken to.

"Aye, then, you mean Campbell o' Glenorchy? Yon one. What's your complaint against him? To mysel'. *Ard Righ nan Alban.*"

"Like his father before him, who beheaded *my* father, he has already taken most of the MacGregor lands, Glen Lyon in especial. By devious means. But the small property of Roro, in the midst of that long glen, is still held by the Gregorach. The Campbell wants it. And will have it, he says."

"He would buy it off you?"

"MacGregor does not sell lands!"

"Ha! Hoity-toity! How, then?"

"He will have Roro by fair means or foul. By using, twisting the law. As he has done before. He is Justiciar. And his chief, Argyll, Lord High Justiciar."

"So-o-o! And what do you want o' me, MacGregor?"

"But a single word of warning in the Campbell ear, Sire. That the King's Grace is concerned for other clans' rights and well-being than just the Campbells'! That is all. I think that I speak for the Macnabs, Maclarens, MacNaughtons, MacAulays, Menzies and others, Your Grace."

"All, eh – all! Hech, hech – here's a right girn, a compleen! A' those? Weel – we'll see. We will consider the matter. Aye. I'm no' promising aught, mind." The monarch waved the subject away. "Noo – this o' the poetry that you canna write! Is it true, man? No' just havers. Poetry's no' that easy, as I ken. It's a right labour o' the spirit. And if you canna set it doon on paper, how d'you mind it? Mind what you've gien birth to?"

"It comes from the heart to the head, Highness. And there is held. In the memory . . ."

"Och, you'll no' mak right poetry yon way, man. You'll no' be able to go ower it, improve on it. And that's right necessary."

"I do so, yes. Many times. But in the head. It is all done in the head, is it not? The memory serves."

James looked more than doubtful. "If your memory's that guid, gies an ensample, then. Let's hear your poesy."

Alastair shrugged. "I do not claim it to be very fine, Sire. And . . . it is better in the Gaelic, the old tongue. And you will not want any long verses, I think. But here are a few lines I made up, as I travelled to this Falkland. Over this of Roro and Glen Lyon." He paused.

> There's sorrow, deep sorrow, heavy sorrow down-
> weighing me,
> Sorrow deep, dark, forlorn, from which nothing can
> raise me:
> Yes, my heart is filled with sorrow, deep sorrow
> undying,
> For MacGregor of Roro, whose due is Glen Lyon.

There was silence for a moment or two after that. Then the King nodded his head, hat and all.

"No' bad," he admitted. "Ower much sorrow, but no' bad. How say you, Patrick, man? Ower much o' the sorrow?"

"Perhaps, Sire. But it is a sorry story, after all."

"Aye – and tell't to me to mak me greet, I warrant! Greet for the puir MacGregors! But there's poetry in it, aye. It could be improved, mind. If you were to put sadness and maybe anguish in place o' a' yon sorrows, it would sound better, and no lose the lilt o' it."

"It does sound better in the Gaelic, Highness."

"I'll hae to tak your word for that, man! Mind, I hae *some* o' the tongue. Yon ill Maister Geordie taught me – Buchanan, that is. He who was *my* fell tutor. He was a hard maister, was Geordie Buchanan – he gave me my paiks! Och, I still hae some o' it. How is this? *Eisd ris an duine. Chuala mi na thubhairt thu.*"

"Ha – excellent, Sire. Do you mean that you do believe me? Or otherwise? It could be either, could it not? Who would have thought that you, that Your Grace could speak the old language. *Ard Righ*, indeed!"

"Och, I tell't you, man. I'm no' ignorant. Like some!" And he glanced at the other listeners. "I speak the Greek and the Hebrew as well as the Latin. And the French, to be sure. You'll no' ken a' these? You canna write!"

Alastair shook his head. "None, Sire. I greatly admire your Highness's abilities. It is greatly to be wondered at."

The extraordinary young man on the bed nodded vigorous agreement to that. "Aye, so. I'm the Lord's Anointed, you see. And need the tongues o' men and o' angels. 'Every tongue shall confess to God.' That's Paul, to thae Romans, you ken. Every tongue. And your Gaelic, mind, is a right special tongue. You'll no' ken, but I've worked it oot and I've decided it's the language o' heaven itsel'; aye, heaven." He emphasised that by pointing upwards.

Alastair looked not altogether convinced but did not put his doubts into words.

James, launched on one of his favourite themes or theories was not to be denied. "D'you no' believe me? Hear this, then. Adam and his Eve – what tongue did they speak, think you? What *could* they, but the language o' heaven itself? And whaur was their Eden? Some place on yon Euphrates River. And when their descendants moved oot o' there, they moved west, aye, west. No' east – yon were the folk o' the Land o' Nod. You'll ken your Scriptures? The folk o' yon Nod werena the same, no made in the image o' God, like Adam. They were there first, mind, had been long, long. But were no'right fashioned, different some way. So Adam's seed moved west, after a time, multiplying, see you. And went on moving, doon the ages. Round the north side o' the great Middle Sea, yon Mediterranean. And they left their Gaelic names behind them as they went – Galatea, Galicia, Gallipoli, Galada, Gaul, Galway – yon's in Ireland – and then ower to Alba or Scotland, to Galloway. There's a river they ca' the Gala Water in the Borders; maybe yon's the way they cam north. So there you hae it – the Gaelic is God's ain tongue." The King gazed round him, to observe the effect of his lecture on his four hearers.

All looked suitably impressed, however much they might privately question the reasoning.

"Aye, weel, enough o' that," the monarch decided. "I'm busy. Off wi' you. I'll consider the matter o' this o' Campbell and your bit glen. I'm no' convinced, mind – but we'll see." He waved a dismissive hand. "You hae my royal permission to retire."

Thus abruptly dismissed, all bowed and backed to the door, James reaching for his pen and ink again.

As they returned down the corridors, Patrick Gray found occasion to congratulate the distinctly bemused MacGregors. "You are fortunate, I think, my friends. Do you not agree, Vicky? You have our sovereign-lord well disposed towards you. Or you would have been out of there long since. You reached him in two regards – the poetry and the language. Both obsess him. He is no poet, in fact, but believes that he is. And is greatly proud of his knowledge of languages, as indeed he is entitled to be. I can think of no other monarch, past or present, who could speak so many. That George Buchanan, who schooled him, was a hard man, but clever."

"So, will he heed our plea, sir?"

"That remains to be seen. But I will do what I can. And no doubt my lord Duke will also. Your Glenorchy – I cannot say that I like him, nor would trust him. Nor young Argyll, his chief. And the Campbells make a close company, strong as they are many. Too many of them altogether! And hungry! But there is one Campbell that I like: Sir John, of Cawdor. I wonder? He might be of some help in this. I did him some small service once. He is . . . unlike the others. More Cawdor than Campbell perhaps! And living so far from all the others. But he is one of the six guardians of the young Argyll. He might be able to help, in some measure. Do you know him?"

"I have met him, yes," Ewan said. "He did seem different, whatever. Not eyeing a man to see how much he might get from him!"

"Exactly! I might seek his aid. To influence Argyll to keep Glenorchy in bounds."

"You are most helpful, sir," Alastair acknowledged gratefully. "What should we do now?"

"Wait, meantime. James may take some time to make up his mind in the matter. If he does anything at all."

"I will remind him," the duke said. "Not say too much, but keep it before him."

The further good offices of their new and lofty friends were in fact not necessary to produce a development of sorts, for the MacGregors were settling down for the night, at the orchard, when a messenger in the royal livery arrived at their encampment, to announce that the King's Grace expected the MacGregor and his tutor to attend him on the hunt next morning. They would ride at sun-up. Just like that.

This, of course, threw them into a quandary. It might represent good news, in that the monarch was interesting himself in them. But it also presented problems. Neither of them had ever hunted deer on horseback, and did not know the procedures. Moreover, their shaggy Highland garrons, although strong, and admirable for long-distance travel over rough ground, were not speedy, and would look odd indeed amongst all the finely bred mounts of the courtiers. But it was now near to midnight and there was nothing that they could do about it.

So, amidst the mists of sunrise the pair presented themselves on their garrons at the palace forecourt, where already a number of the hunt-followers were assembled, standing to their handsome steeds, silent, yawning and looking depressed – looks which turned to astonishment at the sight of the newcomers. None spoke to them, however, no doubt assuming that they were some strange addition to the hunt-servants whose duty was to find the deer and try to drive them to where the hunt could take up the chase.

Presently James arrived, clad as before, high hat included, and went straight to mount his horse without acknowledging any of the bows and salutations which greeted him. Once in the saddle, however, he seemed to count the company, discerning who was there and who was not. Frowning, he could hardly help noting the Highlanders, but he gave no sign of it. He waved to the chief huntsman, who sat his mount apart, and who then raised a horn to his lips and blew a long, ululating blast, presumably to announce that they were moving off rather than to awake heavy sleepers, for the King was not the one to wait for late-comers. There was no sign of the duke or the Master of Gray.

Preceded by half a dozen hunt-servants, James led the way, alone, out of the town, where the first morning fires were beginning to send up their blue columns of smoke, going south-by-west. Soon they were climbing the quite steep grassy slopes of the East Lomond Hill, which overhung the fair vale of the Eden Water, the MacGregors riding well to the rear, none addressing them. They wondered what their role was in all this.

If they were shunned, it was not for long, for presently Duke Ludovick came pounding up behind them, to rein in beside them and assert that this was no way to begin a day. He seemed interested to hear that the MacGregors had been summoned to attend, declaring it to be a good sign. He told them that James would expect him to be riding up front with him. So, to the surprise of the rest of the hunt, the Highlanders, with Lennox, spurred up past all. This they accomplished without difficulty, at least the garrons did, for these were much more sure-footed and nimble on steep slopes, being used to mountainsides, than the fine mounts of the others; indeed they had to hold back for the duke.

James and the huntsmen were leading the way in a slow zigzag progress, for the higher they were the steeper it got. But as the MacGregors neared the front Alastair, without thinking, headed his beast straight up, cutting out zigs and zags both, to reach the King, Lennox making but a poor stumbling job of it and falling behind.

The monarch did not fail to perceive this development, and reined up, to eye them. "Eh, eh – thae critturs o' yourn climb weel, Hielantmen," he commented. "They're no' bonny, but they're guid on the hill."

"They were bred to it, Sire," Alastair said. "There are few level reaches in our glens. They will climb steeper than this. They pick their own way."

"You say so? Vicky, you're late! You're ay late, these days. But – d'you see these Hielant beasts? They're right nimble on the hill. Better than oor Barbary blacks." He pointed. "Here, MacGregor, doon wi' you. Gie's a bit spell on your beast. You take this black o' mine. Treat it weel, mind, for it was a gift frae the King o' France." He dismounted.

So, to the astonishment of all, the monarch and the tartan-clad chief exchanged horses. Whatever James felt like on the broad-backed, short-legged garron, Alastair felt very out of place on the tall mettlesome black. He quickly realised that it was by no means eager to climb the hill, and had to be urged on and a path picked out for it, whereas his own beast had taken the ascent for granted and found its own way. Now the King drew ahead rapidly, with only Ewan able to keep up with him – which he judiciously elected not to do.

When at length they reached the summit ridge, they found James impatiently waiting for them.

"This crittur kens hoo to climb," he declared. "A wise-like beast. I could dae wi' yin o' these, for the climbing."

"Then he is yours, Sire," Alastair told him, greatly daring. "I have others, back in Glen Strae."

"You say so? Maist benevolent, aye benevolent! Mind, I canna gie you my Barbary in exchange just, for it wouldna dae, a gift frae His Grace o' France. Forby, he's guid at the chase. This o' yourn will be ower slow, I'm thinking. But I'll gie you another, aye. I'll hae my ain back noo, see you. Till the next bit climb. Keep by me."

They changed over again, but now Alastair was to ride close to his liege-lord, before all others, an extraordinary state of affairs. He kept well behind the King, of course, but James turned in the saddle to summon him closer, and point.

"See yon banks and bits o' mound? On the ridge, there. Yon's a fort. O' oor Albannach ancestors, the Picts. Yours – but mine, tae. Ramparts. Och, the ditches between hae got filled in, but you can see where the earth wa's were. There would be wooden stockades atop o' each, mind. They kent right likely places for their forts. There's plenties o' them hereaboots, in this Fife."

"Yes, Highness. We have them on our hill-shoulders, too."

"Aye, they were the great yins for forts and standing-stanes and carvings, and the like. Och, they worshipped the sun, but they believed it to represent the Unknown God. Which, as source o' light and warmth and fertility, was no' sae far oot, nae sae daft."

They were heading downhill now, still south-westwards, towards scattered woodlands which flourished more on this sunnier and sheltered face of the range, and where it seemed the woodland stags they sought were apt to be found. Ahead, at some distance, Alastair could see two horsemen awaiting them, huntsmen no doubt, sent to prospect for sport. A group of deer-hounds were with them, straining at their leashes.

When they came up with these, James suddenly became a changed young man, all concentration on the hunt itself. Alastair and the theories were forgotten, as the King conferred briefly with the huntsmen, and then set off at speed without a backward glance, eastwards now, down amongst the trees. Huntsmen blew their horns, as signals, and the hounds were released, to race off, noses down.

After that, Alastair and his uncle were not only ignored but all but lost. Only Duke Ludovick paid any attention to them; there was no sign of the Master of Gray this morning. Never having hunted this way, all they could do was to seek to follow others; but since the said others promptly split up into various groups following different lines amongst the woodlands, this did not greatly help. The King had quickly disappeared.

Young Lennox counselled them. "These hunts are, in truth, for James himself," he informed. "He insists on us all accompanying him. But cares not how much we partake. So long as we arrive to witness him at the kill. So none must get ahead of him and his chief huntsman. *He* must do the killing. Strange, for one who so hates the sight of blood and so greatly fears cold steel."

"He is good with the crossbow?"

"Fair, for his eyesight is not of the best. But . . . the huntsmen are clever at hiding it from him when he misses, ready to put in a secret killing-shot and hailing James as the marksman. He always believes them!"

"I can see *your* bolts, arrows." Alastair gestured towards the duke's saddle-bow quiver. "Shorter than ours. Heavier. Feathered in two. On two sides only."

"Yours are otherwise?"

"Yes. Four sides."

"Himself is a noted arrowsmith, my lord," Ewan put in. "Indeed, his by-name is *Alastair Fleisdear*, the Arrow-Maker.

45

As a boy he concerned himself with arrows. He contrived an arrow-shaft ending with four arrow feathers instead of two. Now all the Gregorach use it."

"I have not seen such. It is better?"

"Yes. As true, but hits harder," Alastair explained. "The ordinary arrow flights straight enough. But it does not turn as it flies . . ."

"Turn? How mean you – turn?"

The other reached over, to draw out a bolt from the duke's quiver. He held it up, and pretended to hurl it forward, like a javelin. Then he rubbed it round and round, between his two palms, so that it twirled. "Yours, shot, will not do this. But four feathers, not two, properly set against each other, will. That sends the arrow forward with much more force. Probably twice as much. And by no means spoils the aim. So the range is longer and the killing-power greater."

"Lord!" Ludovick wagged his fair head. "This is a wonder! I have never heard the like. Wait you until James hears of this! If . . . true?" He coughed, as the MacGregor straightened up in his saddle. "I am sorry. I did not mean that I doubted your word. Only that I could scarce believe it."

"I shall fashion you one, when we get back to Falkland, whatever," he was told. "And you can test the truth."

They had been riding but slowly during this exchange, merely trotting, and most of the hunt had disappeared in front, although there were still other unenthusiastic sportsmen scattered behind. This sort of hunting, with all the killing to be done by one man, was not to everyone's taste.

They further discussed Alastair's theory of rotating, as distinct from straight-flying, arrows. He told Lennox how he had first got the notion from skimming flat stones on the loch-waters, how the stones if made to birl, as he put it, to spin round, flew straighter and faster than the others. He tried this out in his catapult and found it impossible to make the stones rotate, until by chance he found an odd-shaped one doing so to some extent. By trial and error he decided that the pebbles with a definite projection to one side were apt to do it. Then he tried to apply this to the arrow. He made one feather larger than the other. This did make the shaft birl somewhat, but it flew askew. Then he tried three feathers instead of two, then four, with one always dominant. And that did it. So, four graded feathers, one large compared with the others, and he had an arrow which would fly faster, further and as straight. He had tried different kinds of feathering . . .

This disquisition was interrupted by a series of staccato blasts of horns, which the duke explained signalled a kill. They must now all find their way to where the horns blew, to witness this feat. Every now and then a horn blew again, to guide the late-comers, which to Alastair's mind was a nonsense, since it would send any other deer in the vicinity bolting away.

Eventually they reached an open glade where many men were dismounted, for none might remain in the saddle when the monarch was on foot. In the centre, beside the carcass of a large woodland stag with a fair head of eight points, James was haranguing all present on the virtues of deer's guts as a cure for the gout-sickness. The animal had already been gralloched, and its entrails lay in a still quivering, steaming mass by its side. The monarch was gesturing at this unsavoury heap as though in admiration. But he was not sufficiently preoccupied not to notice the arrival of these newcomers.

"Och, you're here, then. Tardy – aye, tardy! Mind, I tell't you that your Hielant nags were guid at the climbing, but slow, slow. You!" He suddenly pointed at Ewan. "You dinna suffer frae the gout, do you?" This was the first time that he had actually addressed Ewan since telling him not to speak until spoken to.

"No, Sire. That I am spared."

The sovereign looked disappointed. "Och, weel – Johnnie Mar does. Johnnie, off wi' your boots, man, and hae a dabble."

The Earl of Mar looked with distaste at the pile of offal. "My gout's no' troubling me the noo, Sire," he declared.

"But it'll be back, man, it'll be back. This'll help. Off wi' your boots."

Unhappily his foster-brother had to pull off his long riding-boots and, under royal direction, stepped barefooted into the smelly mess of entrails, there to paddle up and down while the King explained to all the good effects this would surely have on the patient; something to do with muscle-spasm apparently.

However, James quickly got tired of the non-believing looks of his hearers, and ordered a move on to the next stage of the hunt – to the evident relief of Mar. The chief huntsman gave his orders to his henchmen and hound-handlers, and all remounted.

Once again the duke and his new friends had no ambitions to be in the forefront, but accepted that it was not an unpleasant way of passing the day just to ride quietly through the attractive woodlands in the early summer sunshine, following on the trail of the hunt without seeking involvement. Others were doing the same.

It was some time before there was another kill, in what Lennox called the Glasslie area. This time the King found no sportsmen to admit to suffering from gout or similar problems, and they had to leave the entrails to go to waste. But they did partake of refreshments then, nothing ambitious but welcome for those who had had no breakfast.

The duke went to eat beside his cousin and Mar, the MacGregors left not far off. Presently he came over to summon them to the presence. Apparently he had been telling James about the arrow theory.

"What's a' this aboot birling arrows, man?" the monarch demanded. "You're no' just being ower clever, are you? I dinna like ower clever folk."

"I do not consider myself to be clever, Sire." Alastair smiled slightly. "I leave that to the Campbells! But this of the arrows I can prove to be true."

"You say so? We'll see. Gie's the gist o' it, man. Vicky's no' that clear . . ."

So Alastair again explained his theories and experiments, and had a keen and challenging listener. How fully he convinced he could not tell, for James Stewart made a point always of being sceptical; but at least his questions were apposite and intelligent.

The afternoon's sport, if that it could be called, in the Ballo and Drumain areas, followed the same pattern as the morning's, with all wearied of it save the monarch well before they turned back for Falkland, with five dead deer on the huntsmen's pack-horses. And now, with the Lomond ridge to surmount again, James borrowed Alastair's

garron once more, and forged notably ahead in consequence.

Back at the town eventually, and being fed by the Lady
Marie and Mary Gray – the Master absent on his own affairs
– Alastair lost no time in converting one of the duke's arrows
to his own design, as far as possible, using goose feathers
from the orchard. The ducal impatience to try it out was
undisguised. The ladies, too, proved to be much interested.

There was nowhere to shoot arrows at the Gray lodging
in the huddled town, so all five of them went across to the
palace, where there was ample pleasance and garden space.
Fortunately James had not yet gone to bed, as he was so
apt to do after hunting, whatever the hour, and he examined
Alastair's adapted arrow critically.

"Will these bits o' feather mak a' that difference?" he
demanded.

"I hope so, Your Grace. I think so. But it may not be so
good as I would like. I use a different kind of feathers at home.
And this bolt of my lord Duke's is shorter than are ours."

"Aye, I kenn't you'd hae your excuses!"

"I would not call them that, Sire. It is but that with a longer
shaft and different feathering I could show you better."

"I'ph'mmm. Weel, let's see what you *can* show me!" James
led the way out to a large garden. "What shall we use for a
mark?" he wondered.

"Use this plaid of mine, Sire. Another small hole in it will
never signify."

They hung the red-green tartan shawl over a branch of an
apple tree, and Alastair went to find a leaf of some sort to pin
on it. He came back with a rose-leaf, still attached to its thorn,
which would serve as pin.

"What's that for?" James asked.

"The mark you asked for, Highness."

"But that was the plaid, was it no'? No' this scrap o' leaf."

"It is accuracy we are concerned with, Sire, is it not? As
well as thrust."

"Ooh, aye. Weel – hoo many paces? Seventy?"

"So little, Sire? One hundred? One hundred and twenty?"

His liege-lord eyed him sidelong and said nothing, something highly unusual.

They all paced out the distance, and Alastair took over the duke's crossbow, none other offering themselves as marksmen. He fitted his arrow in place, took seemingly casual aim, and shot.

The watchers had barely been able to see the green leaf at this range, for there was also green in the tartan. Now they could not see it at all. Nor the arrow.

James raised an eyebrow at the MacGregor and then led the way back to the target at all but a shambling run. With weak legs and knock-knees, walking did not become him.

At the plaid, only fragments of the rose-leaf showed around a neat hole in the colourful fabric.

"Hech, hech!" the King observed.

Mary Gray clapped her hands. "Himself has done it!" she cried. "Even at that long distance."

"Excellent shooting," the duke agreed.

"Aye. But that's no' just the point, see you," James averred. "The aim's fine. But what o' the arrow?"

They moved round behind the plaid, looking. Alastair pointed. Another fifty yards or so away, near the garden wall, the arrow had imbedded itself in the trunk of another apple tree.

Forward all hurried to inspect.

"Sakes!" the monarch reached out to grasp the feathered shaft and found it wedged firm on the growing wood. "Yon's deep in."

"A longer shaft and better feathering and it would have gone deeper still, Sire." With some difficulty he tugged the arrow out.

"Umm. Aye. But we dinna ken just hoo far in yin o' oor ain bolts would go."

"I will go back and get one," Mary Gray volunteered. "Then Himself can try it." She ran off.

"I would wish to show Your Grace how much greater is the thrust," Alastair said. "I am trying to think of a suitable mark, which would show it clearly. Something that we can measure." He paused. "Sheepskins," he proposed. "The shaggy sheepskin rugs all use on the floors. Three or four of them. Hang one behind another, hide outwards. That would serve, would it not? A tough mark, with the wool between masking each of the inner hides. Deerskins would be easier, but . . ."

"An arrow wouldna' go through yon, man – no' wi' the saft wool."

"I think that it would, Sire. The drive of this twirling flight would drive it through."

"Try it, anyway," Lennox said. "You have been proved right so far, MacGregor."

James waved over one of the guards, watching from a distance, who so seldom let the monarch out of their sight. "Awa' in and fetch me fower sheepskins. Mats, ye ken. Frae the floors. Instanter, man." He turned back to Alastair. "I dinna understand hoo this birling roond makes the drive so much stronger," he said.

"I scarcely do my own self," the other admitted. "Save that when you seek to bore a hole in wood, you twist the knife-point round and round, do you not? When you draw cork from bottle, you twist then, also. For greater force."

"Aye – and thumbscrews! You screw them, to mak them tighter. I ken aboot thumbscrews. I hae to use them to justify witches. It's the screwing, then. If the arrow screws roond, it gains force. Yon's fell interesting, man."

The sheepskins and the extra arrow arrived together, and there was much to-do to devise a means of hanging the skins one behind another, hides outermost. Eventually it was done by spearing them together at the top with the MacGregors' *sgian dubh* dirks and the points dug into the tree branch where they had hung the plaid. Then they all went back to the shooting-place.

"Try the ordinary arrow first," Mary urged.

"It's ower far," her liege objected.

"It will carry, but may not penetrate," Alastair said and, raising the crossbow, released the trigger.

He was proved right in this, too. The bolt flew, to slam into the first hide, but remained there, impaled, only the head hidden.

"Aye, noo – let's see the differ," James exclaimed, obviously much exercised.

Alastair shot again – and there was no sign of the arrow.

"Ha!"

51

None dared outrun the shambling monarch to reach the target. He hastened round to the back of it.

"Here it's!" he cried. "It's no' richt through, mind. But nearly, aye nearly."

The shaft was projecting from the far side of the fourth skin, its feathering caught in the shaggy, thick wool there.

All were loud in their praises, although Alastair declared that with better feathering it would have gone right through and on. But further elaboration and demonstration were unnecessary. All were convinced. James could find nothing to complain about.

His bed calling, the King unceremoniously dismissed them, saying that he expected to see the MacGregors and their queer-like nags at the hunt in the morning. Alastair thought that he could risk contesting that, in the circumstances.

"Highness, my clansfolk. I have to get back to them. There may be trouble. With the Campbell. And . . . other matters. I am their chief. We have been away for sufficiently long as it is. So, we would ride, with your permission, in two days. But tomorrow I would wish to fashion for you a supply of these arrows. If Your Grace will accept them. Better that than riding far behind your hunt, no? You take the garrons, to be sure."

James eyed him, rubbing his chin. "Aye. Maybe you hae the richts o' it. Dae that, then." And he shambled off.

As they went back over to the Gray lodging, Alastair asked why the monarch spoke as he did, so differently from all his courtiers – save perhaps the Earl of Mar – in the rough Doric of the Lowland countryside? The Lady Marie, who was the King's illegitimate cousin, explained. He had been brought up in Stirling Castle, kept apart from all, from the court, and from his mother, Mary Queen of Scots, a prisoner elsewhere; his foster-mother the former Countess of Mar, always had spoken thus, as did his tutor, the renowned Master George Buchanan. So this was the boy-king's native tongue, and he insisted on using it, partly to confuse others with words and phrases which they did not understand, just as he used Latin, Greek and Hebrew. He found confusing some of his hearers profitable.

Next day, then, the MacGregors were excused attendance

at the hunt and Duke Ludovick took the opportunity to do the same, declaring that they required his help with feathering the arrows. Mary Gray and he went out collecting feathers of various kinds and sizes, and then joined the busy fletchers, as it seemed arrow-makers were called, excellent and friendly company in a most companionable task quite enjoyed by all, the Lady Marie coming to help frequently, and supplying refreshment. Her husband, it seemed, had gone off to his castle of Broughty, near Dundee, on his own affairs.

In early evening, with bundles of improved arrows, they were summoned over to the palace again, where James was loud in his praise of the bolt improved the day before, which apparently he had taken with him on the hunt and had proved it highly effective, much to the astonishment and admiration of all, especially of his chief huntsman. From the monarch's proud account of the day's proceedings it rather sounded as though he himself had accepted most of the credit for this notable development. Alastair by no means begrudged him that.

James, admiring the fine new supply of arrows, was all for the MacGregors postponing their departure for at least one other day, to demonstrate to the hunt multiple progress. But Alastair craved the royal indulgence. It was a long journey back to Glen Strae, and his idling running gillies were getting restive. Time that he was home, and Black Duncan Campbell to consider. He emphasised that carefully.

"Ooh, aye, I've no' forgot yon!" it was acceded. "We'll see what we can dae. Tae clip his wings." There was a tee-heed royal laugh of sorts. "Maybe win some bit feathers frae them, eh? Campbell feathers, to gie him a bit birl!"

They all chuckled dutifully at this sally, which indeed represented a measure of triumph for the MacGregors.

"You'll no' forget aboot yon beasts o' yourn? Your Hielant nags – garrons, d'ye ca' them?"

"No, Sire, they are yours, now. We leave them with you."

"Guid. I'll see that you get decent-like beasts to ride hame on. Aye, Vicky, *you* see to it. You'll ken yins I can spare. Yon grey o' your own would serve. Aye, then. You may come back to my court, Hielantmen, another time. Do so, aye. The court o' the *Ard Righ nan Alban*, mind. We will receive you. And keep up the poetry, mind. You could improve on yon." And without further ceremony they were waved away.

That night, when the MacGregors took their leave of their kindly hosts at the Gray lodging, they were assured that the duke, and no doubt the Master also, would not fail to remind their odd monarch of his promise regarding the Campbell threat. Thanks were waved away, Lennox pointing out that Himself had achieved it all on his own, captivating the King with no fewer than four subjects to intrigue him – poetry, the *Ard Righ*, the Gaelic language, and this of the arrows. James Stewart would be unlikely to forget MacGregor of Glenstrae; and the Campbells would have difficulty indeed in rivalling his interest.

In wishing them well, the duke added that Glen Strae seemed to be not so very far from his Methven in Strathearn, and he would seek to pay the MacGregors a visit one of these days. He might even persuade this Mary Gray to accompany him – a suggestion at which the Lady Marie raised her eyebrows, and the younger woman gurgled one of her infectious laughs.

The Highlanders rode away, then, well pleased, on two handsome horses such as would not have been seen in the glens for many a long day.

4

Doings in Scotland south of the Highland Line did not filter
readily as far north and west as Glen Strae and Loch Aweside,
and word of what, if anything, King James had done about
Campbell of Glenorchy did not reach the MacGregors in the
weeks that followed. But nor did any reports of trouble in
Glen Lyon and Roro, nor indeed any unusual activity of
Black Duncan. Whether the two were linked was a matter
of conjecture; but the MacGregors were prepared to believe
that they were, and give thanks. Life in Glen Strae and on
the Moor of Rannoch to the north went on more or less as
normal, and as far as Alastair was concerned, the interlude
at Falkland soon assumed something like the character of an
odd and scarcely believable dream. But he thought of it, and
the actors therein, often enough.

One event of national import did reach them that autumn.
The almost unheard of had taken place, and the monarch
had left his kingdom and gone off across the Norse Sea to
Denmark, and not going for any brief visit apparently but
for quite a lengthy stay, something all but unprecedented in
Scotland's story. All had heard that, months before, James had
been affianced to Anne, daughter of the King of Denmark,
and had sent an embassage and squadron of ships across to
fetch his bride to her new home. All the poetry the King
was so busy at, it was said, was to and about the said Anne.
However, continued stormy weather had prevented the convoy
from sailing back with the princess, King Christian refusing to
risk his daughter's life thus, James attributing these storms to
the personal intervention of Satan himself, and he, the Lord's
Anointed, alone could put matters to right and the Devil in
his place. So now he had set off in person, with more ships,
taking Chancellor Maitland with him for some reason – the
Chancellor was in effect the ruling statesman of the land –

leaving of all people young Ludovick of Lennox, his cousin, Scotland's only duke, as Viceroy, with the Master of Gray as his principal adviser and guide in affairs of state. This was an extraordinary state of affairs by any standards, but in the circumstances highly favourable to the MacGregors. They had found the right friends, to be sure.

It was obvious, of course, that that peculiar man, the Master of Gray, whom Mary Gray called Uncle Patrick but who all knew was really her true father, would be effective ruler of Scotland during the King's and the Chancellor's absence, although the only style and status he ever used was Master of the King's Wardrobe, a position which gave him access to the monarch at all times. Lennox was only a youth, albeit a pleasant one, with no head nor desire for government, his major aim in life seeming to be attaining the affections of Mary Gray. Although his would be the signature and seal on all national deeds, charters and documents in this interim period, they would be dictated by Patrick Gray. The great lords and officers of state, of course, were powerful, as was the Kirk; but they were divided, disunited, jealous of each other, many of the most potent still Catholic – for the Reformation was only some thirty or so of years old, and counter-reformation was always in the air. The Master of Gray appeared to be most expert in balancing these forces to his own conception of the nation's advantage, and possibly his own. As acting Chancellor he was able to play upon the Privy Council as upon an instrument.

Some proof of all this came to Alastair MacGregor in the autumn, with the unheralded arrival at Glen Strae of four visitors, with a small escort: the Duke of Lennox himself, Mary Gray, the Lady Marie, Mistress of Gray, and a good-looking, grave-faced stranger who was introduced as Sir John Campbell of Cawdor. Alastair, busy with cattle, for this was just before the great droves, his own as well as others', with beasts to be culled and selected for despatch to the trysts and markets, was much surprised by this visitation and scarcely prepared for the attendant hospitality – hospitality on a scale never before offered to a Campbell, too; but the newcomers, who had spent the night at the former monkish hospice of Strathfillan, were nowise demanding.

It appeared that Mary, duly chaperoned by the Lady Marie, was spending what amounted to a holiday at the duke's castle in Strathearn, and Campbell of Cawdor had come to them there, at the suggestion of the Master of Gray, to learn at first hand of the problems the MacGregors were having with his far-out kinsman, Black Duncan. From the way he spoke, he gave the impression of not being over-fond of Glenorchy, but did not underestimate his ability and power.

It was a long time since the MacGregor castle of Stronmilchan had entertained such visitors as these; but Rob Ban his steward coped well, and Uncle Ewan was summoned from Larachan, from his own cattle-gathering, to assist. Over the hastily prepared but adequate meal of soup, beef, venison and salmon from the ice-house, honey sweets, heather ale and whisky, they discussed the King's sudden decision to go to Denmark and the upset this had occasioned in his realm. Also the problems raised by those two difficult but manpower-wielding earls, Huntly in the north and Bothwell in the south, one Catholic, one Protestant, with the need to use the one against the other during this period when they could well seek to make their presences felt, to the disturbance of the kingdom. Fortunately the Master of Gray was notably skilful and experienced in such matters. None knew when James would be home, with his bride.

It was only after the meal, sitting by a log fire in the modest hall – for the autumn evenings were chilly – that they got down to the subject of Black Duncan. Alastair said that, presumably because of a royal warning, the Campbell had made no overt moves in the interim, and Roro had suffered no assaults, nor further spoken threats. The situation looked good, and his thanks were heartfelt towards those concerned.

Three of his hearers looked pleased, but made signs of belittling their part in it all; but the fourth, Cawdor, was less impressed.

"Do not be over-confident, MacGregor. Not yet," he advised. "I know Black Duncan, and he is a difficult man to put down. The Master of Gray recognises this, and urges caution."

"That I understand, sir. But . . . what am I to do? Or not do?"

"Only watch, always. Keep ever within the letter of the law, if you can. For almost certainly it is the law that Glenorchy will seek to use against you. And he knows the law, too well."

"He has been warned of the royal concern," Lennox asserted. "He also will have to watch where he treads."

"Yes. And I go on, from here, to Inveraray, to see Argyll. With the same message. I hope that MacCailean Mhor will be guided by me in this matter. He is hereditary Lord High Justiciar, young as he is, as well as Chief of Clan Campbell. Glenorchy cannot but heed him. Unfortunately, Black Duncan is also one of his advisers, however . . ."

"Will he heed him, above you?" the duke asked.

"That is hard to say. You see, until he comes of age, Argyll has an array of six tutors or guardians, not just one, as have you, Glenstrae. They are, besides myself and Black Duncan, the Campbells of Lochnell, Auchenbreck, Ardkinglas and Neil, Bishop of Argyll. I am senior, in age and next to Lochnell in close kinship. But Ardkinglas is very much in Glenorchy's pocket, a weak and unstable man; and Lochnell untrustworthy. So it is not all simple."

"You are good, sir, to trouble yourself on my behalf," Alastair said.

"It is not only you, MacGregor, but Campbell also. The weal and repute of the clan. There is much good in Campbell, as well as ill. I seek that the good shall prevail."

The MacGregors remained silent. They could think of precious little good in that name, save for this individual.

"But you are not assured of it, even with the royal influence?" Mary Gray put in shrewdly.

"I know Duncan of Glenorchy!" the other said simply.

"I will watch my step, whatever," Alastair assured. "And I have a good adviser in my uncle here, the tutor."

"You come of age in ten days' time," Ewan reminded. "Age, before the law, however much in fact you have been of age for long. Twenty-one years. When you will no longer require a tutor."

"Always I will seek and heed your advice."

"Tell me all of this of Roro and Glen Lyon," Cawdor urged, "that I may put it before Argyll . . ."

When the visitors left next morning, Cawdor to go south, up Loch Aweside, for Inveraray, and Lennox with the ladies east, back to Methven, all parted in mutual esteem.

Two weeks later it was Alastair's turn to travel eastwards, this on a required but distinctly pointless journey, concerned with his coming of age, legal age. He had to be lawfully enfeoffed in the property of Glen Strae, ridiculous as this might seem. So he was going to St John's Town of Perth, for the due duty.

This purely formal legal requirement stemmed from a sorry episode of forty-four years previously, during Alastair's father's minority, when Duncan Ladasach, the then tutor, led a successful and rather bloody retaliatory raid on Campbell territory which had recently been MacGregor's. Sir Colin, Black Duncan's father, had left no stone unturned, legal and the reverse, to avenge this, and one of his moves had been to have his brother-in-law, the then Earl of Atholl and Justiciar of the Sheriffdom of Perth, gain the Privy Council's agreement to enfeoff Glen Strae under Glenorchy, as a warning. This was only a paper device, under feudal law. The MacGregors had always held Glen Strae, along with all their other lands, under the ancient law of the land, always accepted but first set down on paper by the eleventh-century King MacBeth. This other, of feudal tenure, was a much later importation from England, by the Norman newcomers; and however much it had come to apply in the Lowlands, it was all but unknown in the Highlands. But the Campbells knew of it. The enfeoffment did not mean that Glen Strae was transferred to Sir Colin, but the *superiority* was, a feudal term which carried a few privileges. One of the token terms of feudal superiority was that the landholder had to proffer, on coming of age, a token of his enfeoffment to the superior, this before a Justiciar. Usually this was proffered to the crown, but Sir Colin had arranged it otherwise. *He* was the superior. And Black Duncan succeeded him. In the case of Glen Strae the token was, suitably enough, two arrows. If such was proffered, then feudal law was accomplished. Very frequently, in such cases, the feudal superior, especially if it was the crown, did not trouble to send a recipient, so much of a mere gesture was it.

So, Ewan having arranged all, as his final act of tutorship,

Alastair and he made for Perth. It would be interesting to see whether Black Duncan did also.

They called at Methven Castle on the way, but found the duke and his guests gone. It was only five miles or so further to Perth.

St John's Town of Perth lay just before the great River Tay began to widen out to its estuary, not far from Abernethy, a port, since the tide came up thus far – indeed further for three miles, to the ancient Albannach capital of Scone, significantly sited where the life-giving fresh water overcame salt. The former Blackfriars monastery at Perth, notorious as the scene of the murder of King James the First, was to be the venue of the justiciary court. Alastair and Ewan and the MacGregor escort camped for the night on the North Inch, open ground just outwith the city walls, where the famous but dire contest took place between the Clan Chattan and the Clan Cumming, in 1396, before Robert the Third and his whole court, probably the bloodiest entertainment in all Scotland's history. The Highlanders were not stared at in Perth as they had been in Falkland.

In the forenoon, at Blackfriars, they had to wait while a number of more serious cases and causes were held before the Justiciar – who was in fact John Stewart, eighth Earl of Atholl, son of Sir Colin Campbell's friend. It so happened that Glen Strae and Glen Orchy were not in Argyll or Lorn at all, but on the very western edge of Perthshire, and legalities had to be pursued in that sheriffdom, all but hereditary in the Atholl family. But at least the Campbell friendship was not hereditary, for this Atholl was known to be no admirer of Black Duncan.

When at length the MacGregor's name was called and Alastair came forward with his two arrows, there was something of a commotion at the back of the hall, turning all heads. There had entered a group of Campbells, Glenorchy at their head, clad all in black as usual and wearing his cowl. He did not come forward, nor make any sign, but just stood there, silent, watching.

Atholl, looking up from his table, seemed somewhat taken aback. "It is yourself, Glenorchy!" he called. "Do you come forward, to accept the Glenstrae tribute?"

"No, my lord." That was flat, unequivocal.

"No? Then what . . .?"

There was no answer.

The earl shrugged. He turned to Alastair. "MacGregor, you have brought the required offering on your attaining of full age, I see. You proffer this as enfeoffment for your lands of Glen Strae?"

"Yes, my lord."

"Then lay them on this table." He glanced up again. "Duncan Campbell of Glenorchy, do you accept this token of enfeoffment, as you . . .?" His voice faded away as, without a word spoken, Black Duncan turned and stalked out of the hall, his men behind him.

Atholl stared, they all stared. Never had the like been seen in a court of law, and perpetrated by one who was himself a sub-justiciar. What did it mean? Why had the man come at all, merely to do that? It seemed pointless. Unless just to show that he was still to be reckoned with, still determined on his course, royal disfavour or none.

The MacGregors rode back to Glen Strae, enfeoffment accomplished, but far from reassured.

Reassurance was by no means increased on their return, when news reached them of another extraordinary development, and one which could have almost limitless consequences. A messenger arrived at Stronmilchan, from Balquhidder, near Loch Earn, basically MacLaren country but where a small branch of the Gregorach was established. And he brought grievous tidings to tell the chief.

A small party of these MacGregors had been out hunting deer in Glen Artney, none so far from Balquhidder, to the south of Loch Earn. This was nothing unusual, for Highlanders everywhere looked on the deer, which drifted like cloud-shadows anywhere across the mountains and glens, as fair game for anyone able to catch them. But unfortunately Glen Artney was a royal forest; and it so happened that there was a royal forester thereof, one Drummond of Drummond-Earnoch. With a group of his underlings he had come upon the MacGregors at their poaching, and being outnumbered they had been captured. Whereupon

Drummond had cut off all their ears, and sent them home to Balquhidder thus.

The consequent outrage was, of course, almost beyond telling. If Drummond had actually slain the poachers, the reaction would not have been so great. But to mutilate them, and scornfully dismiss them thus, was an affront unheard of. And to the Gregorach, the Royal Race, the Children of the Mist. The entire clan was utterly insulted. This called for drastic measures.

Ewan was especially worried. "This is the worst that could have happened," he told Alastair. "You will have to act. You, the chief. All the clan, and others also, will look to you for retribution, for vengeance. To lead the Gregorach against this Drummond. And this while you are being told to watch your step. It is the work of the Devil himself! I wonder . . . could Black Duncan be behind this?"

"How could he? He could not have known that Drummond would find this poaching party. The chances of that are not to be considered."

"No. But he might have told Drummond. And others. To so punish any of our people, if they could find excuse. Paid them to do it. And these from Balquhidder fell into the trap."

"I can scarcely credit that."

"I cannot, myself. But – it has happened. And *you* must deal with the situation. All will demand it. The clan is mocked, as seldom before, in front of all. And you are MacGregor."

"What can I do? He, Drummond, is the King's forester of Glen Artney. I cannot attack him – as I would, God knows! Not . . . now. And I cannot go running to the Duke of Lennox . . ."

"Perhaps . . . perhaps you could call an assembly of the clan. Put it to them. That, while you would seek due and proper vengeance with our Gregorach broadswords, there are still more serious challenges before the clan. Roro. Other MacGregor lands. Even perhaps Glen Strae itself. Lands, not just ears! Point out that these must be fought for with great care. To keep the King's favour . . ."

"Would they heed me?"

"I do not know. For this is a terrible provocation. I cannot help the feeling that it was meant to be. And . . . so soon after you come of full age. The decision, the challenge, on you. Only *you*, now."

"You remain my adviser . . ."

So an assembly of the clan was called for one week hence. At Balquhidder, since that was where the concern was most fierce. Alastair sought to prepare himself for the first great test of his chiefship. He did not underestimate his task.

Or perhaps he did. For, three days before the meeting, further news reached Glen Strae, shocking news. The Balquhidder MacGregors, a branch of Glen Gyle, had not waited. A party of their young men had gone to Glen Artney, and hidden themselves, to watch for Drummond-Earnoch. And one day they had caught him, alone, up in a high corrie prospecting for a deer-drive. And there they had slain him and cut off his head, not just his ears.

Nor were they content with that. Drummond had married a sister of Stewart of Ardvorlich, a property on the south shore of Loch Earn. It seemed that Stewart was from home and, unmarried, he had left his sister and her husband in charge. The MacGregors had discovered this. Wrapping Drummond's head in a plaid, they had gone down to Ardvorlich and there, finding the wife alone, they had requested the usual Highland hospitality. And while the lady went to get them modest provision, they had taken her husband's head out of the plaid, set it on a platter on the table, and stuffed bread and cheese into the dead mouth. The widow, on sight of it, fled screaming. Then the miscreants had departed, taking the head with them.

Utterly appalled, Alastair and his uncle received this news. Much less so, significantly, were most of their clansfolk, who saw it rather as due justice. And even when reports filtered through the glens that the Lady of Ardvorlich had run off alone into the hills, mad, and none knew where she was now, there was little sympathy. She should not have married such as Drummond, they said, a harsh man who hated the Gregorach. And Ardvorlich himself was far from popular.

Ewan remarked on this attitude to his nephew. "You are going to find the same at Balquhidder, Alastair," he warned. "I fear, I fear . . ."

"What will the King think of this? When he returns."

"God knows! But Black Duncan will see that he hears of it. And will demand the fullest penalties of the law. That you may be sure. We are delivered into his hands."

"So what do I do? Tell me!"

"You have little choice. You are chief, and have to defend and sustain the honour of the clan. That first, whatever else. At whatever cost."

Alastair stared, wits in turmoil, spirits plunging.

There had not been such a gathering of the Gregorach for a century, even for battle. From every airt, near and far, from Rannoch and Ardchoille, Strathearn and Glengyle, Strathfillan, Glen Falloch and Glen Loin, and from places which were no longer MacGregor, with men who could no longer use the name, they had come. St Aeneas's Kirk of Balquhidder could not hold a quarter of them; only the seniors of the clan, the landed men, the *duine-wassails*, could get in, on its shelf above the river, there under the soaring heights of Ben More, Am Binnein and the other giant mountains.

The arrival of the chief, and the Glen Strae detachment, was greeted with prolonged cheering, despite Alastair's grim expression. So those within were warned as he and Ewan entered the crowded church. "Himself!" the cry went up. "Himself! MacGregor! Hail, MacGregor!" Acknowledging the salutations, they moved forward through the crush.

Reformation or none, this was still a Catholic church, and above the chancel-step it was still an altar not a communion-table. Mounting the step, his uncle at his back, Alastair took a further step up, to stand on a long stone which lay there before the altar, carved with ancient Pictish symbols: the *Clach Aeneas*, the stone of Columba's disciple who had founded this church eight hundred years before and which was considered to be very holy and important, so much so that during a marriage or a baptism, the principal actors therein were expected to stand on it, pronouncements therefrom being considered to be of the greatest significance. So Alastair stood on it now, turning to face the company, and raising his hand.

Even so, it took some time for him to gain quiet, so excited and impassioned was the emotion prevailing. And he had to raise his voice unnaturally high to counter the noise which came in from the kirkyard.

"Gregorach! My friends!" he exclaimed. "I, Alastair, greet you all. I salute you. As is my joy and privilege." He scarcely looked joyful nor privileged. "Yet – this is no joyful occasion. We are here gathered for a purpose, a hard and grievous purpose – "

Loud comment interrupted that.

He did not realise how he was frowning, so concerned, so urgent was he. "Hear me," he cried. "We, the Gregorach, have been insulted, yes. And we have in some measure repaid. But . . . less than wisely, I say. I fear." At the murmur which began, he raised hand again. "I say, friends, less than wisely. This of Drummond's head. And his widow turned mad. This will not help our honour, nor our cause. I . . ."

Again the swelling tide of disagreement.

Ewan shouted. "MacGregor speaks! Hear him!"

"I went to the King's court," Alastair went on, "to seek the *Ard Righ's* aid against Campbell of Glenorchy. To save Roro. It was not easy. But with the help of the Duke of Lennox and the Master of Gray, I gained the royal approval. Black Duncan was held. But . . . now we have slain the keeper of the royal forest of Glen Artney and steward of Strathearn. However much he deserved it. The King's representative. And this of the head, and Ardvorlich's wife. That will turn the whole house of Stewart against us. And the *Ard Righ* is head of the house of Stewart!"

Silence.

"So now we call this assembly to decide on what we do now. The King is meantime overseas in Denmark. To wed. But when he returns . . .! Meantime, the Duke of Lennox, another Stewart, is Viceroy. Young. Our friend, up until now. Will he be hereafter? And the King, when he returns?"

Still silence.

"We have to decide," Alastair went on, all but desperately. "All the realm's law will be used against us. Black Duncan will see to that . . ."

"The Gregorach has an older and better law than James Stewart's!" someone called out. "We pay our debts!"

There was a surge of agreement, acclaim.

"Yes. But at what cost? Roro? This Balquhidder itself? The whole clan branded outlaw?"

"Sassenach law! Lowland law!" Glengyle shouted.

"Aye. But the law can proclaim fire and sword against us. Any meeting a MacGregor entitled to slay him, if he can. Women not spared. Amany ready to fulfil that sentence! Campbells in especial."

The growl was vehement there – but it was the name of Campbell which provoked it. Alastair realised that he was gaining little or nothing of support for a careful approach, for taking the longer view.

"What do we, the Gregorach, value most?" he demanded. "Our lands? Our continuing existence as a clan? Or . . . vengeance?"

"Our honour! MacGregor's honour!" Ardchoille exclaimed.

Loudly he was cheered.

Alastair looked at his uncle, who shrugged. He had more or less prophesied this.

"What would you have Himself to do?" Ewan called.

There was a positive volley of shouting, unintelligible.

Ewan pointed. "You, Glengyle – what?"

"The clan's honour above all," that heavy man declared. "The chief must defend it. That first."

"Aye! Aye!"

"How, then?"

"By making this matter the responsibility of the whole clan. Not just of Balquhidder."

"How would that help?"

"The Sassenach law could punish a few, at Balquhidder. But not a whole clan."

"Are you so sure?" Alastair demanded. "I say it could. And it could lose us Roro. And more than that."

"Only if we let it!" That was, of all men, Roro himself, who had just come in, belatedly.

Alastair bit his lip. He had not expected this. He jabbed a pointing hand. "You, Roro! *You* say that?"

"Aye. If all Clan Alpin rallies, with claymores and dirks, to the defence of Roro, do you see any taking it? Ousting us? The Campbell? Or others? It would require an army. And who will send an army?"

Prolonged was the cheering, with no dissentient voice.

Alastair had to accept the inevitable. "The Campbells could muster a large host," he reminded, but without much conviction.

"Could – but *would* they?" That was Glengyle. "They never fight battles, only get others to do that for them. They rely on their laws! How many men can *we* muster?"

Shouts of numbers rose from all over the church. Whether or not exaggerating, these were the men who ought to know, some calling out their own contribution, some assessing totals. Most claimed one thousand to twelve hundred in all.

Roro homed in on that. "Fighting in our own glens. Lyon in especial, around Roro. How many would be required to defeat us? I say three times that! And who is going to send three thousand armed men to attack us? Not King Jamie! Certainly not Black Duncan."

"We would be outlawed. All MacGregors," Ewan reminded.

"If at the first attack on any of the Gregorach wherever, all the clan descended on the attackers, I say that there would be few more attacks!" Ardchoille averred. "And what have we to lose? We might well *gain* back what we have already lost, by being weak and divided. Let us be united, and strong. The Royal Race!"

That roused the company to heights of enthusiasm and decision. Even Alastair was not unaffected.

Into the clamour came action of a sort. Patrick MacGregor of Balquhidder himself, a hot-eyed man of early middle years, came pushing up to mount the chancel-step. He did not join Alastair and Ewan but moved behind them on their stone-slab, to the altar itself. Thereon was draped a plaid of the clan tartan, part-covering it. This he reached out to twitch off, to a great shouting.

Underneath was a man's head, a dark-haired, crumpled-featured, twisted-mouthed head, horribly blackened at the neck – Drummond's, of Drummond-Earnoch.

Many of those present had probably seen it before. Alastair was all but transfixed, gazing.

Balquhidder placed a hand on that bloody trophy. "Before God, all here present, and Himself, MacGregor, I, Patrick, swear to defend and avow the deed done, to maintain the honour and repute of Clan Alpin, unto the death! This I do affirm," he cried.

To resounding applause there was a concerted surge forward to follow suit, by all present, hands outstretched to touch that ravaged head and swear, Alastair almost overwhelmed in the rush.

When all had made their vows, every eye was turned on their chief. For his part, that young man looked at Ewan. His uncle nodded and shrugged in one; but the nod was towards the altar.

"Himself! Himself! MacGregor!" the cry went up.

Alastair bowed his head, took a deep breath, and stepped out, off his stone, hand out. "I swear!" he said. "To avow and defend the deeds done, in the name of Clan Alpin."

It was done. The fateful deed and duty performed, whatever the consequences. Men rushed out of the church to inform the crowd outside. And there the cheering went on and on. Whatever else, the Gregorach did not lack for spirit. As for judgment, only time would tell.

5

Doubtful indeed, Alastair came alone to Methven Castle, feeling that he had to do it, to inform, to explain if he could, to apologise, a man torn. The young duke might not be there, of course; but at least he had to make the attempt to see him.

Less than a week after the fateful meeting at Balquhidder, he came down Strathearn in the early evening, and guessed, by the lack of servitors and attendants about the castle precincts, that Lennox was not present. But, announcing his identity to the doubtful gatehouse guard, he was curtly instructed to wait while the Lady Mary was informed. Taking this to refer to the Mistress of Gray, the Lady Marie Stewart, he was surprised when the younger woman, the girl Mary Gray, came out to the courtyard to greet him, all smiles and welcome. Feeling as he did about his visit, he was stiffer, less outgoing, towards this attractive creature than he would have wished to be.

She, however, showed no such reticence, and haled Himself within with quiet friendliness and no sign of surprise. She explained that Duke Ludovick was at Stirling, or had been yesterday, for a Privy Council meeting; but she expected him back before nightfall. It was only forty miles to Stirling, a medium day's ride. She had waited the evening's meal for his return. Now Himself could share it with them. Had he come from Glen Strae?

While they waited, and Alastair supped wine and nibbled oatcakes, wondering whether to launch out as to the reason for his visit, Mary Gray pre-empted him by doing some explaining of her own, a curiously modest but frank exposition which she seemed to consider the circumstances called for – for apparently, apart from the castle steward and ducal servitors, she was alone at Methven.

"You will wonder to find me here in this house, lacking

other woman, friend?" she put to him. "Not all would approve."

Hurriedly he assured her otherwise, that she should be where she wished to be; and anyway, it was no concern of such as himself.

"Some see it otherwise," she observed, shaking her lovely head. "Some would name me fallen woman! Or worse. But . . . Vicky and I are happy. And my true father, the Master, does not condemn. Although he whom I call Father, David Gray at Castle Huntly, is . . . critical. Which gives me sorrow."

A little embarrassed by this strangely candid avowal, Alastair shook his head. "You are your own woman, are you not, Lady Mary? Need you care?"

"I am, and I am not," she told him. "I am but seventeen years. Not yet of age. My father, David Gray, who has reared and cherished me always, his half-brother's bastard, still considers himself responsible for me. Yet – Vicky and I love each other. So I am well pleased to be here, keeping his house meantime, however much others may disapprove. I care not for most, but David Gray, yes. And his wife, my mother."

Alastair wondered why she was telling him all this. But he liked her, indeed he more than liked her, he was aware. He had never known so delightful and clearly intelligent a young woman. He cleared his throat.

"The duke? He will not wed you?"

"Oh, he would. Indeed he would. He is ever at it. Asking me. It is *I* who will not wed. I cannot, you see."

"Yet you love him, you say?"

"That is why. I am a bastard. And the supposed daughter of a bastard land-steward, David Gray. By no means could I wed Vicky, Scotland's only duke, second person in the realm, next in line for the throne, the King's only legitimate cousin, however many he may have otherwise. And presently Viceroy of the kingdom. Despite himself yet being under age. He needs some great lady for wife, not a bastard girl. If King James was to die, Vicky's wife would be Queen! Think on that!"

Put thus, he could see it, of course. And yet . . .

"Vicky says that he would resile from it all. Abandon his position. He cares naught for titles and statecraft. He says that he would liefer be a country laird, with me as his wife. But that is not possible, for the heir to the throne, whilst there is no other. Save for a far-out Hamilton. The King and the Privy Council would never permit it. The succession must always be assured. If this royal marriage produces an heir, that would be better. But this Princess Anne of Denmark is but fifteen years. So, for years yet, Vicky will be heir-presumptive. Already he has been wed, of course – if only in name. To the sickly Lady Sophia Ruthven. But poor soul, she died, the marriage never consummated. Now they are seeking another wife for him, a suitable lady to strengthen the royal household."

"And if the duke did not wait? Married you out of hand. Then he could not be made to wed another."

"Oh, but he could. Being under age, the marriage could be annulled. And it would be, nothing surer. Even later, when he *is* of age. The King and council would insist on it. The Kirk too, I think. For they have made him a figurehead of the Protestant cause. James's religion is uncertain as so much else about him. So the Kirk needs the Second Person. It is all . . . difficult. So – here I am, at Methven, Vicky's courtesan!"

"How fortunate a man is Ludovick Stewart!" he asserted, greatly daring. "In this, at least."

She eyed him thoughtfully and shook her head. As she began to speak again, they heard noise from the courtyard, the clatter of hooves on cobblestones, and shouts. The fortunate man had come back to his felicity.

Lennox showed no signs of displeasure at the presence of their visitor – so presumably he had heard nothing as yet of the dire affair of Glen Artney and its consequences. Alastair waited until the excellent meal was all but over and the servitors withdrawn before he, reluctantly indeed, came out with the object of his call, somewhat abruptly announced when it came to the bit, neither of the couple having asked him.

"I have grievous tidings to tell you," he jerked, eventually. "To my sorrow, whatever. Hurtful to my cause, to the Gregorach cause. And to your good offices and kind help on our behalf. You, you have not heard?"

The duke looked questioningly. "Campbell? Glenorchy?"

"No, my lord. Not him. Not yet! Ourselves, the Gregorach, at fault. Folly, and worse. We have played into the Campbell's hands, and undone all that you, and the Master, and the King himself, have done for us. This of Drummond. Of Drummond-Earnoch."

"I know the man," Lennox nodded. "Steward of this Strathearn, of the royal earldom. And keeper of Glen Artney, for the King. His is a strong hand, but I have found him . . . difficult."

"No longer, my lord! For Drummond is dead . . ." And taking a deep breath, he plunged into the whole sorry story.

They heard him out, not without occasional interjections and questions, expressions grave indeed. Alastair did not attempt to gloss over any of it, to make excuses, not consciously nor deliberately that is, although he did not play down the notions of clan honour and the duties and responsibilities of chiefship, the inexorability of it all.

There was a long silence when he had finished, the three of them eyeing each other. Mary spoke first, and it was Lennox whom she addressed.

"So-o-o!" she said. "What now, Vicky? What is to be done?"

"God alone knows! The royal forester. The royal Steward of Strathearn. Murder and savagery. On both sides. But the one, on the face of it, within the law. The other sore against it. James is not going to like this. I fear, I fear . . ."

"As do I," Alastair agreed. "I recognise the price to pay. I do not seek your aid again, nor to involve your lordship, after all your kindness and help. Only to inform you. To seek your understanding of my own position. As chief . . ."

"And what does your Gregorach do now?" Mary asked.

"We have no choice. We return, lady, to the ages-old arbiter — the broadsword! What else is there for us? Nothing is more sure than that the Campbells will see all this as their justification. Theirs, the rights of it. They will have us where they want us, before the law. But . . . they are not so good with their swords!"

"Your clan will be outlawed," Lennox said.

"I know it. But outlawry is not greatly more than a word, if it cannot be enforced. In our glens and mountains, who will enforce it? Campbells?"

"In your main places, where you are strong in numbers,

your swords may protect you," the girl said. "But what of the smaller places where there are not many of you? Balquhidder itself? Loch Lomondside. These could be overrun, taken from you. The law enforced." She ever had a very practical mind, that girl.

"I know it. So we will keep a muster of armed men, ready at all times. A roving force. Moving round and round our clan-lands. In especial, the lesser places. Inversnaid, Glen Falloch, Bracklie, Coilettar and the like. I warn off those who might think to enforce the law."

"Could you keep that up, for long?"

"I do not know. We must try. But . . . men will tire of it, yes. In time. In winter. At the hay harvest. At droving days . . ."

"If the council outlaws you, grants fire and sword against you, anyone who aids you is also considered guilty and to be outlawed," the duke pointed out. "You could not sell your cattle to the dealers, at markets. Others selling them for you would suffer . . ."

"I know it. But far-away markets we may reach. And can *thousands* be outlawed, in more than name? In fact? In word perhaps – but in fact? A whole clan?"

"Perhaps not. But certainly you and your chief men can be. And . . . I do not see how I can help you."

"I do not ask it, my lord Duke. I did not come here seeking aid. Only to inform you, who were so kind, before. I owed you some explanation, at least."

"Can you do *nothing*, Vicky?" Mary Gray asked. "You, the Viceroy? And Patrick, who acts Chancellor. There must be something . . ."

"I do not see what. Nothing more sure than that Ardvorlich will appeal to the Privy Council. The Lord Drummond also. And Glenorchy sits on that council, with his chief, Argyll, young as he is. And the council will have to act. It can do no other. I preside, yes, and Patrick acts secretary. It may be that we can delay a sitting for a while. But what would that serve? And James will return before long. And *he* will have to act – his forester and steward beheaded. An atrocious deed. You would have been wiser to have condemned it out of hand, MacGregor, and handed over your Balquhidder ruffians to justice."

"Wiser, perhaps. But, a man can not always take the wise path, when others look to him to lead. Paths can be chosen for him."

"You, Vicky, know that," the girl said. "As when you had to wed the Lady Sophia. When you had to help overthrow Huntly, your sister's husband. And other." Clearly, Alastair had an ally in this Mary Gray.

"Yes, I know it. I will do what I can. See Patrick so soon as I may. He *could* see some way out of it all, with his nimble wits. If any could."

And so he chose. "Some secret way. For it must not be known that *I* have had speech with you, MacGregor. That I, or Patrick, could be favourable towards you . . ."

"No, no. That is why I have come here secretly. Alone. None must know that you are informed. But – I had to tell you, if I could."

"*That* was wise, was it not, at least?" Mary approved. "Whatever else. What do you do next, Alastair – if so I may name Himself?"

"I am honoured! Myself, I go back to Glen Strae as secretly as I came. The clan will be mustering. It is the droving season. Our most busy time: the cattle harvest. But not only MacGregors' – all the Highlands. So we may have some respite from attack. Then winter, with the passes often closed by snow. We may well be spared the fullest assault until the spring. Then . . ."

"Aye, then! And we will, I judge, have James home with his bride," Lennox said. "When the winter storms are over and sea-voyaging possible again. Then, I will be no longer the realm's man, but my own! For which I will praise God! But, at that time, I think, you will be in your greatest peril."

"Much may change before then," the young woman asserted. "In especial, if Patrick can, and will do aught."

"Aye, the Master of Gray," Alastair agreed. "How think you he will see all this?"

"Who knows?" that strange but so effective character's daughter answered. "But if he still will take your part, he may achieve much. Secretly. As he has done so often, in other matters. None in this kingdom has sharper wits, I think . . ."

"Save perhaps one Mary Gray!" the duke interjected.

"I but know how his mind works," she said simply. "Myself, I am not clever. It but comes to me, at times, the way that he will act, use others, see his advantage. And that of the realm and the King – for he does seek the kingdom's weal as well as his own!"

Both young men eyed her, silent.

"So now," she went on, smiling, "our couches call. Himself, I will show to his chamber in the east tower. You have both ridden far this day . . ."

"With respect, Lady Mary – no!" Alastair said. "You are kind – but no. I will be off now as secretly as I came. Not to spend the night here. Go now, in the darkening, riding westwards through the night. Be halfway home to Glen Strae by sun-up. None to see a lone horseman, save only your steward and guards here. And they will not speak of it, I swear, if your lordship commands."

"That is wise thinking, also," Lennox nodded. "For one who can make such wise decisions, it is sad that you had to make that other!"

They left it at that, and soon Alastair made his farewells. The young woman, unexpectedly, came into the MacGregor's arms, however briefly, at parting, and for a moment or two he held her to him, heart lifting.

Riding back up Strathearn through the half-dark, that man's mind was apt to be preoccupied with other than saving Clan Alpin.

6

So commenced a period of waiting, but very active waiting, at least as far as the Gregorach were concerned – and no doubt others also in their various attitudes to the situation and concerns. For, of course, the seasonal conditions which applied to the MacGregors applied to their enemies also, in these southern parts of the Highlands, the Campbells, Drummonds, Stewarts and their smaller allies such as the Buchanans, the Colquhouns and the MacFarlanes. Cattle-breeding, rearing and selling represented the life-blood of the Highlands, hundreds of thousands of the beasts having to be driven south to the Lowland markets, at Crieff, Perth, the Oban, Lochgilphead, Falkirk and the rest. This was the first priority for all, before the passes were blocked for the winter. And the toll-gathering, of course, important also.

Alastair chose to leave this aspect of their affairs meantime to his brother, John Dhu and Rob Ban and others. He himself sought to play the chief rather than the principal breadwinner of the clan in this situation. And however little his heart was in it, he had never been more busy, his Uncle Ewan aiding him.

His first duty was to build up his roving force of swordsmen which was to circumambulate the entire MacGregor country, scattered and in pockets and holdings often quite far apart, as they now were. This demanded a deal of organising, for of course the composition of this force had to be constantly changing, whatever the leadership. All branches of the clan had to contribute and take their turns, in appropriate numbers; and while there was no shortage of volunteers and manpower, the burden had to be spread as fairly, evenly, as possible – for all had cattle to sell, land to till, peats to dig and families to support. So Alastair and Ewan were busy indeed, planning, visiting, adjusting. And, at the same time, leading, demonstrating their strength to all potential enemies.

It was decided that a suitable number for their patrol would be about one hundred and fifty men, enough to warn the entire area that the Gregorach were ready for any eventuality, without seeming to make any specific challenge. Such an armed party, constantly making its appearance throughout this south-east Highland neighbourhood, ought to make the message clear to all.

Alastair himself led the first two circuits, anxious to maintain discipline rather than morale, to keep aggression tamped down – for the payment of old debts, especially in the Campbell lands, would be a major temptation, and inevitably much of their peregrinations would be through territory now occupied by Campbells.

The first sally, indeed, was deliberately so chosen, heading down Loch Aweside, going past Black Duncan's large castle of Kilchurn, and on along the eastern shore some six miles to where the Water of Stacain came in from the east. Up this climbing valley they went, to cross the little watershed into Glen Aray, and down that river. This was true Campbell country, their initial holding, Argyll's own land not the target for possible demonstrations. Reaching upper Loch Fyne, the longest of all the Highland sea-lochs, only a mile or so from Inveraray, the earl's seat, they turned north. Thus far they had encountered and provoked no least inimical reaction, however much interest and heed – which was, of course, what was desired.

Near the head of that fifty-mile-long loch, they had to pass Dundarave, the seat of the MacNaughton chief. Here they halted, and were well enough received, although with unspoken caution. The MacNaughton had to go warily indeed, in much reduced circumstances, with Campbells all around him, Inveraray to the south, Ardkinglas to the east, only too well aware that he was permitted to remain there on suffrance. If he and his opposed MacCailean Mhor, they would be driven out in a matter of days. But just to the north was the small MacGregor holding of Glen Shira, so this visit could hardly be held against MacNaughton. The chief privately wished his visitors well, but made no evident sympathy, nor was desired to.

On round the ultimate head of Fyne, and skirting Ardkinglas

land they went, sufficiently slowly to make their presence known without seeking trouble – not that Ardkinglas himself was strong enough to risk any sort of hostilities. They encountered none.

They struck off eastwards now, up Glen Kinglas, over the great and high watershed and down to the head of Loch Long. Then across the narrow neck of land to Loch Lomondside, all formerly MacGregor land. Lomond was a freshwater loch, unlike the others they had passed, itself some twenty-five miles long. This north and west end of it was Colquhoun country, very much under Campbell sway, this smallish clan indeed hereditary foes of MacGregor. No point in challenging here, although some of Alastair's people would have wished to, while they had the chance. Adamant, he insisted that it was onwards for them.

Round the head of Lomond they were into a mountainous area which had managed to remain Gregorach – indeed, where they were to pick up some reinforcements for their next sweep – Glen Falloch, Inversnaid, and Glen Gyle. No problems greeted them, save over-enthusiasm. The leaders here, of course, had all been at Balquhidder and sworn on that Drummond head. When they moved on through Strath Gartney and the Trossachs, heading now for the said Balquhidder, Glengyle himself, a senior chieftain, came with them.

After Balquhidder, it was back to Glen Strae, by Glens Ogle and Dochart and Strathfillan, now all Campbell land, indeed Black Duncan's, passing without actually threatening his castles of Edinample, Balloch and Finlarig. No opposition showed itself. Then over to Glen Lyon, Roro and home.

They had covered some one hundred and sixty rough miles in the nine days, in an approximate circle, and not so much as having once drawn sword in anger – to the disappointment of many but not of Alastair. This was as he and Ewan had planned it.

After a week's interval, they set out again, the party roughly the same size but differently composed, Alastair again leading, with Glengyle assisting instead of Ewan. This time they made another circuit, shorter, westwards into Lorn at first, then up Loch Etiveside and over to Glen Coe, to cross the wild and extensive Moor of Rannoch, and so back by Loch Tulla and the pass over into upper Glen Strae. The first snows had already fallen and the passes would be closed now for the winter, save for the most determined and energetic travellers. No incidents of any significance developed – but assuredly the message would not be lost on this part of Scotland; and, no doubt, further afield also.

Alastair felt that there was little need to keep up these expeditions over-frequently or in any great strength during the short, dark days and hard weather of the Highland winter, smaller patrols making shorter circuits being adequate for their purposes, surely. The spring would be the testing time.

That, as it transpired, proved to be a miscalculation. For soon after the Yuletide festivities were over, a patrol under Ewan and Alastair's brother John met with trouble. They were coming back down grim, bare Glen Lochy, and nearing the mouth of Glen Orchy itself, when they fell in with a company of Campbells under Black Duncan's steward coming from visiting Kilchurn Castle. The parties were approximately of equal numbers, although undoubtedly the MacGregors were the more effective force; but Ewan sought no confrontation, and would have passed with but frigid salutation. John of Dochard, however, was otherwise minded and spat out some insult as they went by, at the Campbell steward. Instantly there was tension and hands fell to sword-hilts. Ewan then had pushed forward, to come between John and the steward. One of the Campbells, seeing it, whipped out his dirk, presumably judging attack. Raising his dagger, he plunged it into the older man, a fierce blow to the heart. Ewan MacGregor, Tutor of Glenstrae, had fallen and died. Thereafter there had been the unavoidable furious onslaught of the Gregorach, wild fighting, and presently the Campbells fled.

The effect of these tidings on Alastair was shattering. He had been closer to his Uncle Ewan than to anyone else all his life. To have lost him thus was appalling, a friend and counsellor irreplaceable, the man who had reared him. And at this juncture, when the clan was so threatened and in crisis. And him so utterly, pointlessly, slain. The personal loss and the clan's loss was incalculable; and Alastair could not help partly blaming his headstrong brother, heir to the chiefship.

And what would be the reactions on the wider scene, with actual hostilities now seeming to have begun, no longer mere demonstrations?

From now on, Alastair was going to feel very much alone as Himself. He would head the patrols himself, in future.

Extraordinary as it might seem, the next significant development in the clan's concern with its destiny was a non-hostile visit to Glen Strae by a Campbell – Sir John of Cawdor. He arrived one frosty day of late February, unannounced, with only two grooms, on his way, he informed, to Inveraray to visit the Earl of Argyll. And however friendly, he came in grave mood, urgent. And urged to do so, it seemed, by the Duke of Lennox, the Master of Gray and Mary Gray.

There had been a Privy Council meeting, he informed, a week previously, this delayed for as long as the Viceroy and acting Chancellor had been able decently to contrive; and at this the inevitable had happened. The Drummond-Earnoch affair had been high on the agenda, and Duncan of Glenorchy, not a member but personally present as representing his under-age chief, hereditary Lord High Justiciar, had made the most of it all, adding that the MacGregors were now ranging the southern Highlands in armed strength, threatening the peaceful lieges, harrying and slaying, and had even attacked his own, Glenorchy's, steward going about his lawful business, to the effusion of blood. The King's writ no longer ran in this part of the realm.

It had been difficult for the MacGregors' friends, in the circumstances, highly placed as they were, to offer any effective contradiction or defence. The required sentence had been duly passed, almost without other dissent and in much offence. Outlawry of the clan, fire and sword against all of the name of MacGregor, reward for all who might put this edict into effect. In the name of the King's Grace.

So that was now the position – not unexpected but dire indeed.

Most of the Gregorach leadership were inclined to scoff. What difference did it make? Their armed patrolling had demonstrated the realities of the situation. They would continue to so do – and who would the said Privy Council send to enforce their ridiculous sentence? Black Duncan's Campbells? Almost that was to be hoped for! Then they would show who really held the sway in these glens. Not that this was Alastair's attitude.

Cawdor was less assured also. Let them not write off the Campbell strength, *armed* strength, so readily. Black Duncan himself might not risk armed confrontation; but MacCailean Mhor was a different matter. That young man, if so advised and so inclined, could put five thousand men in the field in a couple of weeks, and all but double that in a month. In actual battle, which God forbid, the MacGregors might just possibly dispose of the first; but thereafter, tired and with casualties, what of a second Campbell host? With allies – Colquhouns, Buchanans, MacArthurs? Backed by the law?

That made even John of Dochard look thoughtful.

Cawdor advised caution therefore, where possible. As did those who had urged him to come. Dispense with the patrols meantime, so as not to seem to be challenging the Privy Council ruling. Keep the peace, if they could – at least until the King came home. James was the only one who could overrule the council decision, which of course had been made in his name. They had friends at court, and who knew what might yet be achieved if there was no further provocation? For himself, he would seek to do what he could with Argyll.

Alastair agreed that his clan must be held in check meantime, as far as possible – although that would not be easy.

Cawdor, before leaving, handed over a brooch of silver wire in the shape of a Pictish symbol, crescent and V-rod, which he declared Mary Gray had sent as a token of friendship and sympathy, a great satisfaction for Alastair.

In fact, Sir John was back in only three days, having gone to the trouble of returning south this round-about way in order to acquaint Alastair as to developments. The Privy Council had appointed three of its members to see that its condemnation and punishment of the Gregorach was fully carried out – the Earls of Huntly, Atholl and Argyll; but the latter, being a minor, his guardian-advisers had to act in his stead. However, Huntly, Lieutenant of the North, was far too busy in his far-away north-eastern territories for much personal preoccupation with this matter. And Atholl was, if anything, more favourable towards the MacGregors than to their enemies. So that the carrying out of the fire and sword edict would inevitably fall mainly on the six Campbell advisers. This was both good and bad, with Black Duncan the nearest placed and most virulent. Sir James, of Ardkinglas, was in his pocket. And Lochnell, although the heir, was feeble. That left Auchenbreck, the youngest, although chieftain of broad lands. And Bishop Neil and himself. The bishop, illegitimate, was despised by Glenorchy, and resented it; he had been the only one present at Inveraray on this occasion. So, in practice, it probably came down to three against three, himself and Black Duncan leading – although young Argyll was not to be dismissed, with his own views.

Unfortunately, the Lord Drummond, who was quite influential and eager to avenge his kinsman's murder – also, if possible, to gain the MacGregor lands of Strath Gartney and Balquhidder, no doubt, adjoining his own – had, according to the bishop, already been in touch with Black Duncan urging joint action, a tryst as he called it, a sweep of armed men, to counter the Gregorach ones, attacking with armed force vulnerable MacGregor outlying places. The Drummonds were not normally noted for aggressiveness and Glenorchy's Campbells no major military threat; but they might seriously damage lesser Gregorach communities and provoke fierce retaliation – which could be seen to be against the crown, treason, forcing Huntly and Atholl to do something to fulfil their remit. And the price was high, for the council's decision, naming Alastair, John, their uncles and one hundred and thirty-five other MacGregors could, if taken, be hanged without trial there and then, and their lands confiscated, half to go to the confiscators, half to the crown.

One last point Cawdor revealed. Glenorchy had already applied to his chief, as hereditary senior Justiciar, for specific personal authority to take over Glen Strae in the name of the King.

Alastair, taking all this in, or trying to, could do little more than wag his head. Telling him not to do anything provocative, in the circumstances, was like ordering him to stop a river from flowing. Control of his spirited clan was difficult enough at any time; now it would be a task indeed. He could by no means stop their armed patrols, with the Gregorach perimeter endangered. It would be only a question of time before there was a major clash. His people might well win that. But . . .

Cawdor understood, but could not counsel other than caution, at least until the King got home. Once he did, the duke and the Master of Gray might achieve some betterment, if there had been no further provocation. He still felt that young Argyll was the key – if it could be turned in the lock. He would seek to work on him. And there was one useful ally, probably: the young man's mother. Joanna, Countess of Argyll had been a Keith, the daughter of the Earl Marischal, and still only in her thirties. She and Black Duncan did not get on; indeed he owed her a large sum of money it was said, which he should have repaid long since, for what was not disclosed. That debt might prove to be useful . . .

Cawdor departed for Methven and the south, leaving anxiety and defiance both, behind.

7

Word reached Glen Strae in late May that King James had at last won home from Denmark with his bride – and in a great state of agitation, garbled versions of which came to them. Up until then, somehow, Alastair had managed to restrain his people from major indiscretion, perhaps somewhat fortuitously as much as by his efforts. He was missing Ewan direly, and his brother John no great help.

It was not until June that they gained any detailed news, with the arrival of the Duke of Lennox, Sir John of Cawdor and Mary Gray, from Methven. They came, on the whole, cheerfully, Cawdor congratulating Alastair on so far having managed to avoid major hostilities, the duke friendly, Mary her usual delightful self.

The King, it transpired, was not particularly interested in the MacGregor situation one way or another, for he had more on his strange mind. He had been delayed by unseasonable storms all the way from Denmark, it seemed, and allegedly all but shipwrecked off the Bass Rock, near North Berwick, so close to home. He was convinced that this was the work of the Devil himself, seeking to destroy him, James Stewart, the Lord's Anointed. And his own cousin, the Earl of Bothwell, was Satan's tool, the witch-master and chief dispenser of evil, eager to slay the monarch before he could produce an heir to the throne on his new wife. The earl had even arranged for a sieve-load of witches, in the guise of hares, to sail round the royal ship, the King said, to try to sink it, only his fervent prayers saving them. So this odd welcome for Queen Anne to her new country had turned into a witch-hunt, with trials, questionings, tortures, burnings, Catholics and Protestants finding the occasion apt to accuse each other of complicity, and therefore to be thus disposed of. Chaos reigned – and there was no time for mere Highland follies and cantrips.

Duke Ludovick, hating it all, and no longer Viceroy, was disassociating himself as far as he could from the royal preoccupation and presence, living at Methven. The Master of Gray remained at court, seeking, according to his daughter, to keep some sanity in affairs of state. Mary Gray herself was now openly living with the duke, and thankful to be so far away from all the agonies, the fears and terrors prevailing.

So, as far as feared royal disapproval or anger was concerned, the MacGregors seemed to be safe for the time being. The Privy Council edict still stood, of course, but only the Campbells and their Drummond and Buchanan allies looked likely to try to enforce it. And Cawdor was now going to Inveraray again, with a proposition to put before MacCailean Mhor and his mother. Black Duncan was not having it all his own way.

Lennox and Mary were well content to stay on at Glen Strae while Sir John went on to Loch Fyneside, Alastair happy to have them. Mary was kind, even affectionate, and the young man had to restrain himself from showing too much appreciation. The girl and the duke were obviously in love, but she seemed to be genuinely fond of Himself.

In the early summer weather Glen Strae, and its environs, was a good place to be in.

Three days later Cawdor returned, well pleased. He had made an ally of the Countess Joanna who, having been wife to the late and potent Regent Moray before she remarried Argyll's father, knew how to gain her way. Her enmity towards Black Duncan was a great asset. That man, able and clever as he was, might be his own worst enemy. Together they had convinced the young Argyll that outright battle between Campbells and MacGregors would serve the former, in general, nothing, only bloodshed, only Glenorchy gaining. So MacCailean Mhor was commanding a truce, a coming together – or as nearly such as was possible. And at once. He was sending a special messenger to Glenorchy insisting on it; Duncan would have to obey him, not only as his chief but as the hereditary Justiciar from whom he gained his sub-justiciarship, for this could be withdrawn.

"What does this mean? A truce?" Alastair demanded, the other two almost equally interested.

"A meeting at Kilchurn between you both. With witnesses. Myself, and my lord Duke here. An agreement to be reached, and signed, the peace to be kept thereafter. On both sides. No aggressions. No provocations. Peace, of a sort."

They stared at each other. This was extraordinary, scarcely believable. If Black Duncan would heed?

"He must," Cawdor declared. "He has no choice. The matter is decreed. Thanks largely to the Countess Joanna. She trained in a hard school – not her father's, the Earl Marischal; but her first husband was James Stewart, Earl of Moray, the Regent Moray. The hardest man this realm has produced for long!"

"I knew her," Mary Gray said. "I did not know that she had wed the Earl of Argyll. I would liefer be her friend than her enemy!"

"Glenorchy is a fool to keep owing her moneys," Lennox said. "He must be a rich man, himself?"

"There must be some other reason for this . . ."

It was decided that all four should go down to Kilchurn Castle, warning sent that they were coming.

Alastair had never thought to be doing this, approaching the hated stronghold on its peninsula which jutted into Loch Awe, so comparatively near and so greatly more powerful that his own modest house of Stronmilchan. He had been reared to loathe and fear it, certainly never to enter its frowning walls. Yet here he was, and not coming as any suppliant.

The little peninsula was almost an island, with a defensive marsh between it and the mainland, with a narrow causeway of stone across and a drawbridge beyond, the tall curtain walls, gatehouse and bartisans making a difficult place to assault or besiege, since cannon could be kept well out of range. But today this need not concern them; the Countess of Argyll was more powerful, her range longer, than any cannon.

Their approach could not remain unseen, and a servitor, richly clad for that order and bearing a staff of office – a sort of chamberlain, apparently, and an unsuitable affectation for anyone under the rank of earl – came to meet them at the drawbridge, to conduct them within, in style. The gatehouse arch, through what was actually the castle's main keep, led into a courtyard surrounded by angle-towers and subsidiary buildings, barracks, kitchens, brewhouse and the like. Here the chamberlain left them standing, saying that he would tell his master — itself something of an affront, since all in the castle must have known of the approach. Cawdor frowned.

Presently Glenorchy arrived from behind them in the keep, dressed as usual all in black save for the white neck-cloth but not wearing his cowl, his good-looking aquiline features schooled in a sort of expressionless civility.

"My lord Duke," he said thinly. "Sir John. Lady. Mac-Gregor." That was all.

Cawdor answered. "We come, as we informed you. On MacCailean Mhor's command. Or," glancing at Lennox, "on his request."

"So I understand. I do not think that our business will detain you long, my lord Duke. And lady."

Mary Gray trilled a little laugh. "Oh, but we looked to admire this great house of yours, sir. One of so many, we are told. Seven, is it not? You must have more than you can readily enjoy? Already!" If that was barbed, it was sweetly said.

Glenorchy eyed her quickly, and coughed. "Come within. Refreshments," he jerked.

Upstairs in the great hall provisions were set out, the chamberlain serving. Cawdor did not seek to delay what could be no comfortable session. He produced papers from his doublet.

"Here, Glenorchy, is the missive and wording of the truce which your chief has devised and drawn up, for abatement of the disagreement between yourself and Glenstrae here. For an end to ill will. MacCailean Mhor commands that you sign it. Glenstrae has agreed to do so also. You have pen and ink?"

Narrow-eyed, Black Duncan stared. "The disagreement is between MacGregor and the Privy Council," he said. "I but seek to obey its commands."

"My lord duke is a member of that Privy Council, presided at its meeting, Glenorchy. As is our own chief."

"I believe him to have been misinformed."

"By his lady mother? Bishop Neil? And myself?"

Ludovick of Lennox found his voice. "Would I misinform the Earl of Argyll, sir?"

Silence.

"MacCailean Mhor is well informed," Cawdor went on. "And his wishes are clear as they are strong. In few words they are set down here." He tapped the papers. "There are two copies, one for each of you. Do you not wish to read it?"

Lips tight Glenorchy signed, with no flourishing and flung down the quill. He had not read it.

"Again, Glenorchy. On the other paper. Yours already signed by Glenstrae. Now you, on this, Glenstrae."

Alastair made his mark. He had not spoken a word, so far.

Cawdor offered the papers to the duke. "As witness, my lord," he said.

Lennox signed both, then Cawdor himself. The thing was done.

There was no further comment, no hand-shaking, no lingering, no farewells even. Black Duncan gestured at the chamberlain and inclined his head. Alastair clutching his paper, they were led out, without backward glances. Mary Gray's hand was on his arm. He had a document which said that there would be no hostile actions nor threats nor disturbances of the King's peace, by either signatory or their dependents, for a period of six months, with renewal thereafter anticipated, the witnesses pledged to substantiate this.

There was feasting at Stronmilchan that night. But none there imagined that Black Duncan was disposed of indefinitely.

8

So, contrary to all expectations, the rest of 1590 and the following year passed in unaccustomed peace in the vicinity of Loch Awe, whatever was the case elsewhere in the realm, racked by witch-hunts, trials, torturings, treachery and fear. The King appeared to be slightly mad, but his concern was not with MacGregors and Campbells or other Highlandmen, whom he seemed to consider outwith the range of witchcraft. The duke said that James was in fact writing a book on demonology and sorcery, and looked on the many trials as useful material, and the processes of extracting information and confessions highly relevant.

Alastair saw quite a lot of Lennox and Mary, who found Methven a blessed haven of peace and sanity from the fraught atmosphere of the court and the King's obsession. They could not absent themselves altogether, of course, for Lennox was still heir-presumptive to the throne and Mary had been appointed an extra Woman of the Bedchamber to young Queen Anne. But James was spending much of his time at Stirling Castle, where he had been born, or Falkland Palace, his favourite hunting-seat, and it was only a day's ride from Strathearn to either of these. Alastair found occasion to visit Methven almost as often as the pair came to Glen Strae – although he told himself that this was a sort of folly, for Mary Gray assuredly was never to be for him.

It was on one of these visits in autumn the following year that the steward there, the duke being absent, gave Alastair word of a most surprising development – a royal summons to court, no less. He had been about to bring it to Glen Strae. Astonished, Alastair could scarcely believe that the man was in his right mind; but the steward insisted. The duke had sent a courier from Falkland with this message. He, Glenstrae, was to go to Falkland. The King's Grace required his presence at court, forthwith. A royal command. No further details.

Needless to say, Alastair was in a quandary, not about what to do, since that was decided for him, but why this should happen. Was it good news or bad? He was, after all, outlawed by the council; anyone who could do so entitled to hang him. Was this belated justice catching up with him? Was there to be a trial? Had his enemies persuaded the King? But, in that case, would Duke Ludovick have sent this message? Would he not rather have warned him not to come if a royal summons came? Not himself arranged for the royal summons to reach Glen Strae. He would have to go. But . . .

He waited three days, in case a royal representative arrived with the command. But none such appearing, he set off, this time with only half a dozen running gillies – a chief could scarcely travel with less – to head for Fife, in a very uncertain frame of mind. He halted at Methven in the by-going, but learned nothing new there.

At Falkland again, he went directly to the Master of Gray's lodging, where the Lady Marie greeted him kindly – but indicated that Mary Gray had thought that he would have been there at least two days previously. He could not explain his three-day wait, in the circumstances, but muttered about unavoidable delay. Mary herself, it seemed, was out with the hunt on this occasion. Queen Anne was not averse to this sport, new to her, the hunting of deer not being known in Denmark, and insisted on going with her husband sometimes – apparently to his royal disapproval, for women could only hold up the chase, he asserted. But Anne had a mind of her own, and went – at least often starting out with the main hunt, but was apt to be left behind by her husband's enthusiasts, although not by all the courtiers who were quite happy with a more leisurely and easy-going sport. These did not kill many deer but seemed to enjoy the proceedings. And Mary, Woman of the Bedchamber, was expected to go also, and found no fault.

Alastair could scarcely ask his hostess if she knew why he had been summoned thus, and the Lady Marie did not volunteer information. But she certainly did not seem uncomfortable or concerned about his presence and was entirely friendly –

which surely she would not have been had he been coming for trial and possible execution. Especially as she did speak on the subject of trials and executions, with some distress and sorrow – this witchcraft horror. She said how relieved they were to get away from Edinburgh and Stirling, where these horrible and shameful inquisitions were going on, here at Falkland the King being blessedly more concerned with his hunting of deer than of witches, especially at this autumn season, the best time of the year for his favourite sport. James was her cousin, in blood, yes – but this sorcery nonsense had quite gone to his head, with ghastly results for so many. The red of the fires for burning the unfortunates had been lighting up the Edinburgh and Stirling skies of a night for months now. To Alastair's puzzled demands as to whether there was indeed so much of witch and wizard in the Lowlands – they had none in the Highlands – he was told that his hostess thought that there was really none, of a truth, but that a certain amount of covening and Devil-worship play-acting did go on, meaning little. But James had it firmly in his mind that Satan was seeking to destroy him thus, and any least suggestion or suspicion was enough for him to order trial – especially with his book on the subject to compile. And once arrested, and justified as he named the torture they were put to to gain confessions, the wretched creatures would admit to anything, and implicate others, the witch-testers expert at getting their private enemies implicated. So, let Himself be thankful that it was here to Falkland that he had been summoned.

When the duke and Mary eventually arrived, their welcome was not such as to hint at trouble. On the contrary, they seemed almost congratulatory. All ill was not over, but Alastair's affairs were assuredly on the mend.

It turned out that it was, as so much else, the Master of Gray's doing, with the help of his friend Campbell of Cawdor. The Master was at present at Stirling, but would be back in a day or two. He had convinced the King that his Privy Council had made a grievous mistake, this now emphasised by the Earl of Argyll's order of a truce to Glenorchy.

When the huntsmen got back to Falkland, on the recommendation of the duke, Alastair should not attempt to see the King that night, for the monarch was in a bad mood, as he so often was since his marriage and after a poor day's sport. Although here on James's command, it would be better for him to join in next day's hunt quietly, in the morning, and proceed from there. The duke was not sure what was in the King's mind on this matter, nor was Cawdor, who called in later. They would learn in due course. It was unfortunate that the Master was away.

Meantime all was friendly hospitality.

In the misty early morning, then, and mounted on the fine horse he had been given, Alastair went with the duke to join a distinctly sour and silent company assembled in the palace forecourt. Sir John of Cawdor was already there and greeted Alastair with a sort of rueful warmth.

James appeared shortly thereafter, overdressed as usual, acknowledging the presence of none nor their salutes. Since Lennox was standing to his horse in the foreground and Alastair in his tartans beside him, the monarch could scarcely fail to notice him, but gave no sign. At the chief huntsman's horn-blowing, James led the way off, amongst hasty mounting – and Alastair noted that the two garrons he had presented on the previous occasion were being led along, without riders. If Queen Anne was going hunting today, sensibly she must be doing so later.

This time they rode much further westwards along the Lomond foothills before turning to climb. And here the King got down from his handsome Barbary black and mounted one of the rough garrons. In the saddle he turned, and unsmiling jabbed an imperious finger at Alastair. At his side, Duke Ludovick nudged urgently, and hurriedly Alastair jumped down to go forward to the royal side. Without a word, James gestured to the other garron, and without waiting or speaking, spurred his beast uphill. Alastair mounted and followed on.

Here was an extraordinary situation indeed, the condemned and outlawed MacGregor chosen to ride in front of all, with their sovereign-lord. What Privy Councillors present thought of it was beyond all guessing.

Alastair carefully kept his garron well behind the King's, until he realised that the monarch was speaking – who had a difficult enough voice to interpret anyway, his tongue too large for his mouth.

"Guid beasts, Hielantman," he managed to distinguish as he drew level. "No' bonny, but guid on the hill."

"Yes, Sire. They are bred for it, whatever."

"Aye. Your Hielant hills are steeper than this?"

"Much, Sire. Great mountains. Craigs. Deep corries. Chasms. Screes . . ."

"Aye. I've heard tell o' siclike."

"Your Grace has never seen them? Never visited your Highland realm?"

"Guidsakes, no! Yon ill wilderness! Nae place for decent Christian fowk! God-fearing."

"*I* fear God, Sire." Alastair was greatly daring. He had heard from Mary Gray that the King could accept, even approve of plain speaking, on occasion. "And we have less trouble with the Devil, Satan, I think, than you have in the Lowlands!"

James shot a keen, swift glance sidelong at him from those great, almost feminine eyes. "Ho, ho! Sae that's the way o't! Hoity-toity, eh? You Hielant limmer!"

"No, no, Sire. Only concerned over Your Grace's troubles with this of witchcraft, which I have heard of. Concerned for your royal well-being . . ."

"No' sae greatly consairned that you wouldna cut off the heid of my royal forester o' Glenartney! Yon Drummond."

Alastair swallowed, mind racing. "Not I, Highness. But . . . some of my clansfolk, yes. I, I greatly deplored it. And, and he had cut off their ears . . ."

"But no' slain them."

"With Highlanders, Sire, we would have preferred them slain, I think. Less of insult to MacGregor."

"You say so? Man, that's right interesting. Aye. But you dinna hae sae mony witches?"

"None, Sire. I know of no witches."

"Nae witchcraft! I canna credit that, man. They're a' place. Dinna tell me yon ill Satan doesna find tools in the Hielants? Did I no' hear, some time, the fowk there can foretell what's to come? Is that no' witchery?"

"Not witchcraft, Sire. That is *shealladh. Laimh. Roimh-laimh*. The sight . . ."

"Hech, man, dinna seek to cozen me wi' your heathenish tongue! Gie me guid Scots words."

"It is the sight, Sire – the second sight. Foreseeing. Many have it, the women in especial . . ."

"Aye – witches!"

"Not so, Sire. Good Christian women. My own mother had it, in some measure."

"Eh? She did? She could foresee what's to come?"

"Only some happenings. On occasion. Her own father, she said, had it better . . ."

"You say that? It's inherited, then? Sae *you* could hae it, Alastair man?" That was the first time that the monarch had used his name.

"I, I think not, Your Grace. I am not so blest . . ."

"You hae never foretell't?"

"Not truly, Sire. I have had feelings that some matter might come about. But have not we all? We guess or calculate, without thinking it. That is not foretelling."

"But you get warning? O' ill? Ken something o' what may be coming?"

Alastair wagged his head helplessly. "Not that I can say so, in truth. Only . . . inklings."

"Inklings, hey? Frae you, who canna write!" The monarch chuckled at his wit. "I am fell interested in this, man," he confided. "You see, I am inditing a buik. On this very matter. Or . . . on like matters. Siclike. Maist ken naething o't a'. Belike you can help me. Wi' your Hielant sight. Aye." The King paused. "Hech – was yon hoo you kenn't aboot the arrows? To hae them birling roond?"

"No, Sire. That was but trial, testing. Seeking out the way of it."

"Just so. As I am daeing wi' thae witches and warlocks. Testing. To win at the truth. It's no' easy, mind. They ay lie. They say a' things . . ."

They had come to the crest of the spur of hill which it seemed they had been heading for, and James drew up. The land sank before them in wooded sweeps and undulations, and this presumably was the scene of the day's hunt. The King suddenly appeared to lose all interest in their conversation, witchcraft or second sight. He waved forward his groom with the black Barbary, to exchange with the garron for the actual chase.

Alastair was relegated to suitable obscurity.

For the rest of the day of indifferent sport he remained with the duke and Cawdor. At the midday break for refreshments, he did note the monarch eyeing him, but there was no summons.

That evening he discussed with his friends his strange conversation with the monarch. Lennox saw little in it of significance, in view of James's obsession with demonology, but Mary Gray did.

"He said that Himself might aid him," she pointed out. "That could mean something, perhaps much."

"Or nothing with James. No more than listening to some of his writings. As you had to do with his poetry."

"So long as he does not want me to assist in his torturings and witch-trials," Alastair said unhappily.

"He is not conducting these in person here at Falkland, God be praised! At Stirling and Edinburgh. Even at Cupar, here in Fife. But not in Fothrif, where his sport is all-important."

"No, but he still writes the book," the girl declared. "The Queen complains that he is ever at it. Until late in the night. He does not . . . come to her. He might mean help with that."

"I cannot see how I can aid him. What did he send for me, here, for? Do you know?"

"He did not say. I believe that it was on Patrick's advice – the Master's." The duke glanced at Mary.

That young woman shook her head. "Patrick did not confide in me. But . . . it would not be to Himself's hurt."

"Patrick's mind works in devious ways," the Lady Marie observed. "There will be advantage in it – but for whom?"

"When does he return, lady?"

"Who knows? He was to be at Stirling – from where the realm is presently being ruled. But he could be anywhere. Broughty, or in the Carse. Anywhere. And he prefers the affairs of state to this hunting."

They left it at that.

In the morning it was the same programme almost exactly, James changing to the garron soon after they started uphill, and beckoning Alastair to his side, only the chief huntsman ahead.

"I hae been considering this o' the sight, man Alastair," he started at once, without preamble. "Or whatever ill name you gie it. I judge it relevant, aye, relevant. If you ken what that means?"

"I do, Sire."

"But you tell me that you canna write!"

"Is it necessary to write to understand words, Highness?"

"Eh? Och, weel, maybe no'. I hadna thought o' that. Who taught you, then?"

"My mother. My uncle, later. My Tutor of Glenstrae."

"*They* could write?"

"He could. She, no."

"Why did he no' learn *you*, then?"

"My father had been slain by then. By the Campbells. I was chief, child as I was – as *you*, Sire, were King. It was not considered suitable, or necessary, for a chief to have to write words. So long as he spoke them, gave his commands."

"Guidsakes – d'you tell me that! No' necessar. You rate your chiefs high, you Hielantmen!"

"Not too high, I hope, Highness. The chief has . . . other tasks to learn."

"Yon Glenorchy can write," the monarch observed shrewdly. "He sent a letter to the council. The Master showed me it."

"Glenorchy is not a chief, Sire."

"Ha, so that's it! Can Argyll write, then? He'll be *his* chief, will he no'?"

"His chief, yes. But I doubt the writing, Sire."

"But he's Justiciar, man, even but by descent."

"Need justiciars write? They have clerks for that, I would think."

"So-o-o! You jalouse *I* shouldna write, then, my mannie? Me – who's the chief o' chiefs!"

"Why no, Your Grace. Yours is different, a different place and tradition. Lowland, not Highland."

"Different, aye. Guidsakes, different frae Hielant! The Lord be thankit! Aye, and if I couldna write, how could I pen my buik? Tell me that."

"Your Grace, I am not against the writing, whatever. Just not for the likes of my own self. Although – you could tell your words to a clerk, who could write them down on paper."

"Man, man, yon's no' how buiks are writ or made or indited. The wits dinna work that way. The writer *sees* it a', and canna gie it to ithers to write doon. You ken naething o' it. But never heed. I'll hear aboot your strange Hielant ways anither time. It's this o' foresight I'm consairned wi', see you. How d'you ken you hae it? How you get it? How young, when you start it? I'll need to ken. I'm thinking for to mak a chapter on it – a short bit chapter only, mind. For it's no' a that important in demonology. Sae I'll need it a', frae you."

"Sire, I never thought! Had no notion of this. Would have said nothing. I . . ."

"As weel you did, man. Nane, I vow, hae ever written on this afore. The first, see you. So I hae to hae it right. In fu'. You to tell me."

"I scarcely can, here, Sire. Now. I must think. Consider well. Seek to remember . . ."

"I'ph'mm. You dae that, man Alastair. And since you canna write, you'll need to remember weel, will you no'?" There was a royal chuckle at that.

"Could *you* write your questions, Sire? Beforehand? The duke, or Mary Gray would read them to me. Then I would know what your Grace wanted . . ."

Alastair realised that they had halted the garrons, evidently having climbed as high as they were going. Nobody had come up alongside, however, to disturb the monarch.

James considered the suggestion. "We'll see. Easier just to speir, mind – to ask you."

"If I was to know before, I could give Your Highness better answers, I think." It did not occur to Alastair that he could be arguing with or seeking to constrain his sovereign-lord.

Presumably that did not occur to James either, for he did not seem to be offended. "We'll see," he repeated. "Mind, I'm no' promising anything." He appeared suddenly to become aware of all the waiting hunt behind. "Och, weel . . ."

Turning in the saddle the King waved forward the black horse, and Alastair recognised that the interview was at an end. He reined back, discreetly. He would have liked to have asked what had been the royal objective in summoning him to Falkland in the first place, but felt that this might be too much.

As far as he was concerned, the rest of the day passed pleasantly enough, if uneventfully. He was present at no deer-killing.

When he recounted much of all this to his friends that evening, Mary Gray at least was joyful, actually clapping her hands.

"This is excellent!" she cried. "You are become James's partner and assistant. Closer than any of his lords – who all scoff at his book – although not to him! Himself, the royal scribe! What could be better?"

"But . . . I can, in truth, tell him nothing of this second sight. It is not a matter which can be told. It is a, a gift. That *I* do not have."

"Make it a gift for your advantage, Yourself. May I name you Yourself? Use the opportunity. Even though there is little of fact in it. For, to be sure, there is little of fact in this of witchcraft and sorcery either, I swear. Fact comes little into it. Only the King's folly. So – use his goodwill."

Alastair shook his head, at a loss.

The day following was Sunday, and even James Stewart did not hunt on the Sabbath. So the routine was altered. A kirk service was held in the forenoon at which, it appeared, all the court was expected to attend, whatever their religious convictions. Alastair had never been at a Reformed service, and found it strange indeed and to him rather dreary, although the lengthy, thundering sermon was scarcely that, all denunciations and challenges, accusations and threatenings, extraordinary as allegedly said in the name of their Loving Father. The duke had to go and sit beside the King, at the front; and the Queen, with her noble ladies-in-waiting, had no need here of a mere bastard Woman of the Bedchamber, so Mary Gray had Alastair sit beside her and Sir John Cawdor. At least they had seats, where so many had to stand – which for two hours must have been trying, even to the most faithful.

There was no royal call for any of them to attend at the palace thereafter. James would, it was thought, spend the day at his book. Alastair hoped that his aid would not be required.

In the late afternoon, Patrick, Master of Gray arrived unexpectedly, no explanations given as to why or wherefore.

98

He was nowise surprised to see Alastair there and was entirely friendly. It was, strangely, during the evening meal that, quite casually, he revealed the real reason for Alastair's summons to Falkland – he himself, it seemed, having advised the monarch to command it. He was here, it appeared, more or less as a hostage for his clan's good behaviour. Patrick believed that, with their chief in the King's hands, they would not be so apt to endanger the precious peace which he, with Cawdor and Argyll, had imposed on Black Duncan. That man, he felt, would do everything possible short of outright hostilities to provoke the MacGregors during this autumn period, despite his signature, and blame it on the Gregorach when the latter might well retaliate. But if Himself was in the care of the monarch, and could be held responsible for their behaviour, they might be the more careful.

Alastair was not entirely convinced by this reasoning, knowing his brother John. Also he was concerned over the matter of time. For how long was he here, then? He had thought to return to Glen Strae in a matter of days. But as hostage . . . ?

The Master smilingly dismissed that as unimportant. And when he heard that James was enlisting Alastair as accomplice in his book-writing, he expressed himself as delighted. This would all help. His aim was eventually to win a royal and total cancellation of the Privy Council edict of outlawry, and an overall pardon for the Clan Gregor. This now looked distinctly hopeful.

Grateful as he was, Alastair had his doubts, but he did not express them.

Back to hunting next day, with the high ground again chosen, the garrons were required and Alastair found himself alone with his sovereign once more. James eyed him almost accusingly.

"You hae considered weel aboot your sight and foretelling, man? I've gien you time."

"I have thought much on it, Sire. But there is little to tell . . ."

"Dinna haver to *me*, Hielantman! Dinna seek to cozen me, *your* chief. I'm no' daft, mind. I'll hae the truth oot o' you. Sooth-saying, was it no' you ca'd it? Hielant sooth. And sooth means truth."

"If I knew, Sire, what you wanted to learn . . .?"

"A' thing. Whae does it? And when? Dreams or visions. Hoo you ken it's honest, right, true. No' auld wives' tales. Do they ken far ahead, or no'? Do they use bits o' bones, and the like? Hairs o' the body like yon ill witches?"

"None of that, Highness. They just *see* it, I think. I . . ."

"You'll hae to dae better than that, Alastair man. See – I've writ a bit paper for you. Here it's. Get Vicky or yon Mary to read it for you. And gie me the answers. Come to me this night. Vicky'll bring you. It's fell important. I'm working on this chapter on it."

Alastair took the paper almost gingerly and tucked it in a pocket of his deerskin waistcoat. "I will do my best, Your Grace."

"You will that! See to it."

The hunt proceeded, Alastair's aid nowise required now.

9

So commenced the most extraordinary period in Alastair MacGregor's admittedly not very lengthy life. No one less like a courtier could well have been imagined; yet here he was at court and having to remain there. Not only so, but close to the monarch, closer than most of the true courtiers. That he was an outlaw and condemned Highlander made it the more amazing – and the more objectionable no doubt to the many who would resent it.

It went on for weeks. Whether in fact it was motivated mainly by the Master's hostage-notion or by James's interest in second sight and the like, Alastair could not make out; but although he applied time and again for permission to return from court to his own people, this was always refused, or at least ignored. Patrick Gray was seldom there, he being deeply concerned in national affairs elsewhere and having his own properties to see to, at and around Broughty Castle near Dundee. His wife also was often away at Broughty, leaving the duke and Mary Gray to maintain the Gray lodging in Falkland. Alastair made no complaint about that, needless to say; but it did mean that he had no one to plead his case with the King save Lennox – who obviously preferred him to stay there, as did the girl. And Cawdor was often absent.

Alastair wondered and worried over his clansfolk, always. No least word of them reached him, and there was no one he could ask who might know. Indeed the duke, owning Methven, was probably the nearest to the Highland Line of any Alastair knew, but he seemingly had heard nothing of any import.

Alastair's concern, of course, was that his brother John was headstrong and aggressive by nature; and with no Uncle Ewan there to counsel him, could well react vigorously and toughly to any provocation. And if Black Duncan knew of the situation – and that one would be well informed, for sure – he might see and make opportunity therefor.

That first attempt to answer the monarch's list of questions satisfied neither Alastair nor the King. The queries were just not such as could be replied to in statements. He did his best, and although Mary wrote down what he haltingly told her, there was really nothing sufficiently clear and to the point. So after receipt of that initial paper, James recognised that there was no profit in this, and started a new arrangement. Alastair was to come over to the palace on occasion, of an evening, and actually join the author in his writing endeavours – only for this one chapter, of course. At first apprehensive at this command, he expressed his fears and concern to Mary, who however was as usual far from gloomy. She saw it as a satisfactory development. Not only did it keep Himself safely on good terms with the monarch but it perhaps would enable Himself to influence James to a better, less cruel, attitude towards these victims of the witchcraft trials. Could he not convince their lord that there was in truth no threat to him in this of sorcery and Devil-worship? That the torturings and burnings were pointless, unnecessary, a mistaken policy. If only he could, how much suffering and fear he could spare so many.

Alastair's first evening alone at the palace produced no such opportunities. James, after an initial lecture on the folly of not being able to write, spent the time reading out parts of the first chapter of his book and explaining the subtleties and finer points of his conception of demonology. Most of it sounded nonsense to the listener, or completely beyond all understanding; but he could only heed patiently. The only interruption was when young Queen Anne came into the bedchamber – where the reading was taking place – and was promptly shooed out like an intruder. Alastair saw the young woman frowning on him, and did not blame her. She was not beautiful or graceful, like Mary Gray, but had vivacity and some determination. It was late before Alastair made his escape.

The pattern of climbing the hills together on the garrons persisted, with mainly monologues from James and complaints that the Hielantman was not properly and honestly answering important questions. But on days when the hunting was on low ground and no climbing called for, Alastair might not have existed. Some evenings he was sent for, others not. And all the time he was longing to get back to Glen Strae – were it not for Mary Gray.

There were other matters than deer-hunting and demonology in men's minds over those weeks, however little they affected Alastair MacGregor. Government was being maintained from Edinburgh and Stirling, with the Chancellor Maitland ostensibly in charge and the Master of Gray influencing matters, much as he disliked the sour and stern Maitland of Thirlestane. Constant couriers came and went at Falkland with papers, deeds, charters and other state documents for the King to peruse and sign. Nevertheless the court was by no means insulated here from national events. The Reformation was only some thirty years established, and the Catholic faith was still strong, for much of the nobility clung to the old faith in which they had been reared and their dependants were apt to follow their preferences. Indeed the Romish influence was in the ascendant, growing, much to the alarm of the Kirk and its supporters in high places. James himself, with his own certainty of personal links with the Almighty, as the Lord's Anointed, was not greatly concerned one way or another; but a large number of his courtiers were. For many of them, or their fathers, had received the vast Church lands at the said Reformation, and feared greatly that they might lose them again – while of course their Romish opposite numbers hoped the reverse. This underlying dichotomy was exemplified at Falkland in an odd way, in which Alastair could not help becoming interested.

Two of the greatest earls in the country were the proponents of this religion-cum-landowning tug-of-war – Moray and Huntly. George Gordon of Huntly was the most powerful Catholic in the kingdom, and Lieutenant of the North. His father had been slain in Queen Mary's reign, leading a Catholic revolt, and much of his northern lands forfeited to the then Earl of Moray, the Queen's half-brother and a strong Protestant, who had become regent for the infant James. The present Moray was his son-in-law and relative. He was a very handsome and dashing character, known indeed as the Bonnie Earl, popular at court where Huntly was not. Bad blood between them provided much material for gossip at Falkland.

Unfortunately Moray was the source of more gossip than that. He paid assiduous court to the young Queen who, lacking such from her otherwise-minded husband, was apt to respond less than discreetly. Moray frequently absented himself from the King's hunts to attend the Queen's, and her other activities, and there was much speculation – although Mary Gray, who was in a fair position to know, declared that while he and Anne saw a lot of each other, she did not believe that there was any harm in it.

The gossip, however, could not fail to reach the King's ears.

Alastair's Falkland interlude came to an abrupt close, not only for himself but for the entire court, in early November. And the Master of Gray had much to do with it, undoubtedly. He did not love Chancellor Maitland, with whom he was so much sharing the burdens of government; and as Alastair had reason to know he was as subtle and devious a character as he was able. How much of it all he engineered personally and how much was factual, was anybody's guess. But when the Earl of Huntly had been absent from Falkland for a week or two, and it was assumed that he had gone to his Aberdeenshire fastnesses, the Master turned up to declare that he was in fact at Edinburgh with Chancellor Maitland. This was, of course, strange-seeming to all, for these two had never been friends, with no interests in common, and Maitland was a Protestant. This might not have engendered alarm, but Gray casually added that the Earl of Bothwell was seeing them in Edinburgh also. He, the nephew of Mary Queen of Scots' third husband, and the most powerful of Border chieftains, was the one whom King James believed to be behind all the witchcraft troubles, the chief witch-master himself, Satan's representative. He had been banished, but apparently was back. And he was pro-Catholic, if he had any religion at all other than Devil-worship.

That did it. There must be a Catholic plot to overturn the regime, and they had suborned the Chancellor to their side. Possibly the monarch was to be unseated, even slain, and a Catholic monarch substituted. That could not be the next heir – James thus far lacking a son – Duke Ludovick, for he was approximately Protestant and totally unambitious; but Bothwell himself was a Stewart, only Hepburn on his mother's side. So – Satan's tool! Bothwell to be King!

Huntly was all but forgotten; also book-writing; anyway, the weather was miserably Novemberish. The court to return to Edinburgh forthwith, to nip in the bud this terrible conspiracy.

All to move, then.

Alastair, of course, sought permission to return to his own glens; but this was refused. No royal explanation was forthcoming, so whether it was policy concerning the clan situation or demonology discussion, he did not know. But he had to go to Edinburgh also.

Mary Gray said that she was delighted for him. He would learn much that was new, undoubtedly.

Alastair supposed that it could be called experience. Certainly, travelling in the royal cavalcade he learned much, of the land and its fertility, of the folk and their ways of living, so different to his own, of the tower-houses of even small lairds as well as the castles of the lords, of seeing riches, as well as grinding poverty and misery, such as never experienced in the Highlands.

He was surprised when they did not make westwards for Stirling, where the Forth could be crossed by bridge, but all but due southwards to near Dunfermline, where, at the shore, there were great flat-bottomed scows to ferry them and their horses across the mile-wide estuary, a facility apparently established by Queen Margaret, wife to Canmore, five hundred years before, to enable pilgrims to visit her great new stone abbey. Now there were no pilgrims, and only folk who could afford to pay could use the ferries; but for such it was a great convenience, saving sixty miles or so of detour.

From the southern shore it was but a dozen or so miles eastwards to Edinburgh, which the travellers could soon see – or at least its towering rock-top royal fortress and the mighty hill of Arthur's Seat rising behind, landmarks indeed. This land of Lothian was highly populated, and even more fertile than Fothrif. Alastair could see now why, in a way, these people considered the Highlands to be a barren wilderness, despite being so much more beautiful.

The city, when reached, was strange indeed, running down a mile-long spine of rock from the great castle to the foot of the soaring peak named after the semi-legendary King Arthur, the valley on the north side filled with a long narrow loch. They entered the walled town at the other side, by the West Port, to proceed by narrow streets to a wide market-place below the castle rock on the south side. Alastair assumed that they would be climbing up to the fortress itself, for it was a royal seat, but they continued on along the valley eastwards, most of the town's towering tenements, buildings and churches high on their left. This was the Cowgate, Mary told him, the way the city freemen drove their beasts out to the common grazing. At its eventual foot, at another gateway in the walls, they turned left-handed into what, it was explained, was another burgh altogether although joined to the city – the Burgh of the Canongate which, before the Reformation, had been under the authority of Holy Church, hence the name. This brought them to the Abbey of the Holy Rood, and here the former extensive monastic premises had been turned into a palace, much more commodious and convenient than the cramped quarters up on the fortress rock. This was their destination. Certainly it was pleasingly situated, within the wide parkland at the foot of Arthur's Seat, which spread to south and east.

There had been no signs of alarm or hostile demonstrations thus far.

Large as this Holyroodhouse was, it was clearly incapable of housing all the royal train, most of the members of which would have to find lodging in the town. As it happened, however, the former domestic and refectory wing of the abbey had been given to the Lady Marie's father, the Earl of Orkney, and there was room enough therein for the Gray entourage, the duke choosing to lodge with them, despite the multitudinous household of the said Orkney. So Alastair was installed in Holyroodhouse, a man bemused.

They found the atmosphere in Edinburgh less tense than expected, rumours of plots and warfare not taken very seriously. Bothwell, on whom all seemed to hinge, was reported to be here, there and everywhere, to the monarch's dire alarm but few others equally disturbed. Chancellor Maitland, presenting himself, swore that he knew nothing of it all; and presently Huntly himself turned up, innocence itself. Oddly, the Master of Gray, from whom all the word of plotting stemmed, appeared wholly unconcerned. It all seemed to Alastair to smack of unreality.

But the witch-hunting did not. This evil campaign still went on, now evidently more or less out of control. Even the King was perturbed, not so much at the misery and slaughter, as at it all having gone so far ahead outwith his royal authority. Clearly, unscrupulous men were using accusations of witchcraft to get rid of their enemies, or those whose lands they coveted; even lairdly and lordly families were being accused and involved.

James was not doing much book-writing these days, and Alastair in consequence was seldom alone with him. When he was, the King, having long completed his chapter on second sight, was more interested in reading out his latest effusions – for admiration, needless to say, not for criticism. He permitted questions but only for explanation not for doubts. At much that he heard, Alastair was aghast, so absurd and even contradictory was it, as well as so cruelly misconceived. Admittedly he knew nothing of Devil-worship, demons and witchcraft; and if, as the monarch claimed, bestiality, human sacrifice, even cannibalism did occur at these covens, then they should be put down where possible and their perpetrators punished; but surely it was all not on the scale suggested, with hundreds being accused and burned. Alastair sought to convince his sovereign-lord of this, but of course was told that he was an ignorant Hielantman and quite uninformed – which was true enough. Appeals by him for His Grace's mercy were likewise dismissed. He gave up trying and merely listened.

When was he going to be permitted to return home became his main preoccupation.

News from the Highlands was all but non-existent. At least there was no word of Gregorach clashes or Campbell challenges. The only relevant tidings which did reach them, from the Methven steward for the duke, was that Ardkinglas had died – no loss according to Cawdor; he had been

Glenorchy's ally, but no very strong character, one of the six guardians of young Argyll.

As it came about, the question of Alastair's home-going was resolved, for once, not by the Master of Gray but by the approach of Yuletide. This was, of course, traditionally the season when homes and families had greatest influence and festivities abounded on a local scale. James himself did not seem to care one way or another, and no normal permission to retire from court appeared to be required. Cawdor was one of the first to leave, for his Nairnshire properties, the Grays were going to Broughty Castle, and Duke Ludovick decided to leave James and go to Methven, Mary Gray with him. The pair convinced the King that Alastair's custody should be their responsibility, to that man's great satisfaction. At least he would be a deal nearer Glen Strae.

They left Edinburgh in mid-December, with sighs of relief.

10

Ideas as to custody and hostageship were markedly different at Methven Castle than at Falkland or Edinburgh. To all intents Alastair was a free man, guest of his custodians. The duke even sent frequently to Glen Strae for news for him – of which there appeared to be little of any significance, no hostilities nor unusual violence at any rate. The Gregorach seemed to be able to get on well enough without their chief – which was perhaps less than flattering for Alastair.

More vital news did reach them from the south, from Stirling where, it seemed, James and Anne were passing their own Yuletide. His Grace had decided that MacGregor was indeed a free man and his clan given a full pardon, the Privy Council condemnation at last officially expunged. It seemed that the Master of Gray had recommended this as an appropriate gesture for the season of goodwill and festivity, James agreeing. Alastair could return home. This in mid-January.

The hostage was overjoyed, but found himself sorry to be leaving his so good friends; however they would be returning to court very soon anyway. They parted in mutual esteem, Himself having been absent from Glen Strae for four months.

Despite missing Mary Gray so much, it was good to reach home, to be in his own place amongst his own people. How much he had been missed it was hard to assess. John of Dochard perhaps resigned the supreme authority with some reluctance, for there was no great love between these brothers, but no difficulties arose. Otherwise welcome was hearty, even though few seemed to realise that the clan had been in any danger, and that the far-away and strange monarch's pardon meant anything very much. Black Duncan was the shadow on their horizon, not King James.

However, the said Duncan had apparently lain discreetly low all this time at his distant Lorn castle of Barcaldine.

Then, exactly one month after the good news from Stirling, further word came from there, sent by Duke Ludovick – and it was ill news now, indeed. Sir John of Cawdor had been murdered. He had been enticed to a meeting in Lorn, and there slain by a man called Gillipatrick MacEllar, servant and foster-brother of the new Ardkinglas, which young man was, it seemed, wholly under the sway of his kinsman Black Duncan. The Master of Gray suspected that Glenorchy was behind it, although that would be difficult to prove.

To say that Alastair was distressed and disquieted would be an understatement indeed. Cawdor had been his good, effective and trusted friend and ally – and with no real call to be so. Now, he was gone. And it seemed highly likely that his murder was because of his championing of the MacGregor cause. Which made Alastair feel in some measure responsible. Here was horror.

As well as the loss, there was the other aspect. It almost certainly implied that Glenorchy was by no means accepting defeat. Young Ardkinglas was little more than a boy, and seeing much of Black Duncan. If the latter was going the length of having a fellow Campbell slain, how much further would he go? The six-months-dictated truce was past. What now?

February, the hardest month of the Scots winter, was particularly severe that year, the passes all blocked by snow, the lochs frozen, even some of the rivers. Glen Strae was cut off, as were all the other glens, for weeks, well into March, with no communications possible. This suited Alastair well enough, since it also precluded complications with neighbours. Black Duncan was presumably still at his Lorn castle.

It was the sudden access of spring weather which brought more news – as usual, in the persons of Duke Ludovick and Mary Gray, thankful it seemed to escape again from the constrictions of court life at Edinburgh and Stirling, and come to Methven for another spell. Their arrival at Glen Strae was, in the circumstances, a noble effort, with the rivers now all in flood from the melting snows, and the low ground marshy. They came, full of news, little of it directly concerning the Gregorach but some perhaps with its relevancy.

It had been an eventful as well as a hard winter for Lowland Scotland. The Huntly versus Moray, Catholic versus Protestant, enmity was coming to a head. The handsome Moray was, in fact, dead, slain by Huntly in the most extraordinary sequence of events. Bothwell's part in it was still uncertain, but few believed him uninvolved, along with others on the Catholic side. And Maitland the Chancellor was in dire disgrace, which would please the Master of Gray. Unfortunately King James himself had come out of it all with a reputation distinctly sullied, as it had never been even with the witch-hunting. Moray had been popular, not only with Queen Anne and the court but with the people in general; his bonhomie, good looks and expertise at sports such as boxing, wrestling, ball-play and horse-racing commending him to the commonality. The king was held not to be entirely innocent, the Protestants in especial condemnatory, for that was Moray's faith; and James was a Protestant monarch.

Mary Gray was more eloquent than Lennox, a born storyteller, and gave Alastair the gist of it. Catholic Huntly had played on James's jealousy of Moray, hinting at illicit love-making with the Queen – almost certainly unfounded. And James had ordered Moray from his castle of Doune in Menteith where he had spent Yuletide, to come and answer charges of misconduct – this ostensibly nothing to do with the religious issue. Moray had another house at Donibristle, in Fothrif not far from Falkland, and there he went. The King was not at Falkland meantime, however, and ordered Huntly to go and fetch his enemy to Edinburgh. And Huntly had gone to Donibristle, set that house on fire, and as Moray fled, even his hair alight, had had him caught and stabbed to death, himself adding his dirk-strokes. It was said, the girl recounted, that Moray's dying words were, "Gordon scum – you have spoiled a better face than your own!"

This shameful deed rocked the Lowlands, the assumption being that the King had ordered Moray's death. Also that he favoured the Catholic cause. Few probably believed him entirely innocent, especially as Huntly went unpunished, only told to confine himself in Blackness Castle in Linlithgowshire for a period, where in fact he still dwelt in luxury. Moray's mother, the Lady Doune, through whom he had inherited the

Moray earldom – she was the late Regent Moray's daughter – refused to allow her son's body to be buried, parading the blood-soaked clothing around the streets of Edinburgh, saying that there would be no interment until she had vengeance. The corpse still lay in Leith kirkyard for all to see.

All this, however astonishing and intriguing to Alastair, could seem to have little relevant to his own position – save for one aspect. The Master of Gray believed Glenorchy to be involved, and the murder of Cawdor connected. Cawdor had been prominent on the Protestant side and a friend of Moray, just as Black Duncan was friendly with Huntly. He could well have taken the opportunity to get rid of Cawdor, who opposed him over the MacGregors, and claim it as in the Catholic cause. Whether this was mere speculation on Gray's part or he had reason for it, his daughter and the duke did not know. But he was, of all men, probably the best informed in the kingdom, usually. If this indeed was so, could the Gregorach be implicated in any way? They were all Catholics, like most Highlanders, but . . .

"Patrick thinks that it could be *contrived* to affect you," Lennox said.

"How could it, my lord? We have naught to do with all this, whatever."

It was Mary who answered. "Here is how he sees it. If the Catholic cause wins – and it is gaining the ascendancy at this time, with the King seeming to favour Huntly – then who knows what might be? For see you, the Earl of Argyll, because of his mother, unlike most of his clan, is Protestant. And he has favoured *you*, in this of the truce. Glenorchy now hates his young chief – and if his cause prospers he could be instrumental in bringing Argyll down. And *his* friend, the weak Lochnell, is next heir to Argyll. This thing has gone far beyond Black Duncan's desire for Roro and Glen Lyon, or even Glen Strae and bringing down Yourself. It has become a great conspiracy, with him and Lochnell on one side and Argyll and the Protestants on the other. And if you have been identified with the losing side, Catholic though you are, he would have you. Do you not see it?"

"Do not tell me that even Glenorchy would betray MacCailean Mhor, his own chief!"

"Why not? Argyll made him sign the truce. And sided with Cawdor. And Glenorchy undoubtedly had *him* slain. Why not Argyll himself, to be succeeded by feeble Lochnell? Then *he*, Duncan, will rule the great Clan Campbell."

"Lord! You make him sound the Devil Incarnate, whatever!"

Her infectious laugh gurgled. "You tell that to the King! That should seal Black Duncan's fate. Satan's equal! He might even bring him into his book!"

Alastair shook his head. "Be that as it may, how could *I* be connected with the Protestant cause?"

"Your friends are Protestants. *We* are. Cawdor. Argyll is, and he after a fashion befriended you. Atholl did also. All on the Protestant side. As well indeed, if they win. If not, Glenorchy will use it against you, to be sure."

"You do not truly think that the Catholics can gain Scotland again, do you?"

"They could," Lennox said. "With Spanish help."

"Why Spanish?"

"Philip of Spain wants to avenge the English defeat of his Armada. Bring down Elizabeth Tudor's Protestant England. To gain its colonies and wealth. And to outrank the King of France as Catholic champion, the Most Christian King. He could well use a Catholic Scotland against England."

"A mercy! This is all beyond me."

"It is beyond all. Save perhaps Patrick Gray," the young woman said.

11

If Alastair MacGregor imagined that all this of Catholic and
Protestant, and Spanish involvement, was beyond him, as
well as little concern of his, he learned differently. His next
link with the national scene was a visit from another steward,
this time of the Gray castle at Broughty, sent by the Master
himself, urging that he muster a force of his MacGregors,
well armed, and bring them to St John's Town of Perth just
as quickly as possible. Numbers he left to Himself, but the
more the better. Just like that; no explanations given. The
Broughty steward said that great things were afoot, the nation
rising in arms, but gave few other details. Clearly he disliked
having to visit Highlandmen and this daunting country.

Alastair was in a quandary. He could by no means ignore
the suggestion, almost the command, of Patrick Gray who
had helped him so notably. Presumably there was need for
this demand. But to assemble his clan in arms, after all the
injunctions to keep the peace? And what did he mean by a
force? Fifty? One hundred? Five hundred? And timing? As
quickly as possible. He could be in Perth in two days. But
to assemble men in any numbers would take time. He could
gather fifty in a day from Glen Strae and vicinity, perhaps
more. But to reach the outlying Gregorach lands, even Roro
and Balquhidder, and draw men from there would require
many days.

He decided that he must take the Master's call literally and
go at once, on the morrow, whatever was the reason for it all.
He sent out a call to arms forthwith. His folk would never be
backward in responding, that he knew only too well.

The following morning, then, with sixty men and his
brother John, he set off eastwards, up Glen Lochy, over the
watershed to Strathfillan and so down to Strathearn, halting
for the night at Glen Ogle. They required to carry little with

them save their arms, each man with only a bag of oatmeal. This they could mix with blood drawn from cattle *en route*, an accepted Highland custom, the blood-letting from the beasts' hind legs doing them no harm, the cuts plastered over with clay or peat-mush. Such simple provision could sustain the running gillies day after day if need be, the secret of their astonishing ability to cover great distances at high speed. Only Alastair and his brother were mounted.

They reached St John's Town the second evening. At first there seemed to be nothing unusual about the place, no assemblage of men, no evident excitement. Indeed it was the MacGregors themselves who produced any stir, the citizenry eyeing them warily, reputation well known. They camped on the North Inch Tayside parkland, where the great clan battle had taken place before Robert the Third. Alastair did not know just what was expected of him here. He could only wait and see.

In the event he did not have to wait long. Presently who should come riding to them, with a servant, but Ludovick, Duke of Lennox, who had been told of their arrival. No doubt all Perth knew of it.

Lennox, never an eloquent young man, took some considerable time to explain the situation. He had been left behind, at the Master's behest, to meet and bring on the Gregorach. The army had moved on the day previously, north-eastwards.

To Alastair's bewildered demands as to what army and why, the story came out in bits and pieces, rather incoherently. If Ludovick had started at the beginning it might have been better, and given his hearer less of mental gymnastics in trying to fit it all together and make some sense of it. Eventually, so far as Alastair could judge, this was the sequence of it.

The Earl of Huntly had broken his custody at Blackness Castle and departed for his northern territories. There the Catholic Earls of Errol and Angus had joined him, with sundry other northern lords and lairds. Their men were massing. So it looked as though the dreaded civil war between Catholic and Protestant was indeed brewing. Then there had been an astonishing and alarming development. Betrayed by a resentful colleague, one George Kerr, of the Ferniehirst Catholic Kerrs so loyal to the late Queen Mary, had been apprehended in a ship in the Clyde estuary, on his way to Spain. He carried, amongst other things, a number of sheets of paper, otherwise blank but signed by Huntly, Errol and Angus and addressed to the King of Spain. None, however, in the names of Maitland and Bothwell, who had been thought to be their allies. Put to the torture to extract information, Kerr had admitted that these were letters to Philip of Spain to fill in his own terms in exchange for military and financial aid to Catholic Scotland; also requests for gold, quickly, to help pay for the hiring of troops – this gold not to be in *Spanish* coin, which could result in those obtaining it being accused of conspiracy, but in blank pieces.

This remarkable discovery had immediate and dramatic results. Maitland felt bound to resign the chancellorship and retired to his Border stronghold of Thirlestane. Bothwell was thought to have crossed into England. Even King James was spurred into action, for the Kirk and the Protestant lords were now in full cry. The monarch said that he would be his own Chancellor – although in practice the Master of Gray took charge – and called an urgent meeting of the Privy Council, or the Protestant part of it, and put Huntly, Errol and Angus, with others, to the horn, outlawed. And an army was to assemble, to march north against the rebel earls before any aid could reach them from Spain.

Unfortunately the Lowland lords and churchmen, save for the Borderers whose position was doubtful, were less successful at delivering fighting men than Reformed prayers, whilst the northern earls could provide thousands. James's army, therefore, was slow in growing. In this situation Patrick Gray had thought of the MacGregors, renowned fighters. Not only would these add to numbers, but their adherence would put the monarch and council in Alastair's debt and help in the struggle against Glenorchy. That Campbell, believed to be on Huntly's side, would almost certainly not allow himself to get involved in any fighting – he was far too clever for that; but if the MacGregors, although Catholics, were supporting the King, and Glenorchy was not, then advantage was obvious. So reasoned Gray and so agreed Lennox.

Seeking to absorb all this, Alastair recognised the opportunity, and wished that he had brought more men. But at least he could send back for a greater muster. John would go and bring on another hundred or so as swiftly as possible. Lennox said that the royal army moved only slowly, with marching men and heavy baggage-trains, so the swift-travelling Highlanders would soon catch up.

It transpired that the King was actually with his army, scarcely believable as this was for a young man who was terrified of cold steel and warfare. Gray had convinced him that it was absolutely essential, in that many of the northern Catholics would be loyal enough to the crown and might well not actually join Huntly against the royal person. Patrick must have been very persuasive.

At sun-up, then, the duke, with a few of his own Methven men, joined the MacGregors for the move eastwards, while John of Dochard hastened back to the Gregorach country for reinforcements.

Their route lay across Tay, by Scone and Kinrossie to the head of great Strathmore at Coupar Angus, for apparently they were heading for Aberdeen, which Huntly, Lieutenant of the North, looked on as his own capital city. Aberdeen must be prevented from any aiding of the rebels; that was the first priority.

They came up with the royal host quite quickly, some way short of Coupar Angus, for they were moving at fully three times the pace. Undoubtedly they were welcome, however much the Lowlanders might despise the newcomers on principle, the MacGregors' reputation as hard fighters appreciated. James, that unlikely leader of an army, was much gratified, and greeted Alastair almost effusively, declaring him to be an example to all of his kind in loyal duty. The Master of Gray commended him also, especially when he heard that more Gregorach would be following. Privately he confided to Alastair that he was concerned about the fighting abilities and enthusiasm of this motley host, as against Huntly's Gordon warriors and their allies.

The night was passed at Coupar Angus Abbey, now in the care of one of the King's many illegitimate uncles, Alastair remaining in camp with his men rather than occupying monastic quarters, being uncertain how the Gregorach would react towards their fellow-marchers who so clearly shunned them. He had visitors there, presently, the Master and the duke. Apparently the latter had been telling Gray of the amazing speed of the MacGregor travel and how they would chafe at the pace of the main array; also the risk of trouble between Highland and Lowland breaking out. So the suggestion was that the Gregorach should not remain with the host on the march but go on ahead as a scouting-party, an advisable precaution anyway; that is, if Alastair could keep his people from ravaging the countryside as they went for, naturally, there would be much time at their disposal if they were not to get too far ahead of the army, since it would not be covering more than a dozen miles in a day. This last Alastair thought that he could promise.

He learned more of the genesis of this expedition. The Earls of Huntly, Errol and Angus had been ordered, on outlawry, to ward themselves in St Andrews Castle to await examination before the Privy Council – of which, of course, they were themselves members – and when they had failed to do so, active steps had to be taken against them, before the Spanish help arrived. A number of the more militant Kirk ministers were with the host, to emphasise its godly Reformed character, and the King's authority might well be needed to keep these from exerting too much influence on military conduct, Gray felt. Altogether, this armed sally, their monarch's first, was not without its problems. And if Bothwell decided to make trouble, with his Border mosstroopers, while they were absent . . .

When Alastair enquired why, then, it was absolutely necessary at all, he was told that it was to meet a dual demand – from the Kirk, and of all people, from Queen Elizabeth of England. Both were inordinately exercised over the revelation of the man Kerr's mission to Spain and what was implied – Elizabeth Tudor, always well informed by her spies of what went on in Scotland. She had sent a long, personal letter to James, who was of course heir-presumptive to her English throne, her father's great-grand-nephew, requiring him to take immediate action against the Catholics, for her *English* Catholics were becoming infected by the spirit of revolt, and renewed Spanish intervention dangerous. The threat was implied that if James did not act decisively, Elizabeth would disclaim him as heir, and the hoped-for unity of the two Protestant realms would be lost.

Alastair perceived that he had got himself involved in great matters indeed.

So, in the morning, the Gregorach, given the route by Gray, set off well before the rest were ready to move, east by north along Strathmore. Not that any attack was anticipated at this stage, for these lands, of the Lindsays, Lyons, Ogilvys, Carnegies and the rest, were mainly Protestant, some indeed being expected to add quotas to the royal host. But in the mountains to the west and north there were Highland clans, all Catholic, and these might be suborned by Huntly to make raids down into the wide strath. So the Gregorach scouting was not entirely a matter of policy.

That first day, Alastair, not hurrying, went as far as Glamis, without incident – but carefully avoided the vicinity of the large Lyon castle, whose lord might well not appreciate the presence of wild MacGregors, to camp in a glen-mouth to the west, sending back messengers to inform the King that all was well. In fact they were there before midday, even taking their time. They did not see the following host until just before dusk, so slowly in comparison it moved, with heavily armed men not used to long marching and wagons with provisions, on rough roads. The great ones, of course, were mounted, and these chose to ride only a few hours each day. Even so, as the Master pointed out, they would have been infinitely slower had they brought oxen-drawn cannon from Edinburgh and Stirling Castles, as James had suggested.

There were no communications between scouts and army that night.

The same pattern was followed the day after, Alastair getting as far as Forfar Loch before halting, short of that town. He had a visit from the duke in the evening, to tell him that he was going too far and fast. The host would not reach this far. The Master had suggested that Lennox ride with the MacGregors, to restrain them somewhat – which apparently quite pleased that young man, who found the slow progress boring in the extreme. He would prefer Alastair's company, anyway.

With time on their hands, the two friends were able to do some exploring of this country, new to them both – and a pleasant land it was, the blue Highland bastions to the left, green rolling hills to the right of the wide levels of the strath, with much of woodland and excellent pasture, and great rivers coming down from the mountains – the Isla, the Prosen, the Clova and the North and South Esks. They still made a point of avoiding the seats of the lords of this land, leaving such contacts to be made by the monarch himself. Their progress indeed took on the nature of a holiday rather than any military expedition. Only one real problem surfaced – the Gregorach had to be restrained from bleeding cattle for their oatmeal diet, behaviour which might not be approved of locally, and so had to have extra provision found for them. Fortunately the duke appeared to be well supplied with money, and not loth to use it to purchase victuals and drink – which made him the more popular with the clansmen.

By Aberlemno, with its Pictish stones, so extraordinarily carved, and Brechin, they left Angus at the North Esk and entered the Mearns, the shire of Kincardine, to pass Laurencekirk and Drumlithie, to reach in time Stonehaven. Here, at the Earl Marischal's mighty rock-top castle of Dunnottar, towering over the waves, all halted for a while. This earl was a good Protestant but had uncomfortable links, his great-aunt having been the late Huntly's wife, and one sister married to the Earl of Errol; however his aunt was the Countess of Argyll who had helped Cawdor; and her sister was the said Cawdor's widow. The Scottish aristocracy was like that. But the Marischal proved useful, a handsome and talented man. Not only could he supply a good contingent of men, but he had strong ties with Aberdeen where he had just founded a new college for the university there. That city was only some fifteen miles away, and he was in a position to know the situation there and to influence the citizenry. He believed that there was little inclination there towards revolt and that the royal visitor would be welcomed. He would send messengers to urge the Provost and magistrates to arrange a suitable reception. His information was that Huntly and the other outlawed lords were up in Strathbogie, and well supported by men, but they were showing no signs of marching south; and Aberdeen certainly did not desire to be a battleground.

James's relief was entirely evident.

They stayed a few days in the Stonehaven vicinity, the King at Dunnottar itself, others in the nearby castles of Fetteresso, Ury and Muchalls, the MacGregors ahead at the last, now reinforced of course by John's contingent, and forming a substantial company. On the whole they were well-behaved – but their involuntary hosts were glad to see the back of them in due course.

The news, when it arrived from Aberdeen, was good. The city fathers would welcome the King. And there was word that the rebel earls showed no signs of coming to challenge the royal army, although they would undoubtedly be well-informed as to its presence. The march northwards was resumed.

They came to the fine city which straddled the mouths of the two great rivers of Dee and Don, its stonework all glittering grey granite, its cathedral of St Machar handsome indeed, its university attached and prideful, seeking to outdo St Andrews now that it had the splendid Marischal College, its port extensive and busy. Alastair, for one, had not realised that such a place could exist up in these northern parts.

The army was dispersed, not in the city itself but well outwith the town-walls, where the soldiery would occasion the least upset to the citizenry, the MacGregors in the Dyce area, where they could give early warning of hostile approach from the north and north-west, where lay the Strathbogie area, the Huntly homeland, some forty-five miles further.

James, received with fair ceremony by the Provost and baillies, Church and university dignitaries and a wary populace, installed himself actually in the Huntly town-house, the best in the city, and from there sent the Earl Marischal as envoy to Strathbogie, to order the dispersal of all assembled troops of the rebel lords forthwith, and their masters to come and submit themselves to his royal person and mercy. This last was added on the advice of Patrick Gray, who suggested that an indication of mercy might well be effective in persuading Huntly against the risks of armed confrontation.

All waited.

It took ten rather anxious days, with the MacGregors ranging the country to north and west on the look-out for challenging forces, before George Keith returned. He brought good news – at least, in the main. The royal order for dispersal had been accepted and obeyed, with the Gordon and allied manpower now all sent home. But Huntly, Errol, Angus and the others balked at yielding themselves up to custody, mercy or none. They would remain where they were.

These tidings were received with mixed feelings. The King was actually relieved, for his hostility to Huntly had always been suspect, as evidenced over the murder of Moray without due punishment; and his Protestantism was less than vehement. Patrick Gray, too, seemed noways disappointed. But the Kirk representatives were angry, demanding that the army moved on northwards to arrest these vile rebel leaders. This however the monarch resolutely refused to countenance. The danger to realm and Kirk was over, their great joint cause triumphant. They would return south – and all thank God for His goodness. All to prepare to march.

Anticlimax it might be for some, including most of the Gregorach, not a blow struck. But the majority there undoubtedly were thankful indeed and praised the royal decision.

Alastair took leave of monarch and friends, none holding him back. No point in the Gregorach creeping homeward at the army's pace. Going at their own speed they could be in Glen Strae in four days, across the mountains.

12

Peace reigned at and in Glen Strae – or as nearly peace as such as the Gregorach could put up with. Black Duncan, wherever he was, lay low, like other militant Catholics; after all, he had seven castles to lurk in and did not require to make himself too evident to the MacGregors, at Kilchurn or Balloch. Alastair was now accepted as ranking quite high in the monarch's esteem – and although this was of little help in ruling his high-spirited clan, it did add to his authority and standing amongst their neighbours, especially Campbell ones. John of Dochard was less of a nuisance than heretofore, his part in the Aberdeen expedition having seemingly had a beneficial effect on him, removing perhaps something of a chip on his shoulder about always having to come second to his elder brother, whom he looked upon as lacking fire. It proved to be a good season for both the cattle and the crops; the tolls were therefore also profitable as were the tryst sales. As well as all this, Alastair was happy to be seeing much more of Duke Ludovick and Mary Gray.

How this last came about was odd, both good and less good. Mary had produced a son, if not an heir, for Vicky – Alastair had not even realised that she was pregnant – and James had all but banished his cousin from court. This situation was as extraordinary as so much about their strange monarch. The King was jealous again. His neglected wife, lacking the good-looking Earl of Moray, had transferred at least some of her needful affections to Ludovick, however little that young man encouraged her. But inevitably he had to see a lot of her, and Anne was amorous and less than discreet. Anyway, James found cause for displeasure and allowed his mistaken doubts full rein. The ducal presence was no longer required at court. None could be happier about this aspect of the situation, at least, than Ludovick Stewart, himself now a proud father.

So it was Methven for him and his, not just for a short spell it was hoped, but for more or less permanent stay – until James changed his mind, that was. With Methven only one long day's ride from Glen Strae, the friends could see quite a lot of each other.

Mary was very proud of her son Johnnie, illegitimate as he necessarily was. Ludovick had given up pleading with the girl to marry him; both knew well that it was impossible, or at least impracticable, that any marriage would be dissolved or declared invalid by royal command. The duke was next in succession and the idea of the bastard Mary Gray as Queen was not to be considered. However, Vicky had done what he could to improve the situation. He had given the child *his* name – he was John Stewart, not John Gray. And John Stewart of Methven, at that, for the duke had conveyed the entire estate legally to him, as the best way to ensure that Mary enjoyed it always, whatever might happen to himself. So the baby was laird of wide lands, in his own right, even if he was not Master of Lennox.

Alastair had to go and see the infant, of course, and pronounced him an excellent specimen – although in fact one baby looked much the same as another to him. He was even allowed to hold the small bundle, which he did gingerly indeed, pulling faces and hoping for the best, thankful when Mary took him back. It did not fail to occur to him how different he might have felt had the child been his own.

He received news of Patrick Gray. James had sent him to England, as special envoy to Elizabeth Tudor. He was to tell her, in answer to her so urgent letter, of the triumphant armed sally he had led to the north against the Catholic lords, to announce that the threat was now over, and in consequence to seek to get a firm promise and commitment out of the Queen that James was indeed her undoubted heir and successor – in writing if possible. Patrick, knowing Elizabeth, was not sanguine about this last, but promised to try. After all, the union of the two kingdoms had been his avowed aim always, to ensure permanent peace between the so-long-hostile realms. And if anyone could get such a document out of the Tudor woman, it was Patrick Gray.

So, with Chancellor Maitland in disgrace and Patrick away

and Ludovick at Methven, James was having to rule his realm more or less on his own. What he would make of it was anybody's guess. He was living mainly at Stirling, with hunting-trips to Falkland. Vicky and Mary were thankful to be escaping.

Little news of national affairs reached Methven – and therefore Glen Strae thereafter – even though in theory the duke should have been kept informed, for he was Lord Chamberlain, a member of the Privy Council and hereditary keeper of Dumbarton Castle. But he did have occasion to visit that royal fortress now and then, and consult with its deputy keeper; also to attend to matters relating to his great Lennox estates on Loch Lomondside and the Vale of Leven – whence the name Lennox derived from Levenachs, the folk of the Leven valley. And coming back from one such visit the following autumn, he brought news of a different sort. The young Earl of Argyll was seriously ill, and his mother suspected poison.

This, needless to say, set all agog, not least the Gregorach. If it was true as to the poison – who? Who stood to gain? Campbell of Lochnell was next heir; but feeble as he was, he was scarcely the man to contemplate such a thing. Auchenbreck was friendly with his chief. Young Ardkinglas was vicious but lacked the wits and imagination to plot on such a scale. But he had been Black Duncan's tool for the murder of Cawdor – all accepted that now. Duncan himself, then? Could even he go that far, seek to poison his own chief, MacCailean Mhor? They were at enmity, yes. But poison!

Who else, then? How would any outside Clan Campbell benefit by the young earl's death? None of them could think of any. He was on the Protestant side, of course . . .

If indeed it was poison, and Glenorchy was behind it, then it opened up important new speculations – as Mary Gray, who had inherited her father's nimble and shrewd wits, was the first to point out. Since it seemed unlikely that Glenorchy would seek to slay his chief purely out of personal ill will and resentment, there must be greater purposes behind it. Most of Clan Campbell was Catholic, unlike MacCailean Mhor. And undoubtedly they could produce a larger manpower than most clans and lordships, if so minded. Well then, a Campbell force for a Catholic army would be no modest addition. There could be as many Campbell swords as Gordon, perhaps more. Was that it? Huntly and his allies had not been defeated, only had made a strategic withdrawal meantime. Possibly awaiting the hoped-for Spanish aid. If Black Duncan could offer them a Catholic Campbell host under a new MacCailean Mhor, would that not raise him high indeed? Lochnell was under his thumb, after all . . .

Her hearers, considering this, could not but agree that it all would add up. But only if it *was* poison.

Alastair agreed to have his people make soundings amongst neighbouring Catholic clans, who might well be prepared to support Huntly, to try to learn whether a continuation of the armed uprising was contemplated in the near future. If so, perhaps young Argyll should watch his back indeed.

It was after Yuletide when they had an unexpected visitor at Methven, and Alastair MacGregor was sent for. It was Patrick Gray, not long back from London. He came, not only to see his daughter and little grandson, but to urge Duke Ludovick to return to court where, it seemed, he was needed.

His tidings were as unexpected as his arrival, and disquieting. Maitland was back directing the ship of state, improbable as this seemed. And Bothwell had returned to his Borderland and was making ominous noises. Queen Elizabeth had refused written declaration of James as heir to her throne, but admitted it verbally, and had sent back with Patrick a large sum of money to aid James in his efforts against the Catholics – how much, Gray forbore to disclose. And it was likely to be needed, it seemed.

The Maitland situation had come about by Queen Anne's arranging. She had successfully produced a son, the little Prince Henry Frederick, to James's delight and great concern. His first consideration had been to remove his precious heir from Anne's care to that of his own foster-brother, the Earl of Mar, keeper of Stirling fortress, with the strictest orders that the child was not to be taken outside the castle walls. He was terrified that Anne might try to get her baby back or, worse still, that one or other of his ambitious lords might seek to kidnap the young prince and use him as a bargaining factor;

after all, that had happened to himself as a child, and other young monarchs before him.

The deprived mother, now living at Linlithgow Palace, was desperate to get her son back and, apparently ambitious to take some part in the governance of the realm which she saw as being hopelessly misdirected by her husband, she had personally invited the former Chancellor up from his Border stronghold to be her chamberlain at Linlithgow – an appointment which she was entitled to make under the terms of her marriage contract. And once there, Maitland had been skilful enough to put the King in his debt by quietening the Kirk leaders who, in Patrick's absence, had been waging what amounted to a pulpit war against the monarch, for his apparent leniency towards the Catholic earls, every parish minister being ordered to preach against the royal apostasy weekly. The Kirk's view was that the King should have proceeded on from Aberdeen and laid waste the rebels' lands, and either captured them or driven them out of the country. Somehow Maitland had managed partly to appease Melville and the other Kirk leaders, to James's relief. Moreover, the monarch was in the midst of writing another book, dedicated proudly to his little son, on the duties and privileges of kingship, to be entitled *Basilikon Doron*, and he was finding being his own Chancellor interfering with this important task, in Gray's absence. So he had reinstated Maitland as Chancellor, and agreed that the Queen should be permitted to visit her son periodically in Stirling Castle. This was the situation to which Patrick had returned.

That man, of course, misliking and distrusting Maitland, had his own reactions to all this. He had persuaded James that a parliament was necessary, to clip the wings of the Kirk leadership. Since the Reformation, the clerics had no seats in parliament, having their own General Assembly. He might also manage to check Maitland thereat. This was one reason why he wanted Lennox to be present, as well as to back him up generally. Now that the King and Queen were on speaking terms again, there should be no more trouble in that direction. A pity that Maitland was elderly and so unattractive, or they might have made *him* an object of James's jealousy! There was much needing to be done, in preparation for the next Catholic uprising, which would not be long delayed.

When the others questioned him on that, Patrick appeared to wonder why they had any doubts. Everything pointed to it. The Kirk was right about that, at least. Huntly and his allies were back in their own territories. Messengers were being sent to all Catholic lords to be ready, and with men, funds being offered as inducement. There was plenty of money now. Yes, the Spanish gold had arrived – so the unfortunate Kerr had been replaced as messenger. Gold was circulating, blank gold pieces . . .

When asked how he could be so sure of all this, but newly back from England, the Master shrugged and smiled easily. He had a good Catholic cousin, he reminded them – or approximately good – Logan of Restalrig. It was at his impregnable and inaccessible castle of Fast, halfway down its Berwickshire cliff, that the Spanish gold had been delivered, by sea. Personally, he wondered how much of it had stuck to the acquisitive Restalrig's fingers! But enough was circulating, he was assured, to pay for the hire of many men and buy large quantities of arms and gunpowder – Huntly was strong in cannon. Hence the need for a parliament and a rousing of the nation to imminent danger. Let Himself prepare to muster his maximum numbers of MacGregors; they were going to be needed, and more than they were last time, he reckoned.

Curiously enough, the ever well-informed Patrick seemed to know more about the Earl of Argyll's illness, its cause and consequences, than did his hearers. He had no doubt that it was poison, and Duncan of Glenorchy and Ardkinglas were behind it. MacCailean Mhor himself had no doubts apparently, for fortunately he had recovered; no doubt basing his judgment on his shrewd mother's advice. He had acted the Justiciar and arrested the men who were suspected of the murder of Campbell of Cawdor, Gillipatrick MacEllar and John Og Campbell, foster-brother of Lochnell. Put to the torture, these two had confessed, and implicated Ardkinglas as their instigator. Argyll had promptly hanged both. Ardkinglas however was in rather a different category, a major Campbell chieftain and one of his own guardians. On mere hearsay he could scarcely hang *him*; so he had sent to the Privy Council to arraign him on a charge, not only of this of the poison but of arranging the murder of Cawdor. If Ardkinglas did not compear to answer, he would be put to the horn and outlawed.

All asked the same question then. What of Black Duncan? There was little doubt that he it was who had put young Ardkinglas up to getting Cawdor slain; probably this of the poison also. Surely he would not escape the consequences?

Patrick said not if he could help it – and both he and Vicky were members of the Privy Council. He had little doubt that they were right in their guess that Glenorchy wanted Argyll removed, so that *he* could control the great Clan Campbell, through Lochnell, and provide a huge Campbell force for the Catholic cause.

It was Mary Gray who made the suggestion. Why did not Patrick go on, now, to Inveraray – it was none so far away – and see Argyll? Tell him what was suspected. Advise him. Perhaps turn the tables on Glenorchy, and urge the young earl to provide a Campbell force to aid the *Protestant* cause – as Himself was doing? Would that not be a just outcome?

Her father looked at her thoughtfully.

"You could return to Stirling almost as swiftly from Inveraray as from here," she added.

"I think hardly that. But . . ." Gray changed the subject slightly. "You are willing to aid our strange sovereign-lord's cause again?" he asked of Alastair.

"To be sure, whatever."

"How many could you bring? At your best?"

"Three hundred. Four."

"Excellent. You will have no reason to regret it."

"I hope not," Mary Gray said.

13

To call a parliament demanded forty days' notice, and it was not until the beginning of May that Duke Ludovick left Methven reluctantly, to attend, having no desire to remain at court thereafter despite Gray's urgings. Mary and the child were left at home, with Alastair requested to keep an eye on them. In fact Mary, in the fine spring weather, declared that she would be happy to spend some of the waiting period over at Glen Strae, amongst the exciting mountains – Alastair nothing loth.

That man had sent out preliminary calls to the various branches of his clan to be ready to muster at short notice for the expected campaign against Huntly, and to ensure a maximum turn-out.

Meantime, he greatly enjoyed Mary's company. They were on the friendliest of terms, and by now he had got used to restraining himself from seeming unsuitably affectionate to the young woman – even if perhaps he was less successful at it than he supposed.

Lennox got back from the parliament after ten days. It had been a success as far as the Protestant cause was concerned, most Catholic lords and members staying away, and the burgh representatives fairly consistently of the Reformed persuasion. Chancellor Maitland, conducting it under the monarch's supervision and frequent intervention, had been warily skilful, and there had been no major difficulties. The Catholic earls had been officially attainted, no trial required, their lands and titles declared forfeit and their coats of arms symbolically torn apart in front of all by the Lord Lyon King of Arms. The assembly of a great army had been the principal objective of the session, and that had gone well as to promises. The young Earl of Argyll, making his first appearance at parliament, had declared himself eager and ready to provide a very large contingent of Campbells and their allied clans – MacAlisters, MacTavishes, MacAulays, MacMunns and the like – to the number of at least eight thousand. This resounding offer, no doubt prompted by the Master of Gray's visit, encouraged others, and sizeable numbers were promised. Even the King, whose appreciation of military action, especially against Huntly, was only moderate, was infected by the enthusiasm. However, since all these men were not professional soldiers but tillers of the soil, breeders of cattle and sheep, and land-workers of the lairds and lords generally, with some townsmen, it was recognised that the corn and hay harvests would have to be got in before any campaign started – that is, unless the Catholic earls themselves marched south before that, although they too of course would be faced with the same problems of harvest. An autumn muster, then, and assault.

This suited the Gregorach.

At least arranging the assembly of his Lennox manpower gave the duke excuse for non-attendance at court that summer, with everlasting hunting at Falkland; and Alastair saw much of him and Mary. No word of a Catholic military initiative reached them. Glenorchy remained discreetly out of sight.

In due course they learned details of the forthcoming campaign. The assault on the north would be in two sections. The first and forward thrust would be into the Badenoch area, much inland across the mountains from Strathbogie, where it was said that Errol, Angus and the Macphersons, MacGillivrays and Shaws were to mass, to prevent these from joining Huntly; that army to be under young Argyll himself, since he was supplying the major part of it and nobody could well be put over him. The other force would be commanded by the King in person again, with the Master of Gray, Morton, Home and other lords from the Lowlands, this force to move north further to the east, as before, for Aberdeen, and on eventually to join Argyll's host to assail Strathbogie itself. The Lennox and MacGregor contingents would go with the Campbell array.

In late September, then, the order at last came to move. Mary Gray bade farewell to Vicky and Alastair, adjuring them to be careful and not to show what fine warriors they were, to her possible loss.

The chosen assembly point was at Killin, at the head of Loch Tay, reasonably convenient for the Campbells and the Levenachs, likewise for the Gregorach. Actually this was in Black Duncan's territory, formerly Macnab's; but that man was conveniently otherwhere. Here Alastair met MacCailean Mhor for the first time, older-looking than his nineteen years, slender, almost thin, with long narrow features and a slight cast in one eye, scarcely prepossessing but with a tight mouth and determined chin. Alastair felt no empathy with him, but recognised that he could be a useful friend and a dangerous man to cross.

Argyll had done even better than forecast, having produced no fewer than ten thousand Campbells and their allies. The MacGregor's four hundred and twenty seemed modest indeed; yet even that beat Lennox's three hundred, Highland manpower being more easily mustered than Lowland, the land less demanding of attention. Of the leaders, with Argyll were Lochnell, a shifty-eyed, middle-aged man, richly clad; and Auchenbreck, young, hearty and easy to deal with. There was no sign of Ardkinglas any more than Glenorchy.

It was a strange situation for the MacGregors to be on the march with Campbells – almost certainly it had never happened before. They kept well apart, to be sure, the Gregorach preferring the Levenachs' company, mainly Lowlanders as these were.

On this occasion they did not travel at the usual MacGregor pace. For one thing, so large and strung-out a host could scarcely do so, and with Lowland components. Also, timing had to be to some extent co-ordinated with the King's force, which was unlikely to move very fast. The two armies should seek to reach their target areas approximately together – although Argyll's force did have the furthest to go.

They marched down Tayside, to turn up the Strath of Appin and over the shoulder of mighty Schiehallion to the head of Loch Tummel, then eastwards along that loch to the Pass of Killiecrankie, and so north into Atholl. The Earl of Atholl, they found, had gone to join the King's force.

It was north-by-west after that, on and on amongst the

thronging mountains, up Glen Garry and through the Pass of Drumochter, one of the highest in the land. Ahead now was the great and fair strath of Spey, not exactly Huntly country but that of his allies. Now it was more than just a matter of long marching.

Alastair offered to scout ahead with his MacGregors, and Ludovick elected to go with them. Vicky's position in this expedition was peculiar; Scotland's only duke, and second heir to the throne, he yet had to acknowledge young Argyll as overall commander. Fortunately he was a man with little concern for rank or precedence, and no friction had developed.

The Mackintosh, who was to join them further north, had sent guides to await them at Dalwhinnie, just north of the Drumochter Pass. These had news for them. The entire north was indeed in arms, and mainly pro-Huntly – including unfortunately the Macphersons, whose land was this of upper Strathspey; these were a branch of his own great Clan Chattan federation, of which he was overall head, but Cluny, the Macpherson chief, had chosen the Catholic cause. There was a great and strong castle not far ahead, at Kingussie, called Ruthven, once the seat of the notorious Wolf of Badenoch; and this was now held and garrisoned by the Earl of Errol and the Macphersons. Argyll would find it a hard nut to crack. MacCailean Mhor was warned.

Scouting ahead, Alastair and Vicky emerged into the wide flood-plain of the Spey, the blue giants of the Monadh Ruadh on their right, belying their name of the Red Mountains, the Monadh Liath or Grey Mountains on the left. They could see Ruthven Castle prominent ahead, rising on a mound out of the watery levels, tall and forbidding. Watchers thereon would equally well see *them*.

They waited for Argyll to catch up, and a council was held. With his overwhelming numbers, Argyll was for assault; but other voices urged caution, especially Mackintosh's guides. Lacking cannon to batter holes in the thick walling, the place was too strong to be taken by storm. Only siege would reduce it, and that would take a long time. Better just to bypass it, and head on for the Grant and Mackintosh country.

But MacCailean Mhor was obstinate. To leave the castle

unassailed would be feeble, humiliating. They must surround it and summon Errol to surrender, make a show of strength and confidence. Nothing less was tolerable at their first sight of the enemy.

So the great host moved forward, undoubtedly a daunting sight. But so was the great fortalice rearing before them, its mound much higher and steeper than anticipated, its walls sheer to lofty parapet and wall-walk, its keep dominating all. The three red shields on white of Hay of Errol flew proudly above it.

To surround Ruthven, as Argyll desired, was easier said than done. For the base of the mound was in waterlogged ground, surrounded as though by a wide moat, and only a narrow causeway led steeply up to its gatehouse. And that this causeway was less than accessible was made very evident by a discharge of cannon-fire as the advance party approached. They did not sound like large cannon, sakers probably, but they were more than anything Argyll had.

That young man, annoyed and frustrated, all too anxious that his first military confrontation should not be a fiasco, insisted that they must do something positive, not just proceed onwards. Further gunfire precluding any move to the causeway foot, he could conceive of nothing better than to contrive a white flag and advance, with the duke and a few others, to within hailing distance. There he had a horn blown, and cupping hands to mouth, shouted who he was, and that whoever held this strength should surrender it, in the King's name.

When this produced no least response, he tried again, adding that unless his demands were obeyed, the castle would be besieged and, when taken, all within would be put to death for rejecting the royal command.

Mocking laughter greeted this, and an announcement made that if Argyll thought that he could take Ruthven, let him try. Meantime, if the Campbell did not take himself out of cannon-shot forthwith, he would be fired on, white flag or none.

A dignified retiral followed, somewhat hastened by a bang from the castle, probably a blank, for they saw no fall of shot, and more laughter from the walls. MacCailean Mhor was mortified.

Obviously any prolonged siege would be a waste of time and achieve little. But because of what Argyll had shouted he was faced now with having to eat his words or to leave behind a besieging force, and this large enough to look the part. Fortunately he had such large numbers of men that this was possible without too greatly weakening his array, and he could justify it by declaring that it would prevent the Earl of Errol from possibly leaving to join Huntly. Some five hundred, under Auchenbreck, were therefore left outside Ruthven, with instructions to come on after a few days of it; and the main force resumed its march northwards. Argyll was in no pleasant mood.

They went by Lochs Insh and Alvie to the great pine forests of Rothiemurchus, coming to another of the Wolf of Badenoch's castles, on an islet of Loch-an-Eilean, this one not apparently garrisoned. They camped thereby, to await the Mackintosh, in splendid ancient woodlands.

That great chief, when he arrived with a goodly force of Clan Chattan elements, announced that they would meet the Laird of Grant, and other supporters at Castle Grant, further down Speyside. Then they should turn southwards through the eastern extensions of the Monadh Ruadh, the Cromdale and Ladder Hills, which flanked the River Avon. Thus they would, as it were, approach Huntly's back door at Strathbogie by Glen Livet.

Proceeding down the great river, through more pine forests, the mountains drew back and back. They came at length to Castle Grant, near where Dulnain joined Spey, and there were joined by quite large reinforcements, Macleans under Sir Lachlan of Duart, their chief, and MacNeill of Barra with a smaller following. The Laird of Grant himself was elderly – Alastair was interested that he called himself laird rather than chief, surely a seeking after Lowland status, strange in a Highlander – but he sent a contingent under Grant of Gartenbeg. This last, a youngish man of arrogant mien, now took over guiding and scouting duties, since this was very much Grant country and would continue to be so for some time.

Now they turned away from Spey south-eastwards, to climb over the not-so-high Hills of Cromdale to the steep valley of the rushing Avon, a mountain torrent indeed, cascading out of the high heart of the Red Mountains. Down this twisting glen they went, stretched out now into a column fully three miles long, by the narrows, to camp at Drumin, where Livet joined Avon from the east. Here it was decided to wait awhile. Gartenbeg declared that it was rumoured that King James's army was still far south, indeed in the Dundee area, and they should give it time to catch up. Others argued that this would also allow Huntly to call up support and make his dispositions. However, Argyll agreed that time would serve to summon the Aberdeenshire loyalists, such as the Lord Forbes, the Frasers, the Leslies and the like, which could then threaten Huntly's flank. And a rest from long marching would do his host no harm.

Auchenbreck arrived from Ruthven the next day, to announce that almost as soon as his detachment had left that castle's vicinity they had seen a mounted group leave it and spur off eastwards towards Glen Feshie, no doubt Errol himself, intending to cross the mountains to join Huntly. He, having no horsemen, could do nothing to intercept the escapers.

Waiting at Drumin was all very well and the rest welcome; but in such a place and restricted area there was no provision nor indeed space for so many thousands of men. So the various clan units had to disperse into side valleys and up Livet, some to quite some distance off, Gartenbeg and his Grants the furthest forward, the Gregorach and Ludovick's men up the Tarvie Water.

This waiting period, in fact, did not last long. In only two days Gartenbeg himself came back to announce that there was no waiting on Huntly's part at any rate. A forward patrol of his had in fact clashed with enemy scouts up Glenlivet, with casualties on both sides. A wounded enemy, captured, had told them that Huntly himself had moved north by west from Strathbogie, and was advancing on this Glenlivet area from Auchindoun, well aware of Argyll's presence. He had no comparatively large army however, merely a wholly horsed force of some fifteen hundred. Presumably he was anxious to attack the royalist army before Forbes and the other Aberdeenshire Protestants could join it.

Argyll was only too eager to go meet the enemy. It should not be difficult for his thousands to defeat Huntly's hundreds, even though these were cavalry. To choose, if possible, boggy ground which would hamper horses – that ought not to be difficult to find in these mountains – and their mainly Highland army should be able to trounce the Gordon.

So it was onward up Glenlivet, but only for a few miles. Gartenbeg said that Huntly would be advancing from the north, and they did not want to be caught in the narrow valley itself, strung out and vulnerable to being cut up into sections by cavalry descending upon them. Better to go up into the hills to meet the enemy therein, and try to choose a good area for their purposes, a high slope with waterlogged ground below, bad for cavalry. This seemed good sense, and Argyll turned his host northwards up the Allt Dregnie burn and over between the quite lofty mountain called Carn a' Bhodach on the east and a lower but wider hill, Carn Tighean to the west. This last had a wide east-facing slope, a shallow corrie, drained by a burn called the Allt Chonlachan, which formed typical swampy ground at the bottom, ideal for their purpose. If Huntly attacked, he would have to do it from that low ground. Argyll blessed Gartenbeg.

The army toiled up the side of this Carn Tighean to near its flattish summit, no sign of Huntly's force visible. There Argyll made his dispositions. They would form three distinct forces. Two parallel and forward, apart perhaps half a mile, and a third, the main body, in the rear, ready to advance where most needed. The right-hand forward section to consist of Mackintoshes and Macleans, under their chiefs; the left, Grants, MacNeills and MacGregors under Barra, Alastair and the duke, totalling between them about four thousand. The remainder, mainly his Campbells, under Argyll himself, higher and behind, eight or nine thousand men. It certainly would be a major task for Huntly to attack all this, and a downhill charge for the Highlanders on bogged-down cavalry ideal.

It was chilling up there on the high ground that October night, with no fires permitted to give away their position, but there were no complaints.

To help warm up some of his people in the morning,

Argyll sent men down to dig pits and trenches around those boggy levels, to hamper horsemen further. But these were hastily recalled in mid-forenoon when a mounted host was spotted, approaching from the north over a shoulder of the Hill of Achmore. Now they would see how effective was their strategy.

There could be no hiding the royalist army from the newcomers, of course, as they moved over that bare hillside to their chosen positions. Soon they saw a detachment of about one-fifth of the horsed force spur forward and half-left, in an obvious outflanking move. Argyll's right wing would deal with that.

Alastair, the duke and Barra arranged their men to best advantage. Oddly, Alastair found himself the leader, the most experienced of the three in matters military, or at least in clan warfare, Ludovick having no fighting experience at all, and the MacNeills very little, their isle of Barra not having suffered any invasions for long. So the Gregorach led. They would wait until the enemy horse started to cross that marshy area below, then a Highland charge downhill – the simplest of tactics admittedly, but they ought to be successful.

There was perhaps half a mile of descent between Alastair's force and the corrie floor. The horsemen could not come up at them save by crossing that boggy ground and its trenches. But once across, the ascent was not so steep that the horses could not mount it easily enough. If the enemy waited at the foot, not crossing, it might be possible for the charging Highlanders to get over the wet area, but it would lay them open to dangerous attack by the waiting cavalry, however superior in numbers they were.

Timing, therefore, was of the essence. But there were complications. If Huntly's main cavalry attacked on the other flank, Alastair's force might be needed on this higher ground as a protective threat. This of Errol's detachment – for that earl's red and white banner could be distinguished – might be merely a feint to draw off Argyll's right, and then to swing away back to assist the main thrust. With fast-moving cavalry, that was possible.

Alastair had to watch, then, on more than one front and use his judgment.

In fact, his main trouble was to restrain his own people. Outnumbering the approaching enemy by at least eight to one, they were all for hurtling down the slope and over the bog, whether the cavalry intended to cross it or no.

Errol's squadron duly reached the marshy barrier and halted. Now for the decision. Once they started to cross, Alastair must act; but not until they did.

A horn blew from down there, and the lines of horsemen commenced to pick their way forward.

Alastair raised his hand, sword drawn, and swung it down, to point. He led the way, bounding downhill.

Thousands of men charging and pounding down half a mile of sloping heather and deer-hair grass, and shouting as they went, was not only an awesome spectacle for onlookers but intoxicating even for the participants themselves, a process of ever-increasing wild excitement, almost madness. The effect of that yelling, hurtling, steel-waving host, on men and horses below must have been terrifying, especially as the riders could not be in any formation or front, having to pick their way individually between the water-filled pits and to seek the firmest going. It was not to be wondered at that some faltered and some reined round to turn back to firm ground. Others did press on, to reach terrain more suited to horses' hooves. But it was a very dispersed and broken cavalry squadron which had to face the impact of the Highland onslaught.

The Gregorach led, in their element at last, the MacNeills not far behind, the Levenachs and the Grants well to the rear in this headlong rush. Reaching the foot of the slope, into the soft ground Alastair plunged, leaping agilely from peat-hump to outcrop, tussock to tussock, sword in one hand, dirk in the other – and significantly dirks were held in the right hand, swords in the left. For this was war indeed, and horseflesh no more to be spared than human – in fact, it was horses first.

Riders have undoubted advantages over foot, in length of reach from the saddle and height for heavy down-blows, apart altogether from the frightening effects of lashing hooves and sheer trampling weight. But there are disadvantages also, especially if the ground is not firm, unsure, for the beasts become uneasy then; and noise, yelling and shouting men, can alarm them. And fidgeting, plunging, sidling mounts can be a grievous handicap for cavalrymen in battle. Moreover, the animals' unprotected bellies represent a dire weakness against trained fighters.

The Gregorach were that. However much they might pity the poor beasts, there was no hesitation now. Bounding in and stooping low, they went for those bellies, ripping upwards with their dirks. There was danger from down-slashing swords, yes, and from flailing hooves, but with riders preoccupied with plunging steeds and requiring to bend over very low to get at the crouching attackers, swordery was difficult indeed. With thousands bearing down on them, the horsemen were largely beaten in less time than it takes to tell, their steeds collapsing under them, scattered, disorganised. Those who could fled. By the time that the Grants and the Levenachs reached the boggy area there was little for them to do – save finish off the screaming horses. They could see the Errol banner being borne away from the scene, in haste.

No pursuit was useful, nor possible.

Alastair, the duke and Barra wasted no time in self-congratulation, their eyes turned uphill now, backwards. They could see that fighting was going on. Huntly's main force must have managed to mount and cross a shoulder of this hill, Carn Tighean, and were attacking in flank the loyalist right wing. Gartenbeg had not mentioned the possibility of this. From below, and a mile off, it was difficult to distinguish details, but it looked as though there might be three separate encounters – at least, three masses of horsemen stood out amongst the much more numerous foot.

There was nothing for it – they must ascend that long hill and seek to aid where best they could.

Climbing that slope after their exciting and successful affray was a very different matter from charging down, wearisome, a toil. Also, this time, approaching from below, they would have no advantage over mounted men, the reverse rather. But they had to do what they could.

Halfway up that hill they halted, panting, shocked – shocked by the noise of cannon-fire. Argyll had no cannon. So Huntly must have. Clearly these could not be heavy guns – such could never have got there, oxendrawn; they must be

140

small pieces, carried on pack-horses. More shots rang out, echoing amongst the mountains.

This, of course, changed all. Highlanders were totally unused to fighting with artillery, their broadswords and dirks fairly useless against long-range gunfire. At whom were the cannon firing? The horsemen seemed to be, as it were, entangled amongst the Highland foot, all three groupings; therefore the fire could not be indiscriminately directed into the mass, or Huntly's own men would suffer also.

It was Lennox who produced the likely answer. The cannon could be aimed at Argyll's main body, in the rear, firing into *that* mass, this to prevent them coming to the aid of the Mackintoshes and Macleans of the right wing who were now bearing the brunt of the horsed attack. The Campbell host would be loth indeed to advance in the face of artillery.

None disputed this assessment. What should *their* course be, then? Just to continue with their climb and join the right wing in battle?

Alastair had another idea. If they could work round, on this lower ground, and come up *behind* the cannon, then they might capture these, or at least force them to stop firing.

Some doubts were expressed over this. Would not the cannon then turn on them? Alastair thought that, because of the shoulder of hill, they ought to be able to keep out of sight of the cannoneers until fairly close by. Then a charge. The pieces would not be so very easy to turn around and on to them, repositioned and reloaded, to fire. They ought to have time.

None altogether enthusiastic, they altered course, to contour the middle slopes of the hill. They could be seen, of course, by the combatants up there; but probably the horsemen would be much too busily engaged to be watching the low ground. And although they could hear the cannon, they could not see these because of the lie of the land; so they too ought to be out of sight. They went at the trot now.

Being used to mountainous conformation and the use of dead ground and false summits, all helped. Keeping low on the slope at this stage, they ran northwards, the Levenachs now far behind, Lennox himself having difficulty in keeping up. The cannon-fire continued intermittently. At least, by the sound, this gave them a fair notion as to its position.

When Alastair reckoned that they were directly under it, and went a little further, he turned his strung-out force to climb again, eyeing the hillside ahead for the best covered approach. This was rather like deer-stalking in his own mountains, using the contours and shoulders for unobserved progress. The noise was a help which the deer did not give.

Presently, with the false summits tending to level off, Alastair ordered his people to halt and recover breath, while he went forward alone to spy out the position. The first crest he carefully surmounted showed only one more ahead. But topping this one, he dropped to his knees, his stomach. Now he could see far. Three cannon, with a group of men and horses beside them, were positioned about four hundred yards beyond, on a small mound. Over to the left, half a mile away, the battle was going on. And almost as far, directly in front, was the main mass of Argyll's army, seeking to keep out of range of the artillery. Even as he watched, three more bangs rang out and smoke billowed up. It was too far for him to see whether men fell amongst the Campbells.

Four hundred yards. They ought to manage that.

He slipped back to his waiting array and explained the position to its leaders. Move up to the final crest, then wait just behind it, unseen, until the next cannonade. Then up and over, at their fastest pace. Less than quarter of a mile to go. No shouting at first. There ought to be time to cover the ground before they were seen and the cannon turned round and reloaded and primed. There was no large number at the guns. It should not be difficult.

They moved on, up, to wait below the crest. Evidently it took some time for the recharging of the guns, for there were no more reports in the interim.

When three more crashes did ring out, Alastair was on his feet and waving onwards at once. There was no delay in following him, none desirous of giving time for the reloading and turning procedure.

In the event, it fell out rather differently from what Alastair had visualised. Their presence and advance was spotted, obviously, almost at once. But instead of turning and reloading the smoking guns, the men around became otherwise engaged. As he pounded forward, Alastair perceived what was being done. Those cannon, not large however effective, were being dismounted from their bases and quickly hoisted up into panniers slung on pack-horses' backs, about ten beasts involved. Clearly swift retiral was the priority, not redirection of fire. No doubt those pieces were more precious to Huntly than many men; they must not be captured.

It was a race, therefore, between urgent cannoneers and running Highlanders. The former won, but only by moments – and they left some ball and powder behind. But mounted, they got away and headed northwards at speed. Whether Huntly himself was with them, or with the cavalry, Alastair could not tell.

The entire situation was thus suddenly transformed. Argyll's main force, no longer held up, could advance to the aid of their embattled right wing, unchallenged. As to be sure could Alastair's contingent. Those cannon had represented enormous menace.

Presumably leaders of the fighting cavalry groups also perceived the situation, for horns began to blare therefrom, and the horsemen quickly changed their tactics from riding down the Highland foot to cutting their way out of the press. In a remarkably short time the Battle of Glenlivet was over and the horsed squadrons streaming away northwards after the cannon.

Most of Alastair's wing had not so much as bloodied their swords; nevertheless they found themselves the heroes of the day.

Who, then, had won this extraordinary conflict? It was hard to say. Argyll was left in possession of the field, admittedly; but he had suffered vastly greater casualties, both amongst his fighting right wing and in men mowed down by cannon-fire. Dead were presently estimated at five hundred, and wounded twice that number. Amongst the slain were found to be Huntly's cousin, Gordon of Auchindoun and a kinsman, Gordon of Gight. And, very significantly and oddly, two other bodies amongst the enemy dead were none other than those of Campbell of Lochnell and Grant of Gartenbeg. These had apparently deserted Argyll at an early stage and gone over to Huntly, possibly to inform him as to dispositions, numbers and weaknesses. Both, of course, were

Catholics – but so, in fact, were most of Argyll's army. That both should have fallen was strange, to say the least. It was suspected that Huntly himself might have had them slain, traitors apt to be a liability to one side as to the other.

So now Argyll needed a new heir, and Black Duncan a new tool.

Sadly, at the last moment, MacNeill of Barra had been cut down and killed by a departing horseman whom he had tried to halt. And Campbell of Auchenbreck, one of MacCailean Mhor's guardians, was also dead, hit by a cannon-ball. If it all was victory, it was a costly one – but not so costly as if those cannon had not been seen off when they were. The entire engagement had only taken two hours.

It was not thought that there was much likelihood of Huntly resuming the assault in the immediate future. However Argyll, clearly shaken by it all, decided that he and his host must get away from there, down into Glenlivet and away from possible danger until plans could be made as to further action. There was no delay, a party being left behind to bury the dead in peat-hags.

They got back to Tomnavoulin that evening, on the Livet, where it was felt that they would be secure from any surprise attack meantime. A council was held. Argyll was noticeably less sure of himself than heretofore, still shaken from his first battle and encounter with cannon – as indeed were others. There was much excited talk, blame laid, excuses made, treachery denounced, the presence of those cannon harked back and back to. It was Duke Ludovick who eventually managed to get the discussion on to what should be done now. They were supposed to link up with the King's army, he reminded, to attack Strathbogie.

There was marked lack of enthusiasm shown. The royal force, by all accounts, was still far away, making no haste to join *them*. They had done their part, borne the heat of the day, spilt their blood, in the King's cause. Let James and his Protestant lords from the south do something now. It could be long before that army reached Strathbogie. Meanwhile *they* were in danger. This was too near Huntly's own country. He had produced only those fifteen hundred horse, yes – but he could muster foot by the thousand. Perhaps these were already mustered, only awaiting orders to attack; and they might well have more cannon. Brave enough men all but shivered at that thought.

The duke admitted all that, but pointed out that a firm arrangement and agreement had been entered into. They need not actually seek to challenge Huntly again meantime, but should endeavour to keep their rendezvous with the King. Also seek to find the Forbeses, Frasers, Leslies and their other Lowland Aberdeenshire allies.

The clan chiefs, save for Alastair, were otherwise minded. They had done enough, shown their loyalty sufficiently. Let the Protestants do the further fighting. They were for home.

It was evident that Argyll felt the same way, even though he did not actually say so.

Ludovick could be obstinate. He declared that he and his would abide by the arrangement, seek to join up with King James. Alastair said that the Gregorach would do the same – and found MacCailean Mhor looking at him narrow-eyed. No others spoke up.

So, without any specific resolution being passed, the situation was accepted. The Grants, Mackintoshes, Macleans, MacNeills and the other northern clan forces would retire to their own glens and islands, and MacCailean Mhor would lead his Campbells and their allies back to Argyll, Lorn and Cowal; and the almost eight hundred Gregorach and Levenachs would go to meet the royal army, and if possible try to join up with the Lord Forbes, although meantime not seeking to come to grips with Huntly's main forces.

In the morning, then, it was the parting of the ways. The great majority of the host set off to thread the Cromdale Hills westwards, for Spey; whilst Alastair and Ludovick, with a local guide, led their people further up Glenlivet eastwards, to cross the Ladder Hills, in order to work their way well south of the Strathbogie area, making for the headwaters of the River Don, from which they ought to reach central Aberdeenshire and the Forbes and Leslie country.

The days that followed were a remarkable contrast to those preceding. Suddenly all the pressure was lifted, for the

Gregorach and the Levenach. Haste, clearly, was no longer necessary, battle not anticipated and certainly not to be sought, time to be filled in, rather, in largely empty country. Feeding, at first, was the major problem, the Ladder Hills being notably devoid of population and therefore of cattle and meal. Fortunately there were large herds of deer roaming the long slopes, and the Gregorach at least were expert in winning them, not only in individual stalking but in driving the herds towards what might be called ambushes, narrows, where the animals could be killed in numbers. And they had time on their hands. So they did not starve, although a diet of only venison and a little oatmeal did pall.

Their aim was to head almost due southwards from Livet some score of mountainous miles to the headwaters of Don, where the Ernan joined that river at Inverernan. Then down the strath some twenty-five miles to the Howe of Alford, wherein was Castle Forbes, where they hoped to find, or at least learn the whereabouts of, the Lord Forbes, the chiefest man of this central Aberdeenshire, and now firm Protestant, although his son was a Popish monk. If it was true that the King's army had not left Dundee before the battle, then, at the speed that it was likely to travel, it would be some days before it could reach these parts – that is, if it was decided to come on at all. Patrick Gray, surely, would see that it did, however reluctant a warrior was James Stewart. So Forbes and his allies might well be lying low meantime; and they themselves need not hasten.

In the event it took three days to emerge out of the mountains into the wide vistas of lower Strathdon, in the vicinity of the castle of Kildrummy, a seat of the Earl of Mar – which noble was of course at Stirling, where he was keeper of that fortress and guardian of the young prince – so no aid was to be looked for here. Down the fine river they went, through the Howe of Alford, with no sign of hostilities evident, by Alford itself, Houghton and Keig villages, to Castle Forbes at the entrance to a pass through sudden wooded narrows called, oddly, My Lord's Throat. Here they found the said lord, in no very militant posture, indeed in the bosom of his family, an amiable man in his fifties, less than inclined for warfare, especially as his latest

146

word of the King's progress put the royal army no further north than upper Angus, burning Craig Castle, south of Montrose. Moreover his other information was that Huntly – who happened to be his brother-in-law, although he had divorced that wife and married another, safely Protestant – had in fact retired northwards, after Glenlivet, into Moray, so presumably was not seeking further clash meantime. However, the Forbes manpower was on call to muster at short notice; and the more eager Leslies, Frasers and Leiths were gathered in the Urie valley to the north-east, near Pitcaple – where the newcomers should perhaps join them, after due hospitality. He would send his second son, Arthur, with them as guide.

It was further leisurely progress, therefore, through a pleasant countryside of wide valleys, woodlands and rounded low green hills, skirting the most prominent landmark in all this spreading terrain, the Mither Tap, as it was called, of Bennachie, an isolated thrusting peak of notably feminine aspect. If this was campaigning, in the golden early October weather, then none involved had any complaints. Yet the dreaded Strathbogie area was less than a score of miles to the north, which gave it all something of a feeling of unreality.

At Pitcaple, on the Urie, they found a modest host of about their own numbers encamped, under Leslie of Balquhain, these being quite happy to receive reinforcements, especially under Scotland's only duke, although they looked somewhat askance at the MacGregors, as was usual. Here, in Lumsden country, they decided to wait, pleasingly idle. It seemed a far cry from the bloodshed and slaughter of Glenlivet.

It took four more days for King James to arrive, with a much more aggressive array – aggressive in a punitive rather than a battling way, with fierce Kirk divines all but in control, although the monarch also seemed to enjoy the necessary procedures of burning and sacking the houses of Popish miscreants. This, apparently, they had been doing all the way from Dundee, and the resultant and ever-growing baggage-train of purloined and confiscated goods and valuables partly responsible for their slow progress. According to the Master of Gray, present in head-shaking but philosophic resignation, this rather than actual battle seemed to be the object of the expedition, laying waste the seats of the idolators being the war-cry, James and the Kirk for once in hearty agreement – although the King's concern was acquisitive rather than ethical. Much of Angus, the Mearns and Aberdeenshire smoked behind them.

Patrick, and to a lesser extent James, was interested to hear the details of the Glenlivet struggle, the latter highly critical of Argyll's conduct of the battle and his departure for home thereafter, instead of pursuing Huntly to the death. But His Grace was graciously pleased with the duke's and the MacGregors' parts in it all; they could now gain their due reward by helping to demolish Papist houses they came across on their way north to Strathbogie, with consequent enrichment – this royal prescription less than enthusiastically received.

The combined host moved on next day, spread out over a very wide front, to ensure that as few heretics' establishments as possible escaped godly punishment. Alastair and Lennox witnessed the devastation of Culsalmond Castle, rather than took part. This was a Gordon property, so the fullest retribution was called for; and the treatment of the old laird, his family and retainers, was sickening to watch, the soldiery being given a free hand, whilst their leaders selected desirable contents to add to the baggage-train, before burning the rest.

The friends, to be spared more of this, asked permission to go scouting ahead with their men, now that they were into Gordon territory.

They actually reached Strathbogie Castle, about a dozen miles further, without any challenge at all, to their surprise, and found that palatial establishment, finer than any of the royal residences, completely abandoned, empty, an extraordinary situation. This, the principal target of Reformed hatred and anger for so long, now fell to them without a blow struck. Was it a trap? Was Huntly in fact luring his enemies on, to take it, and then to descend upon them there? Parties sent out to scout the land ahead came back having seen no signs of opposition; indeed the word was that Huntly was retiring still further into the fastnesses of the north, beyond Moray and Inverness, allegedly even to the safety of far Caithness.

So when King James arrived in person, Strathbogie was his, its splendid plenishings, gold and silver ware, furnishings, tapestries, pictures and the like, there for the taking. Never had that less-than-wealthy monarch seen the like. Here, at last, he came into his own and, as it transpired, clashed now with Andrew Melville and the other stern ministers, who were concerned with the righteous burning and demolition of a building full of shrines and images and Popish symbols, rather than with the abstraction of its contents. A tug-of-war succeeded before hammers and crowbars and gunpowder eventually brought low the palace of the Cock o' the North, as Huntly was called, to satisfactory ruin.

This achievement, however, appeared to satisfy James Stewart, if not his spiritual advisers. Enough was enough, he declared – he was for the south, for Stirling. That ill limmer Bothwell might be trying to kidnap his precious young Prince Henry. No point in going on further – they could not pursue Huntly to Caithness. He gave orders for their mile-long train of pack-horses, with the booty, to be most heedfully escorted, and to return to Aberdeen forthwith.

At that city, three days later, Alastair bade farewell to Ludovick Stewart – for, much to the latter's displeasure, James had appointed him Lieutenant of the North, a post up till now held by Huntly himself. Vicky was to remain at Aberdeen and keep the north in order from there, to see that Huntly and the others did not rise up again. With a council of ministers, the Lord Forbes and other local Protestants to advise him, he was to do something useful at last, said his cousin and sovereign-lord, instead of lurking at yon Methven.

James departed southwards, well pleased, and Alastair took the Gregorach westwards, at their own pace now, enjoined to look after Mary Gray.

14

Much as he approved of the assignment, Alastair MacGregor found it no easy commission to look after Mary Gray; not that, he recognised, the said young woman was not notably able to look after herself. The fact was that the Queen had appointed her Extra Woman of the Bedchamber to be one of the nurses of the infant prince, in Stirling Castle, and so she could only occasionally get up to Perthshire. And Alastair was in no position to frequent the court at Stirling, unbidden.

It was Yuletide before he saw her therefore, scarcely the season for upland travel. But Mary sent a messenger to say that she was at Methven and would be happy to see him if he could get there. He was off the next day, weather notwithstanding.

Her greeting was warm as ever, delightfully so – and yet unsatisfying to the man in that, holding her in his arms, he could not but wish that it could be closer still, even warmer. Which was both wrong and foolish, he knew only too well; but nature was strong. He had to make his will even stronger; and Mary had her own strengths, and sought not to tempt him unduly, well aware of his longings as she had to be. The little boy, Johnnie Stewart, was a help. And Duke Ludovick's trust and friendship was never far from Alastair's mind.

Mary was much upset about the said Ludovick's continued absence at Aberdeen. He had sent to the King asking to be relieved of his unwanted responsibility for the north, but to no avail. James still, apparently, harboured doubts about him and the Queen, ridiculous as these were. Vicky was hating being Lieutenant of the North, involving duties so contrary to his nature, ever under pressure from the Kirk ministers to be harsher towards the Catholics, always having to act the judge, the punisher – but most of all, this separation from Mary and his little son.

She had besought her father, the Master, to work on James to have the duke recalled, but without success. He had even suggested, as replacement, none other than the Earl of Argyll whom, he declared, could wield far greater authority, with his great Campbell manpower in the north, than could Vicky; whether that was a good idea or not Mary was uncertain – but no doubt Patrick had his own reasons for putting it forward, for with her too-clever sire one never knew. Argyll was not at present popular at court.

Alastair could only sympathise over Ludovick's enforced separation.

Mary had other news for him. Glenorchy had appeared at court while Patrick was away holding justice eyres in the sheriffdom of Forfar, which he had managed to wrest from his father, Lord Gray, with whom he was in a continuous state of family warfare. She could only account for Glenorchy's arrival in connection with the King's present displeasure with Argyll over the Battle of Glenlivet and its aftermath. Duncan, of course, had not been at Glenlivet, and now saw opportunity to use their monarch's prejudices to his own advantage. Clearly he was still seeking the downfall of his young chief. His ostensible reason for coming to court was to plead for the release of his friend Ardkinglas, who had been detained in ward at Edinburgh Castle by the Privy Council over his part in the murder of Campbell of Cawdor. Now Duncan had convinced the King that Ardkinglas's confession had been obtained only under torture, and therefore was invalid, his guilt a fabrication of Argyll's. He had obtained the prisoner's release, and presumably impressed their peculiar sovereign-lord sufficiently to obtain knighthood. Had Patrick or Ludovick been on hand almost certainly this would not have happened; but there it was. Argyll had better be on his guard.

So should he himself, Alastair recognised. Black Duncan's lying low appeared to be over. His feud with MacGregor was unlikely to be forgotten.

Mary was unhappy about the Queen. James's permission for her to visit her son at Stirling had proved less mollifying than hoped for. She did not get on with the child's keeper, the Earl of Mar; and seeing little Henry – or Frederick as she insisted on calling him – on occasion only, made her want to see him the more often, indeed to have him in her own care. But the King was adamant. His son was to remain under strict guard in Scotland's strongest fortress, lest one or other, or a coalition of his power-hungry nobles, capture him and use him to rule the land in his name, possibly with an assassination of James himself; after all, it had happened before in the realm's turbulent story, not least with his own mother and himself. All Anne's motherhood instincts were outraged – as Mary could well understand. She was refused any improvement in her association with her child, and was now all but confining herself in Linlithgow Palace, in a state almost of hysteria. Not only so, but James's idea of improving the situation was to try to father on her another child, so that the succession was the more assured, and his visits to Linlithgow were in consequence the more unwelcome. Anne was even talking about requesting her brother, the King of Denmark, to come over and take her home to her own country. In all this, Mary's own position was unfortunate. She was the Queen's attendant and tirewoman, and also a nurse to the prince, one of them, ferrying between Stirling and Linlithgow and looked on with suspicion by Mar and the monarch. How she wished that she and Vicky could escape from court life altogether and live privately and peacefully at this Methven.

Alastair, helpless to aid, would have comforted her more effectively had that been permissible. How far did his charge to look after Mary Gray go?

The young woman had one suggestion for Alastair before she returned to her unwelcome duties in the south. Why did he not go and see Argyll, to warn him of Black Duncan's machinations at court? After all, Argyll had helped him, in the past; and he had been a successful commander in the field at Glenlivet. As excuse for his visit he could say that the Duke of Lennox was willing to negotiate a transference to him of the position of Admiral of the Western Seas. This was one more title which meant nothing to Vicky but which Argyll's grandfather had held and his son known to covet. MacCailean Mhor would undoubtedly be glad to have it, and could make some use of it, situated as he was, which Vicky could not. Thus Alastair would further commend himself to

Argyll, which could be useful; and at the same time possibly strike a blow at Black Duncan.

Alastair agreed to consider it.

In March, with the weather improved and the snows melting on the mountains, he made the proposed excursion. He had some doubts as to the numbers of the tail he should take with him, not wishing to seem aggressive in Campbell country but well aware that the first part of his route must be through Glenorchy's territory – although admittedly they had been seeing little of that man in these parts for long now; after all, he had many other houses to make use of. He took forty as a reasonable escort for a chief.

It was no long nor difficult journey, a mere eight miles down the east side of Loch Awe to Cladich, where a drove-road crossed eastwards over the watershed to upper Loch Fyne, where was Inveraray. They passed Kilchurn Castle without any signs of attention, and on down the lochside.

However, they had barely turned up this side-road when, at a herdsman's cottage they learned that MacCailean Mhor was not presently at Inveraray but at Innischonnel. This was the Campbells' original stronghold in these parts, before ever they were lords of Argyll, only Campbells of Lochow, or Awe, a fairly modest fortalice on an islet just offshore and a mere ten miles or so further down the loch.

When they reached the castleton of Innischonnel, on the mainland just opposite the isle, they met their first challenge, Campbell clansmen in some numbers marshalling to demand what the Gregorach wanted in this territory. But there were some there who had been at Glenlivet and recognised Alastair, and there was no trouble.

A horn blown then summoned the watch out at the castle, which was no more than one hundred yards offshore, and a shouted exchange followed, hard to maintain with dignity. MacGregor Himself come to see MacCailean Mhor was well enough, but demands as to why and wherefore, and with how many men, were unsuitable and received only curt replies. But, after a silent interval, another shout intimated that MacCailean Mhor would see MacGregor. His men, however, could remain at the castleton.

153

Alastair did not argue about this, and he was rowed out in a small boat. Innischonnel Castle was basically a rectangle of very high and thick curtain walls with square towers at two of the angles, stern as it was simple, save that it had a curious irregularly shaped outer courtyard at the north end, which followed the outline of the islet. At the gatehouse here they were admitted, and Alastair was led across to a notably narrow doorway in the main building's curtain wall, only three feet wide. Edging through this very defensive feature, he recognised why this strong but so difficult of access fortalice had made but an inconvenient seat for great lords, and obvious why they had moved to Inveraray.

A chamberlain of sorts now greeted him and escorted him to the larger of the two towers, where he was taken up to a first-floor hall and left to wait. Quite a long wait too, Argyll no doubt desirous of impressing on an uninvited caller just who was what. When at length that young man appeared, he was scarcely affable – but then he never was, and one day would be known as Archibald the Grim.

Alastair, in consequence, was stiff also, inclining his head rather than bowing, and waiting for the other to speak.

"So, Glenstrae, what can I do for you?" That was peremptory.

"Naught that I know of, MacCailean Mhor. It is what *I* can do for you that brings me here, whatever."

The younger man blinked, given pause. "How so?"

"Two matters of some import." Alastair was not going to my-lord him, as one chief to another. "Important to yourself, I think. If you wish to hear them?"

Belatedly Argyll, considering that, thought of the traditional Highland hospitality and gestured towards a table on which stood flagons, with oatcakes and honey. "You will partake?"

"If you so wish."

Shrugging, the other moved over, to pour out two beakersful of whisky, and brought one to his guest, who took it, sipped rather than quaffed, and inclined his head again. So far, as an interview, it was hardly encouraging.

"Well, sir, your tidings? It is not often that MacGregor comes to Campbell!"

"No. And with good enough reason, whatever! But I come

now at the behest of . . . others. In effect, from His Grace's Lieutenant of the North, my lord Duke of Lennox."

"Ha, your friend Lennox. Still in Aberdeen?"

"Yes. His concern for the north, and his duties thereto, brings me here." Alastair was speaking carefully indeed. "He hears that the great Clan Donald of the Isles is stirring."

"It is, yes. Stirring dangerously. Many war-galleys mustering. For what purpose is not yet clear. But calling on other island clans to support them. Well may Lennox, and the King, be concerned."

"And MacCailean Mhor also! MacDonald does not love Campbell, I think."

"So?"

"The duke, as well as being Lord High Chamberlain and now Lieutenant of the North, is also Admiral of the Western Seas. He is prepared to consider the transference of that style to yourself, sir."

He had the younger man's fullest attention and interest now. "Admiral! Aye, my grandsire was that. It, it should be mine, by right. He, Lennox, would part with it?"

"Yes."

"At what . . . price?"

"Only your full co-operation, whatever, in keeping the peace of the north. As is to your own advantage and interest, is it not? And not only in this of the MacDonalds. You control much of the southern isles and this lower seaboard. You have many galleys. You would be seeking to restrain the Clan Donald anyway, would you not? From disturbing the peace of these parts?"

Argyll was searching Alastair's face. "Perhaps. Why this of the Admiral?"

"A gesture of goodwill, just. And to give you greater authority. In the King's name."

"So-o-o!" The other let out a long breath. "I do not fully understand this, MacGregor. But I, I esteem the duke's goodwill, yes, and would accept his offer, if the cost is not too great." He paused. "Does Lennox believe that this of the MacDonalds is linked with Huntly and the Catholic cause? They are all Catholics."

"As am I! That I know not. Nor, I think, does the duke.

155

It may be otherwise. Just Clan Donald taking advantage of troubled times to line its own nest! And at the Campbells' expense."

"Campbell can look after his own interests, MacGregor."

"It may be so. But perhaps not so well – if Clan Campbell is divided?"

"Eh? What do you mean, man? Divided?"

"That, sir, is the second matter which brings me here. This, of my own will, because you aided MacGregor that time, against Glenorchy's wiles and threats. Now Glenorchy is on the move again – and it is yourself, I think, that he aims his dirk at!"

"Glenorchy? Black Duncan! What is this?"

"You have not heard, then? Of his recent activities? At court."

"Court? You mean the King's court?"

"That, yes. He has appeared there, and is seemingly in the King's favour – with the duke and the Master of Gray absent. Maitland may have had a hand in it . . ."

"How can this be? Glenorchy has nothing that James Stewart wants. He did not join my host against the Catholics and Huntly. This is folly."

"Be not so sure. At least the King now thinks well enough of him to knight him."

"*Knight!* Black Duncan knighted? I do not believe it." That came out thickly.

"It is true. And not only that. He has obtained Ardkinglas's release from ward. Declaring that his confession to the Privy Council that he had part in the murder of Sir John of Cawdor was obtained only by torture, and so of no substance. So Ardkinglas is free again."

"Devil burn him – how has he done this?"

"I do not know. Mistress Mary Gray, the Queen's woman of the Bedchamber, told me. The Master of Gray's daughter. She is knowledgeable. But she does not know *how* Glenorchy so moved the King. But I think that the how is not so important as the *why*, whatever! Why do it all? For what purpose?"

"Aye. His purpose, God damn him! Ardkinglas also sought to poison *me*. I have little doubt at Glenorchy's behest. So now . . .!"

"Yes – that is why I have brought you this word. He will aim at you, I judge. At MacGregor also, no doubt. But, in the main, at MacCailean Mhor. And so believes Mary Gray. If you were removed, he could control Clan Campbell. And all that means."

The other turned to pace up and down the floor. He took a gulp of his untouched whisky. "The man is a fiend out of hell! Too clever, by half. He got at Lochnell. Had Cawdor slain. He tried to win Auchenbreck, but failed in that. What next?"

"So long as you are on your guard . . ."

"That I will be! I have heard that Glenorchy is seeing much of MacDougall of Lorn. They were ever our foes. That may link with this of Clan Donald. I must needs take steps."

"Yes, So, I think, should I. We could be allies in this, MacCailean Mhor."

Argyll looked at his visitor levelly, but said nothing.

Alastair certainly was not going to press that aspect, pride forbidding. He had done what he came to do, said all that needed to be said. He took another sip at his beaker, and set it down. "I leave you, then, with much to consider."

"You will not bide for . . . refreshment?" That was hardly a pressing invitation.

"I can be back at Glen Strae by darkening if I leave now."

"Very well." He was led to the door. "I will call the clan. To a conference, would be best. Quickly. As well as order all ready to muster at arms. Tell Glenorchy to be there. With Ardkinglas. Then we shall see!"

"I wish it success."

"This of the Admiral. I esteem it well." That was as near to thanks as MacCailean Mhor could get. "When will it be mine?"

"That is for the duke to say. But I think there need be no delay."

"As well, yes. Then I could use it as one reason for the conference. That and the MacDonald threat. And my betrothal."

"Ah! Do I congratulate the lady?"

"She is the Lady Agnes. Daughter to the Earl of Morton."

"So-o-o!" Alastair did not know whether, indeed, congratulations were in order – not from himself, at any rate. For however lofty the match, this lady's father was the former Sir William Douglas of Loch Leven, who had been Mary Queen of Scots' gaoler at that castle, and a harsh one at that. He had succeeded the notorious Regent Morton in the earldom, a cousin. "Sufficiently Protestant, at least!" he said.

The other nodded briefly, and on that note took his guest only as far as the tower door, where he summoned his chamberlain to take him further, without any fond farewells.

Alastair MacGregor would never like Archibald Campbell. Perhaps that had shown.

15

It was not long before Alastair had further news of national affairs which concerned himself, and this time not from Mary Gray, but from her father. Ill news too, for himself and his people, in more respects than one. It was brought by a messenger from Broughty Castle in Angus, sent by the Master, and to the effect that the Privy Council had been approached by Menzies of that Ilk for authority to expel members of the MacGregor clan who were unlawfully occupying his lands in the Rannoch area. Patrick added that there had not long been a meeting of the council, before this request was received, and that there would not likely be another for some time, and when there was, he would endeavour to have the matter either dismissed or made light of. But Glenstrae might well receive a communication from the clerk to the council requiring him either to appear before him to explain the situation and circumstances, or to send a statement for consideration. Knowing Alastair's inability to write letters, he suggested that it might be wise to make some enquiries with Menzies, and be prepared to state his case – if he had a case to state.

Alastair was nonplussed by this message. He and Alexander Menzies had always got on reasonably well together, and there had never been any hint of trouble. The Rannoch lands, well to the north of Glen Strae and Glen Lyon, were a strange, wild territory, extensive and little populated, especially at the west end where was the vast and waterlogged Moor of Rannoch, one of the largest acreages of empty wilderness in all Scotland. The middle district around Loch Rannoch itself was largely ancient pine forest, with clearings, and the heights of mighty Schiehallion. And the easternmost portion around Loch Tummel was more fertile and populous. In all its great area of perhaps four hundred square miles there were few if any recognised boundaries, and ownership limits vague in the extreme. It had almost all been MacGregor land once, but for long the earldom of Atholl claimed the eastern portion, and Menzies the central, with no one particularly interested in the barren, inhospitable and all but useless Moor of Rannoch. A branch of the Clan Gregor had survived on the edges of the moor and some way into the central territory; but Menzies had never found them a nuisance hitherto – indeed they were useful as drovers for Menzies cattle from more settled parts to western markets at Taynuilt and Oban, knowing secret ways across the bogs and morasses of Rannoch Moor, *terra incognita* to others. So this appeal to the Privy Council was utterly unlooked-for.

The Menzies situation was in fact rather an odd one, in the Highlands, for they were not in truth a Celtic clan at all; or at least, their chiefs could not claim to be Celts, although a large proportion of their people would almost certainly be of MacGregor origin. The name was really a corruption of de Meyners, a family from Flanders, warriors who had come over with Norman William for his English conquest, and who thereafter had done rather well for themselves in England and eventually become Earls of Rutland, using the name of Manners. David the First had brought one of these de Meyners north to Scotland, along with so many other Normans and Flemings – Frasers, Stewarts, Lindsays, Gordons and the rest – and given him the lands of Weem just east of Loch Tay. There his descendants had remained, and gradually taken on the aspects and character of a Highland clan – although the true Celtic clans always looked on them as rather different. And the chiefs always called themselves Menzies of that Ilk, after the Lowland fashion.

Alastair, needless to say, decided to go and see Alexander Menzies without delay. The Menzies lands were all but surrounded by those of Black Duncan Campbell.

It was not a long journey, for Weem, where was Castle Menzies, was not far east of the mouth of Glen Lyon, Aberfeldy its township nearby. He picked up Gregor of Roro on the way.

Castle Menzies was a handsome place, comparatively new, quite large and well appointed, for the Menzies lands were on the whole fertile and productive – a notably finer establishment than Innischonnel where Alastair had recently conferred with MacCailean Mhor. It was set on level ground at the foot of a high, steep slope, crag-topped, wherein were the caves which gave the place its name, *uamh*, or Weem. It had replaced an earlier castle not far to the west, burned down.

Alexander Menzies was at home, fortunately, superintending the building of a new cattle-court and range of barns. A man of early middle age, of normally genial character, he was now most evidently embarrassed at the sight of the MacGregors.

Alastair was concerned to keep this interview on as friendly terms as was possible, although Roro would have preferred more forthright methods.

"Greetings, Meinnarich!" he exclaimed. "You are busy, I see. Bless the good work! Your beasts increase and multiply?"

The other mumbled something, clearly at a loss, and Roro barked a laugh.

"Thinking to increase his herds from Rannoch, whatever!"

"No, no. Leastways . . ." Menzies' voice tailed off, as he looked from one to the other. "Welcome to Weem," he got out. He gestured towards the castle. "My house. Refreshment?"

"No need to take you from your work here, Meinnarich. We will not keep you long, at all. We come to discover what is this of Rannoch?"

"Aye. No doubt. It, it is a difficult matter, see you."

"It is? Since when has Rannoch become difficult, friend?"

"Your people there – they are on my land . . ."

"Always they have been that – since it ceased to be MacGregor land, no?"

"Perhaps. But now it is necessary to make a, a different arrangement."

"Necessary? Why?"

"Your people, Glenstrae, have spread over eastwards. Over Menzies land. This must cease. They must go back."

"Back where? They have always been in Rannoch."

"Back to the moor."

"The moor! The Moor of Rannoch is empty, desolate, more water than land. What would they do there? What *could* they do there?"

161

"That . . . is not my . . . concern. So long as they leave Menzies land."

"But why? Why this now?"

"Because Black Duncan of Glenorchy told him they must!" That was Roro, forcefully.

There was a pause then. Menzies looked unhappy but said nothing.

"How could Glenorchy do that?" Alastair asked. "He cannot command the Menzies."

"No. But . . ."

"He can threaten Menzies with trouble if he does not do as Duncan says," Roro observed.

All eyed each other. That was so evidently the situation that there was no need to confirm it.

Alastair actually felt sorry for Alexander Menzies. "What can Black Duncan do to threaten *you*?" he wondered.

"It is the Appin of Dull. Lands there. I need them – Candloch, Torricharddy and Turbroichs."

"The Appin of Dull was always yours, was it not? The Abthanery. Has gone with Weem."

"Aye. But Glenorchy says that he has found a charter, of fifty years past, in favour of his father, Sir Colin, which includes in his barony of Lawers these places in the Appin of Dull. They are not large, but they are most damnably situated."

"You mean . . .?"

"I mean that they are astride the entrance to the Strath of Appin, right at its southern mouth. They flank the drove-road down the strath, on either side, the road from the north. From Rannoch. And no way past them. So . . ."

"So if they are in truth his, the Campbell could close the strath and road at will?"

"He could. And all the beasts from my lands of Rannoch and Foss must come down that road, to market. All coming and going up the strath, for herds, he could stop."

"*Dia!* So that is it! Tolls. He could charge what he likes."

"Yes. And more than that. He could hold me to ransom. My greatest herds are up in Rannoch, the Braes of Foss and Strathfionan. The Strath of Appin is my road to them, my only road."

They considered that, frowning. The Strath of Appin was

scarcely well named, for it was in truth no wide and open vale but a narrow, climbing glen, more of a pass, eight miles long, linking the great parallel valleys of Tay and Rannoch, a steep alleyway through the mountains. At this southern end was the Appin of Dull, a level and fertile area where the Keltney Burn met the River Lyon and both flowed into Tay. This Appin was indeed a place of great significance in Scotland's story, despite its name – for Dull was merely another form of Dal or Dale, and the Appin a corruption of Abthanery. Here, nearly one thousand years before, in 661, St Cuthbert, as a young man suffering from the yellow plague, had set up a hermitage and prepared to die. But, recovering, he went on to lead the life of a most active missionary – and his little monastic foundation grew into a major Celtic Church establishment and college for the training of the Keledei, the Friends of God, commonly called the Culdees, which Adamnan, a successor of St Columba's at Iona, instituted, called the Abthanery, or Abbacy, of Dull. Here was educated the famous Crinan the Thane, leader of the Celtic Church in his day, who married the Princess Bethoc, elder daughter of Malcolm the Terrible, and had a son Duncan who succeeded his grandfather as Duncan the First, a haemophiliac, who died bleeding after fighting MacBeth. When Queen Margaret put down the Columban Church and replaced it by the Romish one, the Abthanery declined, and a modest parish church was erected on its site, the extensive lands passing to secular proprietors, and in time to de Meyners or Menzies. This, of the special and strategic part of the property being granted to Glenorchy's father, for some reason, seemed odd indeed.

"You did not know of this before?" Alastair asked.

"No. These properties have always been tenanted by my Menzies folk."

"It may not be true, at all," Roro said. "Just Campbell lies and devilry. Forgery."

"I think that Black Duncan is too clever for that. He would not risk being exposed as lying if he was challenged on it. Not with the Privy Council brought into it."

"No. He showed me the charter," Menzies agreed. "It dates from my grandsire's time. My father never mentioned the matter to me. But it seems true enough, these places named."

"That Colin Campbell was as great a devil as is his son!" Alastair asserted. "He had *my* father slain, to get Glen Lyon. So, now Duncan threatens you with this?"

"If I do not have your MacGregors driven out of my Rannoch, he will take over these holdings in the Appin, put out my tenants, put in his own, and be able to close the strath. I, I have no choice."

"He wants the MacGregors forced over into the *Moor* of Rannoch, you say? Useless tract as that is. He told you the moor, did he?"

Menzies nodded.

"Why that? He always has his reasons, has Black Duncan of the Cowl. I wonder? His most northerly property, Achallader Castle, is on the southern edge of the Moor. Could it be that he wishes to claim the Moor of Rannoch for himself? None other will want its empty desolation. And if the Gregorach are occupying parts of it, however uncomfortably, he would have them! More of my people unlawfully roosting on his land. It could be that. The Gregorach the target still, not truly you, Meinnarich. *Us* – MacGregor!"

"It could be, yes. I am sorry. But I cannot fight him. Glenorchy has ten men for every one of mine. I have no choice . . ."

"You have, man!" Roro declared. "You can snap your fingers at Black Duncan. So long as *I* hold the centre of Glen Lyon, at Roro. For I have my own pass over to Rannochside, the Lairig Chalbhath. *We* use it, and so could you. From the Black Wood of Rannoch, at Carie, on the lochside, to Roro. Then over, southwards, to Loch Tay. It is higher than the Strath of Appin, yes – but shorter. And your drovers would have Gregorach protection, all the way."

Alexander Menzies stared at him. "You would allow that?"

"To be sure. I would allow more than that, to trip Black Duncan! I would *rejoice* in it, whatever! And you would have no tolls to pay."

The other chewed his lip.

"It is a fair offer, Meinnarich," Alastair urged him. "Accept it. That way you could cheat Glenorchy of his scheming. Tell him that you will in future drove by Roro's passes, west of Schiehallion, not east, and so avoid any closing of the Strath

164

of Appin at Dull. You have him, then. I doubt whether he
will then indeed go ahead with the expelling of your tenants
in the Appin. To have Menzies *and* MacGregor allied against
him, in these parts, will give even Glenorchy pause. Especially
with his chief, Argyll, presently frowning on him. The man is
being just too clever, this time!"

"We, the Menzies, are not a warlike race . . ."

"*We* are sufficiently warlike for both!" Roro told him,
grinning.

"Will you do it?" Alastair demanded. "Tell Glenorchy that
you are withdrawing your request to the Privy Council, on
good advice. And let him do his worst. You are Protestant – use
that. Atholl, your neighbour in Rannoch, is also Protestant.
He will back you, I think. He does not love Duncan. *He* may
well wish the Strath of Appin kept open, also."

"Very well. I, I never wished to do this, Glenstrae. I was
weak, perhaps. But . . . I am a man of peace."

"With Black Duncan as neighbour, peace can be expensive!
As *we* well know," Roro observed. "Here is my hand on it.
Use my passes freely – if you need to."

"And MacGregor will see that you are not unlawfully
harassed," Alastair added.

They all shook hands on that. Refreshment was now
acceptable and suitable.

Alastair sent his own messenger to Broughty Castle to inform
the Master of Gray of the situation. And thereafter no word
came to him from the Privy Council. Also, as a precaution,
he sent a courier to MacCailean Mhor, to tell him of what had
transpired. It might possibly be further ammunition for Argyll
at his projected clan conference in dealing with Glenorchy, in
tune with his tentative suggestion of a sort of alliance. Now
he had Menzies to add to it. Also, it occurred to him that the
earl might well have reservations about Glenorchy perhaps
thinking of taking over the Moor of Rannoch, if that indeed
was so, since this would bring him uncomfortably near to
Argyll's own territory of upper Etive and the Black Mount.
Every little might help.

He had no reply from Argyll, but word reached Glen
Strae from another source. He had a visit from a far-out

kinsman, Aulay MacAulay of Ardencaple, who was in fact of MacGregor blood, but inheriting Ardencaple through the female line, a property actually in Lennox but on the borders of Campbell land in Cowal, had chosen discreetly to change his name, though not as far as making it Campbell. His Campbell neighbours had told him of a great assembly of Clan Campbell, held recently at Dunoon in Cowal. The principal object of this gathering, they said, was to prepare the clan and its allies for an armed muster against the MacDonalds, Macleans, Macleods and other island clans, who presently were raiding the north Ireland coasts in their galleys, ostensibly to aid their fellow-Catholics there against Queen Elizabeth's Protestant governors but mainly to enrich themselves with booty in the process. There were fears that, emboldened by easy success there, they might well turn their attention to the Campbell lands nearer home; they had indeed boasted that they might do this – and after all, Campbell Kintyre was only fifteen sea-miles from the Antrim coast, and all the Cowal area vulnerable. Campbell plans had been made. But as well as this, the news was that there had been a notable confrontation between the two wings of the Campbell clan, the main one of Argyll itself and the Breadalbane one of Glenorchy, Lawers and the rest. Just what had been said in private, of course, was not known; but Glenorchy in especial had been much offended, and showed it, trying to whip up feeling against their Protestant chief amongst the preponderant Catholics – but with marked lack of success apparently. Oddly enough, the division had been made open and accentuated by a great football match ordered by MacCailean Mhor, in which he himself took an active part, against the Breadalbane faction, in which the latter team was soundly trounced. Thereafter Black Duncan and Ardkinglas had promptly left the assembly. So now there was an open breach between the two factions, and Glenorchy in especial discredited before the clan at large.

Whether this would help the MacGregors remained to be seen. But Alastair gained some satisfaction from it, at least.

Soon thereafter he had pleasing news from Mary Gray at Linlithgow. Duke Ludovick was taking a short break from his trying duties as Lieutenant of the North at Aberdeen, however disapproving the monarch might be, and was to be at Methven for a few days; and she had got leave of absence from the Queen to join him. She hoped that Himself would find it possible to come there and visit them, short notice as it was, and at the cattle-droving time.

Other folk could deal with the cattle, Alastair had no difficulty in deciding, and set off for Methven without delay.

He went by Glen Lyon and Weem. At Roro he saw Gregor, who told him that so far no Menzies droves had come over the Lairig Chalbhath; but it was still fairly early in the season. And at Castle Menzies, its laird said that he was in fact still droving down the Strath of Appin, that he had had no response to his message to Glenorchy that he was not going ahead with his appeal to the Privy Council and would use the Roro passes if the Appin of Dull was closed; or perhaps response was there, but of the negative sort, for there had been no attempt to displace his tenants or otherwise interfere with the drove-road. So that was satisfactory, and Menzies grateful indeed.

Over the Aberfeldy heights, by Glen Cochill and down upper Glen Almond, Alastair came to Methven. His friends had already reached there, from north and south, and there was a happy reunion. Alastair had not seen the duke for a year.

There was, of course, a great exchange of news and views. Vicky and Mary were delighted to hear of Glenorchy's defeat in the Menzies situation, and of the liaison between Alastair and Argyll, which should help. They had, however, themselves heard word as to Black Duncan. When he had been at court and received his knighthood, he had, perhaps in an unusual rash moment, informed the Lowland Campbell, Sir Hugh, of Loudoun, that before he died he intended to be able to walk, or rather ride, from salt-water west to salt-water east, across the Highlands, on his own grounds – by which he meant from the Firth of Lorn to the Firth of Tay – and no other man in the kingdom could do that. So his ambitions were by no means moderating.

The duke's report as to the northern situation was good, save in that he still greatly misliked his appointment there, and the separation it entailed from Mary. The Huntly and Catholic position had improved notably, and he would have hoped that James would have now been agreeable to accept his resignation from the lieutenantship. But, no. Huntly and Errol, marooned for all these months up in far-away Sutherland and Caithness, he had summoned to appear before him at Aberdeen, under safe-conduct; and at length they had come. The meeting had been less difficult than Ludovick had anticipated. The Catholic earls had recognised the realities of the situation and, whilst by no means abandoning their ambitions for the future, had agreed that meantime the nation's well-being would best be served by them leaving the country for a period, on condition that their people were not made to suffer oppression. This had been gladly acceded to, and the earls had taken passage on a merchanter from the port to France.

So approximate peace reigned in the north-east, however much otherwise it might be in the clan territories of the north-west, where the Clan Donald federation was on the rampage. But there was little that he, Ludovick, could do about that last, save to urge Argyll to action. He was perfectly content to yield up his purely decorative appointment of Admiral of the Western Seas. Hence this brief vacation at Methven.

Mary had very different tidings to relate, from court – and it was court, the *King's* court, for now James was making Linlithgow his headquarters, a highly unusual location for him, the Queen's own palace. There had been much upset and trouble, and it had all arisen out of the monarch's insistence on keeping the young prince immured in Stirling Castle, and allowing the Queen only occasional and limited visits to see her son. Fretting over this, Anne had made herself ill, with frequent bouts of hysteria, railing against her husband; and these bouts had actually culminated in a miscarriage. This was bad enough in itself, but it had left the young woman – she was not yet twenty-one – in a dire state of mind as well as of body, declaring one moment that she wanted to die, the next that she was going home to Denmark, and that she never wanted to see James again. Such announcements, made to all and sundry, greatly displeased and offended her husband who, always having his own odd ways of demonstrating his feelings, had come and installed himself and his whole court at Linlithgow, not so much out of concern for Anne, apparently, as to ensure that another child was on the way with as little delay as possible, and no nonsense as to suicide or departing overseas. Even so, young Henry Frederick still

168

remained cooped up at Stirling. Sometimes, Mary judged James Stewart to be slightly mad, although at others she recognised that he had his own cleverness. She herself was still ferrying back and forth between Stirling and Linlithgow, a score of miles apart, taking turns at acting nurse to the prince and tirewoman to the distracted Queen – and no more happy with her situation than was Ludovick.

Alastair put it to them – why did they put up with it all? The Duke of Lennox, even though he was second in line for the throne, was surely powerfully placed enough to resign from court and lead his own life? Could the King actually forbid that? Or, at least, make his command effective? And Mary – her position was not so important to either the Queen or her son, was it, that she could not be let go? He understood about the ban on their marriage, that it could and would be annulled by James. But this of leading a private life was surely not impossible?

It was the ever more eloquent Mary who explained for both of them. The blood-royal was something which just could not be washed away – not when it was legitimately conceived, that is; there were plenty of nobles with royal blood, but on the wrong side of the blanket. James *had* to keep Ludovick close to him, one way or another, or at least in close association. For in the nature of things, the King could be kidnapped, even got rid of, likewise and more so his infant son – why Henry was so closely guarded – and an alternative monarch elevated by power-hungry, unscrupulous lords, and used to their own advantage. Vicky could be that alternative monarch. It was of no use to say that he certainly would not wish to be; that would be no safeguard. In a way, therefore, he was almost a hostage, and would remain so, even though James did have other children. This had happened before, in the Stewart family, Vicky's own ancestor having to flee to France for the same reason. She did not want Vicky to go back to France, where he was born. As for herself, while she was not important on the hierarchical scene, because she desired to be near Vicky at most times she had to remain about the court, where he was. Moreover, her so influential sire, the Master, left her in no doubt that he needed her there, to keep him informed, to act as his eyes and ears when he was absent – not that she by any means always agreed with his policies or necessarily told him all that she knew. But she was fond of him, and recognised that most of his scheming and manipulation was intended for the ultimate good of the realm. So she was tied also.

Alastair had to accept all that, and to perceive that even his own problems of being chief of the Gregorach were less involved.

He stayed with them for two days before returning to Glen Strae and the cattle-droving.

It was the cattle which touched off Alastair's next confrontation with his own problems. He did not normally go droving, or even attending the trysts or cattle-markets, although he did usually help with the singling out of the breeding-stock to be kept over the winter months on the limited fodder available in these high territories, and the larger herds which were to be sent for sale. But this year there was a complication. His brother, John of Dochard, who normally attended the sales and brought home the takings, wanted to go a-courting. Whether he was actually in love, or merely had decided that he had found the right wife, with a suitable property as dowry, was unclear – he was not a man for confidences; but he had come to the conclusion that Elizabeth, daughter of Murray of Strowan, in Strathearn, was the woman for him, and her portion was the property of Stronvar in Balquhidder, most convenient for a MacGregor. So, having performed the main task of rounding up all the herds and driving them down the long road to Crieff tryst, in Strathearn, he was for off to Strowan, a few miles away; Alastair could, for once, attend the sales.

Crieff, the main town of Strathearn and former seat of the royal line of earls, was a fair-sized community, pleasingly placed on the south-facing slopes of the mountain range which rose between Tay and Earn, looking towards the Lowlands. Always one of the greatest of the Scottish cattle-fair centres, its autumn Michaelmas Tryst was the most notable of the year, when the Highlanders necessarily emptied the glens of all surplus beasts, for lack of winter-feed; and as many as thirty thousand animals could be brought for sale to the Lowland buyers. There were other tryst-sites, of course, along the Highland Line, east and west, but Crieff held pride of place and, at this Michaelmas, was a hive of activity, its population suddenly swelling to ten times the normal; drovers, buyers, merchants, itinerant tradesmen and vendors, and clan notables – for this was the principal money-producing occasion of the Highland year, and the chiefs and lairds thronged the town to collect their dues in person. The many taverns and alehouses did a roaring trade – in fact, roaring was an all but literal description of the fair-days, for the noise was apt to be almost deafening, with lowing, bellowing cattle, barking dogs, shouting drovers, haggling buyers and sellers and the drunken revelry which marked either successful transactions or sad disappointments. This went on for days, and it all became something of a holiday for many.

The Glen Strae herds, on this occasion, numbered some nine hundred beasts, in three droves, including those of Roro and Balquhidder. These trysts were seldom trouble-free, for clan rivalry frequently surfaced, especially when one clan's cattle fetched a better price than another's, and fights between Highland and Lowland drovers were part of the scene. One of the main problems for leaders, therefore, was keeping their clansmen in approximate order once payment had been made and siller was circulating. There was a notably large gallows decorating the market-square of Crieff, capable of accommodating up to a score of miscreants at a time; also stocks for less grievous offenders.

Alastair found Roro a great help in this matter, with his tough and assertive character. Nevertheless, it was these same useful attributes which touched off turmoil. After a bargaining session with a south-country buyer, when a parcel of Campbell cattle had fetched a slightly higher price than a similar lot of MacGregor beasts, and jeering and altercation commenced, Roro moved to impose peace by his own methods. Unfortunately, Campbell of Balnearn, whose animals they were, made some personally slighting remarks anent Gregor of Roro's bull-like appearance and nature being more suitable for the servicing of MacGregor cows than for associating with decent folk, and this was probably responsible for the poor quality of the beasts just sold; whereupon Roro promptly knocked the injudicious Balnearn down with a single blow

– which of course set off a further bout of general fisticuffs between the rival drovers, with any available Campbells and MacGregors moving to join in. While Alastair was seeking to restore order, Balnearn picked himself up and ran off; and just as matters were being brought under control, turned up again, accompanied now by officers of the town guard, with the Provost himself, who needless to say was a Campbell. Not only that, but behind this official group came none other than Black Duncan of Glenorchy.

It had been long since Alastair had actually seen his enemy, not since the occasion when they had signed the pact at Argyll's behest, at Kilchurn. Now they stared at each other, animosity undisguised.

"So, brawling and rioting in your usual MacGregor fashion, Glenstrae!" Glenorchy said coldly, in his most magisterial voice. "We might have known that any disturbance would be of your making! Provost, have your officers do their duty!"

Alastair's eyes narrowed and he turned to the Provost. "Yes, do, sir. Have them take this man, Campbell of Balnearn, whom I, Glenstrae, hereby charge with creating a riot and disturbing the peace by deliberately insulting MacGregor of Roro, as witnessed by all here present. He will not deny his offensive words, which no Highland gentleman could accept. Take Balnearn in charge."

"He struck me!" Balnearn exclaimed. "I but spoke of the poor quality of the MacGregor beasts just sold, that they made a poor price – as all can see . . ."

"Liar!" Roro shouted. "You named me bull to service our cows! All here heard you. I . . ." The rest was lost in a snarling outcry from the MacGregors, with Campbells quickly raising voice in retaliation.

The Provost, a tanner in the town, looked distinctly alarmed at the prospect of a full-scale riot developing before his eyes there in the cattle-market. He did not speak, but turned to Glenorchy beseechingly.

That man held up an authoritative hand for silence. He did not get it entirely, but enough for those near at hand to hear what he said.

"Roro *struck* Balnearn, whatever words they may have exchanged beforehand. That is an offence against the law, where words need not be. I, Justiciar-Depute, so declare. Roro to be taken and held for trial, Provost."

Gregor's hoot of amusement was eloquent as Duncan's measured words. "*Take* me? Aye, then – come and take me!" he challenged. And he held up one great clenched fist, while the other fell to the dirk at his belt.

MacGregor shouts of support and threat filled the air, above the lowing of cattle. From all around men flocked to see, hear and share in the excitement.

Alastair's concern grew. The last thing that he wanted was a battle in this Crieff town, against Campbells or any other, wherein inevitably the MacGregors would be accused by the Justiciar-Depute of being the instigators of unruly and unlawful behaviour. That the said MacGregors would probably win in any such struggle, being the more warlike race, was no comfort, even the reverse. Unfortunately this was Perthshire, not Argyll or Lorn, and the Justiciar of Perthshire, John, Earl of Atholl, had recently died. So his deputy, Glenorchy, whom he had by no means loved, would himself conduct any trial, with predictable results – and results which could go far beyond Crieff and Perthshire.

Alastair held up his own hand, and at their chief's sign his own clansmen at least sank their voices, even if the Campbells did not.

"Here is folly!" he called. "We are here to sell cattle, not to bicker, whatever. We all have many to sell yet, Campbell beasts as well as MacGregors'. Roro was insulted, yes. But he struck back. And gained his point, I say. So – let it be – no more stramash." He did not look at Glenorchy.

Roro grinned. "Another time then, whatever!" he said.

The Provost at least looked relieved.

Black Duncan's features were expressionless. He was no fool, and with calculating wits. Probably he recognised that the Gregorach would never let the officers take a resisting Roro, even if they were inclined to try; and in any subsequent physical struggle, the MacGregors would probably triumph, with unpredictable consequences in the short term, whatever might be made out of it later. No one would accuse him of cowardice, but Duncan Campbell had shown on many occasions that he had no taste for physical conflict, whether in battle or in more personal controversy, wits, scheming and manipulation of others being his preferred role. Presumably he calculated that way now. He spoke flatly.

"Provost, warn these troublemakers that any further display of insolent and barbarous behaviour will result in the fullest rigours of the law being enforced against them. Disgraceful conduct will not be tolerated. The full town guard, and all law-abiding citizens, will be called upon to support due authority, and I will use all *my* power to ensure the apprehension and punishment of offenders. Tell them so." And he looked coldly from Roro to Alastair.

The Provost mumbled something, and half turned away.

Alastair nodded, even though Roro barked another laugh. "You are wise, Provost. And you, Glenorchy. Here is no time, nor place, for settling mere squabbling. We can do that othertime and elsewhere, if need be! I bid you good-day." And he turned away.

"Wait you, Glenstrae," Duncan said. "Think not that you and yours can avoid your due deserts so easily! In this, or other respects. As you will learn. And quickly. I warn you now that I am applying to the King and council for royal authority to dispossess you from occupying the lands of Glen Strae."

Alastair stared. They all did.

The other shrugged one cowl-hung shoulder. "I am superior of those lands, you will recollect! Also remember that I did not accept your token tribute of arrows, at Perth, on your coming of age. So you are not lawfully enfeoffed in those lands. I can claim them as mine, and will do so. To King and council. You will no longer call yourself Glenstrae, sir, and your unruly, troublemaking MacGregors will have to find themselves new holdings elsewhere – if they can! I misdoubt whether we shall see any MacGregor cattle coming for sale at *next* year's trysts!"

There was appalled silence from all who could understand the language used, Alastair amongst them. Here was threat indeed. Admittedly Glenorchy had not accepted the arrows tribute at Perth, at the enfeoffment ceremony, and had walked out. But the Justiciar and High Sheriff, Atholl, *had* accepted the customary offering as valid, and pronounced Alastair as duly enfeoffed as of Glen Strae. But Atholl was now dead, and Glenorchy perhaps could claim that that judgment was faulty and invalid, his own acceptance necessary. It was all only a paper device, to be sure – but paper and the law could go hand in hand. Perhaps the feudal superior *could* repossess the land? Glenorchy's father it was who had contrived the transference of superiority, in law, at the time he had personally had Alastair's father slain as rebel. So – it might be possible, under the said law.

Roro it was, typically, who broke the hush. "More lawmen's havers!" he cried. "Do you take us for bairns, Glenorchy? I told this small bit Provost-man to take me – if he could! And did he? I tell you the same, Duncan Campbell. Come and *take* Glen Strae! If you can. Aye, come you!"

There was a surge of shouted agreement, acclaim and challenge from the Gregorach present, even though their chief did not join in.

Glenorchy shrugged, both shoulders this time. "I shall," he said. "With this realm's authority and power behind me. I have warned you." And swinging about, he strode off.

Hurriedly the Provost, officers and Balnearn followed him.

Alastair stood biting his lip, however much his clansmen jeered.

He rode home from Crieff next day, a thoughtful man, for all Roro's bravura.

16

Alastair had to wait, with some impatience, for the weeks to pass until the usual Yuletide visit of the duke and Mary Gray to Strathearn before he could seek advice on how to counter this latest dire threat of Glenorchy's, since he did not see what he could do to any effect on his own. He took the threat seriously, but did not think that the danger was immediate; Black Duncan was not likely to appear in Glen Strae with a host of his Campbells to seek to dispossess the MacGregors – that was not his style. He would seek to use other methods, the "authority and power of the realm" that he had talked of, and that would take time to arrange and marshal. Nevertheless, Alastair fretted, although none of his people appeared to share his anxiety. If Mary and Vicky did not come to Methven for Yule this year, then somehow he would have to reach them, and the Master of Gray, at court.

However, the Methven steward duly arrived a few days before Christmas to announce that his master and lady were come, and hoped that Himself would join them for the festivities of Hogmanay and New Year, and indeed the sooner the better. With nothing holding him back at Glen Strae, he accompanied the steward back, there and then.

It was always good to see his friends, and to remark on how little Johnnie Stewart of Methven was progressing, a happy and uncomplicated child, with something of his father's appearance and his mother's wits. Welcome was warm.

It did not take long, of course, before Alastair came out with Glenorchy's latest menace, to his hearers' concern. They did not underestimate the threat, as Roro and the other Gregorach did, recognising that Duncan would not have made it publicly, as he had done, were he not fairly confident of success. They must take steps to thwart him somehow, therefore. How best?

The duke thought that MacCailean Mhor might be a hopeful helper. He had aided Alastair before, and they had established some sort of mutual co-operation. And Argyll now esteemed Glenorchy as *his* enemy also. If he was to persuade the rest of Clan Campbell to, as it were, shun Black Duncan and his ally Ardkinglas, that might help, especially as Argyll was now Admiral of the Western Seas and in a position to aid King James against the Catholic Clan Donald federation, the present activities of which were worrying the monarch, council and Kirk.

Alastair agreed with that, save in that he did not altogether trust MacCailean Mhor. It was not, he averred, just traditional MacGregor suspicion of all Campbells; something about that young man warned him to be wary. That one would, he felt, just as readily sacrifice him as aid him, if it was in his own interests. Still, in the present situation, he might well find it convenient to display his undoubted animosity against Glenorchy.

Mary, whilst not contesting this, felt that her father could well do most in the matter. He was back at court, and high in the King's favour, indeed acting Chancellor again. Maitland had died suddenly, unexpectedly, in October, and James had appointed no other as yet. The Master preferred to *act* the part of Chancellor without accepting the style and title which, he indicated, would limit his activities in other directions. He was content to be called merely Master of the Royal Wardrobe. Admittedly the King seemed to be favouring Black Duncan these days, why was unclear; but with the Master of Gray, the Duke of Lennox and the Earl of Argyll against him on the Privy Council, and he being a Catholic, the Gregorach cause ought not to founder.

Alastair was grateful, and to some extent relieved. Should he seek to see the Master, as well as visit Argyll?

Mary advised him to wait. She would speak to her father, and if and when he felt Alastair's presence at court would be helpful, she would send him word. In theory, one could not appear at court without a royal summons, and James could be fussy about such things. Better to wait.

The couple had their own news to impart. The duke hoped to be quit of his unwanted Lieutenancy of the North in a month or two – indeed he had almost persuaded James to appoint Argyll in his place – Himself might make something of that when he went to see that young man. After all, if as admiral he was now responsible for the north-west, he might as well be so for the north-east also. Protestant magnates in both areas were in short supply.

Alastair reserved judgment as to this. He felt that perhaps MacCailean Mhor might be getting altogether too powerful.

There was surprising news also as to the errant earls of Huntly and Errol. With Maitland's death and Bothwell's renewed banishment, Patrick Gray, for reasons unspecified, had worked on the monarch to recall the pair from exile in France, in exchange for written and signed promises of no further rebellious behaviour, James being not very difficult to persuade, for he always had had a personal fondness for Huntly. Mary was doubtful about the wisdom of this; and of course the Kirk leaders were angry. She had a notion that it was to prevent Andrew Melville and the other militant ministers from gaining too great an ascendancy in the realm that her father had contrived it. Anyway, the two Catholic earls were expected back so soon as the winter storms made voyaging practical.

Other tidings were that the Queen was pregnant again, to her husband's satisfaction if not her own; and this situation being now in order, James no longer felt it incumbent to reside at his wife's palace of Linlithgow, and was returning the court to his usual haunts of Stirling and Falkland. Mary and her little son would presumably have to resume their journeyings back and forth from Linlithgow to Stirling, although she had hopes that once Ludovick retired finally from Aberdeen and went back to court, she could convince Queen Anne to release her from her own unwanted duties as Woman of the Bedchamber and extra nurse to the prince, so that she could be with Vicky again.

Alastair enjoyed his Yuletide at Methven, and regretfully took his leave to return home. He agreed to go and see Argyll shortly.

MacCailean Mhor, he learned, was back at Inveraray, his "capital" on Loch Fyneside, and thither Alastair made his way a week or two later. There was quite a sizeable town here, pleasingly situated at a small promontory of the loch-shore, with two churches, one Catholic and one Protestant, and some quite handsome stone buildings as well as the usual timber and thatch houses, mills, tanneries and brewery. There was even a justiciary court-house, and of course a gaol and gallows.

Inveraray Castle, however, was half a mile away to the north, in a strong position near a bend of the River Aray, a later and more ambitious structure than stern Innischonnel on its island in Loch Awe. Here he met with the anticipated delay in obtaining interview with the young earl, who clearly had his own notions as to behaviour. The eventual reception was no more warm than on the last occasion.

"What do you require of me now, Glenstrae?" was the greeting – and the visitor had difficulty in restraining himself from pointing out that in their previous meeting he had been bringing Argyll helpful information and the Western Seas admiralship, not seeking aid.

"As before, I come with word of activities which concern us both, MacCailean Mhor," he said, level-voiced. "Word which may not have reached you yet."

"I am not ignorant of what goes on, sir," he was answered stiffly.

"Of that I have no doubt. But I do not think that you have been hearing from the Duke of Lennox of late?"

The other did not reply.

"I have seen him recently, myself. He gives me authority to tell you, if so you wish, that he is intending to resign his appointment as Lieutenant of the North very shortly, and is prepared to recommend yourself, MacCailean Mhor, to His Grace as his successor in the Lieutenantship. If so your lordship desires?"

Argyll drew a long breath. "I . . . I . . . it would be most suitable," he got out. "I *should* be Lieutenant of the North. As well as Admiral. The two should go together."

"Perhaps. But others might seek the appointment."

"Who has such as my Campbell manpower? On both this seaboard and inland? Even up to Cawdor in Moray? And my galleys and sway in the isles?"

"MacDonald could claim as much, sir, but appears to be working *against* His Grace's interests at this present. Although

179

he might be persuaded that he would gain more from being the King's friend, and Lieutenant!"

That had Argyll's strange eyes flashing. "MacDonald!" he jerked, at mention of the name of the Campbells' traditional enemy and rival. "He . . . Donald Gorm, would never . . . he *could* not! Never that!"

Alastair was taking a chance on this one. He did not want to go too deeply into the suggestion. "It might be a bargain he would consider, consider well," he observed. "More profitable perhaps than aiding Irish rebels against Elizabeth of England. But – " now he delivered his carefully prepared thrust – "there is Huntly, is there not? Huntly was Lieutenant of the North before. Looks on it as belonging to his Gordon family."

"Huntly! That felon is banished the realm! An outlaw."

"No longer, I fear. Huntly and Errol are pardoned, and return to this land, indeed to court. The King has ever had some liking for the Gordon, as you will know. Now he sees this as a move to reunite the realm. Nothing surer than that the Cock o' the North will seek again to be the Lieutenant of the North!"

"God in His Heaven!" the younger man swore. "Huntly again! No, never that!"

"As you say, sir. So thinks the Duke of Lennox. So, he is prepared to put *your* name to the King as his successor. Before Huntly arrives back from France. If so you agree? And if the Master of Gray, his friend and my own, adds his voice . . ."

"Yes, yes. To be sure. I would esteem it well. Tell my lord Duke so."

Alastair nodded. Satisfied that he had, as it were, prepared the ground for the suitable reception of his own needs, he went on. "Then there is the matter of Glenorchy again."

"That scoundrel! What now?"

Alastair had thought well how best this might be put, to involve Argyll as much as himself, or almost. He could scarcely invent more poisoning or murder, but there was the matter of the Moor of Rannoch and the Black Mount of Etive, MacCailean Mhor's territory.

"You heard, did you, that Glenorchy threatened to close the Strath of Appin, at Dull? To Menzies and his droves if

Menzies did not drive my own people in Rannoch over into the moor. And why should he do that, Glenorchy? In order to claim that the MacGregors were unlawfully then occupying *his* land of Rannoch Moor. He owns no other land in Rannoch. But his Achallader Castle is on the southern edge of the moor. That moor itself is worthless as land – but the Black Mount, its western flank, is not! *You* own the Black Mount of Etive, do you not? Or is it MacDougall of Lorn?"

"I own it."

"And do you want Black Duncan creeping so close? And perhaps taking it over also? As he and his father have done so much, so often?"

"Why think you that is what he aims to do?"

"Because he has also threatened to have me and mine evicted from Glen Strae and Glen Kinglas, the lands that flank the Black Mount on the south. As superior. Saying that he does not accept the enfeoffment I made. That would give him control of all the land from Tay to Etive, from salt water to salt water, and from Atholl to Ardchattan. More land than even MacCailean Mhor controls! In Argyll, Cowal, Kintyre and the Isles. No longer Black Duncan of the Seven Castles, but of the seventy almost!"

The other stared and stared.

"The duke knows of this. As does the Master of Gray. And they believe that Glenorchy should be halted. Do not you?"

"Aye." That came out on a long sigh. "He is calling himself MacCailean Mhic Donnachaidh, I hear! It is time that his wings were clipped, damn him!"

"So think we all. The duke and the Master can prevail upon the council, with your help. But not necessarily upon the King, who has knighted Glenorchy. His Grace seems to have a fondness for such as Huntly and Black Duncan!" That was put in less casually than it sounded.

"James Stewart is a fool! A slobbery-mouthed fool!"

"But with his own cunning. You heard that Maitland, the Chancellor, is dead? And no new Chancellor appointed, but the Master acting it. James plays off Catholic against Protestant, to gain his own ends. These two are both Catholics."

"As are you, sir!"

"Indeed yes. But *I* seek no advancement, no appointments, no increase in lands. Only to hold what is MacGregor's."

"Aye. So you come to me!"

"*We* come to you. And for your own good, as well as mine, and the realm's. If you are Lieutenant of the North you have added control over Glenorchy, do you not? You can act in the King's name. And disobedience to your express command could be treason against the realm. And outlawry."

Digesting that, Argyll inclined his head. "I will do what I can," he said. "I am superior of certain lands which Glenorchy holds – Glen Falloch and Strathfillan."

"Could you claim his wrongous enfeoffment?"

"The enfeoffment was not made to me but to my father. I have not claimed it anew since I came of full age. I could make something of that. Also against his friend, the wretched Ardkinglas . . .!"

Reasonably satisfied, the visitor took his leave, receiving no invitation to stay.

Alastair's next journey was of a very different nature – to Balquhidder for the wedding of his brother, John Dhu of Dochard, to the daughter of Murray of Strowan. This was what might be called a suitable marriage, for the groom at least, for the bride brought with her the property of Stronvar, in Balquhidder, near the foot of long Loch Voil, no major estate but quite a substantial acquisition, and near to the Kirkton, the centre of the glen. So now John would be a laird in his own right, and the less dependent on his brother. Alastair did not begrudge him that; but it might well mean that, headstrong, he would be still less inclined to do as he was told in clan matters.

The last time that Alastair had been in Balquhidder Kirk was on that dire occasion when he had had to swear on Drummond-Earnoch's bloody head that he would accept responsibility, with all his clan, for the man's death; so today's was a notably different atmosphere. The company present made a strange admixture, for Murray of Strowan was scarcely a Highlander, Strowan being near to Crieff, none so far from Methven, and most of the bride's guests were Lowland lairds and their families – although her mother had been a MacLaren of Stronvar, hence the dowry property in Balquhidder. These guests eyed the local MacGregors with some reserve, which was returned with interest. No doubt most thought that Elizabeth Murray had made a strange match.

Alastair, his cousin Patrick of Larachan, Ewan's son, and Rob Ban were the only attenders from Glen Strae. But the Balquhidder MacGregors turned out in force – and they were a distinctly wild lot, as they had proved over the Drummond-Earnoch affair, and there were a lot of them, for Balquhidder was a long, if narrow glen, ten miles of it, and mainly now in their hands. There would be high old goings-on that night in the Kirkton.

There was indeed drama before ever the ceremony commenced – this on account of the MacLaren situation. All Balquhidder and its numerous side-glens had been MacLaren territory once, but the clan, the Sons of Laurence, had declined; now they had no recognised chief, although MacLaren of Ardveich on Lochearnside claimed it. As a result, MacGregors had moved in over a century before, pushed out of their own lands by Campbells; also Stewarts from Appin of Lorn had gained a foothold, by marriage, in the side-valley of Glen Buckie. There were still a few MacLarens in Balquhidder, however, and they were strong in upholding their ancient privilege that none should enter Balquhidder Kirk before the MacLarens had done so, a tradition which had led to many unseemly brawls before divine service. It had not been anticipated that any of that clan would wish to grace a MacGregor wedding with their presence, although the bride's mother had been a MacLaren; but MacLaren of Invernentie, a property towards the head of the glen, did put in an appearance, he claiming to be a chieftain of the tribe. And on entering the church he discovered numerous MacGregors already inside. Promptly he demanded that all these should take themselves out, and stay out until he himself had taken his accustomed seat at the front – to the affront, needless to say, of all concerned. Whereupon MacLaren, in righteous wrath, came striding down to where, at the bridge over the river, the bridegroom's party was assembling, pipers tuning up and order of precedence being arranged, to demand hotly that the church be cleared, as was his right, or he would forbid the priest's entry to celebrate – the said priest's manse being on MacLaren ground.

Naturally, this produced angry reaction, especially from John Dhu, who all but exploded in fury, hand dropping to belt where a dirk would have hung had he not been dressed for his nuptials. With the pipes of the bride's party already sounding from the direction of Stronvar, a most unseemly altercation looked like developing into outright fisticuffs, when Alastair felt bound to take a hand, for decency's sake. He spoke, low-voiced but sternly, to his brother and then, taking the MacLaren's arm, led him back to the church.

"I do not congratulate you whatever, Invernentie," he said stiffly, "on your behaviour as a Highland gentleman. A wedding is no occasion, surely, for prideful display by uninvited guests! But, that all may go fairly and kindly on this young woman's day, I will seek to satisfy you."

"A right is a right, Glenstrae!" was all the other said.

At the kirk door, Alastair stepped in and raised his voice. "All present here heed me, Glenstrae!" he called loudly, stilling the chatter. "I, your chief, ask you to step outside meantime, and to welcome my brother's party to his marriage from there. With cheers – which should not be given inside this sacred building. Then to follow him in, and there wait to receive the bride's company. I do not command you, but I *ask* you."

With some muttering and reluctance the early-comers did as they were bidden, to line up outside.

"Do you wish to be the only one to welcome the bridegroom within, Invernentie?" Alastair asked.

That man frowned and hesitated. Then, shrugging, he marched within, without a word spoken, to growls from the onlookers.

Alastair waited, with the others. The pipers were already leading John Dhu and his little group up the hill. The waiting throng duly cheered.

After that all went well, despite ferocious glares between groom and MacLaren. When the bride arrived, there was no indication of trouble. Elizabeth Murray was a sonsy, bouncing girl of plentiful proportions and a ready smile. She looked as though she would make a good wife, whatever sort of husband John made.

There was feasting after the ceremony at Stronvar for the guests, and celebration of a different sort for the clansmen and their families, with sports, bonfires and liquor and viands aplenty. Alastair, with over twenty-five rough miles to ride home, did not wait until anywhere near the end of the noisy festivities. He wondered how John and Invernentie would get on as near neighbours. It was Kenneth MacAlpin, who united Picts and Scots, who had given Balquhidder to the Sons of Laurence; and Kenneth's brother Gregor who was the progenitor of the Gregorach, or the Clan Alpin as they should properly be called. Perhaps there had been jealousy from the very start, seven hundred years before?

17

Alastair's expected summons to court, that July, came not
through the Master of Gray, as anticipated – although perhaps
that scheming man had something to do with it – but from
the monarch himself; and there was an ominous rather than
a hopeful ring about it unfortunately. James sent an officer of
the council to command MacGregor of Glenstrae to compear
before himself and the Privy Council at Dunfermline within
ten days' time, to declare why he and his clansmen should
not be evicted from the lands they were occupying in Glen
Strae and Glen Kinglas, at the behest of the lawful superior
of the said lands, Duncan Campbell of Glenorchy.

Here was an unlooked-for development. Presumably Black
Duncan had reached the King again and managed to impress
their unpredictable sovereign further, despite Gray's influence
otherwise. Unless, of course, the Master himself was behind
this also, and it was a device to defeat Glenorchy before the
council itself?

Either way, it was unlikely to be a pleasant experience
for himself. No word had come from Gray, Mary or the
duke.

Alastair had no option but to obey. He would go by Roro
and Balquhidder, inform Gregor and John of the situation
and have them see to clan matters in the meantime, since
this affair might keep him away from Glen Strae for some
little time, if he knew James Stewart, his *Ard Righ*.

Dunfermline seemed an unlikely venue for a meeting of the
Privy Council, in Fothrif, inland from the Forth coast near
Queen Margaret's Ferry. There was an ancient royal palace
there, the said Queen Margaret's home, beside her great abbey,
but it was no favoured residence of her present descendant.
However, it was not so far from Falkland, and it might well
suit James to instal his Privy Councillors and their inevitable

trains of men-at-arms and servitors there rather than have them cluttering up the limited accommodation at his beloved hunting-seat.

In the event, Alastair reached Dunfermline well ahead of the ten-day limit, to find the town in its normal state, no influx of great ones yet arrived, the King and court certainly not in residence. Uncertain as to procedure now, and learning that the court was indeed presently at Falkland, he decided to ride on there some twenty miles, in the hope of seeing Mary Gray and the duke and consulting with them.

At Falkland, he found all as though he had never been away since his previous visit, the little town full to overflowing, Lady Marie and Mary occupying the Master's lodging, the duke away hunting with the King, and Patrick Gray himself otherwere on state business meantime. Mary was delighted to see him, but surprised. She knew nothing of the command to appear before the council, nor did Vicky, she was sure. As to her father, who could tell? But if so, he had not informed them. This was all very strange. Yes, Sir Duncan Campbell *had* been at court, at Stirling, before they came to Falkland, but so far as she knew he was not here now.

The Lady Marie acted the usual kind hostess for the uninvited guest. When Lennox got back from hunting, he was equally at a loss, although warm in his welcome. But concerned. James had mentioned nothing of all this to him, nor to the Master he was sure. Which made it look like some sort of secret arrangement, and this was less than hopeful for Alastair's cause. When James was secretive, trouble was apt to loom. At least, thanks to his own especial position, he could take Himself to see the King that evening, and try to get to the bottom of this.

Meantime, the visitor learned that the duke had indeed got out of being Lieutenant of the North, and had Argyll confirmed in his place; and that Mary had managed to resign her appointments with the Queen, on the plea that young Johnnie's care was now demanding all her time – he was here at Falkland and indeed active and adventurous. Also the Queen was due to give birth in about a month's time, and James was insisting that she be brought from Linlithgow to

Dunfermline for her confinement, in order that she should be suitably near him for the occasion – that is, of course, without interfering with his hunting. So she should be at Dunfermline, not Falkland, any day now.

They all shook their heads over their sovereign-lord and his attitudes. Alastair was scarcely looking forward to his interview that evening, if James would see him.

In the event, Ludovick gave his cousin little choice in the matter for, requiring no permission to enter the monarch's presence, he led Alastair past the various guards in corridors and at doorways, right to the royal bedroom door, where he instructed the officer and page on duty to announce the Duke of Lennox. As this was done, he took his friend's arm and ushered him straight inside, without waiting for any consent, and firmly shut the door behind them.

Alastair was again struck by the sense of this being merely a replay of former experiences, by the same smell of unwashed humanity, the same blast of heat – for although it was high summer, a well-doing log fire blazed on the hearth – the same hatted, untidy figure sitting up on the great canopied bed amongst a litter of papers. The years between might never have been.

But he had no time for dwelling on such phenomena. James was staring, and not only staring but pointing an accusatory hand holding a quill pen.

"Vicky Stewart," he spluttered, licking his slack lips. "Who hae you got there? It's, it's yon ill limmer MacGregor! Glenstrae himsel'!"

"No ill limmer, James, but your ever loyal subject, who fought so well in your cause at the Battle of Glenlivet. And who aided you with your book on witches and demons," the duke returned.

"Aye, weel, mebbe so. But he's ay a trial to me, forby. Leastways his heathenish clan is. Ay making trouble. Disturbing my realm's peace. Being ay where they shouldna be. You shouldna hae brought him here, Vicky."

"You summoned him, James."

"No' to court. No' to my ain bedchamber! To the council, just. At Dunfermline."

"A strange summons, is it not? For one who has served you well, in sundry ways."

"Och, here's no place and time to chaffer ower the council's business. I'm inditing a poem, see you."

"Glenstrae could perhaps aid you even in that. He did before, did he not?"

"I do not wish to disturb Your Grace," Alastair put in. "Only to learn what you, or the council, have against me? That I may prepare my defence before the council."

"Hech, hech, you ken fine, man. I sent you word. This o' occupying Glen Strae land unlawfully."

"But the MacGregors have always occupied Glen Strae, Sire. Since King Kenneth's brother's time. King Kenneth gave us Glen Strae, and much else . . ."

"That may be. But Glenorchy is superior o' thae lands now, by the law. And he says that you occupy them against his will and orders."

"I made due enfeoffment before the Earl of Atholl, Sheriff and Justiciar, Sire."

"Atholl's deid!"

"So this is the *Campbell's* case before the council, not yours, James?" the duke asked. "Yet *you* sent the summons. Why, I wonder?"

"Vicky Stewart, I'm no' here to be put to the question by you or any other, I tell you! Mind it. And in my ain bed! I'm busy, can you no' see?"

Alastair thought to try another tack, hopefully tactful. "May I ask, Sire, full humbly, what is the subject and burden of this your new poetic labour? Is it work of deep thought? Or for . . . edification? Or but for pleasing, whatever?"

"For a man who canna spell or write his name, you hae a fine command o' words, MacGregor!" That sounded more like an accusation than a compliment. "I dinna pen pleasurings."

"Although others may gain pleasure therefrom, Highness." Was that spreading the honey too thickly? "For what will we all be indebted, this time?"

"It's aboot the responsibility o' kings to God and no' to men, that's what. A crowned and anointed monarch is no' like other folk, see you. Some folk forget that! You mind it, Vicky! Hear this . . ."

189

> The Lord above is lord of all,
>   He works through kings on earth.
> Realms may rise and realms may fall
>   If monarchy's in dearth.
> But God is kind and builds a wall
>   Round realms where faith has birth.

"Mind, I'm no' just happy wi' that last, '. . . where faith has birth'. It's no' just right, some way. There's no' that many words rhyme wi' earth and dearth that's suitable. And *you* come interrupting me!"

Ludovick glanced at Alastair, shrugging a shoulder helplessly. The other stroked his chin.

"Sire, I hesitate, I greatly hesitate, to make suggestion. I am no poet. But it comes to me, admiring the rest of your verse, that if the last line was changed a little way, it could go thus:

> Round realms with kingly girth.

Girth means a sanctuary . . ."

"Girth? I ken fine what girth means. Or garth, as some say it. Realms o' kingly girth? Aye, that's no' bad. That's possible. It's no' just perfect, mind – but it might serve. 'Realms wi' kingly girth.' Aye, I ever seek to build a kingly girth round this Scotland. Against Satan and a' his works, his witches and warlocks and demons. I'll consider it. Nae use asking *you*, Vicky, you dinna ken poetry frae hucksters' babblings! There's a girth at yon Torphichen, where Jamie Sandilands bides. And another at Solsgirth, nigh Dollar. Sols will mean solus, a beacon, mind. A sanctuary lit by a beacon. Och, aye."

"You are very learned, Sire." Alastair thought that on this high note it would be best to depart. He glanced at Lennox, who obviously thought likewise.

"Have we your permission to retire, James?" the latter asked.

"You have, aye. I hae to finish this afore I sleep, this night. So – off wi' you."

They bowed themselves out.

On the way back to the Gray lodging, they discussed not

so much what the King had said as what he had not said. He had given them no inkling of what they might expect to be faced with at the Privy Council interview, save that Glenorchy's case would be on legal rights. No indication as to why he, James, had sent the command to appear, not the clerk to the council. Nor what his own attitude would be at the enquiry – if indeed he chose to attend. Alastair feared the worst, but the duke thought that James would not be so hard on him, especially after this poetry incident. It was still three days until the meeting. Let them hope that Patrick Gray would be back by then; after all, he was acting Chancellor and so should be directing any council.

There was a lesser problem before Alastair, more immediate if less vital. That was, the next day's hunting? Should he attend, or should he not? He was, it seemed, not invited to court – James himself had pointed that out – only ordered to attend the council. So perhaps he would offend by joining the royal hunt? Ludovick did not think so; but Mary agreed that it might be wise not to appear. The next day was Saturday, and there would be no hunting on Sunday; so there would be time to try to discover the King's real attitude. The council meeting was on Tuesday.

So next morning, when a distinctly grumpy Lennox had to make his unsuitably early start for the chase, the visitor stayed behind, happier indeed to spend the day with Mary than in pounding along behind the monarch in so-called sport.

Presently, leaving young Johnnie in the care of the Lady Marie, the girl took Himself on a different sort of riding, along the strath of the River Eden, known as the Howe of Fife, where he had never visited, showing him a pleasant countryside, fertile and populous, by Freuchie and Pitlessie and Tarvit to Cupar, on the south bank of Eden and back on the north side, by Ladybank and Lathrisk and so to Freuchie again, explaining how this last community, inoffensive as it was, had got a sad reputation for, less than three miles from Falkland, here it was that the King sent courtiers and visitors with whom he was less than pleased and would find no room for at crowded Falkland, using the term "awa' to Freuchie, wi' him!", this becoming a common term for rejection. Mary made an excellent guide and instructress, and the man enjoyed every moment of it all; so much so that he almost, but not quite, was able to forget the ordeal which loomed ahead – for he had no doubts that it would indeed be an ordeal.

When the duke got back from the hunt, he said that James had not mentioned the MacGregor or his absence, and had been in a bad mood all day, the sport having been notably poor. For everyone's sake, not only Alastair's, it was to be hoped that this would improve, for their sovereign-lord in sour spirits could be a disaster.

Himself was not cheered.

At church next morning his hosts said that Alastair should not absent himself, even though a Catholic – as indeed would be not a few present. James was very strong on religious observance, however curious some of his dogma. The visitor would have preferred to remain as inconspicuous as possible, sitting well to the back; but Mary and the Lady Marie said that he must sit with them, and that was, as before, prominent in the front, as befitted their station – although not as prominent as Ludovick, who had to share what might be termed the royal box up in the chancel itself. When James came in, it did not take long for him to be staring fixedly at Alastair, frowning. But then, he arrived frowning anyway, and everybody feared that it would be an even more difficult service than usual.

In the event, however, it proved to be the most uneventful that Alastair, for one, had attended. For early on the King fell asleep, and remained so throughout, snoring audibly, head on chest and high hat precariously balanced; indeed, Mary whispering that if it fell off Satan would triumph, so say a prayer! As a consequence, no doubt, the Reverend James Melville, from Anstruther, the Reverend Andrew's nephew, hurried through the proceedings, low-voiced – as certainly his uncle would not have done – and gave one of the shortest sermons on record, presumably anxious not to wake the royal worshipper.

At the end, after a reverently hushed benediction, the problem arose – what to do now? James still slept. None might rise and leave before the monarch. The congregation stirred, eyeing one another. Some coughed. Whispering sounded, even some sniggers. The only reaction was little puffs from those slack lips.

Ludovick it was who solved this problem. Rising, he bent to tap on more securely the royal hat so precariously balanced on the royal head. James opened his eyes at once, immediately wide awake.

"What you at, Vicky?" he demanded, thickly.

"Your hat, Sire. It might have fallen."

"I'll thank you to keep your hands to yoursel'!" The King looked around him crossly. "Yon was a gey dreich sermon," he observed. "No' much fire to it." With no further comment on the situation, he rose, and tottering just a little, stepped down from the chancel and shambled off, while everybody rose.

"The Lord works in mysterious ways," Mary murmured. "We are released much earlier than usual!"

The Master of Gray arrived that evening, apparently from Edinburgh, his usual affable and courteously confident self, although surprised to see Alastair there. This in itself was surprising for its indication that he knew nothing of the item on the Privy Council agenda referring to the Glenorchy-Glenstrae situation, extraordinary for the man who had in fact compiled that agenda. It set Patrick thinking indeed, and he declared that it must represent some private arrangement between the King and Black Duncan. How such had come about was intriguing, in more ways than one. What influence had the Campbell over James, what promise or hold or threat, which could account for what amounted to a secret device? He, Patrick, would endeavour to discover it, if possible. He knew that Glenorchy had been at court, yes, while he, also Ludovick and Mary, had been absent, but had heard no reports of any special association or intimacy.

Alastair again did not attend Monday's hunting uninvited, although the Master did, an activity he normally sought to avoid. Instead, Mary took Himself to Corn Ceres and other places of interest in the green hills which separated the Howe from the Firth of Forth, this time the Lady Marie accompanying them, leaving Johnnie in the care of her own son Andrew's nurse. She said that her husband was much concerned over this Glenorchy affair, not only on Alastair's behalf but because it implied that James was acting deviously, secretly, regarding himself. It might not be significant, of course, for the King's behaviour was frequently unpredictable; but it could represent problems on a wider scale for the acting Chancellor.

As early a start, the following morning, as for the hunting, was necessary for those attending the council to reach Dunfermline by noon, some twenty miles. Two officers of the royal guard appeared at the Gray lodging to escort Alastair, an unnecessary proceeding surely, making it look as though he was something of a prisoner for trial. Patrick and Ludovick both sought to dismiss them, but they said that they were there on the King's express command. It was not an encouraging sign.

So Alastair rode at the rear of the royal cavalcade between his guards, the duke and the Master up-front with the monarch and the other Privy Councillors who were with the court at Falkland. He carried with him the urgent good wishes of Mary Gray and the Lady Marie.

At the old palace of Dunfermline he was put into a small upper room, with his officers, and told to wait. There was no sign of Sir Duncan Campbell.

He had a long wait and, with his guards scorning to converse with a Highlandman, a boring one. Presumably the Glenstrae case had been consigned to a late stage in the proceedings.

Summoned eventually, he was taken down and led into the lesser hall of the palace, amidst a chatter of voices. About a score of men sat at a long table, the King lounging at the head, Patrick Gray at the foot, goblets and tankards in front of all. At a smaller side-table clerks with papers and pens sat. Ludovick was placed at James's right hand. He smiled encouragingly as Alastair entered. James made no acknowledgment of the newcomer's bow.

From the side-table the clerk to the council spoke, reading a paper. "Your Grace and my lords, the matter of the lands of Glen Strae in the county and sheriffdom of Perth, in dispute. Here is the occupier of the said lands, Alastair MacGregor, calling himself of Glenstrae, rightly or otherwise." He turned to the Master of Gray.

"Yes. We are many of us aquainted with Alastair of Glenstrae, Chief of his Name." Patrick nodded. "We have to ask him, does he wish himself to present his cause in this matter to the council, or does he desire the service of another?"

194

"What has to be said, I can say, whatever, my lords," Alastair answered.

"Very well. The cause has been brought at the instance of Sir Duncan Campbell of Glenorchy, superior of the said lands, who claims wrongous occupation and desires eviction of the said MacGregor of Glenstrae and his clansfolk from the said lands. Is Sir Duncan Campbell or his representative attendant to present his cause before this council?"

"He is," the clerk said, and turned to one of his underlings. "With His Grace's permission, bring in Sir Duncan."

Patrick gestured towards one of two chairs set some way back from the tables. "You may sit, Glenstrae," he mentioned.

"I prefer that I stand," Alastair said, steady-voiced.

That produced a snigger from the head of the table. "No' worth the sitting, he judges – for this'll no' take long!" James observed. "And should you be naming him Glenstrae, Master o'Gray, when that's the matter in debate?"

"Is he not Glenstrae, Sire, until the council decides otherwise? If so it does."

The door opened. "Sir Duncan Campbell of Glenorchy," the clerk intoned. Black Duncan came in behind another officer. He made of it an excellent impression, respectful but quietly assured, carrying himself well, richly dressed as any in the hall. He made obeisance to the monarch and a comprehensive bow towards the councillors. He did not look at Alastair.

"Your Grace! My lords!" he said easily.

Patrick coughed. "Sir Duncan, we understand that you seek the authority of His Grace's Privy Council in order to change the occupancy of certain lands. This is an unusual step to take, on a matter normally the concern of a sheriff or justiciar. You must have some especial reason for this approach to the highest authority in the land. We await your explanation."

If Glenorchy was offput by that introduction he did not show it. "Yes, Sire, and my lords. I have especial reason. For this approach to your council is not merely a matter of land occupancy. It is on account of a direct contravention of the expressed will and command of parliament by the broken men of Clan Gregor. In the General Bond Act of 1587, of which your lordships will be well aware and must be gravely concerned."

195

That gave even Patrick pause. The Act known as the General Bond was an extraordinary measure passed almost ten years before to seek to deal with the disorders in the kingdom at the end of James's minority, and after the execution of the notorious Regent Morton, to make the lords, landowners and chiefs responsible for the misdeeds of all dwelling on their lands. It had been a very drastic decision, passed only reluctantly by parliament and in fact never really put into operation, indeed largely forgotten by most as order became restored. But it had never been repealed. Every man round that table was a landowner and therefore in law responsible for the misdemeanours of his own tenantry.

There was considerable stir and frowning. Only the King chuckled.

"Hech, aye!" he said.

Patrick recovered himself quickly. "The General Bond, Sire – yes, we most of us know of that long-past parliamentary Act. Even though I for one have not heard of it referred to in the years between. During which, to be sure, His Grace's government has been sufficiently well and strongly maintained without resort to its, shall we say, difficult provisions."

"Nevertheless, my lords, it was and still is the expressed will of parliament, never rescinded. And so the law of the land. Is it not?"

"No doubt. And do you claim, sir, that this present matter of the occupancy of certain lands merits the invocation of the General Bond Act? It seems on the face of it . . . excessive!"

"I do, my lords. I am superior of the said lands, this MacGregor occupying them, owing his enfeoffment to myself. I refused to accept his tokens of enfeoffment on his coming of age some years ago. But did not then have him evicted, as was my right, out of patience and forbearance. Although I warned him and his MacGregors as to the results of any misbehaviours and infringements of the law. Since then, as all know, there have been dire and shameful excesses by these people, notably in the slaying and beheading of His Grace's own forester of Glenartney, Drummond-Earnoch, invasions of my other lands and those of neighbouring owners, lawlessness in Balquhidder, outrages by MacGregor of Roro supported by

Glenstrae. I have, in consequence ordered the removal from these lands of MacGregor and his people as, under the General Bond Act provisions is my right and indeed my duty, to uphold the King's peace. This order of mine has been not only ignored but rejected with contumely by MacGregor. So I come before the King-in-Council for authority to put the law into effect."

"Ooh, aye," James said, examining his fingernails.

"However law-supporting you sound, Sir Duncan, save in the matter of Drummond-Earnoch's death you are notably vague in your accusations," Patrick said. "And may I remind you that Glenstrae and the MacGregors have in fact received a full royal pardon for that offence."

"I can, if required, give the council fullest details of other offences, my lords."

"Perhaps that will not be necessary! When we have heard Glenstrae. Alastair MacGregor, you have heard Glenorchy's charges. What have you to say anent them?"

Alastair spread his hands. "Little, my lords," he answered. "Save that I deny having broken any laws since the sorry matter of Drummond-Earnoch, I or my people. I have indeed been most careful that there should be no possible claims of transgression, in despite of the threats of Campbell of Glenorchy. Public threats. Grateful for His Grace's generosity over Glenartney, I have sought to use my clan's power in the King's good cause, in battle as in all else, as all here will know . . . where others held back!" And he glanced at the Campbell. "As for Glen Strae, it was given to my ancestors outright by King Kenneth mac Alpin, from whose brother Gregor our royal race is descended in direct line, with no superior other than the crown itself. Along with other lands. It was not until my father's time, slain by Glenorchy's father, that this of superiority was imposed upon us, how lawfully I do not know. But I have abided by its terms, as did my tutor before me. I submitted the required enfeoffment, of three arrows, for the superior, before the Earl of Atholl, as Justiciar, when I came of age; and he accepted it as right and lawful. Although Glenorchy was present, he left the court at Perth against the Justiciar's ruling. That was seven years ago, whatever. In what have I transgressed the law, my lords?" Proudly, he raised his head. "I am Glenstrae – as my fathers have been before me, for seven hundred years. Before ever a Campbell came to Lorn or Mamlorn. That is all."

There was silence for a little at that.

"We have heard you, Glenstrae," Patrick said. "You also, Glenorchy. Can you now tell us why you invoke the General Bond Act at this present, before this council? What new situation calls for it?"

"Continuing transgressions and offences, my lords. The MacGregors are broken men, obeying no laws but their own! But the King's and parliament's laws must be maintained. I am superior of these lands and can be held responsible for the behaviour of those dwelling on them. I can demand it, by right. There is at present no Justiciar for the county of Perth, the Earl of Atholl being dead. So I come to this council."

Patrick shrugged. "My lords, you have heard the two sides of this matter. Has any a point to raise or a question to ask?"

Lennox spoke up, at once. "I say that this has been a wasting of the time of this council. If Glenorchy believed that the Act should be invoked he should have done it long ago. Not waited until his Justiciar was dead, so that he could bring it here. I say that the matter should be dismissed, forthwith."

There was a murmur of agreement from round the table. Into it another voice was raised, although levelly, that of MacCailean Mhor himself, the Earl of Argyll.

"I am superior of certain lands occupied by Sir Duncan," he said. "Also by his friend Ardkinglas. Under this act *I* am responsible for the behaviour of these. I must mind it!"

That, from the Campbells' chief, was significant indeed, as none there required to have pointed out. There were glances exchanged.

The King licked his lips. This was his council. He need not attend its meetings but if he did, he could take part.

"I'm no' just happy aboot this o' the MacGregors," he observed. "They're a wild and unruly clan, aye unruly. They made an affray at the last Crieff Tryst, I'm told. Maist riotous. The Provost-man had to bring his officers to keep my peace. They occupy lands in yon Rannoch that's no' theirs. Balquhidder's ay in an uproar, folk say. My peace maun be kept, see you all. This Glenstrae's their chief. He'll need to keep a secure haud on them."

"To be sure, Sire. No doubt he will heed your Grace's apt warning." Patrick drew a paper from a pocket, and unfolded it. "But, before we record this council's decision on the issue before us, hear this. Here is another bond from the General Bond which Glenorchy cites. Not passed by any parliament but drawn up and signed by the brothers MacTarlich, in the county of Dunbarton and addressed to Sir Duncan Campbell himself. I have obtained a copy of it from a reliable source." And he looked over at Glenorchy, smiling.

That man did not smile back. Set-faced, he stared.

"Your Grace and my lords, I think that you should hear this. It is in lawmen's words, most legal indeed! Or is it? It goes thus – I will spare you some of the repetitions. I quote:

"Be it known to all men by these patent letters, we, Donald MacTarlich and Douglas MacTarlich, brothers, are bound and obliged and do bind and oblige ourselves faithfully and truly, during our lifetime . . . to the right honourable Duncan Campbell of Glenorchy and his heirs, that, inasmuch as the aforesaid Duncan is obliged to give and deliver to me, Donald, a letter of land-lease during my lifetime and to male heirs lawfully begotten of my body . . . the entire two-mark land of Glen Eurin and the one-mark land of Elir . . . in the lordship of Lorn . . . and the entire half-mark land of Glen Katillie, to be consequent on our performance of the following conditions and not otherwise. Therefore we, being of a mind to do this before we ever shall crave possession of the said lands . . . understanding Clan MacGregor to be manifest malefactors and His Majesty's declared rebels . . . we bind and oblige us that with the whole company and forces we may or can make, we shall immediately enter into deadly feud with the Clan Gregor and shall continue and endure therein and in making slaughter upon them both secretly and openly, and shall in no manner desist until that the aforesaid Duncan Campbell of Glenorchy is satisfied and content with the slaughter we shall do and commit upon them . . . so that thereafter we may possess and enjoy the benefits of the said lands. Subscribed with our hands at Balloch, the 18th day of May, the year 1590, before these witnesses . . . etcetera . . ."

There was absolute silence as the Master finished that

reading. Seldom can a legally phrased land contract have produced such an impact.

It was King James who found his voice first, as he searched the faces of his councillors and then gazed at Glenorchy.

"Reprehensible! Aye, reprehensible. Maist certainly so!" he said, even more wetly than usual.

"Indeed, Sire. You put it . . . moderately!" Patrick commented. "Here is a rent of lands, Glenorchy's lands, to be paid in blood, not in moneys or service. Blood – the blood of your Grace's subjects. And at the express behest of this man, Duncan Campbell himself. Never have I heard the like. Has any here?"

"That, that was years ago. After Drummond-Earnoch's murder. When the MacGregors were put to the horn." Black Duncan's voice, for once, was uneven, thick. "It, it was to maintain the King's law."

"Na, na, man – dinna bring *me* into it, Glenorchy! No' wi' the likes o' yon! It was ill done."

"It was more than that, Sire," Ludovick declared. "It was, is, incitement to murder, mass murder. The slaughter of a whole clan aimed at. Men, women and children. Here is dastardy! Against all law and humanity. I say that this must be punished, with all rigour. A rent in blood!" It was not often that the Duke achieved such eloquence.

All around were cries of agreement. Some there might possibly on occasion have wished for the same kind of contract against their unfriends; but none surely would ever have put it down in writing.

Patrick pocketed his paper. "I propose that this matter be looked into by the Justiciar for the county of Dunbarton, where the contract was signed – which happens to be my lord Earl of Argyll! For due and proper action. And meantime, I think that we can dismiss the issue of Glenorchy versus Glenstrae as irrelevant, and calling for no action by this council. Is that agreed, my lords?"

No voice was raised in objection, not even the monarch's.

"Very well. Sir Duncan Campbell, with the King's permission you may retire. But I suggest that you hold yourself in readiness for investigation over this contract. And have the MacTarlich brothers available also."

Black Duncan of the Cowl lost no time in leaving the hall, drawn-featured, tense, only recollecting to turn and make a quick nod towards the monarch as his officer opened the door.

Alastair, bemused, looked around him, and for guidance to the Master of Gray.

"Alastair MacGregor of Glenstrae," Patrick said, easily now, "I think that we need no longer detain you. This council has a further item to consider. You are, I feel sure, free to go."

"Aye, but bide a wee, bide a wee," James put in. "I said I was no' just happy about thae MacGregors. No' this Alastair himsel', mind, but his folk, unruly chiels as we a' ken. Glenorchy went ower far, aye – but that doesna mean that we can let the MacGregors run riot and make stramash! They'll be the worse after this, I'm thinking. So, I say that this Alastair, their chief man, shall remain at my court, held as token and warranty, aye warranty, for their guid behaviour. No' just a hostage, mind, but a guaranty just. Och, he was here before, and got on fine. That, that is my royal will and decision. Aye."

None could controvert that, least of all Alastair MacGregor. Patrick inclined his head.

"Very well. Glenstrae, you have heard. See you to it. You may leave us."

Alastair bowed himself out, mind in a whirl.

That evening, back in the Gray lodging at Falkland, they made what amounted to a celebratory party, all agog to hear how Patrick had achieved what he had done. Airily that man dismissed his activities as minor. One Aulay MacAulay of Ardincaple, near to Dumbarton town, really a MacGregor and no friend of the Campbells but owing superiority to Argyll, owed him, Patrick, some small thanks. He had told him that the MacTarlich brothers – who had actually threatened *him*, MacAulay – had boasted in their cups, in a tavern in Dumbarton, of this bond with Campbell of Glenorchy. So he, Patrick, had gone to Dumbarton town, where there were only two lawmen, and had no difficulty in discovering the one who had drawn up that contract. The acting Chancellor's authority had easily overcome any reluctance on the part of the lawyer to show him a copy of the contract which he had wisely or otherwise kept. That was all, simplicity itself.

His hearers were duly impressed.

But it was something quite different which was really preoccupying Patrick Gray. This was how it had come about that Glenorchy had managed to influence the King to arrange this Privy Council hearing; indeed also to have himself knighted? Unearthing this had taxed his wits considerably more than the matter of the blood-rent contract, since he could scarcely openly cross-question James himself on the matter. But he thought that he had got to the bottom of it. All hinged on a visit paid by Glenorchy to the Continent, where he had gone to avoid being called upon to support his chief's armed assembly of Clan Campbell and the warfare against Huntly – this after the Dunoon rally. So he had gone, playing the cultured sightseer – for he was a man of some culture admittedly. Anyway, his travels had taken him as far as Padua in Italy, where he had met a fellow-Scot, the young Earl of Gowrie. They would all know how Gowrie had been more or less exiled for the sins of his father, the former Lord Ruthven, High Treasurer of the realm, who had been indiscreet enough to lend his monarch eighty-five thousand pounds – which had never been repaid. Hence the need to get rid of the lender and exile the son!

Gowrie was a most talented and clever young man, and at the age of twenty-one had actually become Rector of the University of Padua. He and Glenorchy seemed to have got on well, and the latter learned something that he realised he could use on his monarch. For Gowrie was an expert, amongst other things, on necromancy, magic, judicial astronomy and the like – the sort of thing which James revelled in. So Duncan picked Gowrie's brains, and came home with all sorts of esoteric information and defences against the diabolic. He even brought a secret elixir against deviltry for James, and an esoteric design to be worn next to the skin – the sighting of which, when James was in his bed, had enabled him, Patrick, to elicit most of this information by seeming most interested. According to Glenorchy, Gowrie was able, with his esoteric knowledge and devices, even to cause snakes to dance! So James, of course, had been enthralled – and was no doubt writing another book on the matter! Hence Glenorchy's advance in the royal favour – until now! On such could the fate of realms depend!

Wondering all, they retired for the night, Alastair's relief great, however much he was concerned over this of having to remain at court again, surety for his clan's good behaviour. At least it would mean that he would see a lot more of Mary Gray. And, to be sure, of Ludovick Stewart.

18

So commenced another curious interlude in the life of Alastair MacGregor, of unspecified duration and most uncertain character and status. He was at court, yes, but not by any means a courtier, not exactly a prisoner, a hostage, but not a free man either. He never knew just how much he was expected to take part in the court's activities, how much he should be seen by the monarch. James, after all, had presumably been prepared to see him brought low at that Privy Council meeting, until the blood-contract revelation had made it evident that Glenorchy's cause could no longer be seen to have the royal support. There was no summons to the royal bedchamber, on the subject of poetry, second sight or other, no commands to attend the hunting. Ludovick sought to advise on procedure, but even he found it difficult to gauge James's attitudes and wishes in this matter, as in much else. Patrick Gray was no great help in this, for he was seldom there, chancellorship business taking him away most of the time, to Edinburgh, Stirling, the Borders and elsewhere. He had done his part.

Mary, to be sure, was Alastair's support and comfort, making up for all. Sometimes he wondered whether Vicky might be a little jealous of her kind care and attention, for Alastair was almost inevitably more in her company than that of anyone else; not that he indulged in any unsuitably intimate behaviour, however tempted he might be on occasion, but they were very close friends and their association a joy, and clearly not only to Alastair. They largely explored Fife and Fothrif together, sometimes with Lennox or the Lady Marie with them but more usually alone.

At least there was no problem about Glenorchy's presence now, for he disappeared immediately after the council meeting, presumably back to his own territories.

Alastair sent messages, by one of Ludovick's men, to his brother John at Balquhidder, to Rob Ban at Stronmilchan in Glen Strae and to Gregor at Roro, acquainting them with his position and urging the utmost care and unprovocative behaviour on all his clansfolk, lest he be made a sacrifice for them. When he would be able to return he could not say. They must hold the fort for him.

That James, however little he seemed to look in Alastair's direction, was not unmindful of his presence was proved by the fact that when, after a few weeks, Ludovick requested leave of absence to visit Methven to attend to his estate's affairs there, he was refused permission to take the MacGregor with him even though he guaranteed his safe return. So the duke had to go alone, for a brief stay, leaving Alastair in the care of Mary Gray at Falkland.

For the court remained at Falkland throughout that summer and autumn and into winter. So long a stay was unusual and was caused in the main by the Queen's condition – or at least by the King's reactions thereto. Anne was expecting the delivery of her new child in July, and James was greatly concerned for the infant's well-being. Brought from her palace of Linlithgow to that of Dunfermline, so that the lying-in could be near at hand without interfering with the monarch's other activities, especially the hunting, there had to be much coming and going between the two palaces, not so much by James himself but by his emissaries and physicians, to report on progress, Mary Gray being frequently used as courier, as former tirewoman to the Queen and knowledgeable about births and infants, Alastair always accompanying her. In the event, the delivery was delayed until mid-August, to the father's agitation and annoyance – and when it came to pass and it proved to be a girl, to his loud disappointment. He had wanted a second heir to the succession, and felt that Anne had, as usual, somehow let him down. However, he rallied and made the best of it, seeking to use the infant as an asset by calling her Elizabeth as compliment to the English virgin Queen, whom he was so eager to have name himself as heir. So nothing must happen to the baby, and she must remain at Dunfermline until he was satisfied that she was strong enough to be moved back to Linlithgow; not, in her case, to Stirling beside young

Henry Frederick, for nobody was likely to try to kidnap a mere female child.

In the midst of all this there was a most unlooked-for development – the arrival back in Scotland of the Earl of Huntly no less, and his immediate call to court. Most were astonished, since the Gordon had been banished the realm after Glenlivet, and sentence of outlawry had not been officially lifted. Mary Gray thought that her father might just possibly have something to do with this, for reasons of his own; but James had always had a weak spot for Huntly. But if Patrick was indeed involved, he had reason to regret it, for James, receiving George Gordon with every demonstration of favour and affection, promptly bestowed on the erstwhile treasonable outlaw the abbey-lands of Dunfermline, quite the richest prize that the Reformation had thrown up, and which Patrick had been angling for for long. Not only that, but he created him *Marquis* of Huntly, something new for Scotland, a rank which the English had instituted above that of earl and below that of duke. So now Huntly was Scotland's first marquis, to the much offence of most of its earls and other lords. James Stewart had a notable faculty for giving offence to his nobility. Patrick wondered, in the circumstances, how long it would be before Huntly was seeking to regain his Lieutenancy of the North from Argyll.

When Ludovick came back from his visit to Methven, he gave proof of his continuing friendship towards the MacGregors by announcing that he had taken the opportunity to go on to Balquhidder, where he had found Alastair's brother John gone to Glen Strae, and had taken the trouble to follow him there to discover how matters went with the clan. He had ascertained that all was reasonably well and in order, with no major problems, even though John had scarcely welcomed his enquiries. Glenorchy was indeed back, seemingly installed at Finlarig, one of his castles, at the head of Loch Tay, but did not appear to be actively making trouble meantime. So Alastair could rest more easy in his mind.

One echo of the Glenorchy affair did reach them, in that the King, still intrigued over the Gowrie expertise in counter-diablery, had summoned that young earl back to Scotland. Whether or not he would come remained to be seen. He might, for he was hereditary Provost of Perth, and his younger brother, Sandy Ruthven, was known to be but a reluctant deputy. But the royal debt of eighty-five thousand pounds must still make Gowrie wary.

The return and restoration to favour of Huntly had an odd side-effect, and something of an embarrassment for Ludovick Stewart. His friends were apt to forget that he had a sister, and she had been wed, almost as a child, to none other than George Gordon. A quiet, retiring creature, she had made a strange wife for the ever-dramatic Huntly, never coming to court but apparently well content to immure herself in the wilds of Strathbogie whatever her husband's activities elsewhere. Ludovick had scarcely seen her since her wedding. Now Huntly brought her south, for some reason; and almost overnight the Queen took Henrietta, Marchioness of Huntly, to her heart. Anne, to be sure, needed a close friend and confidante, with the spouse she had – but perhaps not quite so close as this relationship quickly developed. For soon they were sharing the same bed, and Nicholson, the English envoy, was writing to Queen Elizabeth that Henrietta "had the plurality of Anne's kisses". Not only this, but the new marchioness proved to have become a fervent Catholic, and Anne, who had been tending that way anyhow, now seemed well on the way to becoming a convert to that faith – to the dire offence of the Kirk, more especially as the Queen put the new princess in the care of the Lady Livingstone, another strong Catholic. Needless to say the court was soon buzzing with talk of this liaison. James himself did not seem greatly exercised – after all, he himself had a distinct fondness for young men, and his religious views were vague anyway; but Lennox found it disturbing.

And not only Ludovick, it transpired. Elizabeth Tudor, by now become a crotchety and difficult woman of sixty-three, from her ambassador's reports, became much upset. She wrote in her own hand demanding that her cousin James put a stop to all these shameful tendencies towards the Romish Church, or else she could by no means nominate him heir to her so Protestant throne.

This last did distress James mightily, for the English succession, and the hoped-for wealth and prestige which would accrue therefrom, was now a major preoccupation with him – so much so that he frequently complained that Elizabeth was an unconscionable time in dying. Now, to reassure her as to his sound Protestantism, he sent the Master of Gray down to London to use his utmost efforts and well-known persuasive powers.

That Yuletide, largely because of Alastair's situation, Ludovick and Mary did not go to Methven, but remained at Falkland. There was still no indication from the monarch as to when Himself should be allowed to go home. When Ludovick approached him on the matter, James's attitude was that the system seemed to be working well; the MacGregors were refraining from misbehaviour, so why terminate a successful experiment?

The King, however, had a further notion on the subject of the Children of the Mist, and not only them but other trouble-makers. Early in the New Year, he at last actually commanded Alastair into the royal presence, after all the months of carefully ignoring him, instructing Vicky to fetch him into audience. It proved again to be a bedchamber interview. James, at Falkland, seemed always to be either hunting or in his bed, with much of the realm's business conducted therefrom.

On entry, the King spoke as though there had never been the least interruption of their former association, all as it had been before the Privy Council meeting.

"There you are then, man Alastair," he greeted, wagging an ink-stained finger at him from the untidy bed. "A word wi' you, just. I hae a bit poetry to read to you. No' mine. Did you ken that yon Argyll was something o' a versifier, the man? No' a right poet, mind, but no' bad for a Hielantman. He sent this to me, see you, because o' Geordie Gordon, I jalouse. Geordie was Lieutenant o' the North, mind, and maybe wi' a stronger hand than Argyll. He's likely feart that I'll gie the lieutenancy back to Geordie. So here's to mind me o' his services! Aye. Where is it?" He groped amongst a scatter of papers. "Here it's. Heed you."

> I, MacCailean Mhor, came from the west,
>   With many a bow and brand,
> To waste the Rinnes I thought best,
>   The Earl of Huntly's land.

I swore that none should me gainstand,
    Except that I was fey,
But all should be at my command,
    That dwelt benorth of Tay.

"Weel, what d'you think o' that, Alastair man?"

"It is very good. Apt, Sire. Referring to his services at Glenlivet in Your Grace's cause. MacCailean Mhor has the gift, to be sure. And some . . . appreciation of his position, whatever!"

"Gift? Och, I'd no' put it so high as gift, see you. But he has a smattering o' it – like yoursel', maybe. Aye. But it's no' just his poetry I'm consairned wi', the noo. The man's Lieutenant o' the North noo, and Admiral o' the Western Seas – yon was *your* doing, Vicky Stewart, and I'm no' right sure that he's the richt man for it, the Campbell! But let that bide a wee. He's in right trouble up there, in thae heathenish parts. Thae MacDonalds are as bad as your MacGregors – worse, for there's a sight mair o' them! Ower many. Them and their friends the MacLeods, and the rest. MacDonald, that's calling himsel' Lord o' the Isles – a title o' my ain, mind, the limmer – is in league wi' the Irish rebels against England, Tyrone and the others. Aiding them to rise against Elizabeth Tudor. Subjects o' mine, aiding Elizabeth's enemies! She's fair annoyed, and holds *me* responsible, the woman! So, something has to be done, I've tell't Argyll. So here's a ploy, a guid ploy, guid in mair ways than one. A threat's what's needed, see you. Against yon MacDonald's flank. Up in thae Hebrides. To keep him looking ower his ill shoulder, no' to go stravaiging to Ireland to help the rebels. And to get rid o' some o' the barbarous folk who aid him up yonder. And at the same time do some guid hereaboots. Lewis. You ken o' Lewis, man Alastair?"

"I know where it is, Sire. The largest of the Outer Isles, is it not?"

"Aye. Lewis and Harris are joined, like. But Lewis is the biggest. And the worst, for there's mair folk on it. Full o' MacLeods, allies o' MacDonald. They've been having right troubles amongst themsel's, a right scoundrelly lot. So we'll use that to guid effect, see you. There's been trouble in this Fife, as you'll ken, ever since yon bad harvest. Near to famine, and some o' the lairds hard put to it to keep their folk in bread. No' only Fife, mind. Weel – I'm going to use this o' Lewis and the MacLeods. Send a pack o' Fifers, armed mind, up to Lewis, to get rid o' the MacLeods, or some o' them. Put the fear o' God into them, and settle there. Make a decent-like place o' it – colonise it, just. Och, it's no' just barren land, I'm told. And at the same time, gie yon MacDonald a fright and hae him feart to go sailing his folk off to Ireland and upsetting Elizabeth Tudor. Is that no' just a bonny ploy?"

Alastair blinked, and looked at Ludovick. "It sounds . . . clever, Sire. Notable. If . . . possible?" he said cautiously.

"Possible? Why should it no' be possible? It's my royal will. There's ower many hungry folk in Fife, and lairds' sons wi' no' enough to do! They'll get free land in Lewis, to improve and mak a decent place o' it. What's no' possible aboot that, man?"

"It is the Lewis folk, Sire – these MacLeods. They will not like such . . . invasion by Southrons. Highlanders themselves. They may well resist. Fight, whatever."

"Ooh, aye. But they're no' the only ones who can fight! And that's where you come in, man – you and your MacGregors. You could go wi' them. Your MacGregors are the great fighters, we a' ken ower weel! You'd hae something guid to fight for, there. And then tak ower some o' the lands for yoursel's. Nae mair trouble wi' your superior, Glenorchy. Nae superior there but mysel', the King. Broad lands in Lewis and Harris. How say you to that?"

Alastair bit his lip. "Sire, I do not know what to say! The Outer Isles! My clansfolk – they, I fear, would not wish to become Islesmen. Always Clan Alpin has belonged to Lorn, Mamlorn and Strathtay. These parts. For seven centuries. They would not take kindly to any move to the far isles amongst the island clans – MacDonalds, MacLeods, Macleans, Mackenzies and Macraes. Who would not welcome *them*! I fear . . ."

James frowned, jabbing his pen again. "I'm no' that consairned wi' your fears, man. I've got to consider the weal o' this realm, see you – aye that. The weal o' it a'. And this o' the MacDonalds, the MacLeods and Lewis is important, fell important. You could be some help to your sovereign-lord in this, you and your MacGregors, no' a hindrance and makers o' trouble for once! It's a right worthy ploy and you could do weel out o' it. You mind that."

Alastair was silent.

Ludovick spoke up. "James, this is a notable scheme, as you say. But it requires a deal of thought. Not only on the part of the MacGregors. The Fifers also. Folk from Fife would find it difficult to settle in the Outer Isles. Distant islands in the ocean, utterly unlike their own lands here. Far from their own kind. Everything different. Hated by all around them as incomers, invaders. Apart from the MacLeods themselves, and they are a large clan, the MacDonald federation would be set against them. Their great galley-fleets would harry them. The MacGregors are fighters, yes – but *they* are not a large clan, not now. They . . ."

"Och, Vicky, hud your tongue! You dinna ken what you're at. Argyll will aid them – he has galleys, too. He's Admiral o' the Western Seas, is he no'? Wi' plenties o' Campbells and the like. He kens o' this ploy, and favours it . . ."

"Since it could hurt his enemies, the MacDonalds!"

"Mebbe so. But that's naught against it. Some way, that Tudor woman has to be shown that I'm seeking to aid her. This'll dae that. And at the same time aid my ain realm. Clip MacDonald's wings and bring some worth to those isles. Aye, and get these MacGregors oot o' my hair!"

"You cannot move a whole clan against its will, James."

"Can I no'! I'm the King, mind, and they're in unlawfu' possession o' lands. I'm offering them free lands, wi' no superior but mysel' in return for protecting thae Fifers. D'you tell me I canna dae that, Vicky Stewart?"

His hearers eyed each other and their monarch, wordless now.

"Aye, then. That's that. Be off wi' the pair o' you. And think weel on't, for I'm fair set on this. A guidnight to you – I've work to dae!"

Bowing, they retired.

The door was barely shut behind them when Alastair burst out, "My people will never accept this, Vicky! Never. It would be the end of Clan Alpin. To be exiled to the Outer Hebrides! Against the will of all the other island clans. I cannot even put it to them. Go there to protect a landing of the Fifers perhaps – some of us. But never to remain there."

"I know it. Folly it is. I wonder . . .? Could this have been Glenorchy's suggestion in the first place? It could well suit his cause."

"It might well have been him, yes. What shall I do, Vicky?"

"Do nothing meantime. It may well all come to nothing. The Fifers may refuse also. I cannot see *them* wishing to become islesmen! Nor other Lowlanders. Nor their lords and masters. No, no – I do not see this coming to pass. So spare yourself the worry of it, meantime."

Which was excellent advice – but not so easy for Alastair to follow, nevertheless.

Whether Alastair's so evident opposition to the Lewis scheme was responsible or not, the King thereafter returned to his ignoring attitude towards the MacGregor – which was a relief in one way. So life at court went on, with the hostage becoming increasingly discontented and frustrated, despite all the kindness of his friends. This was no life for a young Highland chief.

James did not enlighten Ludovick further on the Lewis colonisation project, and it was not until Patrick Gray returned from his visit to London that they learned that the plan was indeed intended to go ahead. The Master was a little surprised at this himself – not at the notion of the plan, but that the King was taking it so seriously. It had been one of the matters he had been told to mention to Queen Elizabeth, as another token of James's goodwill, but for himself he had never believed that it would come to anything. It might well have been Glenorchy's idea, in the first place – it certainly was not his own – but he had assumed that it was little more than a reassuring gesture towards England.

Patrick's embassage had been only partially successful, it seemed, in convincing Elizabeth that James was her suitable heir. Most of her English advisers were against it, especially those religiously inclined or linked with the Church, headed by the Archbishops of Canterbury and York, fearing that Scottish succession would bring with it the danger of Presbyterian Church government as against Episcopal. Even while Patrick was in London a despatch had arrived from Nicholson, the English envoy to James, reporting on a sermon preached at St Andrews by the prominent divine, the Reverend David Black, denouncing Queen Elizabeth as an atheist and her religion vain, that all kings were the Devil's children, and their lords cormorants. The word of this extraordinary effusion had not helped, needless to say, especially as Nicholson added that other Scots Kirk ministers were applauding these sentiments. Patrick had been instructed by a furious Elizabeth to inform James that such wretched bigots must be punished and put down forthwith, and to urge him to establish the rule of bishops in Scotland instead of presbyters.

This last, actually, coincided with James's own ideas as to Church government, and he was quite prepared to work to that end. He would take active steps in the matter, apparently; but first he had to see to the more urgent need to dispose of the MacDonald aid to Elizabeth's rebels in Ireland, which aid would surely resume on the abating of winter storms, to make galley navigation in the western ocean practical again.

So, with the spring weather reasonably good, it was to be action. Not the Lewis plantation quite yet, but large-scale armed intervention in the north-west. Troops would have to be carried in the only other large galley fleets available, those of Argyll and Maclean of Duart – who had been receiving English gold to help restrain MacDonald for some time. Argyll, as Lieutenant of the North and Admiral, had to be in command of this expedition, of course; but James did not entirely trust him nor his military prowess, after Glenlivet, and ordered that Ludovick should go along as personal representative of the crown, little as the duke relished the prospect. The King was adamant, however, so Vicky had to become a reluctant warrior. And Mary Gray surprised them all by declaring that she was going to accompany him, to seek to ensure that he came to no harm. She did not propose to go into actual battle – and hoped that Vicky would not either – but if she was with him, he would be the less likely to run risks. Despite the pleas of Patrick and his wife, and of Alastair also, she was quite determined on this, to leave young Johnnie in the care of Lady Marie and to make, with the duke, for Inveraray and Argyll's mustering array.

It made a sad parting for Alastair when they departed from Falkland, with sundry others of the lords. Not only was he going to miss them direly, his so good friends, but it left him in a more ridiculous and pointless situation than ever, a sort of pariah, at court but not of it. The Grays said that he must continue to stay at their lodging – for James apparently was not prepared to release him yet. Lady Marie was kind, but her husband was so often absent. It was going to be a grievous interlude.

Alastair, to be sure, had offered to go with the expedition, and take a contingent of his MacGregor fighters with him, but unaccountably this was turned down by the monarch for reasons unspecified.

It made quite an emotional farewell, with embraces, kisses and shoulder-patting, Mary asserting that they would not be gone long, and Ludovick declaring that once he had got this over, he would get his friend back to Glen Strae somehow. Then they were gone.

After that the days seemed endless and without object. Patrick took Alastair on one or two not too distant excursions, once to Broughty Castle and once to St Andrews where he went to urge moderation on the Reverend Andrew Melville, Principal of the University. But the Master was never long at Falkland, and their lodger spent most of his days alone.

Then one day in May, Patrick arrived with news which altered the situation, at least for many at court. The Reverend Black, who had made the assertion that Elizabeth Tudor was an atheist and kings the spawn of Satan, had been summoned to appear before the Privy Council, and had refused to attend. This refusal was publicly backed by the other leaders of the Kirk, who declared that the ministers of Christ obeyed God's laws above man's, the Presbytery of Edinburgh going so far as to send out copies of Black's statement to every other presbytery in the land, urging its declaration from every pulpit. James had to act, or Elizabeth would write Scotland off entirely. He would go to Edinburgh, with his Privy Councillors, and interview the Kirk leadership in person.

So, suddenly, Falkland was all but deserted – but with neither release for Alastair nor orders to go to Edinburgh. Presumably he was now the responsibility of the keeper of Falkland, with his section of the royal guard – although he was not actually told so.

When the Lady Marie announced that, in the circumstances, she was going to the Gray family home at Broughty with the two children, her own son and Mary's Johnnie, she asked would Alastair wish to approach the palace keeper, and ask if he might accompany them? Surely he would be considered secure enough in the acting Chancellor's household? But that young man said thank you, no. He had made up his mind – it had been getting made up for him for long, now. He would cut loose, depart, quietly leave for Glen Strae. This situation had become intolerable and had lost all meaning.

Lady Marie looked at him, nodding. "I understand. I wondered if it would come to this – *when* it would come," she said. "I, for one, do not blame you, Alastair. Nor indeed will Patrick, I think. He said to me, before he left for Edinburgh, that if it was *his* position, he would do that. He was not advising it, see you, but understanding it. What James will say or do, of course, we know not."

"I am all but past caring, whatever. Go you off to Broughty, my lady, and the next evening I shall steal quietly away!"

"And God go with you!" she told him.

19

The return to Glen Strae was happy, almost joyful, Alastair scarcely aware of the esteem in which he was held by his clansfolk, as distinct from mere respect due to a chief. Except from his brother John, that is, who seemed less than jubilant; no doubt he had found satisfaction in playing the chief all these months, and had his own ideas as to how this should be done. He departed for Balquhidder – where oddly enough he had left his wife in the interim – with no great display of affection.

However, John had at any rate kept the clan in order, if somewhat heavy-handedly apparently, and there seemed to have been no major troubles or problems. Except at Balquhidder itself, as it happened, where one John Galt MacGregor, a tacksman of quite extensive land, had been making a nuisance of himself towards his neighbours, some quite far afield, as distant as Loch Tayside evidently; for there was a complaint, in the name of Campbell of Glenorchy, before the sheriff court at Perth, not the higher justiciary court significantly, of John Galt's lifting of cattle from various places in the area, from tenants of Black Duncan, only two or three at a time, no large numbers, but a provocation. Since Alastair was not officially free from his royal hostageship, he thought it best not himself to appear before the sheriff, so he instructed his brother to go, since he was the senior at Balquhidder and these stupid thefts had taken place during his period in charge. He told John to inform the court that MacGregor cattle would be sent to the victims in replacement, plus one or two more by way of compensation. It was to be hoped that this would serve to cover the matter without further and wider complaint, John Galt to be suitably punished.

Otherwise all was well enough, and Alastair slipped back into his normal routine readily, paying visits to the various MacGregor "colonies" to remind all that he was back in charge and to emphasise the continuing need for circumspection and unprovocative behaviour. With Roro and Glengyle and some of the other chieftains, he discussed the King's suggested Lewis scheme, and as expected met with unanimous rejection as impracticable and unacceptable folly.

Black Duncan was evidently lying very low, as well he might, out of favour with the Privy Council and his own chief. There was word of him at Balloch, Finlarig, Edinample, Glendochart, Barcaldine and Achallader – but not at Kilchurn, so near to Glen Strae, which gave the impression that he was deliberately avoiding that neighbourhood meantime, probably wisely. Alastair did not publicise the MacTarlich-Glenorchy blood-rent bond for fear of whipping up MacGregor fury and what that might well result in. The Campbell had had a fright over that, and it was almost certainly as well to let sleeping dogs lie.

Of national doings in the months that followed they heard no great amount at Glen Strae. Rumours spread through the Highlands, of course, but these tended to lack coherence and detail. There was little interest anyway in what went on in the Lowlands; but the west Highland and Isles situation was different. The word was that there had been two major battles there, one on land, in the vicinity of Tobermory on the Isle of Mull, and one at sea, between the MacDonald and combined Campbell and Maclean galley fleets. The former had been a victory for Argyll and Lennox, the latter apparently indecisive. The campaign was still going on and had now moved over to Northern Ireland, it was said. Alastair was anxious for his friends and wondered often how Mary fared, praying that that resolute young woman kept out of danger.

News of the royal doings came eventually from Church sources – Catholic Church, that is. Wandering friars still survived in the Highlands, where the Old Religion remained general, and these travelling priests, descended as it were from the old Trinitarian friars who had used to drum up contributions to pay for the Crusades, were often the only priestly presence in the glens and straths, performing the necessary baptisms, marriages and commemorations for the dead – as well as being the great carriers of news and gossip from all over. One of these gleefully told Alastair of the trouble

217

the so-called Reformed Kirk was being to King Jamie, with dire ongoings. Apparently James had duly gone to Edinburgh and summoned the Kirk leaders to appear before him in the Tolbooth there, where there had been a notable scene, the ministers thundering denunciations and the King threatening to impose bishops over them, to keep them in order. Andrew Melville had in fact called the monarch "God's sillie vassal"; and David Black had, amongst other wordy assaults, declared that the Queen's association with the wretched Marchioness of Huntly was a disgrace and intolerable, and announced that although they were required by law to pray for the monarch and his wife and family, they could not in honesty do so for her, as she would never be of any good to God or the realm. This had provoked James to wrath and an angry termination of the interview; and the ministers ejected had rounded up a mob to come and riot outside the Tolbooth and later outside Holyroodhouse, to the sovereign's much alarm. The following Sunday the Reverend John Welsh, who had married John Knox's daughter, preaching in the High Kirk of St Giles, had denounced the King as possessed of the Devil. The good Marquis of Huntly was now advising the monarch on how to put Scotland's spiritual affairs in order; and there was growing hope for some return to the true faith.

All this seemed far removed from the MacGregors and Glen Strae, where Catholicism was of the vaguest variety.

Further news brought by the friars was of an enormous clan battle fought in the south-west Lowlands. Highlanders were not apt to think of the Lowlanders as having clans, or what they understood by the term; but apparently great families there, and their tenants, could behave in much the same way. The Maxwells and the Johnstones had been long at feud in Annandale and Nithsdale, and this had erupted in a mighty conflict wherein no fewer than two thousand died, the Lord Maxwell himself amongst them. The Johnstones had won, and Johnstone of Dryfesdale had thereupon assumed the Wardenship of the West March, hitherto held by Maxwell – and King Jamie was in no position to assert otherwise. Alastair had never heard of a Highland clan battle producing such a casualty list.

It was early autumn before there were repercussions –

or at least until such reached Glen Strae – from both Alastair's absconding from Falkland and the Perth sheriff court proceedings. Unpleasant repercussions, in the form of a missive expressing royal disapproval and the demand that caution must be produced to the tune of ten thousand merks, or the Clan Gregor would be put to the horn once more.

This, needless to say, was a shattering blow. Alastair could no more produce ten thousand merks than fly in the air. James would know that, and had chosen this way of demonstrating his ire at the leave-taking without his authority, and used the John Galt affair as convenient excuse. What was to be done? Ludovick would have helped, no doubt – although Alastair's pride would prevent him from asking for moneys; but Ludovick was far away. Patrick Gray? The same applied there, only more so.

He called a meeting of his chieftains. They were no more able, conjointly, to raise ten thousand merks than was he; anyway, they would not have paid it even if they could. There was a Lowland saying that you canna tak the breeks off a Hielantman, since he wore a kilt! Let the King try to collect his merks! Being put to the horn was no great harm; they had been so before and suffered but little. Unless some great lord with large manpower, like Argyll, came against them, they were safe enough in their glens – and Argyll was otherwise occupied. Glenorchy was not strong enough to assail them in force. Let Himself just do nothing and see what happened.

Himself was not quite so confident. Argyll would not be away for very much longer probably, for the winter would make campaigning in the Western Ocean impossible; and he was Lieutenant of the North, and it would be his responsibility to enforce any outlawry and dispossession of the MacGregors. He had proved helpful, if hardly friendly, in the past; but in a matter of this seriousness, against direct royal command, it would be different. Alastair was not hopeful, and did not relish the thought of being more or less besieged in his glens, even if nobody was actually able to turn them out.

Curiously, a sort of relief came from an unexpected quarter, after a few weeks: no less than a raid on those MacGregor tenants of the Menzies lands of Rannoch by a party of Macleans. The reason for this was not known, so far away from the Maclean Hebridean island of Mull, but it was sufficiently serious, with two MacGregors dead, some wounded, women abused, cattle stolen and premises set afire. No doubt the Macleans suffered casualties also, MacGregors being what they were, but that in no way mollified their fellow-clansmen. Alastair was faced with vociferous demands for vengeance – which, of course, was not easy to impose on islanders far away. Just what could be done was not clear, any more than the reason for this outrage.

In this predicament, Alastair was relieved to have a messenger come from Methven Castle to say that the duke was back there, and urging Himself to visit so soon as he might. In the circumstances it did not take him long to fulfil that invitation.

Seeing Mary and Ludovick again was a joy, both safe returned from their adventures and glad to be so. Alastair's reception was rewarding indeed.

Recounting the couple's experiences over the last months took a considerable time, of course, before they got on to the MacGregor troubles. The visitor heard about the battles and the voyaging, the stratagems and tactics, the successes and failures, the behaviour of leaders and led, what had transpired in Ireland, the doubtful outcome of it all. Argyll was claiming it as a triumphant campaign, but Ludovick was not so sure. The MacDonalds and their allies had been shaken, yes – but by no means finally defeated; and the Irish were still in revolt. But it had probably served its main purpose: that is, to convince Queen Elizabeth that James was seeking to aid her interests actively. He was not greatly concerned as to whether the Irish rebellion succeeded or failed; what he was concerned with was *his* succession eventually to Elizabeth's throne, with his nomination meantime as her successor and undoubted heir. That presumably had been advanced by this Hebridean venture. The Master of Gray had been sent once more down to London to acquaint the Tudor woman with its alleged achievements. And there had undoubtedly been achievements, even though hardly on the scale James was now claiming. For that they had to thank

Sir Lachlan Maclean of Duart rather than Argyll himself, an older man and seasoned warrior. Unfortunately he had been slain in wretched circumstances towards the end of the campaign, this indeed hastening its close.

In all this Mary apparently had managed to play some small part, not in the actual fighting of course, although she had been in one of the galleys during sea-battles, but in influencing Ludovick who in turn influenced Argyll, if not Maclean. The Countess of Argyll, the earl's mother, was a vigorous and venturesome lady, as befitted a daughter of the Earl Marischal and former wife of the late Regent Moray, who had ruled Scotland for the young James and been assassinated for his pains, and she had also accompanied the expedition. Mary and the Countess had become good friends, together making their mark on proceedings apt to be considered the province of men only.

Alastair was the more impressed with that young woman.

The mention of Sir Lachlan Maclean led him to bring up the subject of the Maclean raid on Rannoch. The duke was much concerned to hear of this, and could not understand the reasons behind it. The idea that Black Duncan might have some hand in it occurred to all, of course, but this seemed hardly likely. What links could he have with the Mull Macleans? But then, why should the islanders have come all the way from the Hebrides to Rannoch, in the centre of the mainland Highlands, for raiding? So far inland from their salt water, with easier to reach and more productive areas for pillage? Ludovick thought that it might represent upheavals in that clan following on the death of their chief. Sir Lachlan had left a number of sons, who were known to be at odds with each other; and lacking their father's firm hand, one or other might have gone raiding on the mainland. He supposed that if they chose to sail up either Loch Etive, from the Dunstaffnage mouth thereof, or Loch Leven from Ballachulish, they could get their boats to near Glen Coe, north or south, and the Moor of Rannoch was not so far from there. Why? Glenorchy might . . .?

Anyway, they would have to do something about it.

When Alastair went on to tell of the John Galt affair and the ten thousand merks caution, his hearers looked grave indeed.

Somehow that money would have to be found; they must not have the MacGregors outlawed again – that would play into Black Duncan's hands. Ludovick recognised that Alastair could by no means raise any such sum; James had undoubtedly made it so high with that in view. He would see what could be done to produce it. Alastair of course was vehement in his refusal to allow Vicky even to consider paying *his* debts, and the inevitable argument arose.

It was at this stage that Mary intervened. "Do not talk of debts," she urged. "This is a *caution*, is it not? Not an unreturnable sum. For the good behaviour of the MacGregors. Let two or three, including Vicky, make themselves responsible for finding the moneys. If required . . ."

"It *is* required!" Alastair declared.

"Wait you. This of the Macleans could be made to help, I think. You are the injured party in this, Alastair. If you make due complaint to the Privy Council for retribution against the Macleans, and for compensation for damage done, men's lives and property, it could come to more than any ten thousand merks! Could it not?"

Alastair stared.

"He would have difficulty in getting moneys out of the Macleans, whatever the Privy Council said!" the duke observed.

"No, not out of the Macleans. The council would recognise that. But if Himself was now the complainer and entitled to compensation, might they not cancel the ten thousand merks caution? This of the Rannoch raid and deaths is a far greater offence than that of the Balquhidder man, whatever his name was. The council could well, to get it off their hands, declare the ten thousand merks caution unnecessary and invalid, in the circumstances, and leave Himself to try to get his own damages from the Macleans?"

"On my soul, I believe you have it," Ludovick exclaimed. "What a notion, girl! That might well serve."

"Myself? Go to the Privy Council? Would they hear *me*?" Alastair doubted. "Would the King not stop it, whatever?"

Vicky looked thoughtful. "He might, yes. And Patrick is away in England. See you, I have another notion. Not the Privy Council. Go to the Court of Session instead. In

Edinburgh. This is what they call, I think, a civil case – compensation for damage done. Appear before the Court of Session judges in Edinburgh, in due complaint. James could not halt that, especially if he did not hear of it beforehand, as is unlikely. He would if it was Privy Council business. The senators of the College of Justice operate quite distinct from the council. But they could rule in this, I think. That would be the way."

"How could I appear before these men of the law? I would not know how to do it, what to say, any of it."

"We would find you a lawyer, to speak for you, to guide you. Yes, yes – I have it. I'd get you the man Duncanson, in Dumbarton. Who drew up that MacTarlich blood-rent bond that Patrick discovered. That was an ill document for any lawyer to indite. He will not want that held against him, in high places! If I threatened him with exposure if he did not plead your case before the Court of Session, I think that he would be glad enough to do it."

Mary smiled. "Good for you, Vicky! We will get Himself out of this hole that way. And teach King James a lesson for his deceitful part in all this. He is a strange man. He can be likeable and yet hateful too. Sometimes I think that the Kirk ministers could be right – the Devil can possess him!"

"As he would tell you himself, my dear, kings are not as other folk! Different rules and laws apply. And he will resent Himself's departure from Falkland without permission, however little blameworthy it was."

"It may be so. But this large sum for caution shows a meanness of spirit. You will be able to find two or three other guarantors for the moneys meantime, will you not?"

"I shall myself. And others belike . . ."

"I do not want you finding moneys for me!" Alastair insisted.

"No actual money will be required, I hope – only the guarantors' word. Until the Court of Session's ruling. Then we shall see."

"Why are you so good to me, at all?"

"Because we love you," Mary said simply, and touched his arm. Vicky did not amend that.

Three weeks later another messenger came to Glen Strae, this time from Stirling, saying that the case, MacGregor against Maclean, would come before the Court of Session in Edinburgh on 20th November; and Glenstrae was ordered to be present in person with legal representative. The Duke of Lennox would meet him the previous evening at the Earl of Orkney's lodgings at the palace of Holyroodhouse.

Alastair faced this ordeal, so kindly arranged for him, with some trepidation. It would be a totally new and trying experience for a Highland chief. But he had to go through with it.

He took Rob Ban with him, for moral support, and rode south by way of Balquhidder, to inform his brother, and to let his folk thereabouts know what John Galt's actions had brought upon them all. Carefully thereafter they avoided the Stirling crossing of Forth, in case King James got word of it, riding on eastwards into Fothrif, to Dunfermline, and across salt water at Queen Margaret's Ferry, and so the further ten miles to Edinburgh.

It seemed strange indeed to be making for the royal palace of Holyroodhouse in the circumstances. But the old monastic quarters of the former abbey had been handed over at the Reformation period to Robert Stewart, Earl of Orkney, one of James the Fifth's bastards and the Lady Marie's father. He was an elderly man now but retained these premises, and had filled them with a motley crowd of his own offspring and their partners, largely also illegitimate, a cheerful, noisy, unruly throng, notorious throughout the city. But no doubt it made a convenient lodging for Patrick Gray and Ludovick when the palace itself was not in use.

The Highlanders, presenting themselves, were greeted with some hilarity by Orkney's brood, but not denied admittance. They were conducted through the untidy establishment to a chamber where the duke and Mary Gray, Alastair was pleased to see, sat at table with the old earl himself, a red-faced, corpulent, jovial character, wearing a bedrobe over nondescript clothing, untidy as the rest of these quarters, but with an air

224

of authority about him nevertheless, as befitted a king's son and uncle of the reigning monarch. He greeted the newcomers with bellowed goodwill and grins, especially when Mary rose to embrace and kiss Alastair, punching Ludovick on the shoulder and warning him to watch out for his young lady.

Rob Ban was abashed.

However, the visitors were soon put at ease and provided with excellent food and drink.

The duke explained the morrow's procedure. The day's hearings of the Court of Session would be held in the Canongate Tolbooth, quite close to the palace. The MacGregor-Maclean case would be taken first, at noon – no doubt in deference to the ducal sponsorship, an excellent sign. The Lord of Session, one of fifteen, chosen for this hearing would be Sir John Hamilton – a decent-enough body for a lawyer, Orkney interjected – and so far as was known, no response had been forthcoming from the Macleans in answer to the summons. Which again looked very hopeful. Ludovick did not think that there would be much doubt about the verdict: in the MacGregors' favour; the crux of the matter would be the question of compensation awarded, if any, and how it would be arranged for in view of the fact that almost certainly no moneys would be forthcoming from the Macleans, whatever the judgment. Orkney seemed to find the entire affair hugely amusing, and declared that all would be well. Ludovick informed that meantime he and Sir John Murray of Tullibardine, a kinsman of brother John's wife, and Alexander Murray, Comendator-Abbot of Inchaffray, had between them guaranteed the ten thousand merks caution, should it have to be produced – to Alastair's much embarrassment.

Nevertheless he spent a hilarious evening in the former abbatical quarters where music, dancing and capers of various sorts seemed to be the rule of that odd and multitudinous household, some of the ongoings rude, not to say indecent by Highland standards, so that Alastair was concerned for Mary's feelings, although that young woman seemed to take it all as acceptable enough. It was scarcely how the uneasy litigant had visualised spending the night before his trial. Rob Ban had never imagined the Lowlands would be like this.

In the morning, after all too short a sleep, the MacGregors, used to fairly early rising, found the establishment still abed until a late hour. Indeed Alastair began to worry about getting to the Court of Session in time. However, Mary Gray appeared, and assured them that a hearty breakfast would be provided presently; and to this the guests sat down in due course, unaccompanied save by a single young man, all yawns, of uncertain identity.

When they were about to set off for the Canongate, they were surprised to be joined by Orkney himself, who seemed to be anticipating something in the nature of an entertainment. Mary Gray was not to be left out either.

So the plaintiff proceeded up the Canongate in illustrious company.

At the handsome towered Tolbooth, fairly recently erected, they found Thomas Duncanson, the Dumbarton lawyer, awaiting them, a sad-looking cadaverous individual who scarcely inspired confidence. He did not seem to be very interested in Alastair, his attention all on the duke and Orkney. He gave his client no real instructions, seemingly already having been given *his* by Ludovick. An usher took them upstairs, with much bowing, and led them into a large chamber, empty as yet, furnished with a long table, many chairs and little else. Orkney promptly sat down and called for wine.

They all took chairs, and while Duncanson arranged papers, Ludovick explained that the Court of Session, the supreme civil court of the land, had no jurisdiction over criminal charges. This case, therefore, must relate to damages sustained by the plaintiff, decision on responsibility, and compensation to be awarded if so adjudged. Actually the court consisted of fifteen Lords of Session, but for individual causes such as this, the fifteen appointed one of their number to hear it and make decision; and only if that decision was contested would the others meet to hear the appeal and consider it. The judge selected for today's hearing was this Sir John Hamilton.

Two men arrived, bearing flagons of wine, goblets and plates of oatcakes. While this was being placed before the visitors two more came in, to sit down beside them, one with papers placing himself at the foot of the table, the other bowing to the duke, Orkney and Mary, seating himself

226

nearby and entering into conversation. All partook of the provision.

Alastair wondered where the court was to be held, and when. Mary smiled across the table to him.

Presently, goblet still in hand, the one of the last pair without the papers cleared his throat and waved to the other. "Proceed," he mentioned easily.

The individual at the foot of the table stood up and read from a document, in a flat and monotonous voice.

"My lord. Herewith complaint of one, Alastair or Alexander MacGregor, calling himself of Glenstrae, in the sheriffdom of Perth, against persons unidentified but said to be of the name of Maclean, from the Isle of Mull, in the sheriffdom of Argyll, claiming damage and hurt to person and property committed against the said MacGregor and servants of his, on the property of Rannoch in the sheriffdom of Perth on the last day of September, which hurt and damage being contrary to law, public weal and the peace of the realm, and for which the said Alastair or Alexander MacGregor hereby claims due and sufficient compensation and indemnification." The clerk sat down.

Astonished, Alastair realised that this was to be the court hearing, unlike anything of the sort he could have imagined. Presumably the man who had spoken first, elderly, well but soberly dressed and sitting at ease supping wine, as he had been himself, was the Lord of Session Hamilton.

That individual nibbled an oatcake and nodded. "Is the said Alastair MacGregor of Glenstrae present in person to speak to this complaint and damage?" he wondered conversationally.

Alastair rose. "I am, sir."

"Very good. No need to stand." He waved his oatcake. "Do you wish to present your cause yourself, MacGregor? Or are you represented?"

"I represent the plaintiff, my lord," Duncanson said, rising. "Thomas Duncanson, notary, Dumbarton."

"Yes. And who represents the defenders in this action?"

Silence.

The judge did not seem in the least disconcerted. He took another sip. He pointed at Duncanson. "The complaint alleges the misdemeanours on the part of persons unnamed but alleged

227

to be Macleans. Can you assert any proof that this is the case? Not . . . others?"

Duncanson looked at Alastair. They all did.

"They were Macleans, whatever," Himself said simply.

Orkney chuckled.

"Perhaps. But that is scarcely proof, sir."

"MacGregor does not fail to know who attacks him."

"Perhaps not. But your unsupported word is scarcely enough for a court of law, Glenstrae."

Alastair glanced at Rob Ban.

"I am Robert MacGregor in Stronmilchan," that man said, a little uncertainly. "I know that they were Macleans from Mull, indeed and indeed."

"You saw them?"

"I saw their bodies, sir."

That produced something of a stir. "H'rr'mm. Bodies! This is not a criminal court, MacGregor. I am not concerned with criminal slaying, if that is what is implied, save insofar as such could affect a claim for damages. But . . . I would wish to hear what you mean by bodies, and how you identified them!"

Rob Ban spoke with a little more assurance. "I visited Rannoch when we heard of this raid. With John of Dochard and Stronvar – that is Himself's brother. Himself was at the King's court at the time. I saw the bodies of three Macleans killed in the raid."

"Indeed. And how did you know that they were Macleans?"

The other stared at his questioner. "Think you we do not know such things, sir? MacGregors!"

"That is not proof."

"Only Macleans wear crowberry, my lord," Alastair put in. "On their bonnets. And their war-cry is 'Another for Hector!'"

"Is that so? Then, I have no option but to take your word for it!" The judge turned to his clerk. "The defenders have been notified of the charges and required to be represented at this hearing?"

"Yes, my lord. By over three weeks past."

"And that is sufficient time for notice to get to this, er, Mull? And for the defendants to reach this court thereafter?"

"We are so assured, my lord. A sufficiency."

"They could be here in four days, from Tobermory," Rob Ban mentioned helpfully.

"Is that so? Then we must assume that they do not seek to defend the cause. Which much eases our task, does it not? What damage and hurt do you assert, Glenstrae?"

"Two of my clansmen slain. Sundry injured. Seven women raped. Six cot-houses burned. Others ransacked, whatever. Forty-two beasts taken."

"Beasts . . .?"

"Cattle, my lord."

"On my soul! All that! And only three of these Macleans died?"

"Only three bodies were left behind when they went." Orkney chortled.

"Ah. And can you support this claim of damage and hurt by any evidence, Glenstrae?"

Alastair frowned. "You have my word," he said quietly.

"M'mm. In a court of law, MacGregor, one man's word, however certainly given, is scarcely sufficient."

"I say the same," Rob Ban added loyally. "Only, och, there were the sheep, see you. Slaughtered. Plaids and gear taken, forby. And much ill done to plenishings."

"Indeed. And the wherefore of all this evil? Some clan feud?"

"We are not at feud with Maclean," Alastair said. "We have had no dealings with them at all. Why they came to Rannoch we know not. Unless . . . some enemy sent them."

"Enemy?"

Ludovick cleared a warning throat.

"We can think of no other reason, my lord." Alastair shrugged. "But it may not be so."

"So this assault was unexpected and unprovoked? Purpose unknown. Save for plunder?"

"That is all that we can assert. And they did steal the cattle."

"Yes. This is a difficult case, you will concede. No defence from the Macleans, no denial either. Yet no supporting evidence save the word of the claimant." Sir John glanced at Lennox and Orkney, of whose presence there he was obviously very much aware. "In the circumstances, I can only assume the Maclean guilt and the MacGregors damaged." He refilled his goblet. "What is claimed by way of damages and restitution?"

Alastair looked at Duncanson. It was time, surely, that the lawyer played his part.

"It is no simple matter to place a value on men's lives and on the women's bodies abused, my lord," that man said flatly. "A substantial sum is called for. The cattle and the plenishings are different, and can be assessed . . ."

"How much, sirrah? You must have come here prepared to claim some specified sum?"

Duncanson looked unhappy. "I have not been so instructed, my lord."

"The Macleans will pay nothing, to be sure," Alastair observed.

"Then what is the point of this hearing and plea, Glenstrae?" the judge asked, wagging his head.

"May I speak?" Ludovick put in. "I have no standing in this court, but I know and respect the plaintiff, Glenstrae. He and his have suffered grievous hurt, and are entitled to generous compensation. But, as he says, and as your lordship will know, the Macleans having already ignored your court will ignore any penalty it imposes. And there is little possibility of enforcing any payment from the Isle of Mull by your court. Soo . . ."

"All this I recognise, my lord Duke. And regret the circumstances."

"Aye, but mair than regrets are needed, man!" That was Orkney, joining in. "This MacGregor's right injured."

The Lord of Session smoothed mouth and chin.

Rather hurriedly Ludovick went on, "There is something that can be done. Glenstrae has to find caution for a trespass committed by one of his own clansfolk. Against neighbours. Guarantors are forthcoming – *I* am one. For ten thousand merks. If the caution was to be transferred, in law, to the chief of Maclean, at Duart in Mull, then it would release both Glenstrae and the said guarantors. And if this caution was refused, against the order and authority of the Court of Session, then it would be a matter to go before the Privy Council, would it not? Of which I am a member."

If Alastair was prepared for the judge to balk at this ingenious suggestion, he was pleasantly surprised. Sir John nodded, almost relievedly, and took some more wine.

"Excellent, my lord Duke!" he exclaimed. "A very suitable solution and decision for this court. Who is the present chief of these Macleans? Who must be taught to keep his people in order."

"Sir Lachlan, a good chief, was slain in the recent fighting in the Western Ocean – hence the unlawful behaviour by some of his folk, I would think. But his eldest son, Hector Og, will now be chief."

"Very good. This Hector Maclean must needs order his clan better. I so declare. This court orders the caution of ten thousand merks to be transferred to the said Hector. And another ten thousand merks to be paid to MacGregor of Glenstrae in compensation for damage suffered, on penalty of further escheat and possible forfeiture." Sir John waved to his clerk. "Note that," he ordered. "Now, my lord Duke, I understand that you were yourself engaged in the recent fighting in those far waters. And in Ireland. How went it . . . ?"

Alastair came to realise, although scarcely fully taking it in, that the case was finished, that the law had spoken, his own position thus suddenly improved enormously. Not that the Macleans would ever pay, or accept the caution-imposition. But the responsibility was now theirs. The MacGregors could breathe freely again – if any others than himself and Rob Ban had taken all this seriously. What would King James say?

20

What their curious monarch had to say about all this Alastair did not hear for some time. Anyway, James Stewart had more to concern him than the MacGregor doings that winter and spring. Queen Anne's brother, the Duke Ulric of Holstein, arrived from Denmark, apparently in response to her appeals to her elder brother, King Christian, to come and aid her against her husband's unkindnesses, Ulric proving to be a rather gross young man with gargantuan appetites, especially for wine and spirits and women, indeed seldom seen sober. With the errand he came upon, James was at pains to impress him with kindnesses, hospitality and the like, and as a result life at court became an all but continuous round of banqueting, pageantry, masquerade and dissipation. Falkland and Stirling were both unsuitable for this sort of thing, and Dunfermline and Linlithgow too small, so Edinburgh and its Holyroodhouse became the venue for this all too prolonged visit, the Earl of Orkney more or less master of ceremonies, apt for the task. What Queen Anne thought of it all was not recorded; but it could hardly have come up to her expectations as improving her conditions and relationship with her spouse.

And during it all, other matters were boiling up, in especial the imposition of bishops on the Kirk, to please Elizabeth Tudor, and the Lewis colonisation venture. The King, strangely, had grown very enthusiastic about this last, and was even talking about taking charge personally, once this Ulric was gone, saying that he would supervise all from Kintyre – which seemed a long way south of Lewis for anything of the sort. However, as Ulric lingered, clearly in no hurry to return to Denmark, James decided that Ludovick must deputise for him in this matter, as in so much else, unenthusiastic as that man was.

At least there was no pressure for the MacGregors to take part, the monarch presumably washing his hands of them. The idea had started as a means of relieving hardship and distress in over-populous Fife; but now other Lowland areas were involved, although the majority of the colonists were from Fife and Fothrif. The assembling and equipping of this host took some considerable time. It would have been absurd to march all the would-be settlers and carry their worldly goods right across the width of Scotland to the Western Sea, at Dumbarton or Kintyre or elsewhere, when Fife had a dozen of its own little ports. The settlers could sail with their belongings up the east coast northwards and round through the Pentland Firth to the Hebrides much more conveniently. So James was able to supervise some of the assembling from Falkland that spring, with Duke Ulric in tow, before sending Vicky off to the west. There he was to help Argyll muster a force of armed men, in galleys again, to ensure that the colonists were able to land and settle in, despite any opposition from the local Lewismen. It was on his way to Inveraray that Ludovick was able to inform Alastair as to all this. He was not happy about the entire notion, having had some experience of the fighting qualities of the MacDonalds, MacLeods and other islesmen who, he was sure, would not take this invasion of their territories lying down. The colonists, or their leaders, were in theory to have free possession of the whole of the Isle of Lewis for seven years, holding direct from the crown; and thereafter they were to pay the King an annual rent of one hundred and forty chalders of victual, that is some one hundred thousand gallons dry measure, mainly of oats and barley presumably. Another group of Lowland lairds had offered to do the same for the Isle of Skye, more MacDonald and MacLeod land; but it had been decided, wisely, to see how the Lewis scheme went before embarking on this.

Ludovick had other news to impart. This matter of introducing bishops into the Kirk of Scotland was provoking grievous outcry and denunciation from the ministers, needless to say. The divines were declaring that it was the beginning of an attempt to bring back the Romish Church and papal domination, bishops anathema, it all being engineered by Huntly and the Catholic-inclining Queen Anne. Actually it was not, Elizabeth Tudor being behind it, she as anti-Rome as they were, and James doing this mainly to please her, to try to prove that he was the obvious and only logical successor to her throne; the Church of England, although Protestant, had bishops, so the Church of Scotland should have them also, royally appointed. James tried to point out to the angry ministers that bishops were an integral part of Christ's Church from the very beginning; and here in Scotland the original Columban Celtic Church had its bishops and abbots, at odds with Rome as it had been. But the clerics would not listen. Three bishops had been appointed so far, but were by no means being accepted by the Kirk, although the Privy Council somewhat doubtfully agreed that they should sit in parliament amongst the lords temporal.

All this scarcely affected the MacGregors, although Alastair at least realised that side-effects might reach even them. For his part, he was able to tell Ludovick that his brother John's wife had now borne him a son; so there was an eventual tanister, or heir to the chiefship of the clan. When the duke asked when Himself was going to produce his own heir, that man shrugged eloquently. He would have to find a wife first; and to satisfy him, that would be difficult indeed, with Mary Gray as the standard to measure up to!

The duke departed for Inveraray.

Strangely enough, it was from Inveraray, some six weeks later, that Alastair received his next information as to national concerns – but not from Ludovick Stewart. The Earl of Argyll himself arrived at Glen Strae, one day in mid-summer, an unheard-of event. MacCailean Mhor did not normally visit lesser men, preferring to summon them to his presence.

He was scarcely genial on arrival, but then he never was that. By his manner he was obviously not prepared to stay long – he had brought quite a troop of horsemen with him – but did not vouchsafe where he was going thereafter; Alastair wondered whether it might possibly be to one of Black Duncan's castles? Argyll and his company did accept drams and refreshment, but the impression given was that this was something of a duty call and to be got over as expeditiously as possible. Alastair wondered.

Argyll revealed that the Lewis invasion had gone reasonably well. The islemen had resisted, of course, and there had been casualties; but his own force had been sufficiently strong to overcome them, and they had thereafter seen the colonists safely settled on their new territories – although he did not envy them their task in subduing not only the Lewismen but the land itself, to peaceful productivity. He and the duke had left a fairly large contingent of Campbell men-at-arms to protect the settlers meantime, as far as possible. It was to be hoped that the project might prosper. Argyll hardly sounded enthusiastic nor optimistic.

However, this was not, obviously, what MacCailean Mhor had come to tell him, Alastair recognised. He waited.

At length it came. "Glenstrae, you owe me some service, for aid I have rendered you and yours. Now you may repay me. I have been having considerable trouble in lands of mine in Cowal, Rosneath, Rhu and Kilmun. Insurrection, failure to pay their dues, hership of my tenants. Two men in especial are behind this – Colquhoun of Luss and MacAulay of Ardencaple. I suspect that Ardkinglas acts with them, that traitorous wretch! These must be taught a lesson. I esteem you as the man to do it."

Alastair stared. "Me, my lord? Why myself? When you have thousands of Campbells at your call?"

"I have my reasons, MacGregor. This is something that *you* can do for me."

"But . . . I do not understand, whatever. Luss, Ardencaple and thereabouts Rosneath and Rhu – these are in the Lennox, not in your Cowal. Near, but not in Cowal and Argyll. The Duke of Lennox is superior of these lands, surely. He . . ."

"Precisely. The Duke and I have to work together in much. But he is not being helpful in this, as he ought to be. Weak. This is the best way."

"What do you want me to do?"

"Teach MacAulay and Colquhoun a lesson, a hard lesson. That they cannot play their games with MacCailean Mhor! Get rid of them, if need be. I will see to it that no hurt comes to you if blood has to be spilt. Ardkinglas also – if you can catch him, for he is as slippery as any eel, that one . . ."

"And one of your own Campbells!"

"Even so. He tried to poison me. Me, his chief!"

"Ardkinglas I might seek out, on your behalf, my lord. *He* is not any man of the Lennox. But Aulay MacAulay is. Colquhoun I do not know. His lands of Luss and Rossdhu are on the *west* side of Loch Lomond. Is that in Lennox or just out of it? I know not . . ."

"What matters it, man! They cause me trouble."

"I cannot take up arms against Aulay MacAulay, my lord. He is my friend."

"He is a MacGregor in truth, is he not? Only his father took the name of MacAulay. Therefore you bear some responsibility for him and his works. So I come to you."

Alastair shook his head unhappily but determinedly. "I cannot do this, my lord. I cannot go behind the back of the Duke of Lennox, who has greatly aided me. That would be treachery, base betrayal . . ."

"Because he *is* your friend you could do it, man. And put it right with him afterwards. As another could not. You he would accept. He himself should keep his folk in order. If he does not, others must."

"But not MacGregor! I owe him too much, whatever."

"You owe me, also, Glenstrae, I'd remind you!"

"I do not deny it. But . . . not turn my hand against my friends. Forby, I and my people are in no position to take arms against other folk. Any others. We were put to the horn. We still are, maybe. I know not how it goes. The King and council ever threaten us with dire pains if we break the peace, if our behaviour seems against their laws. *You* know that, as a member of the council. I cannot do this."

"You will be sorry, Glenstrae, if you do not!"

Alastair drew himself up. "You threaten me, my lord? You may be MacCailean Mhor. But I am MacGregor, Chief of Clan Alpin. Of the old royal race. Here when there was no Campbell in all Argyll! I take unkindly to threats."

They eyed each other.

The younger man shrugged. The earl was, after all, only of twenty-three years, difficult to remember by the way he acted. "So be it," he said shortly. "We shall see. I bid you good-day, Glenstrae." And turning on his heel, he strode off to his waiting company.

Alastair gazed after him, chewing his lip. One of the last things that he wanted was to make an enemy of that man. But worse was to fail his friends, to betray them. He was trapped. What was he to do?

Long thereafter he pondered. He had to do something. He did not know where Duke Ludovick was meantime, to consult. Nor Mary Gray. *She* would have advised him well. They could be anywhere – Edinburgh, Stirling, Linlithgow, Falkland, Broughty. If they were at Methven they would have let him know. Vicky might still be up in the north-west, of course.

He decided that he should go to see Aulay MacAulay. Partly to warn him of Argyll's active enmity; but also because he could then inform Argyll himself that he had sought to do something to help improve the situation – if that was not being too optimistic. Colquhoun of Luss he knew little of; and Ardkinglas was a friend of Black Duncan's. But MacAulay at least he could approach and influence.

He wasted no time. Taking Rob Ban with him only – no others, for he wanted to travel as inconspicuously as possible through country where MacGregors might not be welcome – he set off on quite a long journey. To reach Ardencaple, at the mouth of the Gare Loch in Lennox, they had to travel fully sixty difficult miles, avoiding as far as possible Glenorchy's land, and going down Loch Aweside some little way and south-eastwards across the intervening high ground to the head of Glen Shira, an empty valley amongst barren hills which led down to the head of Loch Fyne, MacNaughton country, keeping well north of Inveraray. Then round the head of that long sea-loch, the longest in all Scotland, and so, still eastwards up Glen Kinglas, so near to Ardkinglas, and over the watershed pass, under Ben Arthur, to Arrochar at the head of Loch Long. Then down the east side of Long, to the head of the Gare Loch, down near the mouth of which, opening on to the Firth of Clyde, was Ardencaple, near to Rhu. By so doing he would be in Lennox, rather than Argyll and Cowal, for much of the way.

It took them two days, stopping overnight at a shepherd's cottage in upper Glen Kinglas.

Ardencaple proved to be a quite substantial lairdship with

a good house, almost a small castle. MacAulay himself was not there when they arrived but his wife, a cheerful, motherly woman and herself of the MacGregor stock, welcomed them kindly, saying that her husband would be home by evening.

They had not long to wait. Aulay MacAulay, a big, good-looking man of middle years, was happy to see his chief for, although his name was changed, he still paid "calp", or token dues of manrent, like a lesser form of enfeoffment, to Glenstrae, as a gesture. He listened to Alastair's account of Argyll's visit and demands, grave-faced, shaking his head.

Then he explained the true situation, as regards his own position. Argyll, like all Campbells, was eager to extend his lands and power, already vast. This had to be at the expense of the Lennox territories, which bordered Cowal and Argyll on the south-east. Here were the Gare Loch properties of Ardencaple and the larger Loch Lomondside areas of Colquhoun of Luss. Both in a dangerous position inevitably. Colquhoun, in the circumstances, sought to play both sides, to keep a good relationship with his superior, the Duke of Lennox, and at the same time try to be friendly with Argyll, not with entire success. For himself, MacAulay was too near to Argyll's property of Rosneath for comfort, and he also tried not to give MacCailean Mhor cause for offence – but it was difficult, for the latter sought to cause trouble through others whilst maintaining ostensible good-neighbourliness.

Matters had deteriorated when one of his own tenants had died, leaving only a daughter who had married a Campbell and assumed the tenancy. And quite soon the husband had begun to create disharmony, and brought in other Campbells to work for him, for it was quite a large farm. And one winter night, MacAulay was waylaid and beaten up. He was certain that it was by these Campbells, and was in the nature of a threat and warning, with others of Argyll's people desiring to move in as tenants of Ardencaple land, the beginning of the end as he saw it. So he evicted his cuckoo-in-the-nest, and gave the farm to a cousin of his own.

For a little there was no reaction. Then two neighbouring lairds from beyond the Lennox, Galbraith of Culcreuch and Buchanan of that Ilk, descended in force on Ardencaple, grievously assaulted MacAulay, indeed left him for dead, and harried his property. This was some nine months ago. He had recovered and complained to the Privy Council. He could not prove that Argyll was behind it, although sure that he was. The council had fined Galbraith and Buchanan, and given him, MacAulay, certain compensation. But oddly enough Campbell of Ardkinglas, who as far as he knew had had nothing to do with it all, was ordered to find caution of ten thousand merks. Ardkinglas came to him later, from a remote property of his where he was hiding, near the head of Loch Fyne, and told him that Argyll had indeed arranged it all, and had falsely implicated himself, Ardkinglas, to the Privy Council, out of spite, and had paid the fines of Galbraith and Buchanan.

That was the situation. Obviously MacCailean Mhor was not doing all this for nothing. It looked as though he was manoeuvring to take over the western part of the Lennox and using others to effect it whilst not himself coming into open clash with the Duke of Lennox. And absurd result of it all was that the council ordered Argyll himself, as Justiciar of Argyll and Lieutenant of the North, to bring all to order in the King's name.

All but aghast by this catalogue of deceit, treachery and violence, Alastair recognised why he had been approached to aid in it all, and the danger he was undoubtedly in by refusing. The Campbell passion, almost mania, for the gaining possession of more and more lands and domination, was evidently not confined to Black Duncan. Argyll could be an even worse enemy than Glenorchy, being that much more powerful and highly placed.

Much disturbed and uneasy, Alastair set off back to Glen Strae next day, assuring Aulay MacAulay that he would try to improve the situation for him if at all possible, through the Duke of Lennox. What else he could do, he knew not. He almost felt sorry for the wretched weak Ardkinglas, used by Glenorchy and abused by Argyll.

21

Back in the seeming safety of his own mountain fastnesses, there was a distinct temptation for Alastair to do nothing, just to sit tight, until he could see Ludovick and Mary Gray, presumably at Methven. Whatever the threats against them, the MacGregors in fact could not be forcibly ejected from their remote and wild upland glens save by a major armed force, and even then with great difficulty, since there were scores of side-valleys, high passes and hidden corries where they could retire, with their beasts, all with splendid ambush places to trap invaders. This was why he always had the greatest difficulty in persuading his clansmen that they were in any danger and that the ill will of others should not be ignored – if not returned in active reprisal.

Nevertheless, he realised that this was short-sighted, and that as responsible leader of his people he had to take the longer, wider view of it all. The trouble was to know what, other than seeking the duke's guidance, he could achieve. And how to reach Ludovick and Mary, short of going away south to court, wherever that might be at present, with no certainty of finding Lennox there – and at the risk of being arrested by the King's command. He could, in fact, only wait, however impatiently.

Then, in late autumn, with no out of the ordinary events afflicting the MacGregors, the longed-for messenger arrived, to say that the duke was at Methven and that he and Mary would be happy if Himself would join them for a day or two. It was not long before Alastair was a-horse and on his way.

As ever, the reunion, after a long interval this time, was joyful, heart-warming, little six-year-old Johnnie Stewart contributing his vociferous welcome. It was a pity to dispel this happy atmosphere with current problems.

Ludovick it was, indeed, who started the dispelling, with

reporting on echoes of the Fife Adventurers scheme in Lewis. The first positive reaction of the Hebrideans to the invasion by Lowlanders had been signalled by the arrival at court of two sackfuls of heads, a dozen of them, delivered by night anonymously – the heads of leaders of the expedition, sent with MacDonald's compliments. And as news came down thereafter, it was of disaster, massacre, abandonment of settlements, the settlers giving up and coming home. James was most annoyed and offended, and inclined to blame him, Ludovick, and Argyll, for not having wiped out the wretched MacDonalds, MacLeods and the rest while they were up there. It looked as though there would be no more colonisation schemes meantime. At least the MacGregors had spared themselves this fate – although possibly, if they had been there in force, this might not have turned out quite so badly.

Alastair doubted whether his two or three hundred Gregorach would have made all that difference against the Clan Donald federation.

Anyway, the duke was going through a period of royal disfavour, since James had to have someone to blame, the fact that he had been against the scheme from the first being no excuse. Hence his being able to leave court and come here to Methven meantime – although he would have to go back to attend a parliament in two weeks' time. Mary said that she feared that it would not be long, unfortunately, before James found that he needed his useful cousin for something else, and recalled him.

Vicky added that at least it gave him time and opportunity to pay more extended visits to his inherited lands in Lennox, which he admitted he had very much neglected. Too much land and property could be a grievous responsibility, in his opinion – however differently thought Argyll!

That, of course, gave Alastair the opportunity to unburden himself. He recounted MacCailean Mhor's visit to Glen Strae, his own refusals, and subsequent trip to Ardencaple, what he had learned there, and the threat to them all from Campbell greed.

His hearers, used to plotting and double-dealing as they were, were shocked.

What to do, then? Not only the Gregorach, but Lennox himself? Could they allow Argyll to take over his lands bit by bit, whoever he used to effect it? Mary Gray answered that with a decided negative.

Ludovick was much perturbed. But he was, in essence, not a man of action, and certainly no schemer or plotter, such as clearly was required to deal with such as MacCailean Mhor. Patrick Gray would be the man for that – but Patrick was again down in England, seeking to convince Elizabeth's advisers and statesmen that she ought to end all speculation and intrigue by naming King James as her undoubted heir – which she was so manifestly reluctant to do. She had been reported as declaring that to do so would be to sign her own death-warrant, as James's scoundrelly Scots would have her assassinated promptly thereafter, so that they could take over her England. Gray's task was to dispel such fears.

If the Master of Gray was not available, at least his daughter was, with so much of her father in her. When the duke averred that he could hardly challenge Argyll, his Privy Council colleague, with all this, face to face, when it was after all only hearsay, the assertions of lesser men, with nothing that he could actually pin on the Campbell, Mary suggested that Argyll's request to Himself to raid and if necessary dispose of MacAulay and Colquhoun was something to use against him. Were these not both vassals of Lennox?

"Ardencaple is, yes – but Colquhoun is not. His lands of Luss and Rossdhu are in Lennox, yes, but he holds direct of the crown. But, anyway, Argyll would just deny it. Or claim that these two were causing trouble for *his* people. And had to be taught a lesson. That is the way he put it, was it not, Alastair? And did you not say that he declared that *I* was not keeping the Lennox men in order – and somebody had to do that? This would be his line, for sure, and hard to rebut, before the council. As I say, I have neglected my Lennox interests. They were my father's lands, and I have never felt much for them. Save for the revenues they bring me!"

Mary shook her head. "Not through the Privy Council, Vicky. That is not the way. Not how Argyll works. He is much too clever for that. He works through others. *You* will have to use his kind of weapons to beat him. Himself, too.

Wits! Argyll must have his weaknesses – use them!" She paused. "He has, yes. Weaknesses. Some of his own people. Glenorchy, and this Ardkinglas. They tried to poison him. They slew his guardian, Campbell of Cawdor. These. These, somehow, you might use to get at him. Use his enemies."

They eyed her, wonderingly.

"Black Duncan would never aid us against Argyll – never aid *me*, anyway," Alastair declared.

"No. But he has been lying low of late. That blood-bond with the MacTarlichs cost him dear. No, he would not willingly aid you. But you might be able to use *him* against Argyll. He is strong, yes – but this Ardkinglas sounds weak. And they work together, it seems. Could you not use Ardkinglas somehow?"

"How?" they both demanded.

"Let us think. There must be some way. He is a Campbell laird, whose lands march with Lennox. Did you not say, Alastair, that you went to this Ardencaple by going up Glen Kinglas and over to Arrochar? Arrochar is in Lennox, is it not, Vicky?"

"Yes. It is Colquhoun land," the duke agreed. "In Lennox, but not mine. And I would not trust Colquhoun of Luss. He is said to be too friendly with Argyll."

"It does not sound as though Argyll thought that – if he wants Himself to get rid of him! But perhaps this Colquhoun *has* to seem to be, placed as he is. If Ardkinglas and Colquhoun and this Ardencaple *did* work together, in a firm alliance, they could cause Argyll much difficulty. That is what he fears, no doubt. They would form a solid barrier all the way along Argyll's lands to the east, from Loch Fyne right down to the Gare Loch and the Clyde."

Alastair wondered at the girl having so much knowledge of the lie of these lands; but of course she would have visited the Lennox area with Ludovick.

"That might be possible," the duke agreed, guardedly. "But what of those other two, whom Argyll seems to have used against your MacAulay? Would they not act to spoil any such arrangements. Friends of Argyll."

"The Buchanan, and Galbraith of Culcreuch? They are based some distance off," Alastair said. "Both on the other side of Loch Lomond. Both in the sheriffdom of Stirling, not Perth or Lennox or Argyll. What hold MacCailean Mhor has over them I know not. Buchanan could threaten Colquhoun, yes, across Lomond. But scarcely openly, in large armed force."

"Armed force is not what we would want," Mary asserted. "We must be more clever than that! We want to prevent Argyll from encroaching on your territories, the lands of your vassals, Vicky. And to save Himself from the Campbell's ill will. It matters not to us whether somebody, this Buchanan or other, attacks Colquhoun, who is no friend of yours and no vassal. So long as these three great lairds, Ardkinglas, Colquhoun and Ardencaple, with any smaller men who can be brought in, form an alliance against Argyll's expansions towards the Lennox. Their properties do that, make a barrier, do they not? You then, Vicky, support them – as is your right and duty. Without any open clash with Argyll. He works through others – so must you. No?"

"Perhaps, my dear. But Ardkinglas is a scoundrel, and weak. And I do not trust Colquhoun."

"Does that matter? They are but tools to use. They have their lands to protect from Argyll. Use that. I see Ardkinglas as the key to it. He is in hiding from Argyll, is he not? Somewhere?"

"I have heard that he roosts in a corner of Glenorchy's land. On an island in Loch Dochart where there is a small castle which used to belong to Macnab. Near where Glen Dochart joins Strathfillan," Alastair told her.

"Then why not go to see him? Tell him of all this, that Argyll approached you to have him disposed of. That this way, with the Duke of Lennox's help, he can regain his lands. Work with Colquhoun and Ardencaple and others, to hold Argyll back."

Alastair looked doubtful. "This is all too, too cunning for me! Crafty. Guileful. Not how the Gregorach work!"

"But how the *Campbells* work! Fight them with their own weapons."

The men exchanged glances, not contradicting but scarcely convinced.

They left it at that, meantime.

Alastair enjoyed three pleasant days at Methven before returning home.

Other matters arose to preoccupy him soon thereafter, problems nearer that home. His brother John had elected to go raiding in Strathtay, lifting sundry cattle and horses and taking them back to Balquhidder, allegedly in reprisal for some injury done him by one MacLachlan. But Strathtay was Black Duncan's land, and this was indeed asking for trouble. Alastair had to go to Stronvar in Balquhidder, and all but came to blows with his unruly brother. He insisted that the beasts should be returned to their owner, and on John's refusal, took them himself. The brothers, never close, had seldom been in such disharmony. And John was tanister, heir to the chiefship.

When Alastair got back to Glen Strae it was not long before he had a visit from Ludovick and Mary. They were on their way to Lennox, and had come this round-about route with grievous news. The duke had attended the parliament, rare as these were nowadays, called by King James in order to get its authority to impose bishops on the Kirk and to give these seats in parliament and on the council – acceded to only very doubtfully by the nation's representatives. And at this session, Sir Duncan Campbell of Glenorchy had been present, commissioner for Breadalbane and Strathtay, and had surprised all – but evidently not his monarch – by proposing a motion to disallow all persons, save the representatives of the crown and the law, to carry offensive weapons, on pain of death, this to limit the shameful activities of limmers, broken men and law-breakers who were becoming increasingly bold and outrageous, especially in the Highlands, where only recently his own lands of Strathtay had been raided and ravaged. This motion had been seconded with acclaim by some, and warmly supported from the throne by James himself, and thereafter passed by a fair majority, few wishing to seem to be in favour of swordery and violence. So this was now the law, and its implications for such as the MacGregors notable indeed. So Black Duncan of the Cowl was still to be reckoned with.

The duke was much perturbed for his friend, and for others

so placed. The clause permitting the King's and law-officers' nominees to bear arms where others could not, of course allowed Argyll, Lord High Justiciar, Glenorchy a Deputy Justiciar, and their like, to arm whom they would. Most of the lords, indeed, held some office under the law, so that they were exempt, and even baronies, with their powers of pit and gallows, could claim lawful status. But few Highland clans, save the Campbells, had had their lands erected into baronies by the crown – so the Highlanders were, in theory, to be disarmed.

Alastair, for one, did not see his MacGregors ever yielding up their broadswords and dirks voluntarily – but it would be one more offence to charge them with.

Mary Gray declared that this reinforced the need to do something positive to halt the Campbells, Argyll equally with Glenorchy, for the former had voted for the measure. It was time to approach Ardkinglas and the others – all now, in theory, disarmed.

Alastair could not deny it. He would go and see Ardkinglas, little as he relished the task. Since his friends were going south to the Lennox he would accompany them as far as Crianlarich in Strathfillan, where he would branch off for Loch Dochart. He took Rob Ban with him, a useful aide, and a half-dozen running gillies, as they would have to return through Glenorchy land. They did not go unarmed.

Twelve miles up Glen Lochy to Tyndrum and another seven down Strathfillan, and Alastair left his friends. They would proceed southwards down Glen Falloch to the head of Loch Lomond and so along the lochside into Lennox, to lodge in royal Dumbarton Castle meantime, of which the duke was hereditary keeper. Also leaving the gillies at Crianlarich, so that they would not seem to threaten Ardkinglas, Alastair and Rob went on eastwards for a mile or so, under the shadows of Ben More and Am Binnein, mighty mountains, into Glen Dochart, where two smallish lochs were linked by a channel, Dochart the first, Iubhain the easternmost and larger. These lakes were in fact only a sudden widening of the River Fillan, flowing in from the west, yet the river which flowed out from the eastern one was the Dochart, curious naming. Near the head of Loch Dochart was a small islet on which rose a little castle or rather tower-house, a former seat of the Macnab, now taken over, like so much else, by Glenorchy.

There was no castleton or hamlet in evidence at the lochside, Crianlarich presumably being the local community; and although the castle was entirely evident, being only a couple of hundred yards from the shore, there was no boat to be seen. So how did one get out to it? Or attract attention? There seemed to be nothing for it but to shout, undignified for a Highland chief as this might be. Rob Ban volunteered.

No response forthcoming to his cries, although smoke was rising from chimneys out there, Alastair joined in with a variety of halloos and yells, which echoed from the surrounding braesides. Hoarse, they were almost giving up when a small boat appeared from round the back of the islet, rowed by an elderly man. This came to about seventy yards from the shore and there stopped. The oarsman called out to demand who they were and what they wanted.

Rob Ban answered. "It is MacGregor of Glenstrae. Himself. Come to speak with Campbell of Ardkinglas. In peace and good fellowship, whatever. Is Ardkinglas there?"

The rower did not reply, other than by turning the boat round and heading back whence he had come.

The horsemen waited, as patiently as they might.

It was some time before the craft reappeared, now with two men in it, one much younger. Rowed to a little nearer this time, once again it stopped well back from the shore.

"What does the MacGregor want with Ardkinglas?" That was still the old man shouting.

"A word or two, for the benefit of them both," Alastair called back.

"Ardkinglas does not see what Glenstrae can have to say to him, of benefit or otherwise, at all!"

"He will see. And hear. But hear the better if we can speak without this shouting, whatever!"

There was a pause, and then the oarsman pulled the boat nearer – but halted again about a dozen yards from the bank.

"What do you seek of me?" That was the younger man now. He was a thin, reedy individual, probably a year or two younger than Alastair, peering narrow-eyed, wary indeed, unprepossessing and slovenly dressed.

"If I sought any hurt to you, Campbell, I would come other than thus! I have come from Glen Strae to talk with you. On an important matter."

"Talk, then."

Alastair nudged Rob Ban, who spoke. "Himself does not usually talk at such a distance, Ardkinglas."

"And I do not usually talk with MacGregors, at all!" No move was made to come nearer.

Alastair shrugged. "If we cannot speak together like gentlemen, whatever, I must needs shout aloud like some cattle-dealer. Words of a vital matter which not all this land should hear!" he called. Not that there appeared to be anyone but these two in sight anywhere. "I come on a matter concerning your chief, MacCailean Mhor."

Silence.

"Also concerning the Duke of Lennox. I think that you are at present not on the best of terms with MacCailean Mhor, Ardkinglas?"

"My terms with him are no concern of yours, MacGregor."

"Be not so sure. Argyll came to me and besought me to make armed raid on you, on Colquhoun of Luss and on MacAulay of Ardencaple. If I cared, to *dispose* of you, he said! How think you of that?"

"I do not believe you."

"It is the truth. He says that you tried to poison him. You and Glenorchy. He has bided his time, whatever, to deal with you. Why think you he would act now? And why to dispose of Colquhoun and MacAulay as well as yourself? Why, think you? And now?"

No reply again.

"I can tell you, if you do not see it, man. Ardkinglas and Luss and Ardencaple properties stretch from Loch Fyne right down to the Gare Loch, forty miles. Macfarlane has some small lands amongst them, but these three form the barrier between Argyll's Cowal lands and those of the Lennox. And Argyll wants them. Wants to expand his territories eastwards. He cannot expand westwards, for there is the sea. So he wants to move into Lennox. He thinks that the duke is weak, cares little, will not withstand him. But your three large lairdships stand in his way. He would be quit of you. And have the MacGregors do it for him."

"I do not believe it, I tell you."

"You had better. For although I refused him my own self, he will find other tools. I did not believe it myself, at first. But it is true. I have just left my lord Duke of Lennox but an hour ago. He, the King's cousin, told me to come to you. To warn you, and to urge that you take steps to protect yourself and your lands and people. And these others also."

"What . . . if this is true . . . what can I do against MacCailean Mhor?"

"Do not roost here on this swan's nest of an island, man! Warn the others. Act with them. Muster your people. Show Argyll that you know what he aims at, that you are not all so easy meat!"

"If this Lennox is so concerned, let him deal with Argyll himself. The great man!"

"The duke is held in by his position. He acts Viceroy of Scotland in the King's absence. He is Lord High Chamberlain. He was Lieutenant of the North, as Argyll is now. They sit on the Privy Council together. They cannot seem to come to blows. So Argyll would use *me* and my MacGregors. These great ones work through others."

"I care nothing for the Duke of Lennox . . ."

"But you care for your own life and lands, do you not? And these others." Alastair gestured. "Can we not speak together better than this? This shouting."

"I am very well where I am, MacGregor. I can hear you."

"Then hear and heed! Warn Colquhoun. You are now wed to his sister, are you not? And both of you should work with MacAulay. And Macfarlane, if he will join you. And any others who may be threatened. Ready your people. You can keep Argyll at bay, if you act together."

"I will think on it."

"Do more than think, Ardkinglas. Argyll could use others than the MacGregors. He has already used Buchanan and Galbraith against MacAulay. These could assail you, from the east. And more than these – Drummonds, Lamonts, MacLachlans, MacArthurs, MacNaughtons . . ."

"Think you that he has not already assailed me! He had the council fine me ten thousand merks, and when I could not pay, violently debarred me from my lands, insulted my wife and beat my servants. That is why I bide here, in this hold. Glenorchy will not aid me now . . ."

"This is *his* house, is it not? One of many."

"Aye. But that is all he will do for me. Every hand is against me!"

"All the more reason to unite with Colquhoun and MacAulay, is it not? Hit back. An alliance with these, threatened also, should halt Argyll."

"Will anything halt him? With the power he has. MacCailean Mhor – he is Lieutenant of the North, Admiral of the Western Seas, he can sway the council and the King . . ."

"The King does not love Argyll. When the Master of Gray returns from England, he who acts Chancellor, he, with the Duke of Lennox, could clip Argyll's wings, I say. *You* can start the clipping, no?"

"I will think on it."

Alastair saw that he was not going to get any further with the man at this encounter. He shrugged. "Think well, then. Think too of the cost of *not* doing it. Finding the ten thousand merks is the least of it. *I* was so fined, and the duke found me cautioners. Do you have any such?"

The other only scowled.

"Argyll no doubt wants you to sell your lands to him, to pay the fine. Is that what you would rather do, whatever?" Alastair raised a hand in farewell – a gesture not returned – as he and Rob Ban reined round and rode off.

By no stretch of the imagination could that be considered a satisfactory interview. But he did not see how he could have bettered it. The man was feeble, untrustworthy and a coward. But he was trapped, and here was a way that he might get out of it. On due consideration he might recognise his opportunity.

Back at Crianlarich they picked up the gillies and turned for home. Alastair could see no point in proceeding on to visit Colquhoun. That man's clan and his own were traditional enemies, almost at feud, although there had been no major hostilities during *his* years of chiefship, apart from some petty raiding perhaps by the Glengyle MacGregors. Better to leave this to MacAulay, whom the duke said that he would speak with. He had done all that he usefully could, at this stage.

22

Up until the turn of the century, the months were uneventful, save that John Galt MacGregor did some more raiding, on a petty scale admittedly, but on Menzies land this time and Alastair had again to smooth things over and to order his brother to punish the offender. Then Ludovick and Mary came back to Methven for their usual Christmas break – and brought ill tidings.

The seeming calm had been superficial. Argyll had not forgotten his rebuff by Alastair over the Ardkinglas-Colquhoun-Ardencaple raiding, and had complained to the Privy Council that the MacGregors were still misbehaving, out-of-hand and a menace to all law-abiding folk, and demanding sanctions against them. Ludovick had stood up for them as best he could, but Argyll's claim that the Gregorach were rejecting the Disarming Act told against them. There were claimants for drastic action, even the death penalty. There was no point in imposing further fines, which Alastair could by no means pay. The best that the duke could do for him was to agree that he should produce three hostages, to be detained during the King's pleasure at Stirling and who could be executed if there was further MacGregor raiding; and for the three previous cautioners, including himself, to promise a sum further in earnest of good behaviour. So, he feared that Himself must produce three of his clansmen, of some standing, to send as hostages meantime, and fairly promptly. It was only at Lennox's own pressure that Himself was not taken into custody, as Argyll had urged.

Needless to say this greatly concerned them all. Almost, Alastair would have preferred to be a hostage again himself, than to condemn others to that fate. After all, it had not been so unhappy an experience on the previous occasion, although he had been then required only to be installed at court, whereas the three now demanded were to be held at

Stirling Castle, very different. But one thing was sure – John Galt MacGregor would be one of them.

Alastair was sorry about the cautioners' involvement again, the duke, Tullibardine and Inchaffray; but after all, they had not actually had to pay out any moneys, only to guarantee it if required, so Ludovick was able to brush that aside.

Mary said that they had heard nothing of any move by Ardkinglas and Colquhoun, as yet. Of course mid-winter was not the best time to take such action as they urged. She and Vicky were interested to hear about Alastair's unfriendly reception by Ardkinglas, but hoped that self-interest would impel that unsavoury individual to do something about it nevertheless.

They had news of a different sort to impart. The Master of Gray had come back from England, to inform that Queen Elizabeth was ailing. Her spirit was still strong and obstinate, but she had largely taken to her bed and was ruling her kingdom, after a fashion, from there, her health obviously failing. This, needless to say, gave additional urgency to negotiations as to the succession. There were really only the two likely contenders who would be acceptable: James and his cousin, Arabella Stewart, the daughter of Darnley's brother who had become Earl of Lennox before he died, and whose earldom, advanced to a dukedom, had been conferred thereafter on Ludovick's father. They were both great-grandchildren of Henry the Eighth, Elizabeth's father. This Arabella had been brought up in England and France and was unknown in Scotland, James never even having met her. He was of course outraged that there could be any suggestion of her superseding him as heir to England; but Elizabeth, who was not fond of her, nevertheless might well have a leaning towards being succeeded by another woman. And not a few of her advisers were against the idea of a Scottish king taking over in their England. So Patrick Gray was not having an easy time of it in London, and had come home to urge more backing-up, a larger and distinguished embassage. He was being sent south again, with some supporting lords, but James was now talking of sending Ludovick himself to Elizabeth, as his personal representative and cousin. Ludovick did not want to have to go, but might have no option.

This concerned Alastair also, of course, for if both the duke and the Master, his friends, were away in England, his position would be much the weaker. And now he had Argyll *and* Black Duncan against him, even if they were enemies of each other.

Court news was not particularly interesting, to Alastair at any rate. The Queen was pregnant again, and the King was seeing much of a youth called John Ramsay, who was thought to share the royal bed on occasion. The Earl of Mar, with whom James had always been friendly – they had been more or less brought up together, both pupils of George Buchanan, and the earl's mother the royal foster-mother – was now keeper of Stirling Castle; but Mar's younger brother, Sir Thomas Erskine, was exerting a greater influence on the monarch, which did not please Ludovick, for Erskine was a strong but unscrupulous character, and James all too readily led astray. The young Earl of Gowrie was back in Scotland, from Padua, and although not frequently seen at court was, perhaps naturally if not altogether wisely, requesting the repayment of the eighty-five thousand pounds lent to the King by his father, intimating that he would not press for payment of interest however. There was word that Glenorchy had bought large lands in Menteith from Balfour of Boghall – just why he was moving now so far southwards was not clear, but evidently his ambitions were nowise abated. And he was making good use of all his lands, actually improving them, going in for drainage, reclamation of moorland, tree-planting and so on; also encouraging his tenants to farm better and produce more. It was even suggested that he was aiming to be richer and more powerful than MacCailean Mhor himself, and possibly seeking to take over the leadership of Clan Campbell. None of which was calculated to cheer Alastair MacGregor.

When the friends parted, Ludovick advised Himself not to delay too long in sending his three hostages to Stirling, certainly before the next scheduled meeting of the Privy Council, set for April. And by all means possible to keep his clansmen in order. Which was excellent counsel, to be sure – but not so easy to follow, with the Gregorach to handle.

It was March before Alastair managed to effect the so difficult task of persuading his people that hostages were necessary, and of selecting the three individuals and convincing them that they had to go, for the sake of all. It so happened that all three were named John, or Iain the Gaelic equivalent: John Galt MacGregor, who certainly deserved the role and was given no option; John Dubh MacEwan MacGregor; and John Patrick MacGregor. These were assured that their ordeal would not be for over-long, and that they would be replaced by others if the council insisted on a hostage situation. It was that, or the whole clan being put to the horn again, and with this Disarming Act in force, becoming more or less besieged. The Glen Strae and Roro regions might hold out; but the lesser septs in Balquhidder, Glengyle, Loch Lomondside and Rannoch almost certainly would fall. This of hostages was much the lesser of the evils.

Alastair decided that he must himself accompany the trio to Stirling, the least that he could do. There was a certain risk in so doing, he recognised, in that whoever received the hostages might judge that having got Himself, the chief, into their hands was an added security, and so detain him also. And they could not go armed, to resist anything such.

So, with Rob Ban again, the three set out, a not very happy group, to pick up John Galt at Balquhidder in the by-going. From there they could make Stirling in a day. They stayed the night with brother John at Stronvar – who strongly disapproved of the entire proceeding, saying that *he* would never have agreed to this of hostages; let the wretched Lowlanders do what they would. Nor would he accept any disarming, whatever the King and council said. Clearly he judged Alastair soft, feeble. Would John have made a better chief?

At Stirling they climbed the steep, narrow streets of the town to the great fortress on its rock, the strongest in all the land. At the gatehouse, eyed with unconcealed mockery by the guards, as Highlandmen, they were kept waiting for an unconscionable time before they were admitted, and conducted, like felons, up to the handsome palace-block, built by the King's grandfather and, shut in an ante-room there, left to kick their heels. No Highland hospitality here.

At length the door was opened and a heavily built man of little more than Alastair's own years came in, flanked by armed attendants, to look them up and down less than welcomingly, wordless.

Alastair drew himself up, chin raised. He knew this man, and did not like him.

"Glenstrae, my lord," he said stiffly. "I give you good-day. And bring you these three friends of mine, as requested by His Grace."

The other hooted. "*Requested* by His Grace! Prisoners, commanded into my custody, mair like! As you all should be, I swear! Or, better still, hangit!"

The MacGregor exchanged glances, hands reaching down for where their dirks should have been had they not come carefully unarmed. John Erskine, Earl of Mar, keeper of Stirling Castle, was a tough, not to say coarse, character, all but a foster-brother of James, reared together here in this castle by the stern George Buchanan, who had whipped them indiscriminately for every fault and failing. James had been the more rewarding pupil undoubtedly, his remarkable erudition and command of languages not achieved by Mar, although both always affected the braid Scots speech.

"Your humour, my lord, is all your own, whatever!" Alastair said levelly. "My instructions were to put my friends in your care here for three months or so, in token of our acceptance of His Grace's policies as regards the clan. Assured of their good care and comfort while they are with you."

"Guid care and comfort! Sakes, Hielantman, are you gone clean gyte! These are prisoners, to be held."

"Not according to my lord Duke of Lennox, who gave me His Grace's instructions, sir."

"Lennox? Ooh, aye – him! Och weel, your friend Lennox has mair on his mind than MacGregor caterans these days! He'll be ower occupied wi' yon Jeannie Campbell, to consairn himsel' wi' the likes o' you!"

"Campbell? Jean Campbell?" Alastair blinked. "What mean you? Who . . . what is this?"

Mar grinned. "You havena heard, then, up in your barbarous Hielants? Our Vicky Stewart's wed again. To Jeannie Campbell, that was Mistress o' Eglinton, Campbell o' Loudoun's daughter. Nae mair than two weeks past."

"I do not believe it! You cozen us!"

The earl frowned. "I dinna waste my time cozening the likes o' you, MacGregor! He married – by royal command."

"But – what of Mary? The Lady Mary Gray?"

"His bit doxy! Ooh, she'll hae to mak the best o' it. He'll just hae to tak her on the side, noo and then! As Jeannie Campbell will dae, nae doubt, wi' her ain paramours!"

Alastair stared. "This I cannot credit, at all!" he said.

"It matters little whether you credit it or no', Hielantman. It's true. Jamie ordered it so. For guid reason, nae doubt. Lennox had nae choice. He's o' the royal blood, so his marriage is in the king's hands, whether he likes it or no'."

"Wed! Ludovick! And to a Campbell!" Alastair swallowed. "Who, who persuaded the King to do this?"

"Guid kens! But I'm no' here to chaffer talk wi' the likes o' you." Mar turned. "Tak these awa'," he told his attendants. "Four is it? I was tell't three."

"Rob Ban MacGregor is my uncle. He returns with me. The others are Gregorach gentlemen, one my cousin. Treat them well, my lord – if His Grace, and yourself, desire no trouble from my people!"

"What do you mean by that, man?"

"I mean that the Erskine lands of Cardross and Gartrenich in Menteith are none so far from MacGregor lands to the north! It would be a pity, whatever, if anything was to spoil . . . good relations!"

Mar clenched fists, glared, but said nothing. Swinging on his heel, he gestured for his henchmen to take over, and stalked out and off.

Alastair and Rob shook hands with their distinctly apprehensive clansmen, assuring them that they would not be forgotten nor left in durance for over-long, that the whole clan would rise if they were mistreated.

The news of the duke's remarriage, needless to say, had come as a great shock to Alastair, who still could scarcely believe it, the effect on Mary Gray in especial troubling him. He decided to risk going back by Falkland, where he ascertained the court was at present, to try to discover the facts of the matter.

So they rode along the north side of the ever-widening Forth eastwards to Dunfermline, where they passed the night, and then northwards round the Lomond Hills of Fife, familiar ground now, to Falkland. They made for the Master of Gray's lodging, as usual, wondering whom they would find there.

It was the Lady Marie who greeted Alastair, and as warmly as ever. There was no sign of Mary Gray.

It did not take Alastair long to ask his questions, his hostess most clearly troubled by having to answer them. It was all a folly, she declared, a miserable piece of manipulating on James's part. Vicky was forced into it, James making the marriage a royal command, declaring that being of the blood-royal, the duke's marital state was of vital concern, and at his disposal; for if his own two infant children were to die, as infants so often did, Vicky would be heir to the throne and his offspring in the succession, his *legitimate* offspring – and, God willing, not only to Scotland's crown but to England's also. So he had to be properly married, and not to any bastard like Mary, but to an heiress of notable line who, after all, might one day be a queen. Why the Lady Jean Campbell should have been chosen was unclear to Marie, widow of the Earl of Eglinton's heir; but the fact that she was a Campbell was probably significant. Ludovick had stood out hotly, furious, but James had threatened imprisonment, and that they would be wed in prison if necessary, whether he agreed or not. Vicky had declared, as before, that he wanted to marry Mary Gray, but James had again promised annulment of any such union and, moreover, imprisonment of Mary also should it be attempted. So the thing had gone ahead, wretched nuptials as it had been.

It was at this stage that the unwilling bridegroom appeared, come back early from the inevitable hunting. The duke was set-faced, sour for him, and welcomed Alastair's presence less genially than usual, clearly an unhappy man, almost guilty-seeming. Before ever his visitor could broach the subject, he launched into a somewhat incoherent diatribe.

"I am the most accursed of men!" he all but shouted. "Forced into a shameful marriage. By my fool of a cousin! Wed to a woman I know naught of – save that she lives loosely. All but at dirk-point! For what? For nothing. That or be imprisoned. And separated from Mary. She also to be imprisoned. I tell you, it is beyond all belief. James run mad! I, I am accursed!"

"Do not take it so hard, Vicky," the Lady Marie urged. "You could do no other than obey. And this way, you can at least still see Mary . . ."

"And where is she? Gone! Gone back to Davy Gray. At Castle Huntly. Hating me, belike!"

"No, no, Vicky! Mary loves you – will always love you. She understands, I swear. But she is best with Davy, who brought her up." She turned to Alastair. "Davy Gray is Patrick's elder brother, illegitimate. Who reared Mary when my husband, young, did not acknowledge her as his . . ."

"She should have gone to Methven! Methven is hers. I put it all in Johnnie's name. So that whatever happened to me it would always be hers. When I was wed to Sophia Ruthven, who died – if you can call that wed! She should be there, not at Castle Huntly. She, she fled. Mary fled!"

"It is best, meantime. With little Johnnie. The time will come, Vicky."

"And I must remain here, with James, that slobbering fool! Was there ever such madness . . .!"

Alastair managed to get a word in. "And this . . . lady? The new wife. What of her?"

"Who knows? Or cares? Gone also, now. She is nothing to me, I tell you."

"She is now your lawful wife, nevertheless, Vicky," Marie reminded. "You have *some* responsibility for her. She is gone back to her father, meantime. Campbell of Loudoun, in Ayrshire. I think that she was no more eager than you were for this match."

"She has a name for sleeping with whom she will . . ."

"Is there not some advantage for you, in that? Looked at frankly? If she can take other partners, so can you. She will not decry you for continuing to live with Mary, on occasion. She will be Duchess of Lennox, yes, but in all other matters Mary will be as your wife. And Mary could never have been duchess – that would never have been permitted. And she always knew it."

Ludovick glared at them both, a man trapped by his birth and blood.

"What advantage does the King gain from this marriage?" Alastair asked. "To a Campbell! There must be some reason for it."

"Lord knows! But . . . Loudoun is rich. He may have paid James siller! James is ever short of money. And now the young Gowrie is asking for his father's eighty-five thousand pounds back! It could be that. Loudoun paying for his daughter to be the only duchess in Scotland!"

"You do not think that Black Duncan could have had anything to do with it, whatever? Or Argyll himself? A Campbell! If the lady has a child by you, it will be half a Campbell! That could . . . constrain you, could it not?" Alastair put that to him almost diffidently.

"I do not know. It is all crazy . . ."

The Lady Marie tactfully changed the subject. "Himself has been placing his MacGregor hostages in Stirling Castle. He tells me that Mar was less than friendly."

"That I can believe. But they will not be maltreated. I will send strong word."

"How long, think you, that they must remain there?" Alastair asked.

"Who knows? James may well lose interest in them. Or change his mind. Let them bide for three or four months. And if he still demands hostages, change them for others."

"Yes. So I intended. I have heard of no move by Ardkinglas and the Colquhoun. Have you?"

"No. MacAulay was to send me word if anything happened. He has not done so."

"I fear that nothing will come of it all. Ardkinglas skulking on his island. A sorry creature!"

"Yes." Obviously the duke's mind was not really on other matters than his situation vis-à-vis Mary Gray. "I will go see her. Mary. At Castle Huntly. Whatever James says . . ."

"Do that, yes," Marie agreed. "Explain that it will be little different from before when you were wed to Sophia Ruthven. In name only. Tell her she must go to Methven with Johnnie. That is where she belongs. Go to her there, whenever you can. This other woman never taken there."

"Yes. And *I* will visit her often at Methven," Alastair put in, almost too eagerly. "She will be very well there."

260

Ludovick nodded, and they left it at that.

The MacGregors slipped away before sun-up next morning, in the hope that their odd monarch would not hear of their visit.

Whatever sort of a summer the unfortunate hostages passed in Stirling Castle, and however trying and frustrating it was for Ludovick Stewart, it proved quite a satisfactory one for Alastair MacGregor. For in early June the Methven steward arrived at Stronmilchan to say that his Lady Mary Gray was now in residence at her castle and would be happy to see Himself when he found it convenient to visit. Himself was preparing to ride almost before that message was completed, and indeed went back to Strathearn with the messenger.

There was a particularly moving and emotional reunion thereafter, the man showing less restraint than he usually achieved with this young woman, and Mary herself responding with frankest affection and pleasure to his embraces and kisses. They undoubtedly felt the need for each other, in the circumstances.

It all came pouring out from the girl, even while he held her, the shame of it, the mean unkindness of James, who, she said, still harboured suspicions anent Vicky and the Queen, absurd as this was; the heart-burning she had suffered, and Vicky too, the sheer folly of it all. She told how Vicky had come to Castle Huntly, that she had been perhaps less kind and understanding to him than she should have been, but how he had persuaded her to come here, to live permanently at Methven with little Johnnie, and he would join them as often as he could. No more court life for her. She was finished with all that.

Nodding, wordless, he clutched her.

Later, strolling in the orchard, with the cuckoos calling hauntingly from the trees of the little loch below, she gave him more details.

"The Lady Jean, Mistress of Eglinton, was known at court," she explained. "Oh, she is attractive, yes – and generous with her attractions! Even while her husband was alive. But perhaps I wrong her? She is older than Vicky. Why James chose her, I do not know. But her father, Campbell of Loudoun, is very rich. *His* father married a great heiress. It may be that his daughter was sold! Not to Vicky – to James! Buying her way into the blood-royal! And James ever in debt. It could be that."

"Yes. But I keep thinking that Black Duncan is behind it, somehow. There must be other heiresses and rich brides in the land, other than Campbells! It seems so . . . like the man. Is the King seeing much of him, these days? Glenorchy?"

"I do not know. I have been less and less at court. And with my father so much away in London, I do not hear of what goes on behind the curtains. But I do know that James admires what Glenorchy does on his wide lands – the enriching of the ground, the tree-planting, the drainage and the like. He says that other lords and lairds should do the like. And, of course, Glenorchy is very rich also. So . . ."

"Aye! That, too. Why is the King ever so short of moneys?"

"He wastes his riches. He pays his young favourites. Gives them his lands. Keeps up all these hunting-places. Has so many huntsmen, falconers, horses. And the Queen is extravagant, loves jewellery. Always in debt to Geordie Heriot, the Edinburgh goldsmith and banker. James was never truly rich, for a King. His grandsire, James the Fifth, wasted the royal substance; and his mother, Mary, had so much taken from her . . ."

"So Black Duncan could also be *buying* James's favours – and demanding his price! To avenge himself on Vicky. And weakening me, therefore, and the Gregorach."

"It could be. Poor Vicky – he is hating it all. I am sorry for him more than for myself. Sorry for Jean Campbell too; this was not *her* doing, of that I am sure. She is no hard, scheming woman. Married thus, only in name."

"You must wish, often, that your father, the Master, had acknowledged you as his. Wed your mother. Then you would have been legitimate, the daughter of the future Lord Gray. And could have wed Vicky and become his duchess."

"Ye-e-es." She did not sound altogether convinced of that. "But Davy Gray, who is not my true father, has *been* father to me, always, so good and kind and strong. I love him dearly. Patrick could never have been like Davy. I would not wish to have been without Davy as father to me. He reared me, taught me, loved me. We are still very close. As we would not have been had Patrick married my mother."

"This Davy – he is closer than your mother?"

"He is, yes."

Young Johnnie came running, clutching a kitten, and further confidences were postponed meantime.

Alastair spent three happy days at Methven before going home. He promised to return frequently, and Mary offered no discouragement. Theirs was a curious relationship. The young woman's obviously whole-hearted love for Ludovick Stewart did not prevent her as evident affection for their mutual friend. And it was scarcely a platonic association, for she showed herself to be very much a woman towards him, and he was not good at hiding his almost adoration. But their varied strengths of character prevailed, and they realised much satisfaction with each other without betraying Vicky. Whether Alastair, for his part, could keep this up indefinitely . . .?

23

The fourth of his visits, in mid-August, coincided with one of Ludovick's own. The duke was in much better spirits, and full of news. He seemed to have come to a working relationship with his new wife, each agreeing discreetly to go their own way. The duchess had become a lady-in-waiting to the Queen, and since Anne and James seldom occupied the same palace, this suited the other couple well enough.

There was further talk of Ludovick being sent to London, to support the Master's efforts. He still was reluctant, especially to be so far from Mary for some indefinite period; but at least it would ease the marriage situation. Elizabeth Tudor was still all but bed-bound, it seemed, but stubbornly refusing to settle the succession. What James thought *he* could do in the matter, the duke did not know.

But the most exciting news he brought was of an extra-ordinary affair of the court. The Earl of Gowrie was dead, and his brother with him, and the great Ruthven estates confiscated to the crown, the debt of eighty-five thousand pounds conveniently cancelled.

It had happened thus, almost unbelievably. Earlier in the month, while as usual hunting at Falkland, James had suddenly announced that he must go to St John's Town of Perth, where a man was awaiting him with a pot of gold. Why the man could not bring it to Falkland was not intimated. If this altogether seemed an unlikely story, to say the least, the King did not deem it so. A select party of courtiers had set out for Perth, Ludovick included, a lengthy ride of about twenty-five miles. At that city, they went straight to Gowrie House, the Ruthven town-lodging – the earl being hereditary Provost of Perth – and were there entertained, after a fashion, by that surprised individual and his brother Sandy Ruthven. There was no sign of any character with a pot of gold. Presently, James, with Sir Thomas Erskine and young John Ramsay the present favourite, went up with the earl and his brother to the topmost tower-room of the house, presumably to investigate the gold story, while the others were being refreshed in the garden below. And after a little while, the shutters of a window up there were thrown open and the King's head and shoulders appeared, to shout out that he was being murdered. There was, of course, a concerted rush up the winding turnpike stair to reach the room, the duke leading, to find the door locked, evidently from the inside, cries from within. It took some time to smash the door down, and when they all surged in it was to find the earl and his brother dead on the floor, James unhurt but babbling, being soothed by Erskine, and young Ramsay still with a bloodstained dirk in his hand. Explanations were incoherent, but it seemed that the Ruthven brothers had demanded their moneys from the King and when he could not provide it, attacked him, Ramsay and Erskine gallantly coming to his aid and slaying the miscreants. Ludovick for one doubted the accuracy of this account, especially as the only weapon in the room appeared to be Ramsay's dagger. There was no sign of any gold – only blood. The King's physician, Hugh Herries, who was with the party, pronounced the Ruthven brothers dead.

This quite singular situation was soon added to by another. Servants must have carried the news of their Provost's death to the townsfolk, for presently the street outside was filled with a yelling mob demanding the King and shouting, "Come down, thou son of Signor Davie, come down!" – a reference to the commonly held belief that James was a son, not of Darnley, Queen Mary's second husband, but of her Italian secretary, David Rizzio, an issue on which Ludovick, for one, reserved judgment. The house all but surrounded by the angry crowd, King and company had managed to escape only with difficulty, and lack of dignity, by climbing over the garden wall and across the Tay in a boat, while Tullibardine, who lived nearby, summoned, kept the townsfolk at bay.

And out of all this, Sir Thomas Erskine, whom Vicky thought had probably engineered the entire affair, was now made Earl of Kellie and given large swathes of the Ruthven lands, young Ramsay was knighted, and physician Herries likewise – possibly to keep them quiet as to details. The wealthy Ruthven family was to be trodden into the ground – and eighty-five thousand pounds no longer owed.

The duke's hearers could scarcely believe their ears. Only to James the Sixth could such a happening be attributed.

So court and nobility were set by the ears. If James could actually have one of his earls assassinated before his very eyes, to avoid payment of a debt, what else might he be capable of towards any who might offend? It was an alarming thought.

Alastair did not fail to take note.

He asked about his hostages. He had been sent no instructions as to bringing them home, or exchanging them for others. Had Vicky any information? The duke admitted that he had none, his preoccupations being apt to be elsewhere at present. The council had not met recently and he had not seen Mar. Perhaps those three unfortunates at Stirling should be replaced voluntarily, as it were. They had no doubt had more than enough of incarceration. Thus give a good impression.

Alastair agreed. But should *he* go with them again, with the new hostages? If the King could have the Earl of Gowrie and brother slain, on a mere false story, what might he not do to the chief of the turbulent MacGregors, if he could lay hands on him?

Ludovick admitted that it might be unwise to risk putting himself personally into James's hands. Why not send the new hostages under his brother? Let that one do something to earn his position as tanister of the clan? No, himself not to go meantime. Especially as it looked as though he, Ludovick, indeed going to be sent south over the succession negotiations. He had, in fact, snatched this opportunity to come to Methven beforehand, for James was talking of it as necessary soon.

Mary was concerned at this last, and hoped that, if Vicky could not get out of it, he would see that he was not away for long. He assured her that he would not stay in England one day longer than he had to.

There was much well-wishing, on all sides, when Alastair left, the future looking distinctly uncertain.

Strangely, only ten days later, Alastair had more advice on the subject of his hostages – and from none other than MacCailean

Mhor. He did not come to Glen Strae himself this time, but sent the new Campbell of Auchenbreck. His message was that the council was indeed demanding three replacement hostages, and was allowing the present trio to return home. Glenstrae himself to appear with the newcomers. Argyll's counsel was *not* to accompany the new men. He believed that this was merely a ruse to get the chief himself into the council's hands, to be imprisoned. Indeed, he very much doubted if this replacement should be proceeded with, in the circumstances – who could tell what might happen to any sent? After the present hostages returned, inactivity was probably the wisest course. The word was that Queen Elizabeth Tudor was very ill. If she died, King James would be off to London to claim her throne without delay, and the situation in Scotland completely changed, in all probability, for the MacGregors as all others. MacCailean Mhor advised inactivity meantime.

Alastair pondered this. Why was Argyll suddenly taking such interest in him and his? Especially after his refusal to assail Colquhoun and the rest. This did not seem to be in character for MacCailean Mhor. Yet the advice more or less coincided with Ludovick's. If the three from Stirling were indeed to be sent home, his own inclination also would be to temporise, to put off replacing them, if at all, and certainly not to accompany any new men.

He took the matter to Mary Gray at Methven, recent as his last visit there had been. She also wondered at this unexpected evidence of goodwill on Argyll's part, and suspected Campbell self-interest somewhere. But Vicky had also said not to go to Stirling in person, although he had not recommended no more hostages. She thought that Alastair should wait and see what the returning three had to say about their treatment. Vicky might well also send more word, if there had been a council meeting. It was now September and winter would soon be upon them, when the Highland glens were largely cut off from the Lowlands, and there would be time for reflection and decisions . . .

However, circumstances changed all that, only a week or two later, when another unexpected visitor arrived at Glen Strae: Sir John Murray of Tullibardine, one of Alastair's guarantors, a hearty, friendly character, but not now in his most friendly mood. He came, in fact, protestingly and much upset, from his Perthshire seat, to Alastair's distress.

Why had he not come with the new hostages, as the council commanded, he charged? He had been given until mid-month, and had not appeared. As a result, he and his clan were put to the horn again, and Inchaffray and himself, Tullibardine, had been fined, made to pay up the ten thousand and five thousand merks – the Duke of Lennox was away in London. Ten thousand merks! Six thousand six hundred pounds! What sort of gratitude was that?

Bewildered, Alastair stared at him. How could that be, he demanded? He had had no commands from the council. He was awaiting the return of the three hostages, yes. Before submitting more . . .

"You were not informed?" Tullibardine wondered. "No instructions came? From the council?"

"None. When the duke was last here, or at Methven, there had been no council meeting. Argyll sent a message . . ."

"He did? Then you *must* have known, man!"

"No. That was some time back. No instructions to appear. Nothing from the council. Indeed Argyll advising . . . otherwise!"

"You say so!"

"Yes. He thought that it would be wiser not to appear. At Stirling, or otherwise."

"M'mm. Argyll said that? Man, I do not like this!"

"What means it, think you, Sir John?"

"I am not sure. Argyll was at the council, I was told . . ."

"And the duke was not? Nor the Master of Gray?"

"No. Both gone south to London."

"So-o-o! You say that we are put to the horn again? The whole clan, whatever?"

"Yes. Anyone seeing any of your people is entitled to slay them! As outlaws. Men, women, bairns . . .!"

"No, no! This must not be! For *my* fault. Or on my behalf. It must not be."

The other looked at him, silent.

"And you? You have had to pay the ten thousand merks? You, and Inchaffray. Not just promised it?"

"We have paid, yes. The council's orders."

"Then . . . then my road is clear! I must go. Go to the council. To Stirling. Or to Edinburgh, or wherever. Yield myself up. I cannot pay your fines, Sir John. Paid by you in my cause. But this I can do. And lift the curse of outlawry from my people. Whatever the Campbell may advise."

Tullibardine inclined his head. Obviously this is what he had come to urge.

"You will spend the night here, Sir John, and tomorrow I will ride south with you. If you will go by Methven, I will tell the Lady Mary."

With Tullibardine and his men, Alastair rode up through the tourney-ground to the frowning gatehouse of Edinburgh Castle three days later, and was there handed over to the care of the deputy keeper, one Sir William Hamilton. He parted from his escort on friendly terms, considering the circumstances; indeed Sir John had been amiable throughout, his main complaint having been against King James, whom he felt should have stepped in to absolve him from any responsibility and penalty in the matter, especially after he, Tullibardine, had helped to rescue the monarch from the Perth mob at the strange affair at Gowrie House. Sir John declared that he would now inform the clerk to the Privy Council of the situation, and hoped that a reasonably satisfactory outcome would be realised. It was a pity that the Duke of Lennox, who was now Lord President of the Council, should be away. That, Alastair thought, was putting it mildly.

He was taken to a small room in an angle-tower perched on the cliff-edge, sparsely furnished but not exactly a prison cell – and with a magnificent prospect out over the Nor' Loch, all the Lothian coast, the Firth of Forth and the green hills of Fife beyond; even, if he peered, the shadowy blue outline of his own Highland mountains.

He composed himself to wait.

For a man used to the far-flung immensity of those mountains and valleys, the space of the wild places, his constrictions in that little tower made of it a very long wait indeed. Day after day of confinement, with the vistas almost emphasising the narrowness of the enclosing walls and the enforced inaction of his person. Control himself as he would, he fretted and fumed — that is, for the first few days, until he sank into a kind of lethargy, a protective torpor for the preservation of his wits, even his wide-ranging thoughts and dreams, in which Mary Gray featured prominently, tending to fade into a vague background. He was adequately fed and his physical wants attended to, but otherwise left entirely to himself.

A whole year passed before he had any visitor other than what amounted to his gaoler — and this none other than MacCailean Mhor himself, who arrived unannounced and alone. The door shut behind him, the two men stared at each other, silent.

"So, Glenstrae, we meet again," Argyll said, at length. "I have come far to see you. Although, perhaps I should no longer call you Glenstrae. Since you are no longer that!"

"How say you that? Even *you*!"

"Because you no longer possess Glen Strae. Your people are no longer there. They have been driven out. Are taken to the hills and forests. They are gone."

Alastair swallowed, speechless.

"So, MacGregor, you and yours pay the price of perfidy and ingratitude! You are lost, all of you. Unless . . . unless *I*, whom you have injured, save you!"

"This, this cannot be!"

"I say that it is truth. You are finished, MacGregor, you and your people. Driven out. Glenorchy, on the Privy Council's orders, and with the aid of others, has emptied your glens, taken over Stronmilchan, and the rest dispersed. Finished. Unless . . ."

Clenching his fists, Alastair swallowed, wordless.

"Your friends in high places are gone. Far away. I alone can save you now, MacGregor. If I am so inclined! After your infamy towards me. Your treachery."

"Infamy? What infamy? What treachery?"

"Do not pretend, sirrah! You know very well. Colquhoun of Luss, wretch although he is, came to me. To tell me. That other scoundrel, Ardkinglas, told *him*. How you had come to him, Ardkinglas, and proposed that he, Colquhoun and MacAulay leagued against *me*! Form a federation of rogues to injure me, to strike at my back, to betray me,

MacCailean Mhor! Dastards! And *you* urged it. Can you deny it?"

Alastair hesitated, as well he might. "I . . . I did not betray you. I but said that these should act as a barrier. Their lands. Between your lands and those of the Duke of Lennox. He fears that you may seek to extend your lands eastwards. You have done so already, have you not? Into the Lennox territories. With Black Duncan coming down from the north into Menteith, Lennox threatened. But – these three lairds' lands lie between. They could act, not *against* you, but to keep Lennox secure."

"That is not what Colquhoun said, MacGregor. He said that they were to league in arms against me. And he *has* the arms! He has gained the council's permission to ignore this Disarming Act. The Colquhouns and their friends now go armed, where others may not. This to bring *you*, the MacGregors, to order. It was these who aided Glenorchy to overrun Glen Strae and the rest."

"Dear God! The council did that? Colquhoun!"

"You are at the horn. Outlawed. Somebody had to carry into effect the council's will. Colquhoun and the Macfarlanes were so chosen."

"Chosen! I, I . . ." Alastair could not continue.

"So, you are finished, MacGregor. Imprisoned here yourself. Your clan scattered. Landless. All lost. You could be executed tomorrow. Unless . . ."

Tight-lipped Alastair eyed his visitor.

"Only I can save you now," Argyll reiterated. "I, whom you have so grievously injured."

Silence.

"You do not deserve it. But I think that I could. If you will, in turn, give me some assistance."

"How can I? Here?"

"Not here. I can win you out of this castle, I believe. Into my care. As Lieutenant of the North. Take you back to your glens – or what *were* your glens."

"And . . . the price?"

"Your aid against the dastards Colquhoun and Ardkinglas."

"Aid?"

"Aid, yes. They must be taught what it costs to conspire

against MacCailean Mhor! Colquhoun came to tell me, yes —
but that does not make him any less my enemy. That was but
to curry favour. And to betray Ardkinglas and Ardencaple. He
still endangers me, and my interests. Placed where he is. And
the man he is. I want him taught a lesson. Ardkinglas also.
I care naught about MacAulay of Ardencaple. *You* can deal
with him. He is a MacGregor in all but name."

"How am I to deal with him? Or any of them? In my
present state."

"Use your wits, man. Do you not see it? This Disarming
Act. Colquhoun and his allied Macfarlanes are permitted to
carry arms, to deal with *you*! All others forbidden them. But
who has defied the Act? Your MacGregors! You, and you
alone, could assail and punish Colquhoun as he deserves. *I*
cannot, as a member of the council and Lieutenant of the
North. I cannot defy the Act for my Campbells. *You* already
do so."

"You mean . . .?"

"I mean go back to your former glens. Assemble your
scattered clan again. In arms. And march south against
Colquhoun."

Alastair shook his head in wonderment.

"You could do it. And save yourself and your folk."

"And, and what would the council say to that?"

"Does it signify greatly? Once you are free again, and your
people mustered. You could even retake Glen Strae from
Glenorchy. And take refuge on *my* lands while you do it.
That will be a deal better than the case you are in now."

"I do not know. I cannot say. Without much thought,
whatever. This is a, a matter . . . so much to be considered.
So much involved. My people led into what would be war! And
against the King's peace and the council. The law . . ."

"What are you now? At the horn, outlawed. Broken. Lost.
You could hang, MacGregor, and would, I think! Here is a
way out. Which you scarce deserve!"

Alastair took a turn up and down the room. "I must
think . . ."

"Think you, then. I will come back in one hour. Think
well. And thank me for this opening of the condemned
man's cell!"

Abruptly Argyll turned and left him.

Striding to and fro thereafter, Alastair thought indeed, cudgelling his brains. Should he do it? He suspected, of course, that Argyll had contrived this entire situation for his own purposes. But did that alter the facts? Imprisoned here as he was, he could indeed be hanged tomorrow. An outlaw. This way he could get back to his own mountains and gather his people again. Wherever they were. But, to lead them to their deaths, perhaps. Or some of them. But they were condemned *now*. Anyone who could might slay them. At least better to die fighting! Himself also. All the Gregorach would undoubtedly say the same. Few of his folk would choose differently. And the Colquhouns were hereditary foes. Colquhoun *had* betrayed him, and helped Glenorchy to empty Glen Strae. It would be but just recompense. Yet – Argyll! Trust Argyll in this? Or in anything!

Long he debated with himself; but in fact it was scarcely debate, more a convincing of himself that he was right in accepting this chance and challenge. So that when, presently, Argyll returned, it was to be given an agreement, hardly enthusiastic or grateful, but acceptance.

"Come, then," MacCailean Mhor said briefly, and waited impatiently in the open doorway while Alastair gathered together his few belongings.

They walked out together, side by side, and down to the gatehouse, none questioning them. It was as easy as that for the Lieutenant of the North.

Horses were waiting for them, and Campbell men-at-arms without the arms on view.

Mary Gray reached out to press his arm. "Oh, Alastair," she said, "I do not trust Argyll. Must you do this?" The grave news had muted what would have been a tumultuous reunion.

"I have given my word. What choice have I? Hanging *me*, the least of it! The whole clan crucified! Women, children, all. Homeless, landless, outwith the law. This of battle was the lesser evil, surely? Some will die. I may, my own self. But not all. We are hard fighters, the Gregorach. And Colquhoun deserves it."

"Perhaps. But . . . after? When you have taught Colquhoun

his lesson and gained Argyll what he wants? What then? You will have outraged the council, and probably the King. Broken the Disarming Act. Risen against the peace of the realm. Slain men acting under the royal authority. Do you think that the King's Lieutenant of the North will protect you and yours then? Accept any responsibility for it all? He cannot, and still retain his position. Argyll will deny any part in it, deliver you to the council again, *his* ends gained."

"I have thought of all that, yes. I put little faith in MacCailean Mhor, once he has got what he wants. But – I am *warned*. And the situation will be changed. I will have the clan mustered again. And the Gregorach, mustered in arms, are no easy prey! So long as we remain together, and retire into our hills and glens, who will take us?"

"You cannot always remain fugitives in the mountains. Hundreds of you, women and bairns too. Outcasts . . ."

"We are outcasts now. Fugitives in those mountains. But then, strong, united, armed, we will be in a better position to strike a bargain. The Campbells will not help us. But surrounded by what are now Campbell lands, although they were ours once, they will not hound us down, whatever. *Could* not. What could the council do? They have armed the Colquhouns against us. If we defeat the Colquhouns, who will take up the task?"

"In the end, must not the crown and Privy Council win?"

"Who can tell? Sakes, if it comes to the worst, we might elect even to go to King Jamie's colony in the Isle of Lewis!"

Mary wagged her head. It was not often that that young woman was at a loss.

"If only Vicky was here. And Patrick. Both hundreds of miles away, at Elizabeth's court . . ."

"Yes. Argyll chose his time well! In all this, Mary, it is Vicky that I fail, as I recognise. It is *his* interests that I must seem to work against. If we defeat the Colquhoun, on Argyll's behalf, that leaves the Lennox lands open to the encroacher. Ardkinglas will lie low. And MacAulay is not powerful." He paused. "But if *we*, the Gregorach, could then change over . . .?"

"You mean . . .?"

"I mean take over the Colquhoun and Macfarlane lands!

Fill the gap ourselves. Face Argyll, with our backs to the Lennox. How then? The *Gregorach* help to form the necessary barrier!"

"Could you do that?"

"Why not? Providing that we win the warfare, we will be strong. For the time triumphant. And the Colquhouns low. If the Campbells can take over our lands, can we not the Colquhouns'? At the least, for some time, whatever. Our men will be there, on Loch Lomondside. What, think you, Vicky would say to that?"

"I do not know. It might save some of his tenants' lands from Argyll's encroachment, yes. But could you and your people hold out there? Outlaws, with the council strong against you. Those lands around Loch Lomond and the Gare Loch are softer, more open, less easy to hold, I would think, against assault, than your own wild glens and passes."

"We could hold them for long enough to strike a bargain. With Argyll and the council. And when Vicky and the Master come back . . ."

"If only they would come! This of Elizabeth Tudor is such folly, unending. It is Patrick's one great aim and object, to see James on Elizabeth's throne and so unite the two kingdoms. Put an end to five hundred years of strife and enmity. For that he would sacrifice everything. But I *hate* it! For of course it would mean the court being in London for much of the time, assuredly, and Vicky with it. Not here, with me, at Methven. *I* would never wish to go there. James would never allow Vicky to remain in Scotland, I fear . . ."

"He was Viceroy while the King was in Denmark."

"That was only for a short time. James *needs* Vicky, as I know to my cost!"

"We have our problems, whatever!" he said, and reached to hold her arm, shaking his head.

"Yes. But mine are of a different order from yours. Less dire, less urgent. Only a . . . a long ache!"

"Would that I could help, Mary!"

"You do, you do! Dear Alastair. Without you, I sometimes could all but despair. And now after so long in captivity you are to take great risks, risks to your dear person as well as to your cause. And could well be betrayed. Oh, my dear, you must take care . . .!"

They held each other for a little, wordless.

As always, Alastair had to limit these emotional moments, lest he lost all control. And this was one of the hardest so to do.

So, at arm's length, their eyes locked, and said it all.

24

Alastair rode home, if home it could now be called, by Roro in Glen Lyon. He reckoned that, if any of the Gregorach had been able to withstand the assaults of the Glenorchy and Colquhoun invaders, Roro would, in his tightly embattled community which had to be approached by easily defendable passes. And he was right in that. Roro was still in his own house, surrounded by his own folk – and not a few of the Glen Strae people with him, including Rob Ban.

The reunion was highly charged with a variety of emotions: thankfulness and relief, concern, anger and, in most there all but uppermost, the desire for revenge. So Alastair had no difficulty in persuading all present that a major raid on the Colquhouns was a suitable repayment, and overdue. Indeed great was the enthusiasm and excitement. He warned that Argyll was not to be trusted in this, as in other matters, and who could tell what his attitude might be afterwards. That was brushed aside by his hearers. They would deal with Colquhoun and the Macfarlanes, with scores to settle; and after that the Gregorach, in arms, holding the Colquhoun lands, would look after themselves!

Alastair was, of course, concerned as to the present state and whereabouts of most of his clan. Roro and Rob Ban assured him that the situation was not so grievous as he had feared from Argyll's account. They were dispersed, yes, Stronmilchan occupied, Larachan and Dochard also. But there were scores of hidden valleys, corries and upland meadows amongst the surrounding mountains, as none knew better than Himself, and although there had been some casualties in the invasion, most had got away into the hills and were roosting over a wide area, from the eastern slopes of Cruachan to the Moor of Rannoch. There should be little difficulty in mustering a sizeable force – and every man of the Gregorach thirsting for vengeance.

What had happened in the more outlying MacGregor communities, Balquhidder, Glen Gyle, Inversnaid and the rest, was less certain. Balquhidder itself had been cleared, but it was thought that John and most of his people had got away up into the wild high territory at the head of that glen, where they were not far from Glen Gyle which, so far as was known, had escaped attack, being so remotely situated.

They discussed procedure. Alastair would send out the fiery cross to all parts, to assemble at Roro. This would be much better than mustering at Glen Gyle itself, the nearest to the Colquhoun lands, from which word of the gathering might well seep out. No point in trying to assemble in Glen Strae, where the castle of Stronmilchan would have to be recaptured first, which might delay matters considerably, for although small, it was strong. Hidden Roro would keep all secret until they were ready to march, even though it was scarcely conveniently placed for a descent on Loch Lomondside. Himself would go visiting the eastern side-valleys of Strae, Rob Ban the west, Roro Rannoch and the Appin area, their messengers elsewhere. Then, south!

Alastair found it good to be riding his own hills again after his recent constrictions, even though he still had doubts as to the rights and wrongs of what was ahead, few as others seemed to have. Advisedly skirting lower Glen Strae and his cousins' property of Larachan, he climbed first into the high, narrow valley of the Allt nan Uan and over to that of the Cleft Stone, remote indeed. And here he found about forty of his folk, camping in an upland meadow, with a few cattle, living mainly on venison, for these hills were full of deer. He was joyfully received, with none of the criticism which he had feared for not having been with them in their hour of need; and great acclaim, at least from the men, when he announced the muster and campaign against the Colquhouns, all raring to go. They told him of other groups hiding in the valley of the Allt Choireann to the south, and in some sections of the lofty Fionn Lairig to the north.

Climbing over to these thereafter, Alastair met with similar receptions, men, women and children thronging him, spirits by no means dampened by their misfortunes, and rejoicing at the prospect of vengeance and the regaining of their own homes and properties again. He spent some time with a fairly large grouping towards the north end of the Fionn Lairig overlooking his brother's former lairdship of Loch Dochard, which apparently was occupied by a mixed company of Colquhouns, Macfarlanes and Buchanans. His people were all for making a prompt attack thereon, now that they had their chief back with them, but Alastair did not agree. To do so would be to warn their enemies that the Gregorach were rising again, and this could prejudice the vital attack on the Loch Lomondside Colquhoun and Macfarlane lands. It must all be kept secret as far as possible, until they were fully assembled and on the move.

Next he covered the mountainous area north and west of Dochard, led from one pocket of fugitives to another, all responding in much the same fashion, gladness at seeing him, vociferous approval of the projected expedition, with assurances of urgent co-operation. Whatever the wisdom of it, the eventual prospects, this was what the Clan Alpin wanted.

Later he was back at Roro, to find over one hundred and fifty men already assembled, eager to be on the march, their so evident weaponry making a farce of the Disarming Act.

While they awaited the arrival of further contingents, the leaders conferred as to the strategy. What was *their* policy, rather than Argyll's? That man probably would be well enough pleased with a succession of raids on the Colquhouns and the Macfarlanes and their lands, with at least superficial devastation, driving off cattle and stock and so on. But was this what the *MacGregors* wanted? No. They desired much more than that. Their aim, all agreed, was battle, the clan's suitable and spectacular vengeance on their enemies and despoilers, no mere petty raiding. For this, although some surprise was advisable lest the Colquhouns had time to enlist aid from neighbouring clans such as the Buchanans, Galbraiths, MacArthurs, Drummonds and the like, the Colquhouns themselves must have opportunity to assemble in some force for battle, or it would all degenerate into a series of petty fights, assaults and ravishings.

So what should be their tactics? A march southwards, secretly, by unfrequented ways and if necessary by night, to reach the lesser Gregorach lands of Glen Gyle and Inversnaid, near the head of Loch Lomond. From there, send out a few raiding parties down the west side of that long loch, this to let it be known that the MacGregors were there in some strength, enough for Colquhoun of Luss to marshal a force to deal with them but not for him to be sending all around for support from others. This Disarming Act would presumably apply to the said others – but if the Gregorach knew other Highlanders, no Act of Parliament would prevent swords, axes and dirks from being hidden away in roof-thatches and hay-barns, for retrieval on special occasions. Thereafter, a full advance down Lomond into the Colquhoun and Macfarlane country.

It was Roro, the most experienced warrior present, who pointed out an especial problem. Loch Lomond was twenty-five miles long, with side-glens innumerable entering its main valley on the west. They would come to the Macfarlane country first, centred round Tarbet and Arrochar. Although not a large clan, the Macfarlanes were stout fighters too, and would not just sit idly by without confronting invaders. So the Gregorach might well have to fight a battle with *them* before ever they could get to the Colquhoun lands. There might have to be two battles therefore. And if the Macfarlanes fought well, would the Gregorach be in a state immediately to fight another and larger host? An interval for recovery would have to elapse – and that would give Colquhoun warning and time to summon the help of allies.

That presented a poser which had not occured to Alastair. Pondering, he agreed that there might indeed have to be two battles. If so, would it be possible to spread them apart not only, as it were, on the ground but in time also? Assuming that they beat the Macfarlanes, to return home here. Use their victorious strength to clear out their enemies occupying Glen Strae and the rest – as they would be doing after the main Colquhoun battle anyway, God being good. And wait for a period. So that Colquhoun would assume that any threat was by-with, that he was safe meantime. Then descend on him later, when he had not summoned allies. They would have to inform Argyll, to be sure, or he would think that Himself was breaking his word. But MacCailean Mhor would, it was to be hoped, see the difficulty and accept the situation.

No one there admired MacCailean Mhor, but they did not doubt his wits, and reckoned that he would recognise realities and wait likewise. After all, his purposes would still be fulfilled. So it was decided. They would march in two days' time.

With, for the Gregorach, great discretion, they set off actually northwards, by the high pass of the Lairig Chalbhath for Rannoch, to avoid Campbell land as far as possible, and then turned south again at the head of Loch Tummel down the Strath of Appin, to Dull, a long road indeed. Even in the Menzies land there they marched by night, skirting the Aberfeldy area and over to Strath Braan and Upper Glen Almond. Then they traversed the lofty watershed over to the head of Loch Earn and so to Balquhidder. Resting, they there picked up another sixty men, and John, and proceeded up that glen and over the mounth to Glen Gyle, to near enough the head of Loch Lomond, where they collected fifty more. Now they constituted a force of two hundred and fifty, and these having had enough of skulking travel, spoiling for a fight.

But restraint was the strategy at this stage. Two or three small-scale raids on the Macfarlane country was what was called for, those involved coming back here to Glen Gyle and Inversnaid. Yet these raids must not seem to be by only local MacGregors, or the Macfarlanes might well not mass for battle but content themselves with minor return raids. So Alastair himself, with his brother and Roro, would lead these small sallies, and let it be known that they were doing so. Surely that would rouse the Macfarlanes to full-scale assembly?

How best to go about it? Simultaneous raids on different areas would probably serve their purposes best, as indicating fairly large numbers involved altogether. The Macfarlane chief's main seat was at Arrochar, over at the head of Loch Long, well to the west, although they had a smaller castle on an island in Loch Lomond itself. Their clan lands lay between these two lochs, north of the Colquhoun territories, mountainous land with great Ben Vorlich at its lofty centre. It was decided that three parties should descend – or, in fact, *ascend* – on three of these high glens. Alastair's brother would lead the most northerly, on Glen Sloy just across Lomond from

Inversnaid; his cousins Gregor and Patrick would go further south, to Glen Loin; and Alastair himself would take the more challenging venture, further south still, to Glen Mallochan, which bordered Colquhoun lands, indeed was not far from Luss itself. These, especially this last, ought to ensure that the Macfarlanes, with possibly some Colquhoun neighbours, mustered in major strength to deal with the threat implied.

So, in a wintery early morning of frost and mist, the three groups, amounting to around one hundred men, set out up Glen Gyle and over the little pass to the head of Loch Lomond at Ardlui, a mere four miles. Down the west side of that great loch they marched for another five miles, to Inveruglas, where opened a pass over to Glen Sloy and Glen Loin, and where, just offshore, was the little island castle of that name, Macfarlane of that Ilk probably not in residence there meantime, for it would be in the nature of a summer residence. Here two of the parties struck off westwards for their respective target areas, whilst Alastair's thirty or so continued on down the lochside a further three miles to Tarbet, where another and fairly low and short pass led over to Arrochar and Loch Long. This represented a first major hazard, for although they had passed not a few scattered little communities and houses *en route*, without attacking or being attacked, Tarbet was the seat of one of the Macfarlane lairds, so it had to be dealt with. However, they were fortunate in this, for it proved to be no very strong house and the laird an old man who offered little resistance to the sudden eruption of armed MacGregors, declaring that they would have had a hotter reception had his sons not been away to a cattle-tryst at Balloch at the foot of the loch. Since this venture was all in the nature of a ruse to coax out the Macfarlane strength hereafter, Alastair contented himself with telling Tarbet that he was wise not to demonstrate active opposition, for they would be back, and if he caused any trouble in the interim he and his would suffer. Meantime, he took a couple of dozen of the laird's cattle and sent them back up the lochside in the care of three of his men, more or less as a conventional gesture.

Now they marched on for another five miles to the next major entry to the lochside from the west, Glen Douglas. Here they were all but into Colquhoun country, only a few miles from Luss – and the Colquhouns were not their present targets. So they turned off here, up this glen for a couple of miles, where dusk descended on them at the farmery of Doune. This they took over from its alarmed Macfarlane tenants, without any actual struggle – for they would be coming back this way on the morrow and wanted no refugees rushing off to Luss and rousing the Colquhoun. Making themselves comfortable enough at the farmhouse, they did not unduly harass the occupants.

So far so good.

They were off again early in the morning, leaving four of their number to watch over these Doune people. Now just over a score strong, they climbed southwards over the flank of Sith Mhor, the great fairy-hill, and down into Glen Mallochan, their target area. This was a fine upland valley half a mile across and some three miles long, noted for its excellent high pasture. It was indeed still filled with cattle, the object of the enterprise. The Gregorach were sufficiently experienced in rounding up these, in the upper reaches of the glen, and could have departed with them forthwith. But that was not their sole objective. There were two communities down where this glen joined Glen Luss, one called Mallochan or Mulchan and the other Edintaggart. These had to be given notice of the MacGregor presence and identity, other than merely losing some of their beasts. So thither Alastair led his band. They were itching for a fight by this time, but he had to warn them that this was not the time to display their armed prowess. That would come, he hoped, and soon. The present need was to alarm these people here rather than assault them, so that they would send urgent tidings to their chief at Arrochar. And he, Macfarlane, getting other similar reports, would, it was assessed, muster the clan.

Descending, then, to the glen-foot, the bulk of his party made their presence felt in no uncertain fashion, without actually wounding, slaying or raping, however tempted. They were in fact all but met by a group of locals who, sharp-eyed, had evidently perceived their cattle being rounded up in the distance, and were coming to investigate. But at the shouts of "Gregorach! Gregorach!" resounding from the valley-sides, these turned and sped whence they had come.

Alastair's restraining hand prevented any very serious harm being inflicted and property sacked, although certain goods were purloined, some women partially disrobed and fondled and two barn-thatches set alight. This achieved, the grumbling MacGregors returned up the glen to collect the cattle and drive them off back to Doune in Glen Douglas, and so down to Loch Lomondside again. It was only a forenoon's work.

They were not interrupted on their way north to Tarbet, slowed as they were now by the cattle-droving. There they found the old laird and his people discreetly absent, their remaining stock gone also. Apart from helping themselves to food and drink, the Gregorach pressed on for Ardlui and then to the pass to Glen Gyle. From Inveruglas onwards they perceived that the drove-road was decorated with many cattle-droppings – so evidently the other two groups had preceded them, and not empty-handed.

Glen Gyle was loud with protesting cattle, as well as whisky-stimulated high spirits when they arrived back. All seemed to have gone according to plan with Alastair's brother and cousins – although whether they had adhered as strictly to the no-unnecessary-violence instructions as had he was uncertain. But at any rate no casualties had been suffered by the MacGregors, and since cattle were the clansfolk's wealth, all were considerably the richer. This was what life should be like, most asserted.

Glengyle sent out scouts knowledgeable as to the Macfarlane country to investigate reactions and to report back.

Eventually the reports began to come in. The Macfarlanes were massing at Arrochar. Some Colquhouns with them but as yet no general assembly of that clan. Colquhoun himself was said to be, oddly enough, with Argyll at Inveraray.

They waited.

Then the word which came puzzled them. The Macfarlane assembly, variously reported at between two hundred and three hundred, was moving south from Arrochar, not east or north as anticipated, but down the steep Loch Longside towards Garelochhead. Why? There were no MacGregors in that direction. It must be something to do with the Colquhouns – that way lay *their* territory. Were they seeking to join a mobilised host of Colquhouns, to face the Gregorach together? That could make up quite a major army. Argyll could not have anything to do with that, could he? Alastair now was ever suspicious of MacCailean Mhor; but he could not see how any such move could aid the Campbell cause. Could it be possibly for the Macfarlanes to link up with Buchanans, coming over from the Dumbarton area?

At any rate it was something which fell to be coped with, and the sooner the better undoubtedly. It was time to be on the move themselves.

About two hundred and fifty strong, the Gregorach marched, no more hiding and making gestures. This was to be full-scale assault. It occurred to Alastair that their best strategy would be to make for Arrochar itself. Macfarlane would not have left it undefended, presumably; but if it was now seriously threatened, this might bring the Macfarlanes hurrying back from wherever they were headed, and before they could be reinforced by allies.

So the MacGregors crossed over that pass again to the head of Loch Lomond, and down the western side thereof, pipes playing and spirits high. It was a long time since Clan Alpin had marched in strength thus.

They had some fifteen miles to cover, going the simplest, quickest way, by Tarbet again and then over to Loch Long, most of it fairly easy going after that first stretch to Ardlui. Expert at fast travel – they all but ran, rather than marched – they need allow only four hours for that, if there were no unexpected delays. And who was going to delay quarter of a thousand MacGregors?

In fact, they reached Arrochar before noon, without incident, any Macfarlanes who were not off to the muster lying discreetly low. The castle there was quite strongly sited, where the River Loin in its glen came down to join Loch Long, the same name in fact, and set on a steep knoll protected on three sides by ravines and water. Alastair had anticipated this, and it was no part of his objective to lay siege to such a place. The township of Arrochar was a different matter however, and the Gregorach simply took that over there and then, almost without resistance – for of course most of its able-bodied men were away with their chief. Its women had to bear the brunt of it, although Alastair sought to keep the matter within reasonable bounds. The Gregorach did not make war on women and children.

Despatching scouts southwards, they settled down to wait, most much enjoying Arrochar's enforced hospitality. They had little doubt that Macfarlane would not be long in being informed of the situation.

In fact, the winter's night fell without definite word reaching them of the enemy force's whereabouts. A night-time attack on them here was not impossible – although if the Macfarlanes had been near enough for that the scouts would surely have informed them. Great fires were lit all around, just in case, with plenty of wood available. Relays of guards and sentinels were organised, and well-earned rest for the remainder.

It was mid-forenoon following before the first positive news of the Macfarlanes' whereabouts reached them, surprising news too. They had gone right down to Rhu, where the Gare Loch entered the Firth of Clyde. What could be the reason for this? Admittedly Buchanans, Galbraiths and Drummonds, if these were to come to their aid, would be likely to come that way; but surely it would have been more effective for such to have come up here to Arrochar, rather than the Macfarlanes going to meet them away down there? No, that did not seem likely. The only other explanation was that Macfarlane wanted major *Colquhoun* help, and was carefully going the round-about way to get it, presumably fearing MacGregor attack in the interim if he went by the usual and shorter route to Luss down Lomondside. If Colquhoun himself was indeed far off at Inveraray with Argyll, then Macfarlane might well have decided that he would have to do the enlisting of Colquhoun help himself, and so move his men down this longer way and come up to Luss from the south, where most of that clan's manpower was situated. That was the only way Alastair could see the situation.

What, then, was their own best course? They did not want to have a combined force of Macfarlanes and Colquhouns to face, with perhaps Buchanans and others as well; they could be outnumbered many times over. Therefore, try to intercept the Macfarlanes before they could reach the Luss area. They might well be able to do this by taking a more or less direct route instead of the enemy's circuitous one. Through the mountains with them, then, as MacGregors knew how!

Decision taken, they were off without delay. They marched down Loch Long for about six miles, to Glen Mallon, which small climbing valley would take them up between the mountains of Cruach-an-t-Sithean and Beinn a' Mhanaich, so over to the head of long Glen Luss. They did not want to assail Luss itself at this stage and provoke major resistance, so they would cut southwards over the shoulder of Beinn Ruisg to Glen Finlas, and take that down to the southern end of Loch Lomond, and so, it was to be hoped, confront the Macfarlanes on their way up. Fortunately, MacGregor of Glengyle knew this territory well and could guide them.

It made a strange march for an armed force, seeking their foes in those high valleys and passes, not knowing just where they might be, and trusting that their evaluation of the situation was reasonably accurate. In the circumstances, given the long and wide peninsula between the two great lochs, there was not a great deal of opportunity to guess wrongly, however. The question was – from Rhu, how would the Macfarlanes move? Presumably over to Glen Fruin and to Loch Lomond that way. Would they linger at Rhu, waiting for allies and reinforcements? Alastair hoped for word from his scouts – although these themselves might have some difficulty in finding them, to report.

Their highest point reached, after steep Glen Mallon, found them in a veritable hub of major mountains, with Glen Luss stretching away eight miles down there, very much Colquhoun country this, but largely empty in these higher reaches in winter, with the cattle largely withdrawn from the shielings, their pasture died away. Fortunately there was no depth of snow yet. The first houses they saw were some three miles down, and these the MacGregors carefully avoided, not wanting the alarm to be raised so near to Luss itself. So they climbed again, over another shoulder of great Ben Tharsuinn and so down into Glen Finlas. They had come a dozen very rough miles.

They had just passed the lofty small Loch Finlas, and could see far ahead the wide waters of Loch Lomond, when there was an unlooked-for development. Over the shoulder of the lowish Shantron Hill on their right appeared a sizeable band of men, not far off one hundred at a guess. Who these were they could not tell – but it was highly improbable that they were unconnected with the Macfarlane muster. Why else would such a number be crossing these winter mountains?

Alastair had to make a quick decision. These had to be attacked, halted, or they could warn all the population of the lower Lomond area. Better, probably, if they turned and fled westwards whence they had come, in the circumstances.

But the advancing company did not do so. Presumably they thought, at that distance, that the MacGregors were more Macfarlanes or Colquhouns. They came on.

The two groups approached each other over the heathery hillside, the Gregorach at least very much on their toes, hands reaching down for swords and dirks.

At perhaps four hundred yards the newcomers hesitated and halted. At the sight, most of the MacGregors did not wait for Alastair's orders. Led by the ever-eager John, they leapt forward, shouting their dread slogan "Gregorach! Gregorach!", bounding over the knee-high heather.

That was no battle and certainly not what Alastair had planned. The enemy, if that they could be called, surprised, unready, mostly turned to flee before their yelling attackers, so that the encounter became a chase, and a scattered one at that, every man for himself, the youngest and fleetest of foot the most fortunate. Some indeed did stand and put up a fight, but there was no organised resistance, no forming of a square or other defensive posture. Most indubitably got away into the hills, some wounded, but fully a score fell before the furious MacGregor assault, dead or dying.

Alastair was angry, condemnatory, frustrated. Yet even he did not see what else could have been done, in this situation. And when he found that these were not Macfarlanes at all, but Colquhouns, he was the more troubled. Presumably these were from the western Gare Loch lands of the clan, and had been roused by Macfarlane and were on their way to a muster at Luss. Now they were dispersed, yes – but most of them had got away, and they would soon be rousing the whole country, inevitably. There would be no more surprises. The Colquhouns would be rising in arms everywhere, and with the Macfarlanes already assembled, wherever they were, the MacGregors, in these enemy mountains could be, if not trapped, certainly greatly outnumbered and at a strategic disadvantage. He cursed, and beat clenched fist on targe, his planning made a nonsense by this folly.

It was Rob Ban who pointed out that matters were not so bad as all that. After all, although there had been no resounding battle such as they had envisaged, this would serve their purpose almost equally well. The Colquhouns would now know that the Gregorach were aiming at them in strength, which was the objective. Himself could tell Argyll that he had made a major descent on the Colquhouns, and would make a greater one, in due course. And meantime they could round up a sufficiency of Colquhoun and Macfarlane cattle and horses, and head home for Glen Strae, there to dispossess the wretched invaders. It could all work out well enough.

Alastair recognised that this was indeed so. Swallowing his ire, he ordered a turn-around, with retiral more or less whence they had come, and to collect cattle as they went. By keeping to the high ground between the two great lochs they should get up to the Arrochar-Tarbet pass, and so to the head of Lomond again, without any large-scale attempts at interception or chase, even slowed by the said cattle. It would take time for the Colquhouns to assemble adequately; and wherever the Macfarlanes were, they did not seem to constitute a threat at present – although watch would have to be kept for them.

So back to Glen Gyle, and then to Glen Strae, with work awaiting them there.

25

In the event, the clearing of Glen Strae of invaders and occupiers did not present any very great or bloody task. Word had spread across the distances and vast empty spaces, and it seemed that their enemies here had not failed to learn of the Gregorach rising in arms. And wisely they recognised that it would not be long before there was a vigorous and concentrated attempt to retake these MacGregor lands. Discreetly, those left in occupation saw their best interests served by a quiet slipping away before any such unpleasantness developed; after all, they were but underlings and tools of the greater ones, who would not have to face the angry armed MacGregors. So, although they left considerable devastation and displeasing traces behind them, they were in the main gone ere Alastair and his people arrived. Stronmilchan, Larachan, Dochard and the rest were in a state of wreck and ravage, denuded of anything of value that was portable, and with the livestock gone; but there was nothing which could not be put right in time – and they had, indeed, brought back enough cattle with them to all but replace the losses.

The resettlement of the clansfolk took some time thereafter, and with the weather turning to snow at last in that mountain land, progress was delayed. Alastair would have liked to go to Methven for Yuletide, but with so much to be done, and careful watch kept in case of reprisals by Colquhoun, Macfarlane or Glenorchy, he just could not leave Glen Strae and neighbourhood. He did send a messenger to Inveraray, to inform MacCailean Mhor of developments and intentions, although that man would no doubt be well informed already.

It was late January before he was able to get away to Strathearn. It was to find Mary Gray still alone, Ludovick not yet back from London where, she was informed, Queen

Elizabeth was very ill and sinking, but clinging to life and authority, and not naming her heir finally and beyond doubt. The young woman relievedly welcomed Himself, admitting that she had been grievously worried about his safety on his Argyll-inspired venture – and not a little perturbed that there was more to come. She shook her lovely head over men and their strange ambitions and priorities. But she was glad to hear that Glen Strae was in MacGregor possession again.

She had news for Alastair too. "The Lady Marie keeps me informed as to what goes on at court and in the realm at large," she said. "Your exploits on Loch Lomondside have not gone unnoticed. Indeed there has been great stir, for Colquhoun of Luss took a great company of his folk to Stirling, the women, scores of them, to parade the streets carrying the bloodstained shirts of their menfolk slain in Glen Finlas, on the points of spears, himself to complain bitterly to King James of the MacGregor savagery against the King's lieges, their scorning of the Disarming Act and the intolerable state of affairs this represented in the southern Highlands. This parade of the Bloody Sarks, as it is being called, has created a notable sensation, and the Privy Council called a special meeting to command the Lieutenant of the North, Argyll, to take immediate and vehement steps to right the situation and bring the reprehensible MacGregors to justice." She managed a small smile. "Argyll, who ordered it all!"

He shook his head. "This of the shirts! That was clever! The King cannot stand the sight of blood – save deer's blood! So it all would have great effect on James. And so on the council. That is bad. I wonder . . .?" He paused. "We heard that, during our descent on the Macfarlanes – who, see you, did not lose very many men in what was but a scuffle – Colquhoun himself was at Inveraray, Argyll's castle on Loch Fyne. So . . .?"

"You wonder if Argyll himself put Colquhoun up to this of the shirts? Would that serve his purposes?"

"I do not know. But from all that I have heard, Colquhoun himself is not a clever man, whatever. Or subtle. Whereas MacCailean Mhor most certainly is! It might be. Why, I cannot see. But he plays a deep game, and this might just give him added powers. I do not trust him one yard! So I will keep my Gregorach mustered and at the ready. *After* we have made our second descent on Colquhoun!"

"Oh, Alastair, when will that be? *Must* you?"

"I must, yes. I have given my word. I do not have much to give, but my word is to be trusted. Even to Argyll! We go soon, very soon. Colquhoun will not expect us while the snows linger. We do not want him bringing in large numbers of his allies, Buchanans, Galbraiths, MacArthurs and the rest. So, in a week or two . . ."

"And . . . afterwards?"

"We retire to Glen Strae. Embattled. The whole clan in arms. We shall see what Argyll and the council can do then!"

She bit her lip. "I do not like it," she said. "Oh, Alastair my dear, I do not like it! If only Vicky was here! Though what he could do, I know not."

"Nor I. You have no notion when he will be back?"

"None. James wants him there, at Elizabeth's bedside almost, to plead his cause, to assure her that he, James, will make a good king for the English, that it would be folly to have Arabella Stewart, who lacks strength. That it *must* be James. Patrick has been saying this for long, but James does not altogether trust my father. Strange, because in *this*, Patrick is to be trusted, in whatever else he is not! So, until Elizabeth dies, or makes notable recovery – which is not likely – Vicky will probably have to remain in London. Sadly. While *you* hazard yourself and your people!"

He shrugged. "I seem to have been doing that for some time, whatever!"

"Then, for *my* sake, if no other, be careful, Alastair . . . as I have told you before! Promise me?"

He clutched her to him, grasping her and all but shaking her, by way of answer.

Nearly four hundred strong, the Gregorach marched south in early February, not this time in secrecy but boldly, openly, as to war, caring not who saw them, indeed wishing their advance to be reported to Colquhoun – but not so far ahead that he had time to recruit allies. They went by the most direct route therefore, down Loch Awe, over to Glen Aray –

Argyll, if at Inveraray nearby, would note it – then round the head of Loch Fyne and up Glen Kinglas. That glen had an unusual right-angled bend in it four miles up, with the usual route to Loch Long swinging off to the right, southwards, and the glen itself left, northwards. Here was Alastair's first problem. To take the direct drove-road over the high pass under Ben Arthur and down Glen Croe would bring them to Arrochar; and this they did not want. They had no wish for the Macfarlanes to rise again and come to the aid of the Colquhouns, possibly attack themselves in the rear when they were engaged. So Arrochar had to be avoided. Situated as it was at the very head of Loch Long, this was quite difficult to contrive, coming from this western side. It entailed going up into upper Glen Kinglas and over a remote pass to upper Glen Sloy and so down to Inveruglas on Loch Lomondside, a diversion of some ten difficult miles. It was in crossing this lofty and little-known pass that they had their only real difficulty with deep, drifted snow.

Down at Inveruglas at length they were, of course, still in Macfarlane territory and to some degree risking that clan's mobilisation, although much less so than at the chief's seat of Arrochar. This could not be helped, but if they struck off again westwards into the mountains, once past Tarbet, up Glen Douglas, then they would avoid any dangerous head-on or tail-on confrontation along the narrows of Lomondside, the major hazard of the entire project, where they could be strung-out and ambushed all too easily, Colquhoun before, Macfarlane behind.

They made comparatively empty Glen Douglas safely, and at the Doune again, where they had encamped on the previous occasion, they here passed the second night of their march.

Next morning mere tactics merged with strategy. They could move on down Glen Luss itself, admittedly, and challenge Colquhoun at his seat of Rossdhu there, on the lochside. But that might well be to *his* advantage, for he would be apt to be mustering there; and Glen Luss was narrow and easily defendable. Better to coax him out of his lair, as it were, and into territory where their own military prowess and use of ground might have play – for almost certainly they, the MacGregors, would be outnumbered, here in the middle of Colquhoun country. So they would avoid Glen Luss and even Glen Finlas, and make for the furthest south of the Colquhoun glens, Fruin, where they could spread themselves, be able to outflank if necessary, and cause the enemy maximum difficulty.

From Glen Douglas to Glen Fruin was fully a dozen awkward up-and-down miles. Traversing these, they were bound to be seen by not a few dwellers in the high valleys, who would no doubt send word down to Luss. So Colquhoun would know that they were there, and heading southwards. What would he expect, therefore? Probably that they were seeking to get behind him, as it were, either down Finlas or Fruin. Or perhaps get to the communities down on the Clyde coast, Rhu and Camuseskan, to join forces with Ardencaple. They might well assess it that way. What would he do, then? In his own country, to prevent it all being ravaged by the invaders, he would almost certainly not sit tight at Luss and wait. He would move out and seek to intercept, if possible to ambush and trap. Assuming this, Alastair reckoned that his own best course was to get to the head of Glen Fruin, and there wait, scouts out. According to Glengyle, on the slopes of a mountain called the Strone, they would be in a position to oversee the long and quite wide valley, and down right to the low ground near the foot of Loch Lomond. Four hundred men, they themselves would be visible, of course. So Colquhoun would, in all probability, come up to challenge them with his larger force. So be it.

The Gregorach marched, high above the shores of Loch Long.

Before midday they were on the long eastwards-facing slope of the Strone, Glen Fruin opening before them. There they halted, massed. But not quite all of them. This Strone formed a descending ridge between two valleys, the main Fruin to the south-west and a lesser one to the north-east. Down into this latter Alastair sent his brother John, with about one hundred men. They could come back up, at speed, if required; but they could also slip down the smaller glen to get behind an enemy force all but unseen, if that seemed advisable. So to wait hidden there.

Scouts were sent out, south and east.

It was strange, after all their urgent activity and climbing, to sit there on the open hillside, idle, obvious, unsuitable somehow. Yet, until they were informed of Colquhoun's moves, if any, this was their evident course. The Gregorach, never the most patient of warriors, fretted.

They had a long wait. It was indeed almost two hours before one of their eastern scouts returned to say that a great force was on the move, from Luss, down Loch Lomondside. And much of it mounted.

The news set Alastair, Roro, Rob Ban and Glengyle wondering. Mounted? That was unexpected. A few leaders on horseback was likely enough; but not a cavalry host, in these hills. Almost certainly these would be Buchanans, Drummonds, Galbraiths, men from the lower country at the far southern end of Loch Lomond eastwards, rather than Colquhouns themselves. If they expected to be fighting along the level Clyde coast cavalry would be useful. But in rough mountain territory, horsemen were apt to be at a disadvantage.

The Gregorach leaders were discussing this and debating tactics, when at last they were able to see for themselves instead of relying on the scouts. A mass of men came into view down at the mouth of Fruin – and, yes, the leading ranks were cavalry. And they were turning up into this glen. The MacGregors would be equally visible to them, now.

Alastair gave the word to head downhill.

In a way, this might have seemed to some of his people a foolish move, to give up their strong position on high ground. But he ordered it advisedly. They had not wasted their time while waiting up there, but had carefully scanned the surrounding terrain. And down where this ridge of the Strone sank to the valley floor it was, not unnaturally, soft and boggy ground, hill drainage being as it was. That wet and marshy land could serve them well, with cavalry to face.

It was quickly clear that it was a large force which came to challenge the invaders, some assessed as twice their own numbers. Not that this alarmed most of the Gregorach. As the host drew nearer, Alastair reckoned on roughly two hundred horse and four hundred foot. He still kept his clansmen moving down, almost to the edge of the soft ground. Their pipers played before them as they went, in Gregorach challenge.

Now, so much depended on Colquhoun's immediate decision. He was not famed as a particularly wise or discreet character, but he had been shrewd enough over the "bloody sarks" gesture.

Swords drawn, the MacGregors formed a crescent behind that peat and moss area, their half-dozen pipers strutting up and down before them, blowing lustily, positively inviting attack.

Colquhoun did not follow suit and wait. He would see only three hundred ahead of him, and he had double that at least. And his cavalry was, as always, scornful of infantry, superior, eager to ride them down. With a great shout, the enemy leadership spurred forward at the head of the horsed contingent, while waving on the foot, right and left.

Alastair still managed to hold his men in check. He hoped that his brother was watching from some viewpoint above that hidden side-valley.

Quickly the cavalry was in difficulties as the horses' hooves sank into the soft ground. They did not sink far, of course, for there was inevitably underlying rock. But it was enough to slow down what had begun almost as a charge, and to break ranks and formation, as some hit deeper peat-broth than did others. In mere moments the proud ones were in floundering disarray, with some pressing ahead, others reining aside, some even backing off.

And at last Alastair raised his sword high and brought it slashing down, to point. About half of the Gregorach surged forward at the signal, yelling their slogan, the musicians cast aside their pipes and drew sword and dirk instead. And at their backs, Roro and Glengyle each led half of the remainder to get to grips with the Colquhoun foot, right and left.

Men can leap and dart over ground too soft for heavy horses, and the MacGregors were adept at it. Moreover, by stooping low they could avoid the slashing swipes of the cavalry swords, especially with the horsemen already having difficulties in controlling their frightened mounts and unable to bend as far down as necessary. Gregorach swords and dirks were not at the same disadvantage.

Chaos reigned in Glen Fruin – or seeming chaos, with the MacGregors at least knowing just what they were at. The two wings under Roro and Glengyle fought in straightforward fashion with their Colquhoun counterparts at either side and, outnumbered, did their martial best.

Alastair, of course, sought to engage the enemy leaders, these in no better state than the rest. But he recognised that his responsibility, as commander, lay not in individual combat, however dashing, but in seeking to marshal and guide his forces, difficult as this was in the circumstances.

The MacGregors had the initiative now, and were making good use of it, when there was a sudden eruption of that five-score more men on their left flank, as John's company came racing out of the little hidden side-valley, yelling. And this extra and unexpected assault turned the enemy's chaos into sheer panic and disaster. The foot on that north side saw themselves as trapped, front and rear, and broke, to turn and flee. Those on the other flank, perceiving this, and their cavalry in disorder, did not take long to follow suit. And the horsemen, their leaders picked out by the Gregorach and quite failing to lead, each sought to get out of the morass unscathed rather than make difficult battle. It was, indeed, no battle but a rout, and created in only minutes. Even Alastair could scarcely believe it.

What followed was as incoherent and disorderly. Men and horses were floundering in the mire, heavy riding-boots no help to those dismounted. There were many wounded, who could not flee. Some small groups attempted to rally, but most who could streamed off in any direction which was available to them, some pursued, some not.

Alastair and his lieutenants tried to control the situation as best they could, he himself to some extent bogged down in the soft ground. Roro and Glengyle, on the flanks, were in a better position to order matters and keep their men approximately in hand. But victory is heady stuff, particularly unlooked-for and sudden victory, and the fighting spirit takes some damping down. The victors were little more disciplined than the defeated.

There was of course also a lot of noise to help confuse matters, yells, shouting, groans; but it was a continuing series of high-pitched screams, from over on the left, the north, which really brought Alastair to accept the urgent need for him to take more forceful command. Over there on the outer perimeter of the conflict, part of his brother's hundred had managed to intercept and capture a group of Colquhoun foot; and now these were being stabbed to death one after another, even though their swords had been cast away.

Himself yelling now, Alastair struggled to get over to this shameful massacre. Finding John nearby, slightly unsteady and clasping his side, he actually struck him in his hot anger, pointing and shaking his own bloody sword.

His brother shook his head and raised a blood-dripping hand. "It . . . is . . . MacIans," he panted, "Glen Coe men. They . . . will not . . . heed me! Crazed!" A contingent of MacIans from Glen Coe, at the north end of the Moor of Rannoch, and traditionally in league with the Gregorach, had joined this expedition. Apparently they had their own priorities, and scorned John's authority.

Furiously Alastair ran at them, shouting, to lay about him with the flat of his sword, some of his own folk at his back. At first it looked as though the miscreants would turn on *him* in their blood-lust; but perhaps it was the innate respect of all Highlanders for a clan chief which prevailed, and made the MacIans desist and end their slaughtering, some of the captives still alive.

When Alastair turned back, trying to calm himself, it was to find John no longer standing, flat on his back in the heather, with Rob Ban bending over him. Dropping to his knees beside his brother, staring, gulping, Alastair reached out a hand. John mustered a twisted smile, then his eyes suddenly went blank, and he breathed his last.

After that, it was Roro who took charge for the time being. These two brothers had never been close; but family ties are strong, and this abrupt, final parting, was shattering. It was Rob Ban who, grasping his nephew's shoulder, sought to comfort him.

"It is the way he would wish to go, whatever, Alastair. He was a fighter, ever. More than yourself. He will not complain, where he has gone, at all!"

Gradually order of a sort was restored over the rest of the

298

battlefield, if that it could be called, the only Colquhouns and their allies left in sight being dead, wounded or prisoner, their slain, at a quick count, amounting to one hundred and twenty. Only two MacGregors were dead, including John, although perhaps a score had wounds.

It was a scarcely believable outcome, so swift and so complete a victory, difficult to take in. Elation and congratulation prevailed, with less mourning for John than there might have been for one more popular. There was considerable astonishment.

A deal of self-discipline was required, in the circumstances, for the leadership to turn their minds to further and appropriate action. What next? They had achieved more than they had looked to do, Alastair's word to Argyll more than fulfilled. It was unlikely that Colquhoun – who apparently had escaped unhorsed – would be able to rally, or muster another large force meantime. But his seat of Rossdhu, at Luss, was a strong place and not to be taken without lengthy siege and cannon-fire. Anyway, Colquhoun had been taught his lesson. No point in proceeding against him further.

One aspect of the situation was foremost in Alastair's mind – his projected occupation of the Colquhoun and Macfarlane lands, or some of them, by his Gregorach, to maintain the barrier against Argyll's expansionist tendencies, this to show his gratitude towards Ludovick of Lennox. But he found, now that affairs had reached this stage, that this was not really a practical proposition. To keep a large force like this patrolling these mountains, in winter weather, was scarcely possible for any length of time, especially as his people had no desire to do any such thing. What *they* wanted was to get off home with as many cattle, horses and sheep as they could collect, back to their own glens. They had done their bit; now they would have their reward. Alastair saw this and could not blame them. Anyway, perhaps an occupation force was not really necessary? It would be a considerable time before this area recovered from the MacGregor invasion, and its people would dread a repeat attack. Would Argyll, in the circumstances, seek to acquire it? Probably he would, but not in these winter conditions. They would have a breathing-space. And with the Gregorach back in *their* mountains, and strong now, in arms and morale,

MacCailean Mhor might well recognise that it could be easier to raise the Devil than to lay him! An interview with that man might be advisable.

So Alastair and his lairds accepted that their course now was the obvious one; collect as much stock as they effectively could drove, keep their victorious clansfolk happy, and march for home. Now they need not take the unfrequented upland passes, but go by the most direct and convenient routes, without fearing interference.

Alastair found himself faced with an unforeseen embarrassment. One of the prisoners turned out to be Semple of Fulwood, who was none other than deputy keeper of Dumbarton Castle, Duke Ludovick's lieutenant. What he was doing fighting for Colquhoun was not entirely clear; presumably he considered that this was all in the cause of defending his master's interests in the Lennox. Alastair told him that *he* was also acting in the duke's interests, and wished to counter Argyll. He gave him one of the captured horses and sent him off back to Dumbarton – to the scowls of some of the Gregorach.

Then there was the problem of the enemy dead, wounded and prisoners. In this cold weather the slain could lie there until their own folk came up to bury them. The wounded could be sent back to Luss, aiding each other; and it was decided, after argument, the prisoners freed with them – the normal ransoming process would be too difficult for the MacGregors to implement effectively. They would collect their price in the form of cattle-beasts and horses.

That left Alastair with his brother's corpse to deal with. He considered taking the body all the way back to Balquhidder and the widow and infant sons; but came to the conclusion that John would be best buried here, on the site of the victory which he had helped to win, and had fallen, as had been a MacGregor custom since Pictish times. A cairn to be heaped up over him. This accorded with the general feelings in the matter, and willing hands scraped a grave and gathered a vast heap of stones above, with a long boulder to serve as monolith on top. There, with a muttered prayer by Himself, and little diminution of cheer on the part of the company at large, they left John

MacGregor, and set off down Glen Fruin in the gathering dusk.

They took over Shantron, at the mouth of Glen Finlas, for the night, and celebrated their triumph in various ways, not all to the local inhabitants' approval, the women's in especial; and in the morning were on their way up long Loch Lomondside, much outnumbered and delayed by a half-mile-long drove of cattle. They did not anticipate attack or resistance, and experienced none. By the time that they reached Ardlui, and the parting of the ways, they counted their booty as over six hundred cattle-beasts, two hundred and forty horses and five hundred sheep and goats, a fair recompense for a quarter-hour's fighting. The division of the spoil inevitably resulted in some argument. Alastair left his own Glen Strae and Roro folk here, on their northwards march, to accompany the Glen Gyle and Balquhidder contingents eastwards. He had the sad duty of informing John's widow at Stronvar of her loss.

26

It was almost three weeks later before Alastair found time
and opportunity to visit Inveraray, to see MacCailean Mhor.
He went well escorted this time, for now that Argyll had got
what he wanted from him, who could tell what his reactions
might be? And it would do no harm to demonstrate his
status as a victorious commander, rather than some sort
of outlawed supplicant. So he took two score Gregorach,
bristling with arms – to some considerable alarm of the
townsfolk of Inveraray.

In the event, however, his demonstration was rather wasted,
for MacCailean Mhor was from home, the journey abortive.
The earl had gone to Castle Campbell, in the Ochil Hills
near to Stirling, they were told, a strong Lowland seat built
by Argyll's grandfather. It seemed that there was a great
stir at court. Elizabeth Tudor was almost certainly dying,
and James was awaiting the hoped-for news all but with his
baggage packed, ready. There were likely to be big changes
in Scotland in the near future, and the Campbell chief wanted
to reap any benefits available.

This news put Alastair in a quandary. He desired word with
Argyll, but he could hardly take his Gregorach escort down to
Stirling; and if he went alone, he would almost certainly be
arrested as outlaw, especially after Glens Finlas and Fruin,
and possibly hanged out of hand. So it was back to Glen Strae
meantime.

Spring came to the Highlands, and the MacGregors, with
all the extra cattle to feed, welcomed the sprouting pasture,
their stocks of hay and oat-straw exhausted. No attempts were
made to oust them from their valleys meantime. As far as
repercussions were concerned, for them the Colquhoun and
Macfarlane episodes might never have occurred.

That is, until Mary Gray, with the Methven steward,

arrived. She came concernedly, with urgent news, in early
April. Lady Marie had sent her the tidings. Queen Elizabeth
was dead, James *was* named as her heir, and indeed already
proclaimed as King of England, in London, and was now on
his way south with most of his court. He had left on 5th April.
But two days before that he had presided over a celebratory
Privy Council meeting, which of course had been much taken
up with procedural matters and arrangements for the rule of
Scotland meantime. But it had not been so preoccupied with
the long-waited succession and its consequences as to ignore
the MacGregors and their recent activities. The raids on Glens
Fruin and Finlas, and the slaying at the former, had aroused
King and council to unexampled fury, no word spoken in
their favour by Argyll or others, with Ludovick still in the
south. Terrible punishment was decided upon and made law.
The MacGregors were to be exterminated, one and all, by
every means possible, even the name of MacGregor forbidden,
banished, proscribed. None were ever again to bear that name.
None so calling himself or herself could exist in law, none
could own property, buy or sell, be christened, married or
buried . . .

Alastair's eyes widened. "That . . . is . . . impossible!" he
got out.

"It is now the law, passed by King and council, nevertheless. How they will impose it, or try to, God knows!
But Marie said that it was passed without dissent. And not
only that. The outlawry decrees against you were changed
to Letters of Fire and Sword, which means that every
man has not only the right but the *duty* to slay your
clansfolk and burn their houses and take their property.
All who can claim to be neighbours of your people are
released from the Disarming Act and obliged to proceed
against you. And any taking your part is guilty of treason
against the realm and is to suffer accordingly. I suppose
that *I*, coming here, am so guilty! Oh, Alastair, what have
you done!"

"I have carried out my word to MacCailean Mhor, Lieutenant of the North, whatever. And repaid the Gregorach debt to
Colquhoun and his friends. But, Mary, you should not have
come. Not *you*!"

"I had to. Who else would warn you? Oh, my dear, what are we to do?"

"You, lass, go back to Methven, and bide there. They will not touch the Master of Gray's daughter and mother of the Duke of Lennox's son! As for me and mine, *we* bide in Glen Strae. I bring in my outlying people, and we guard our mountains and valleys as we know how. Let them try to take us! Who, think you, could do it? Not Colquhoun. Not Black Duncan. Not Argyll himself. No Lowland army could win at us. Let them bring their Letters of Fire and Sword! Paper! *We* will do the burning! Burn the Letters! We the nameless ones!"

Brave words, even though Alastair's heart sank somewhat.

Mary looked unconvinced. "For a time you may survive this, Alastair. But for how long? You cannot keep it up always, as in some besieged castle."

"If we show them all that we are not to be overcome here, they will bow to the reality, whatever. They may not *call* us MacGregor – but they will respect MacGregor broadswords and dirks! The time will come when much of all this will be forgotten, I say. Especially with King James down in London. And no doubt many of his lords and great ones with him. For how long has he to be gone?"

"None know. But James has been looking to this for years, always with Patrick's urgings and guidance. I cannot think that he will return to Scotland soon. He has talked so often about sitting on England's golden throne! He will wish to settle into it, I would say. And there will be much to detain him, undoubtedly. Not only a new reign starting but a wholly new situation for both realms. Two kingdoms to try to bring together."

"So much the better, then. For us. And – what of Vicky?"

She took her head. "That I do not know either. To my sorrow. James will not let him go readily. However unkindly he acts towards Vicky, he seems to need him somehow, his nearest kin – apart from this Arabella Stewart, his rival. Vicky sends me letters. He promises that he will come home so soon as he can. But he can say no better."

"Perhaps James will find other councillors and friends in England now . . .?"

They had to leave it at that.

Alastair did not offer to escort Mary back to Methven. Sadly, the less she was seen in his company the better.

It was not long thereafter before word began to reach Glen Strae that Letters of Fire and Sword were no idle threat, even though it was Argyll himself, as Lieutenant, who had been given the main responsibility for carrying them out. First came news that Aulay MacAulay had been arrested and imprisoned, awaiting trial as sympathetic towards the MacGregors. No doubt that was MacCailean Mhor's own doing. Then they heard that Black Duncan was stirring again, actually using bloodhounds to track down any individual Roro cattle-herders who were moving their beasts up to the high summer-time shieling pastures, and then slaying them and taking the cattle. It was this customary seasonal shieling process which now proved the Gregorach weakness. On all the clan's lands, however remote and defensively situated, men had to take their stock off to the scattered high grazings in herds large and small, and these were vulnerable while so doing. Little groups were followed and assailed. Roro suffered worst, for his people's shielings were largely up in the Rannoch area, some on the perimeter of the moor itself; and one such party of drovers was intercepted by a large band, with hounds, under Robert Campbell, Glenorchy's younger son now reached manhood, and slaughtered to a man, their heads being cut off – for there was now a money-bounty on MacGregor heads. Similar reports came in from other areas.

Alastair fumed and fretted. It was all very well to make a fortress area of Glen Strae and Roro and Glen Gyle; but men had to venture out on occasion. Moreover, even if the drovers escaped back to safety, their cattle could now be taken, and cattle were their livelihood. Mary Gray had been right to ask for how long the Gregorach could keep up their defiance.

Then the last straw was laid. A message came to announce that his brother John's three infant sons had been taken from their mother at Stronvar in Balquhidder, and were now in custody.

This forced decision upon Alastair MacGregor. He had been unhappy indeed over his brother's death and its effect upon his wife and children. This latest was beyond all acceptance. Moreover, the eldest boy, of five years, was now tanister, heir to the chiefship. It was quite inconceivable that he, the chief, could let this continue. He must go and see, and if possible, bargain with MacCailean Mhor.

From one of the wandering friars he learned that Argyll was more and more taking a leading part in the rule of Scotland, now that the King and court were in London, and was consequently less often at Inveraray, using his Castle Campbell seat near Stirling. So that was where Alastair must go, and necessarily, secretly, and without escort. So, reluctantly discarding his MacGregor kilt, plaid and tartans, he dressed himself in shabby packman's Lowland clothing, and taking an old garron as mount, set out for the south, leaving an apprehensive Rob Ban in charge at Glen Strae. This was something that had to be done, his chiefly duty.

He went by Strathearn and Methven, a humble traveller, unmolested. He was a little concerned about calling on Mary, in case it got known, but he felt that he had to see her, even briefly. He was no less warmly received than usual, Mary exclaiming at his strange appearance, even laughing at it. But she was in no more laughing mood than was he. She had heard much of what was happening to the Gregorach, and was desperately unhappy and worried about it. She was doubtful of the wisdom of him going to see Argyll, and indeed wondered whether it would be possible for him to go much further south than Stirling, in fact all the way to London, there to throw himself and his people on the King's mercy, with Vicky to speak for him. It would be an extraordinary and difficult undertaking, but it might be worth it.

He shook his head. That would take weeks. And James had as good as signed his death-warrant anyway, before he left. What mercy could be expected there, even with the duke's support? He had nothing to offer the monarch, but he just might have something to offer Argyll. And he could not risk being away fron Glen Strae for weeks, in these circumstances. No, it was Stirling for him.

Mary agreed that he might have something to offer. In a

recent message, the Lady Marie had told her that Tullibardine had suggested to the council that instead of seeking to slaughter the MacGregors, the whole now nameless clan could be shipped off to the Isle of Lewis, there to use their undoubted military skills to keep the MacDonalds at bay and so enable the monarch's fond scheme of a colony to be re-established. Or alternatively, their fighting men could be enrolled *en masse* to go overseas to fight *England*'s enemies, the Spaniards, in their ongoing warfare. These proposals had aroused some interest, she said; and James might well consider them.

Alastair wondered about that, needless to say, but agreed to keep it in mind.

They parted in a state of considerable emotion and only partly hidden distress, words more than usually inadequate.

Next day he approached Stirling cautiously, not entirely satisfied that his disguise would serve his required anonymity. However, no one seemed to be interested in one more packman to add to others thronging the market-place, and he made his way up the steep narrow streets to the castle approaches.

The citadel on its rock seemed to be singularly devoid of activity, no doubt as a result of court and nobility being so largely gone to London meantime. Taking a chance, Alastair went up to the gatehouse itself, and there asked the bored guards whether the Earl of Argyll was in residence.

Astonished, the pair gazed at him. "What's the likes o' you at, spierin' for my lord o' Argyll?" one demanded.

"I have a message for him, from one of the Campbell lairds." That, he hoped, sounded suitably humble.

"Hech – a Hielantman!" No doubt his voice scarcely matched his appearance. "Whit way . . .?"

"Yon Earl o' Argyll's a Hielantman tae, mind," his companion warned him.

"Ooh, aye. Och, weel – he'll be at yon Castle Campbell o' his. That used to be called the Gloum," Alastair was informed. "He's biding there, the noo. Ower by Dollar, yonder."

Alastair had passed Dollar, when riding from Falkland to Stirling, more than once. It was ten miles, no more.

So he journeyed on, along the Ochil hill-foots to Castle Campbell. It was rather an extraordinary place, or at least extraordinarily sited for so large an establishment, perched like some eagle's eyrie up on a rocky promontory between the steep ravines of two cascading burns, all but waterfalls, called the Burns of Care and Doleur. Such a position was apt enough for some small Highland chieftain's tower, but odd for a great earl's establishment, and giving the impression that its builder had been distinctly concerned for his safety – no doubt with reason, for he had been renowned for making enemies. The names of the burns, Care and Doleur, and the former name of the original fortalice which Argyll had converted, the Gloum, gave no very cheerful air to the place.

Yet it was a fine house, tall and commanding within its high courtyard, the shape of which had to follow the outline of the rock-top site. Alastair had difficulty in gaining admittance until the seeming packman announced that he carried a personal verbal message for my lord Earl, from the Chief of MacGregor. That at least got him into the courtyard, there to wait.

When Argyll at length appeared, after first failing to recognise his visitor and then registering evident astonishment, he quickly adopted a frigid attitude.

"How dare you come to my house, man?" he demanded. "This is an affront! You, now a nameless, landless vagabond, sought by the law and all the forces of the realm! To come *here*!"

"I came because I had to, my lord. To report on my doings. On *your* behalf, against Colquhoun and Macfarlane. And so seek your aid, as a consequence, whatever." It is to be feared that that last was said less humbly than the circumstances might have warranted.

"Aid? From me? You will get no aid here, wretch!"

"Yet you owe it to me, MacCailean Mhor, do you not? I and my people are hounded and assaulted and slain for doing *your* bidding! You owe it, if ever man did. You may not show it openly, I recognise, as Lieutenant of the North. But privily you could and should do much . . ."

"I could not, and will not!"

"What then, if I was to shout it aloud to all, *who* had urged, even commanded me to assail the Colquhouns? Testify to the council. Call on others to verify it? That you visited me at Glen Strae beforehand, to order it. I have witnesses . . ."

"None would heed you, a forsworn outlaw and rebel! Forby,

308

you would never be able so to speak, for I can, and will, shut your mouth. Do not doubt that, fool!"

Alastair changed his tone a little, advisedly. "See you, here is folly, yes. *Your* folly. You have gained your desired ends, but you may well need the Gregorach yet. You have enemies still. Glenorchy, Ardkinglas. And you will have the Duke of Lennox against you now, and the Master of Gray also. MacGregor could be of use to you . . ."

"There is no MacGregor, any longer. You are finished."

"Yet my clan, in arms, holds Glen Strae, Roro, Glen Gyle, lands bordering yours. Bring us down – if you can! And who will gain then? Glenorchy, I swear, not MacCailean Mhor!"

"I will ensure otherwise."

"You may try. But more than trying will be necessary to dislodge MacGregor from Glen Strae. You will need an army, whatever, and a large one! And will the lords and council be happy to find one for you? Much blood shed."

"It will be *your* blood that is shed!"

"Mine matters not. But innocent folk. Women and bairns. Does even the Campbell war against such, now? Bairns, yes. My brother's three infant sons have been taken, the eldest but five years. Their mother a widow now. By your orders?"

"I know naught of that."

"But you *could* have them sent back to their mother."

"Why should I? Better that I send you to join them! Before they hang you!"

Alastair shook his head. "You will not do that last, I think. Even you." He tried another tack. "See you, you could serve your own cause, as you ever seek to do, hurt whom it will. And also King James's. He still favours this Isle of Lewis settlement. Tullibardine, I am told, suggested to him that, if the whole of Clan Alpin was given the Lewis, or part of it, then they could all go there and bide there. We would keep the MacDonalds at bay and protect the other settlers. Before, I rejected this whatever. But now, in this pass, I would be prepared to go. The King said, then, that he would consider it. That he was interested . . ."

"You are well informed, damn you! How?"

"All men are not my enemies. You should remember that, MacCailean Mhor. But – how say you? Put that to King

James. It would please him, I think. And do *you* no harm. For although you are Lieutenant of the North, His Grace does not love you, I hear!"

The earl turned away tight-lipped and strode the length of the chamber. When he came back, his features were set hard.

"No!" he said. "It is not to be considered. You will not escape your fate so easily, wriggle as you may. I will not let you and your outlaws go to the Isles. You would still be too near to my Argyll. Indeed, I think that I shall not let *you* go, at all. I have you here now and shall hold you. Till they hang you!"

"I think not." All along Alastair had recognised the possibility of this reaction to his visit, and had taken such precautions as he could. "Others know that I have come to your house, here. They know at Stirling Castle. Other friends of mine. Why should I visit you, in this pass, if I did not know that I was safe with you? That you and I are in league. Hand in hand, whatever. Even though I am at the horn. If you hold me now, all the realm will hear of it, and ask why? Why then did I come?"

"Curse you . . . .!"

"Not only that, my lord. But if I am not back to Glen Strae in four days' time, Roro and my uncle will descend in force upon your Inveraray town, and treat it as you seek to treat the Gregorach! They have their orders, and will not be loth to do it, I promise you."

There was silence.

"So, you will not prevent me leaving here, MacCailean Mhor, I think! As I came. But – consider well what I have said. And do not spite yourself in seeking to spite me. And have my nephews returned to their mother, see you." It was Alastair's turn to swing on his heel and leave the other standing, speechless. "Do not trouble to escort me to your door, my lord," he called back.

He strode out and down the stair to the courtyard and his garron, and out, an unlikely packman. None sought to halt him.

27

Back at Glen Strae, Alastair found that events had not stood
still. Some of Black Duncan's men had managed to trap a
Roro family herding sheep and had slain all six, including
two women and a child, cut off their heads and sent them
in a sack to Glenorchy, claiming the bounty money. But the
sack-bearer had himself been intercepted and hanged, and the
victims' bodies and their heads given decent burial, amongst
vows of vengeance. Which vengeance took the form of Roro's
descent in arms on Achallader Castle, Black Duncan's tower
nearest to the Moor of Rannoch, and leaving it a smouldering
ruin. Inevitably there had been casualties.

Alastair could not blame Roro, but such developments did
not assist him in his cause, even though it might drive home
his arguments with Argyll. He urged that there be no more
major provocations of this sort meantime, in the hope that
his conversation with MacCailean Mhor might bear fruit.

But it was difficult to hold his people back in this spring and
summer as reports came in of savagery and violence towards
MacGregors. The killings were not confined to their hereditary
enemies; rogues and scoundrels of various sorts began to see it
as an opportunity to wipe clean their own slates by bringing
in Gregorach heads to sheriffs and justiciars. For instance,
a younger son of Dalzell of that Ilk, himself at the horn
for murder, delivered two heads to a Privy Councillor, and
was granted remission. And Colquhoun of Camstradden, a
noted cattle-thief and ravager in a large way, outlawed for it,
managed to capture two MacGregor drovers, and although
he hanged both, one was already dead, on his own initiative,
having stabbed himself with his own dirk rather than suffer
the indignity of being hanged by a Colquhoun And so it went
on. The season for sending the cattle up to the shielings and
lofty pastures was inevitably the dangerous time, with the men

no longer able to remain secure in their embattled glens. The droves had to be escorted by quite large companies of armed men, therefore, with consequent delay.

Matters reached such a pitch that Alastair could no longer control his clansfolk when, in August, Roro himself was captured, after a bloody fight with a large troop under Robert Campbell, Glenorchy's son, who was proving a fiercer fighter than his father, taken to Balloch Castle and there hanged. This was beyond all, and fury overflowed amongst the Gregorach. Alastair, mourning his friend, was unable to damp it down this time. Any and every Campbell seen was to be slain, went the word.

No message had come from MacCailean Mhor.

In something like desperation, Alastair went to Methven, although he had been avoiding the place advisedly, lest he got Mary Gray into disrepute. But he found her gone, for a spell, to Castle Huntly to be with David Gray.

Then, word did come from Argyll. At least, it came from Ardkinglas, who announced that MacCailean Mhor wished to speak with Himself. He was back at Inveraray meantime; but recognising that Alastair might not be eager to visit him there in the Campbell capital, in present circumstances, he suggested that they met on, as it were, neutral ground, at Ardkinglas House itself. A secret meeting, necessarily. Himself to send word when he would come.

This put Alastair in a dilemma. He trusted neither Ardkinglas nor his chief, and it all might be a trap. Yet he *was* anxious to speak with Argyll, to try to come to some arrangement with him to improve on this dire and ever-worsening situation. Something *had* to be done. Possibly MacCailean Mhor saw this also.

He decided that he could not refuse this invitation. But he would take precautions. Secret it might have to be, but he was not going to deliver himself into Campbell hands, if he could prevent it, as totally helpless. He would take a company of armed Gregorach with him as far as the head of Loch Fyne, and leave them nearby, as an evident threat to Ardkinglas, and possibly Argyll himself, if there were any underhand attempts or developments, enough men to ensure that Ardkinglas House would provide no shelter for treachery.

A courier was sent to inform Ardkinglas that MacGregor of Glenstrae would come to his house in four days' time. He would come alone, as requested, but a party of his clansmen would not be far away.

He discussed with Rob Ban how he should seek to bargain with Argyll. What had they to offer? The lives of many Campbells spared, that was the obvious first step. But would that greatly concern MacCailean Mhor? Warfare against his hereditary foes, the MacDonalds? That had already been more or less offered over the Lewis colonisation, which had not seemed to impress that man greatly. What else? A fighting force at hand for general use by the Lieutenant of the North and Admiral of the Western Seas? That *might* appeal.

Rob had no faith in any appeal or bargain with Argyll himself. He would abandon any arrangement, break any bargain or promise, to suit his own advantage. This of Ardkinglas, for instance. He, Argyll, had sought for Himself to bring down Ardkinglas, his enemy; now he was using *him* to reach Himself. The man was utterly untrustworthy. No, Alastair would be better to demand to see the King, and throw himself on the royal mercy. Go down to London, where the duke would help him. Argyll was the King's Lieutenant and Privy Councillor. If Alastair demanded to be allowed to see the monarch, who had shown him favour in the past after all, could Argyll refuse to allow it? If he stressed this Lewis project, which was dear to James; and also the notion of a MacGregor standing force at the King's call at any time, in Scotland or elsewhere. If, beforehand, he sent a message to Lennox, to tell the monarch of his offers, and then let Argyll know that James knew that he was coming – would that not force the Campbell's hand? To refuse, then, would be as good as slighting the sovereign.

Alastair saw the point of that. Yes, he would take that line.

Rob Ban with him, then, and fifty Gregorach, Alastair set off for Loch Fyne and Ardkinglas four days later. They went by secret ways this time, up Glen Lochy and over the high shoulder of Ben Lui to the Corrie Aonaich and so down into upper Glen Fyne and on to the head of that sea-loch. Then round to the east side of this. Ardkinglas lay barely a couple of miles down.

The house thereof was no very strong place, standing in the mouth of its glen, where the Kinglas Water joined the loch. They could not approach it without being observed, Alastair recognised, especially with its castleton community of Cairndow to pass first; but there was no harm in letting Ardkinglas see that his visitor was not without support. They passed the Cairndow houses openly, and fairly soon afterwards Rob Ban and his men were left at a wooded spur less than half a mile from the house. Alastair went on alone.

Campbell of Ardkinglas had not been unaware of his approach and stood awaiting him at his door. There was no sign of Argyll.

"Ha, Glenstrae, so we meet again!" he greeted. "Much has happened since last we forgathered."

"To be sure. But should you, a careful man, be naming me Glenstrae? Is that not now a breaking of the law, Ardkinglas?"

"Ah, MacCailean Mhor will be the judge of that! He seeks word with you – for the good of us all."

"He was not seeking *your* good when last I saw him! Nor, I think, mine!"

The other shrugged. "Happenings change attitudes! I see that you have brought a force of men with you. This was to be a secret meeting."

"I have left them some way off. It will be secret enough. We MacGregors, nameless ones, must travel warily, especially in Campbell country! Is Argyll here?"

"Not yet. But you will see him, fear not. Come you inside. A dram? We will have a celebratory feast later."

In the house, Ardkinglas led him to the stair-tower in the angle, where he gestured to the winding turnpike. "Up to the hall, Glenstrae; my wife is there. I will join you for a dram. Have my folk look out for MacCailean Mhor."

Alastair started up the corkscrew of the narrow stairway. Three turns up, beside a slit-window and he stopped. Two men, with drawn swords and daggers, barred the way. He turned. Behind him were others, completely blocking descent.

Cursing, he reached for his own dirk. More men were crowding up and down, naked steel in all hands.

He was trapped, most effectively. Such staircases were built for defence by one man against many. There was no way that he could move. He might stab one or two of these Campbells before their swords got him; but there were more, no doubt, round the bends of the stair. He shrugged, and dropped hands to sides.

Men lunged to grab him savagely, his dirk snatched from him, and he was hustled back downstairs. At the foot, Ardkinglas was waiting, grinning. He said nothing, but pointed his minions along the passage to where a door stood open. Through this doorway Alastair was thrust, and the door slammed and locked behind him. He was in a small, empty, vaulted chamber, lit only by an arrow-slit window, as secure a prisoner as might be.

He berated himself fiercely. Would he never learn? Never to trust a Campbell. Wry or crooked mouth the name meant, and they lived up to it! Here he was, penned like any foolish sheep. Admittedly his men were not far away. But Rob Ban would not come storming this house for some time, assuming a conference to be going on. Seemingly he was to await Argyll as a captive.

He waited.

It was some time before the door was unlocked to admit half a dozen men, dirks in hands, with Ardkinglas at their backs.

"So, felon, it is decided that we take *you* to MacCailean Mhor at Inveraray, not him to come here," he said. "More seemly!" He waved to his people. "Bind him."

The men surged forward, to grasp him, twist his hands behind his back and tie his wrists with twine, securely. He did not resist. At least he could still retain a chief's dignity.

He was taken out and pushed further along that passage to a back door. This opened on to a courtyard, lined by stables. This they crossed diagonally, to a gateway which led out into shoreside woodland. Down there he saw a little wooden jetty – and his heart sank when he perceived a boat there, and rowers, waiting. He was going to be rowed across Loch Fyne to Inveraray, not taken by road round the head of it. So his Gregorach, in hiding, would not be able to rescue him, as he had hoped.

It was a bitter blow. Even when his people saw it, if they

realised what was happening and that *he* was in the boat, a prisoner, they could scarcely race round to the other side of the loch and as far as the town, miles, before the craft got across by water. Here was the worst yet.

Bundled into the boat with five of his captors, so that the craft was indeed overcrowded, he was flung into the stern and they pushed off.

Alastair, betrayed and bound, still had his wits – and his voice. Loud he yelled, knowing well how sound travels over water, at the pitch of his lungs. "Gregorach! Gregorach!" Surely never had that famed Clan Alpin war-cry resounded in less likely circumstances.

A blow to the side of his head knocked him all but unconscious. But not for long. Rallying, he sought to gather his wits. His hands were tied but his legs were not, so that they had not had to carry him down. They were not far from the shore yet. Without hands, could he swim? Not on his front but on his back? Kicking out with his feet. The thought was no sooner in his mind than he was up and leaping backward over the stern of the boat before any could grab him. With a great splash of cold water, he went under.

Desperately active now, he came up on his back and, kicking forcefully, rhythmically, headed for the shore, thankful indeed that he had not come mounted and so was not wearing long and heavy riding-boots.

The shore was no more than one hundred yards away. But to go straight back would bring him again into enemy hands. So he struck off at a tangent, half-left, in the direction in which he had left his escort, and from where, if God was good, they might be coming to his rescue – if they had heard his cries. With the exertion of his back-swimming he had not much breath to spare, but he summoned enough to shout a series of gulping "Gregorachs" nevertheless, amidst his splashings.

The men in the boat, of course, taken by surprise as they were, did not delay in coming after him. But he had leapt off from the stern, and it took a little time to turn the craft's bows and pull in pursuit. Fairly quickly they did catch up with him, but found it less easy to capture a swimming man from a boat than it might seem. They had to ship oars and lean over the side, and the craft lost way. Also Alastair swung off at right ngles before they could grasp him. So they had to use the oars again to turn the boat after him, whereupon he promptly changed direction once more, kicking hard.

For how long he could have kept this up he did not know. He was becoming exhausted. And the shore still seemed a fair way off. Also, when he reached land, the boat could do the same, and its crew, less tired, could probably outrun him and recapture him. He tried another yell or two, but just had not the breath for it.

Then, above the shouts of men and his own panting and splashing, he heard what was like an echo of his own calling, "Gregorach! Gregorach!", repeated again and again. He did not, could not, turn his head to look landwards; but flooding thankfulness came over him as he realised that his people were indeed aware of his plight and were responding. How far away they were he could not tell, but the slogan-shouting did not sound very far off. He flailed the water with legs and feet. If only he had his hands free. And without the weight of his sodden clothing . . .

It was a jarring pain in one foot which at first dismayed him – and then another changed sudden despair into hope again. His feet were striking stone, rock. He was in shallows. And the tide was out. That boat would not be able readily to come in amongst rocks and shallows. Men could jump out and come after him. But he had a chance still.

In fact, the boatmen also recognised their being in difficulties and probably they could see, as Alastair could not, that the two score MacGregors were none so far off, and more than capable of wading in, and even swimming to the rescue of their chief. If they had to face fury, perhaps they preferred that of their master, Ardkinglas to that of the Gregorach. At any rate, the boat swung about and went back whence it had come, leaving the quarry gasping and struggling in the shallows.

Soon strong arms were helping him to his feet, amidst exclamations, cursings and cries for vengeance, Rob Ban's dirk cutting the rope which bound those wrists.

Gulping for breath, Alastair told them to get him away from there, not to think of a raid on Ardkinglas House meantime, as was being suggested. Revenge could wait. Argyll might have been waiting on the other shore, with many men. Best to get back to Glen Strae as quickly as possible, through the mountains. *He* would do well enough. He was not injured. His clothes would dry on him. Home with them . . .

Snarling like a pack of wolves, the Gregorach turned to head back northwards.

28

It was two weeks later that Alastair had an unexpected visitor at Glen Strae, none other than his erstwhile guarantor, Sir John Murray of Tullibardine, riding with only four of his men, and being brought up to Stronmilchan by a score of suspicious Gregorach, who always now were on the watch for intruders. The greetings were wary, in the circumstances.

"You are brave, Sir John, to risk being seen in the company of so black and wretched a character as the outlawed and condemned chief of the nameless Children of the Mist! Welcome, however, to the beleaguered Glen Strae!"

"I much regret it all, Glenstrae," the other said, dismounting. "But you have been foolish, headstrong. You must have known that this would happen, after your massacre of the Colquhouns. The folly of it! What made you do it, man? I have taken your part in the past. But now . . .!"

"Argyll made me do it. And it was no massacre but a battle of sorts. Colquhoun outnumbered us two to one."

"Argyll? What mean you?"

"I mean that Argyll besought me to do it. For his own ends. He wanted Colquhoun brought low. If we, the Gregorach, would do it for him, he would have the outlawry on my people lifted, cease our persecution. I played *my* part, but he has not played his . . ."

"Argyll! Dear God, is this truth? *He* ordered it?"

"*My* word is not to be doubted, Sir John!" That was stiff. "It was all of his secret devising. Now, he repays me by rejection. He sought to capture me at Ardkinglas's house under pretext of conferring with me."

"No, there you wrong him at least, Glenstrae. That was not his doing, but Ardkinglas's. He assured me of that . . ."

"You have seen him, then? Talked with him? Since?"

"I come from him. He came to *me*, at Perth. Besought me

me to visit you here. To tell you that. Tell you that it was Ardkinglas, seeking to ingratiate himself with him, Argyll . . ."

"I do not believe it, whatever!"

"He swore it. He sent me to tell you. And to offer you terms . . ."

"His only terms, when I visited him at his Castle Campbell, were to take and hang me!"

"He has had time to consider. I do not love Argyll – few men do – but I believe that he has thought better as to you and yours. In token of which he has had your brother's young sons handed over into my keeping at Huntingtower. Their mother, after all, is my kinswoman. They will be safe with me, meantime."

"For that I am grateful, at least. If their mother could remain with them?"

"I will see to it. They will have to be called Murray now! But, Argyll would have word with you . . ."

"I have heard that before, to my cost!"

"This time I judge he means you no ill. It is this of the Lewis colony. Argyll, as Lieutenant and Admiral of the Western Seas, is being held responsible by King James for the failure to subdue the MacDonalds and MacLeods and protect the settlers. *I* suggested to James, before he left for London, that you and your MacGregors might redeem yourselves in his eyes by going and settling there and opposing the Clan Donald and MacLeods. He, the King, did not dismiss the matter. Now Argyll is considering it, for it would undoubtedly aid him in his duties in the Hebrides."

"I told him so, at Castle Campbell. He scorned it."

"Well, he has thought again. Now, he offers you the chance to discuss it. He cannot himself give you the necessary pardons and permission to go to Lewis, for the King signed the letters of Fire and Sword against you, and only he can revoke them. But he will allow you to go to England, as I proposed, to plead your case with James. And with the Duke of Lennox's help, I think that you may well win out of this tangle. You and yours would settle into the Hebrides well enough, I swear. And be no longer hunted fugitives."

Alastair shrugged. "It could be so, yes. But how am I to believe Argyll? Trust his word?"

"He sends me with a firm promise to convey you across the border to England. Gave this before myself and Inchaffray, as witnesses. And he has already given, as token of his good faith, the three bairns into my care. And will have Aulay MacAulay released also, to go to England, if you agree to it all."

Alastair drew a deep breath. "Very well. I will do it. Although I still do not trust Argyll. But – something I *have* to do. This cannot go on as it is."

"Can you persuade your people to go to the Western Isles? All of them?"

"I think so, yes. I have discussed it with Glengyle and my uncle Rob Ban. They see it as better than always being hunted outlaws. Yes, given lands there, Clan Alpin could begin a new life in the Hebrides. After all, Alpin himself came from those parts, King of Dalriada."

"Good! Then, let us hope that King James will see where lies advantage to his Scottish realm. You will go to England?"

"If that is how it must be brought about, yes. But how do I get to the border in safety?"

"Argyll himself will provide escort. But there is a condition. He must have hostages for your sure return from London. He fears that you might be tempted not to come back. Seek to make some other arrangement with the King, against his interests. Not return . . ."

"The fool! And abandon my clan?"

"*I* said that, yes. But he insists. He must have securities, he says. And notable securities, to impress the Privy Council that he acts in accordance with their interests also. To suspend letters of Fire and Sword, lacking the King's signature, is no light matter, indeed impossible. So there must be token submission, in the interim, to make it seem lawful. He wants thirty of your people, to be held as hostages, until you come back with the royal decision."

"Thirty . . .!"

"Yes. Why thirty, I know not. But it must be an impressive number to make it seem sufficiently important, adequate to the occasion."

"But . . ."

"They are not to be prisoners. They will be well housed

321

and treated. But you may well be away for a month and more. Some such proof of good faith is necessary . . ."

"Good faith! The Campbell talks of good faith!"

"It is for the council's concern. He must carry the council with him in this matter. You must see that, Glenstrae."

"I will have to think on this, whatever. Consult others . . ."

"Then do so quickly, man. For I cannot linger here."

Alastair did consult Rob Ban and his cousins. There was little disagreement. All saw this scheme as a possible way out of a hopeless situation – the *only* way out in evidence. None trusted Argyll, but they did trust Tullibardine, who had proved his goodwill in the past with gold and silver. And risked royal disfavour on the Gregorach's behalf. They would do as he advised, lacking alternatives.

Tullibardine went off, as satisfied as the circumstances warranted.

At least, ten days later, marching south with thirty of his men, volunteers all, Alastair need not fear interference, however askance were the looks cast upon them. Disarming Act or none, they went armed.

They were bound for Stirling again, where Highlands met Lowlands, and this time MacCailean Mhor was waiting for them. From the lofty fortress-citadel, of course, their approach could be seen for miles, even though they had crossed the Forth at Fords of Frew rather than by Stirling Bridge itself.

Argyll was scarcely affable – but then, he seldom was. However, he was civil, and did not greet Alastair as wretch, fool or scoundrel, not even making reference to the so evident Gregorach swords and dirks; nor yet to the two pipers who led the way up to the castle gatehouse blowing their vehement challenge.

"You have come, then," he said, carefully avoiding giving Alastair a name, although he frowned at having to wait until the music died away to make himself heard.

"We have come at your behest, Tullibardine bringing it. With your sworn word."

"Come, then."

"A moment, my lord. Before we enter this castle, where we could be held against our will, I seek your word from your

322

own lips. Before these others, as witnesses. Word that I will be conveyed safe to England; and that these, my people and friends, will remain cared for and unharmed until I return."

Argyll's frown was darker. "That was the message I gave Tullibardine. It is sufficient."

"Sufficient to bring us *this* far! But I want to hear you swear it, MacCailean Mhor, before we enter this fortress."

"Insolent! But so be it. I swear it. Swear that you shall be taken over the border into England. And that these others will be held here, unharmed, until you return."

"And if I do not return, with the King's pardon? What then, for these?"

"That will be for the council to decide. I can say no better."

"I require better. I bring them, my people, only as bond and pledge of my return. When I do so, they have served their part. I will not have them to remain prisoner here."

"Very well. I say that, when you return, they shall not remain prisoner."

Alastair raised his voice. "All hear that! MacCailean Mhor pledges his word."

A cheer, somewhat derisory, rose from the Gregorach ranks.

Argyll turned away. "On the morrow we go to Edinburgh," he threw back over his shoulder. "These will lodge there, in that castle. Until you return . . ."

They followed him into the fortress.

The journey to Edinburgh, thirty-five miles, was a piecemeal affair. Argyll was not going to demean himself by journeying with the outlawed Gregorach, and rode off with his mounted escort, leaving a foot detachment to accompany the hostages; but neither were the MacGregors going to demean themselves by marching at the pace of these latter, themselves used to covering ground at a considerably smarter pace. So although they all set out together, they quickly separated into three parties, with the guards, if that is what they were, very much in the rear. How long MacCailean Mhor took to cover the distance they did not know, but the Gregorach made a point of displaying their prowess as travellers, and whilst not seeking to go thirty-five miles in one day, did twenty-five afoot, reaching Niddry-Seton for the night and arriving at Edinburgh Castle by mid-forenoon next day. After all, most of them would be cooped up, with a minimum of leg-stretching presumably, for some time thereafter.

They found the quarters allotted to them in that great citadel on its rock not exactly prison-like but less than comfortable or extensive, food plain but adequate. There was no sign of Argyll.

Next morning there was a surprise for Alastair. A young man came, to announce in arrogant fashion that he was Colin Campbell, Younger of Glenorchy, and that it was his duty to escort the former Glenstrae to the Borders and into England. A horse would be provided.

Alastair stared. So this was Black Duncan's elder son and heir, brother of the savage Robert Campbell. They had never met previously – and Alastair did not much like what he saw, nor the implications of using this individual as his escort. But he could scarcely refuse to accompany him. Apparently they were to go forthwith.

He said farewell to his people, there and then, and followed young Campbell out into the upper courtyard before St Margaret's Chapel, where another surprise awaited him, in the shape of a half troop of the Edinburgh town guard, mounted and waiting, with a spare brown horse of no great quality for himself. At least, apart from young Glenorchy, he was not going to travel with Campbells. But it seemed an odd task for the town guard, who looked but doubtful horsemen.

Mounting, without remark or waiting for the others, Campbell rode off. The guard formed up around Alastair, eyeing him warily, and they followed on.

That was a strange ride. Glenorchy the Younger stayed well ahead throughout, keeping his own company, aloof, seeming to want nothing to do with his party. Although the escort stayed close to Alastair, none conversed with him, his few remarks to them unanswered. He felt more a prisoner, a man condemned, than he had done hitherto, despite being on his way to see his sovereign-lord.

Berwick-on-Tweed, where they were heading, was fully

fifty miles from Edinburgh, and with the horseflesh provided this was not to be covered in one day. They got as far as Coldinghame by nightfall, where they were put up in the former priory, now apparently a Home possession, where Colin Campbell installed himself, in the King's name, in the former prior's quarters, the rest looking after themselves as best they could. Alastair, used to hard living, made no complaint.

They were at the Tweed by mid-forenoon next day and, where once they would have had great difficulty, as Scots, in gaining entry to the walled town, once Scotland's greatest seaport but long now in English hands, they found the gates wide open and only token guards on duty – thanks to James's accession to the English throne.

Down through the crowded streets to the wide river-mouth they trotted, Alastair interested in all he saw. The port area at the waterside was thronged with shipping; and out from amongst it all a long, spidery bridge of timber projected, with a central portion which could be raised to allow vessels to proceed further upstream. It seemed a fragile link between the two nations, perhaps symbolical – and this no doubt had occurred to King James also, for Mary Gray had said that the monarch, on his way south those few months ago, had commanded it to be the first charge on his new English treasury that a fine stone bridge be built to replace it. No sign of the replacement was as yet evident, testimony to the all but empty treasury James had in fact inherited, to his grievous disappointment and offence.

Distinctly gingerly, young Glenorchy led the way across the creaking timbers.

At the far side, on English soil, Campbell reined up and turned in the saddle. "Dismount!" he commanded briefly, abruptly.

They escort did as it was bid. But Alastair, misliking being thus ordered, and by a Campbell, remained seated.

Scowling, the younger man pointed at him. "I said dismount! You are in England now, fellow. I have carried out MacCailean Mhor's promise – conveyed you into England. That is what he agreed to do, and that is what I have now done, in his name." He turned to the guard. "Have him down! Seize him!"

The Edinburgh men, obviously prepared for this, flung themselves upon the astonished Alastair and dragged him out of the saddle and down, holding him fast.

"Bind him!"

For the second time Alastair MacGregor had his wrists bound behind him with twine, despite his struggles. Then he was hauled and hoisted back up into his saddle again, a difficult proceeding. What the good townsfolk of Spittal, the community on the south bank of Tweed, thought of it all there was no knowing.

Back across the rickety bridge he was taken, guards hemming him in closely now and leading his horse, the Campbell behind. Up through the streets of the walled town they went, clattering. If any perceived that the one tartan-clad horseman was now a bound prisoner, no sign of it was evident. Out through the same North Gate by which they had entered so recently they passed, and onwards on to Scots soil.

Alastair's mind was in turmoil indeed, seething with fury, resentment and self-criticism. Might he not have guessed that something of this sort would eventuate? He might have known! Campbells! He rode, fists clenched behind his back.

It was only midday when they passed Coldinghame, without halting, Colin Campbell well in the lead again. How far they might be going that day Alastair was not informed; indeed no words were addressed to him at all. But he was determined to try to do something to retrieve the situation, possibilities restricted as they were, to put it mildly. It was on the high wastes of heather and gorse on Coldinghame Moor that it came to him that Mary Gray had often spoken of Fast Castle, an extraordinary stronghold built halfway down a precipitous cliff hereabouts, all but impregnable and belonging to Logan of Restalrig, the Master of Gray's cousin. If, by any stroke of good fortune, he could reach that . . .?

What could he do, bound as he was? The only circumstance that he could see in his favour was that crossing this lofty moorland amidst the heather and peat-bogs, their drove-road had degenerated into a mere track which, narrow as it was, forced the horsemen into riding only two abreast and therefore well strung out. If he could find a spot where the track crossed really broken ground, he might be able to kick and knee his mount abruptly away from the man holding his reins, and make off, gaining some lead on the inevitable chase by the surprise. The trouble was, he did not know just where this Fast Castle was situated, save that its cliffs flanked the moor; but there were miles of this moor. Actually, looking eastwards, seawards, he could see where the land fell away suddenly, perhaps a mile off. That would be the cliff-tops, presumably. But where along there was Fast?

He was still pondering the issue when there was shouting in front. There was a dip ahead, and he could see Campbell reined up beyond and pointing back and down. Some of his score or so of captors were here out of sight in this dip, but five still behind him. There might just possibly be some chance here. It was probably a burn in its shallow declivity.

Reaching the lip of this, Alastair saw that it was indeed a burn in a fairly steep little valley. Their track crossed this at an angle, by a tiny ford. But evidently the bottom was boggy, in this wintery weather and Campbell was directing his horsemen to cross a little further down from the path itself, where the beasts' hooves would not sink in so far. Presumably he had no high opinion of the Edinburgh town guard's riding abilities.

Alastair decided that it was now or never, as he slanted down. The man holding his horse's reins edged in front to lead the way across the burn and, his own beast requiring urging and guidance at the water, for moments he was less in control of the captive than heretofore. The next man behind was two lengths off. Suddenly kicking his heels into his horse's flanks with all his might, and leaning forward bodily over the animal's neck to nudge and turn its head sideways, to the right, he managed to get the alarmed and town-bred creature plunging off in that direction, dragging its reins out of the preoccupied guard's grasp. On down the little valley, Alastair kicked and drove his mount.

Shouting behind arose immediately, but he did not look back. Would individuals come after him right away, or wait to form a group?

On he urged that unhappy horse, himself shouting at it

now to speed it on. It was not good at covering this sort of country, over rough and broken ground. But, probably, neither were the guards' beasts. It was the Campbell's mount that he feared, well-bred and used to hill country.

He wondered whether to remain in this little valley, with the burn, or to get up on to the open moorland again, to head more directly seawards? It was the trailing reins, catching on a stunted hawthorn bush, of which there were many in this declivity, that wrenched the horse's head round anyway, and decided him. Up there would probably be better.

Climbing out, he did glance back briefly. Men were much scattered in pursuit but, a curse on it, Young Glenorchy was now in front of the chase, not seventy yards behind.

Alastair could not hope to outrun the Campbell's horse on this animal, which was labouring already. His hands tied behind him, he could not fend attackers off, save with his feet. What, then? How far had he to go to those hoped-for cliffs? Half a mile and more. It did not look hopeful. But if he did get there, he would rather throw himself off and risk tumbling down the cliff, possibly to his death, than to yield himself up again.

He pounded on, his mount making heavy going of it. The creature had to pick its own way since he could not reach the trailing reins to guide it. Alastair could hear the Campbell's beast drumming ever closer.

The edge of the land was now clear enough, but it still seemed a long way off.

The snortings of the following horse and the beat of hooves sounded now all but alongside.

"Fool! Think you . . . you can . . . escape your fate!" Colin Campbell shouted. "Halt you – or I ride you down."

Alastair kicked his mount the harder.

Then the other was there, close, cantering neck and neck. Campbell reached over to try to grip the fugitive.

Alastair kicked out, not at *his* horse now but at the other's.

It swerved away.

"Curse you!" Young Glenorchy cried. "Dastard!" He dragged his beast's head round again, and tried to ride it directly at the would-be escaper.

Both horses had senses and wills of their own, and well bred as this one was it would not charge headlong into another animal if it could help it. The horse swerved at the last moment.

Campbell retained his seat with difficulty, yelling fury. He had lost a few yards in his efforts.

But he made them up again, with his superior speed. This time he attacked from the rear, where Alastair could not turn to kick backwards effectively. He beat down a fist on the other horse's croup, dirk in hand.

It was that unfortunate animal's turn to swerve, in a panic. Unfortunately, the ground they were covering, moorland, was rough and uneven indeed. Plunging, the beast swung into a hollow, small but enough to upset its canter and balance. Over it pitched, throwing Alastair headlong and itself falling over in sprawling crash.

Winded, part-stunned, Alastair had difficulty in rising, wrists tied behind him. By the time that he was on unsteady feet, others of the guard had caught up and, leaping down, grabbed him, panting.

Campbell did not dismount. Reining close, he bent in the saddle to smash the same dirk-hand across Alastair's face three times in his rage, drawing blood. He poured out his wrath by word of mouth also.

When he had somewhat recovered himself, he turned to the fallen horse, still on the ground and kicking three of its legs only. The fourth, a foreleg, was obviously broken.

"That devil-damned brute! It will not carry anyone again. Leave it," he ordered. "*You* – put him on one of your beasts. This dastard. A cord. Tie his legs also. Together, beneath the horse's belly. All of you. See to it. One of you will have to ride pillion. Do not stand there gaping! Get him up. On that horse. You, there, with the cord – get him up and then tie him, I say. Numbskulls!"

So, somehow, Alastair was bundled up on to another animal and, kick as he would, his ankles tied and linked thus underneath the beast, a painful and difficult process – but he was in such pain anyway that he scarcely noticed this addition. Two of his guards now on one mount, and all thronging him so closely as to make their own riding difficult, they turned and headed back to the track across Coldinghame Moor. Alastair did spare a thought for the injured animal left kicking helplessly in the heather.

They made a slow ride of it to Dunbar, where the prisoner was flung into one of the stinking cells of the Tolbooth, without food or drink, and left to come to terms with his fate.

Next night he was back in Edinburgh Castle, but this time in another prison cell, cold and alone.

29

Guards came for the prisoner next forenoon, to take him to a considerably more comfortable chamber in the fortress where, before a well-doing fire, three men sat at a table, all clerkly-looking, papers before them. They eyed Alastair slightly askance, assessingly, bloodstained and mud-streaked as he was. The best-dressed of the trio, a slenderly built man of middle years with a pursed-up mouth, dismissed the escort with an authoritative flick of the hand.

"I am James Primrose, Clerk to His Grace's Privy Council," he announced in a clipped voice. "You are the former Alastair MacGregor of Glenstrae?"

"I *am* MacGregor of Glenstrae, Himself."

"H'rr'mm. Sit here, then. The council commands that I take from you a disposition anent sundry misdeeds and breakings of the law over these last months. Your own testimony and account is required. You will give it."

That sounded like an order, but Alastair treated it as a question. "I will, and gladly whatever," he said, through thick lips, still swollen from yesterday's treatment.

"You do not have a hand-of-write, I understand?"

"I do not. I am not a clerk."

"H'rr'mm. These others, then, will write down for the council what you have to say." He gestured. "Sit."

"I prefer to stand."

"As you will. All that you aver and testify will be written down. There are many occasions when the council has decided that you have broken the law in the past. But this present enquiry and testimony relates to the grievous and murderous raids on Glens Fruin and Finlas by you and your people, contrary to all law and the peace of the realm, in which many of the Clan Colquhoun in especial were slain. What is now required is what *you* may say as reason and excuse for this outrage."

"That you shall have. But first I do make strong and vehement protest that I should be here at all. I was given the sworn word, before many witnesses, of the Earl of Argyll, Lieutenant of the North, that I would be conveyed safely to the border and into England, there to travel to London to make submissions to the King's Grace himself, and to make offer of my clan's services in the matter of the colony on the Isle of Lewis. I was indeed taken to the border at Berwick-on-Tweed, but once on the English soil I was attacked, and bound prisoner, and brought back here, in violation of Argyll's sworn promise and assurances. I do therefore protest. And say that you have no right to question me now."

"H'rr'mm. That, sir, is no concern of mine. I am here on the Privy Council's orders, to receive your testimony. The circumstances of you being here are not for me to consider. Your protest will be noted and passed on, for the council to judge. Now, your sworn testimony, as before God, as to the outrages against the Colquhouns, Macfarlanes and Buchanans."

"And if I refuse to testify?"

"Then you will be very foolish. This testimony can be only to your advantage. You will be brought to trial. Others will testify against you, no doubt. Not to speak in your own defence will serve you nothing."

"Is this, then, part of my trial?"

"Not so. It is for the Privy Council's consideration."

"Very well. I will tell you the truth of the matter. All of it."

"As God is your witness?"

"As God is my witness, yes. The facts are these, whatever. I, Alastair MacGregor of Glenstrae, declare before God that I have been persuaded, moved and enticed by Archibald Campbell, Earl of Argyll and Lieutenant – "

"Wait, you. You go too fast for these to write it. Speak more slowly. And, I warn you, choose your words with care indeed, when you speak high names!"

"Is the Campbell name higher than that of the Chief of Clan Alpin! *My* race is royal, I would remind you, clerk!"

"H'rr'mm. Proceed then."

More slowly, carefully, Alastair went on. "I was persuaded,

332

moved, to what I am now presently accused of, by the Earl of Argyll himself. Also, indeed, if I had used the counsel and command of that man who enticed me to it, I would have done and committed sundry deeds more – ”

“More slowly, man, slowly!” That to the scratching of quills.

Alastair, in his anger and resentment, did not hide his scorn for clerks and their slow scrapings on paper. “I swear that, Archibald, Earl of Argyll, urged me to use my clansmen to bring down Colquhoun and the others, for his own advantage, promising me that if I did so he would prevail on the council to have the outlawry passed upon us lifted and – ”

“Wait, wait!”

So it went on. Alastair, in fits and snatches, detailed the whole sorry story, or the vital parts of it, relating Ardkinglas's treachery, Argyll's invitations to the Macleans and Camerons to attack MacGregors in Rannoch, his attempt to have him, Alastair, bring down MacAulay of Ardencaple, and all the other provocations. He ended by declaring that he was telling all this in order that the council, and the King's Grace, should know the truth of it, and that innocent men, women and bairns, the King's subjects, should be allowed to live their lives in peace and under the will of Almighty God.

It all took a long time, with much interruption and requests for repetition, Alastair's Highland speech being very different from the clerks' Lowland Doric. But eventually it was done, he made his mark, and was returned to his cold cell.

The following morning he was taken out and led under guard down into the city, through the Lawnmarket and the High Street to the Tolbooth. Passing the Mercat Cross and the west gable of the High Kirk of St Giles, he noted a feature not before seen by him, an enormous black crucifix in painted wood with very extended arms, workmen still hammering at it, and townsfolk staring up in wonder.

At the Tolbooth, Alastair was thrust into one more cell and left. What next?

After a lengthy wait, he was taken out and upstairs to a large chamber which appeared to be the city courtroom. Here at least he saw friends, four of his MacGregor hostages, two his own cousins, all like himself with hands bound behind backs. They greeted each other warmly in their own Gaelic tongue, despite commands from a lengthy table, at the head of the room, for silence.

At that long table sat no fewer than fifteen men, facing down the chamber, with another at one end, facing inwards. At a smaller table nearby were clerks with papers, one of whom Alastair recognised from the day before's interlude.

He scanned the long line of individuals at the main table, seven on either side of one robed as a judge. He did not know most of them, but those he did struck him as ominous indeed – for one was Colin Campbell, Younger of Glenorchy; another Semple of Fulwood, deputy keeper of Dumbarton Castle, who had been his prisoner at Glen Fruin; a third was the Captain of Dunstaffnage, a Campbell fortalice; a fourth was Thomas Fallasdale, burgess of Dumbarton, whose two brothers had died at Glen Fruin; and a fifth was none other than Menzies of that Ilk. If the others were equally carefully chosen, then any proceedings today were a foregone conclusion.

The central robed figure wasted no time. "I am William Hart of Little Preston, Lord Justice-Depute," he announced flatly. "We are here, in assize, in the King's name, to try for treason, mass murder, infringement of the Disarming Act and other reprehensible offences against the laws of this realm, the following." He consulted a paper. "The former Alastair MacGregor of Glenstrae, outlaw and chiefest offender. Patrick Aldoch MacGregor. William MacNeil MacGregor. Duncan Pudrach MacGregor. And Alastair MacEwan MacGregor. These here before us. They represent many others of the former and proscribed name. All notour law-breakers, now apprehended." He turned towards one end of the table. "I now call upon Sir Thomas Hamilton of Monkland, Advocate-Depute, to detail the charges."

A handsome youngish man rose, bowing to the court. "The crown's case, my lord and assize, is exceeding simple this day, and the issue should not detain you for long. These former MacGregors, I assert and charge, are guilty of wicked raiding, murder, ravishment, stealing of cattle, bearing of arms and other grievous offences. Also high treason, in that Letters of Fire and Sword were signed against them by King James himself, and they have made mockery of the declared royal will. However, your task, my lord and assize, is made easy and simplified by the confession of the principal accused, this Alastair, which indeed concedes all that you require to make judgment. The clerk will read it out to you, and you will no doubt perceive your due course and duty." He turned to the clerks' table. "Proceed."

He whom the day before had been so busy with his pen, cleared his throat and picked up his papers. "My lords," he said, faltering a little at first, "Hear this. 'I, Alastair MacGregor of Glenstrae, confess before God, that I have been persuaded, moved and enticed, as I am now presently accused and troubled, also –'"

Alastair interrupted him forcefully. "I protest! This is not a confession. It is a testimony, a statement, made by myself for the Privy Council, at their request. To explain my actions – "

"Silence!" The Justice-Depute banged his gavel loudly. "The accused will not speak unless instructed to do so. There will be no interruptions of this court. Proceed with the confession."

"Yes, my lord. '. . . also if I had used the counsel and command of the man who so enticed me, I would have done and committed sundry murders more –'"

"That man was Archibald Campbell, Earl of Argyll and Lieutenant of the North," Alastair announced, as strongly as before. "I – "

The gavel thumped and went on thumping. "I said silence!" the judge thundered. "One more word from you, sirrah, and you will be removed from this court and judgment made in your absence. My last warning. That applies to you all. Proceed, clerk."

The long testimony went on. Alastair recognised that it would serve no purpose to be banished from the proceedings, and with difficulty held his tongue. But he recognised also that his testimony had been most skilfully edited and amended. Most of it was indeed his own phrasing, but here and there vital words had been changed or cut out to make it sound like a confession of guilt. His references to Argyll, although not entirely deleted, were much reduced and toned down, to sound like the strivings of a guilty man to lay the blame on another, the fulminations of desperation and hatred. Alastair, fists clenched behind his back, shook his head at his fellow Gregorach helplessly.

At length the reading was over, and the Justice-Depute held out his hand for the papers, and then raised them.

"You, sirrah, admit that you wrote these words? And that the mark at the end is yours? You may speak – but only to this question."

"I wrote nothing. I do not write. I am MacGregor! I spoke most of the words there – but many have been changed, made to read differently."

"Enough! I said answer my questions only. You spoke much of this wording. And the mark at the end, a cross within a circle, is yours, as signature?"

"It is Christ's cross within the sun of life everlasting! To signify truth, as I value salvation. But these changed words – "

"Silence! We have had a sufficiency. The course is clear. No more wasting of time is required." The Justice turned to the fifteen on either side of him, none of whom had so far so much as opened their mouths. Presumably they constituted a jury, or assize. "You have it? This man confesses to the crimes libelled, and signs with his mark as truth, as before God. What need have we for more?"

"None! None!" came in a chorus from all of them – save one. The Menzies gazed down, unspeaking.

"So be it. The law is satisfied." The judge waved. "These other accused are mere tools of their chief. They are covered by his confession. No need to deal with them separately. All are murderers, ravishers and outlaws, meet for the most severe sentences of this court. Is that agreed?" He turned to an elderly man sitting on his right. "Your verdict, sir?"

This man rose. "I am John Blair of that Ilk and I speak for this assize. We find all guilty as libelled, for the crimes specified." He sat.

Colin Campbell raised his voice. "Agreed! Meet, right and our bounden duty!"

The others nodded and supported. But not Menzies of that Ilk.

Alastair raised *his* voice, since it could do no harm now. "The Menzies has not spoken!"

"Silence!" That was automatic. But the judge did glance at the Menzies chief.

That man seemed to take the command as applying to himself, for he did not open his lips. But he raised his eyes, to meet those of Alastair MacGregor, and for moments they gazed at each other, words unnecessary, agonised both in their different fashions.

"God pity *you*!" Alastair got out.

"Enough! This court declares all the accused guilty, and pronounces sentence of death for all. I call on the Doomster to do his duty, and to declare the sentence in detail as by law required."

From a corner of the courtroom an onlooker came forward, a stooping, old man clad all in black and carrying a black staff. This he thumped on the floor four times and then a fifth, and walked over to touch each of the accused briefly on the brow.

"I, James Henderson, Doomster, pronounce this for doom. The accused here before you will all suffer death by hanging. They will be taken to the Mercat Cross of this royal burgh of Edinburgh and there hanged by the neck on a gibbet until they be dead, the former Alastair raised a man's height higher than the others. Thereafter, heads, legs, arms and remaining parts to be quartered, and put upon spikes in public places about the realm, and their whole lands, heritages, rents, steadings, possessions, corns, cattle, goods and sums of moneys forfeited and taken for our sovereign-lord's use. This I do declare for doom!" The creature banged his staff again, bowed to the Justice-Depute and went back to his corner.

Alastair no longer sought to speak, nor did any of the condemned. Dignity, as Highlanders and descendants of the royal race of Alpin, was all that they had left. They stood, heads high, silent.

The judge rose, pointing to the guards.

Before they were hustled out, Alastair sought the eyes of the jurymen. Only those of Glenorchy the Younger met his own, steely, gleaming triumphant. They were exactly like those of his father, Black Duncan of the Cowl. No words were spoken.

The prisoners were hustled out of the Tolbooth and back up the High Street. And reaching the giant crucifix beside the Mercat Cross, they saw that, although hammering still went on completing the structure, it was already in use. For dangling on ropes from the long cross-bar were six tartan-clad figures, swinging in the breeze. These Gregorach had at least been spared the farce of that trial.

The prisoners eyed each other.

In his cell that night, alone again, Alastair pondered. He knew no despair now, no heart-searchings, no fears indeed – for he was in fact reconciled to his fate. He could acknowledge now that for long he had more or less anticipated and subconsciously prepared himself for some such ending to it all. He had struggled against it, yes, as had all his people. But their doom had been writ large long before ever that Doomster had pronounced it, the Children of the Mist bound for the mists of eternity. Whatever he, their chief, had done or failed to do, was highly unlikely to have averted the ultimate end. But they had put up a fair fight.

What he pondered was why? Why? Not that, or what, but why? Why evil, treachery, greed, falsity, should triumph? As so often it seemed to do. If a man believed in a loving God, as *he* did, why this? Man was given free will, yes, and so largely chose his own fate, at least here, in this life. And many chose the ill. Perhaps in the next life, the better one, they would learn better? Was that it? This one all but preparation for the next? How one coped with evil and hurt here, important for the next? It could be. If there was no evil, no hurt, no sorrow, what proving would there be? But . . . what of the evil-doers? What of them, when their time came? Would they receive their just dues? Due punishment? They had chosen the wrong road, not by chance or error but by intention. Would they have to tread that wrong road for all eternity? Surely not. Some retaliation, yes? Some remorse, at the least. Or, was that itself wrong thinking, wishing? For that God of love. What did *he* wish for Argyll, then? And Black Duncan? And Ardkinglas? And that young Colin Campbell? Endless suffering, one day? No, not that. That would make him black as he esteemed them! Not even he would wish that. So – forgiveness? Was that what the evil was for? Here and now. For forgiveness, for giving opportunity for forgiveness? Could *he* forgive? As he hoped to be forgiven his own sins and failures? He could try, he could try . . .

He was not afraid to die. Even thus, by hanging. And what they did to his body afterwards mattered not. He would be on his way, new ventures and prospects ahead. The dying was merely the gateway to that shining, better road. And hanging, dying on a gibbet, as those of his friends had done that day, and he would do on the morrow, was no worse than the dying they had all risked so often in warfare and the field of battle; better indeed, as a quicker death, with a broken neck, rather than slow, painful death after sword-thrust or dirk-stab. A better death than so many Gregorach had died. The shame of it was not theirs, but those who decreed it.

So they would go unafraid, and if *he* could, forgiving. He would have liked to say his goodbyes, especially to Mary Gray. Or . . . would he? That would have been an agony, worse than any neck-breaking. Misery and pain indeed. Why wish for that? Better this way. Theirs was a strange relationship. But good, good. One day, he somehow felt sure, they would meet again and take it onward. And Ludovick, that man forced to live a life he did not want because of his birth? Was he, Alastair, going thus, not in the end more fortunate than that duke? Going on to better fulfilment, where Vicky faced only long years of being that strange King's near kin, with all its constraints – and no marriage with the woman he loved. Who was the more to be envied?

Thus pondering, Alastair eventually slept, and peaceably.

They came for him in the later morning, and again his wrists were bound. Outside his four friends were awaiting him, bound likewise, but holding themselves proudly. Under heavy guard they were marched down into the town behind a single young drummer, who gave a regular, rhythmic, slow beat at every second pace.

It was not a long parade for them, with the populace already thronging the streets to watch, the word clearly spread through the city. Down that Lawnmarket again and into the High Street, where stood the Mercat Cross near the west gable of St Giles Kirk. There the huge crucifix-gibbet stood, cleared now of its six previous victims, noosed ropes already dangling. At one side was a platform on wheels, with a ladder incorporated.

The guard had to clear a way through the crowd to get to the gallows. Always the folk turned out to watch executions, sometimes angry, mocking, noisy. On this occasion there was only silence, save for the stirring of feet and the occasional child's voice raised in question.

At the foot of the gibbet stood three men, the Doomster, James Henderson, and two others, presumably the hangmen. Usually a clergyman was provided to hear a last confession of guilt and remorse and to commend to God's mercy; but in Reformed Scotland, no Catholic priests were to be encouraged to come and console their erring co-religionists. Anyway, these today were only Hielantmen.

So it was to business, without unsuitable delay, no lofty ones to wait for now, even though no doubt some might well be waiting and watching from convenient High Street windows. The drummer continued to beat, but paused when the Doomster thumped with his staff on the cobblestones. Henderson did not speak, but simply pointed upwards, at the gallows, effectively enough.

Alastair turned to his four companions. He was the Chief of Clan Alpin and must show an example. He mustered a smile of sorts, head high. He had the gesture returned.

"Gregorach!" he said simply.

"Gregorach! Gregorach!" came the response, strongly.

That was sufficient.

The two hangmen stepped out, to grasp and push. But this was not necessary. Alastair moved forward of his own accord, his friends following. Now that it had come to this, he was not uninterested to see how it all was done. He had never witnessed a hanging.

The wheeled platform with steps was trundled forward to stand below the great black crucifix, and the victims gestured to climb the ladder one of the hangmen leading, Alastair and the others next, the second executioner bringing up the rear. That made seven of them to take their places on the platform, fully thirty feet above the heads of the onlookers.

It was something of a crush, in that limited space. Carefully then the hangmen went to work with the five dangling ropes, placing the nooses round each neck and drawing the knots sufficiently tight and exactly placed at the back, where the jolt of the fall should break the junction of spine and skull. Alastair's rope was the shortest, and it hung from the top of the cross, whereas the others were attached to pegs in the transverse beam. That meant that these would fall in a swinging motion, where Alastair's would drop straight down. It was to be hoped that this sideways initial fall would not alter the knots' positions and effect the neck dislocations.

The drummer had resumed his dolorous beating.

The hangmen, first part of their duty accomplished, descended the steps, for the second and simpler part.

Alastair looked upward. He was facing westwards anyway. Up there was that castle, inevitably, of sorry experience; but far beyond and somewhat northwards, one hundred miles as the crow might fly, was Glen Strae and home. And, thirty miles nearer, Methven. Would he go winging that way in a few moments, on his road to a better land than even Scotland? He thought that he might. This forgiveness, now . . .? He could speak the word, at least – however unsure he was that he meant it.

The Doomster raised his staff, the drummer stopped, and the two hangmen stepped out to put shoulders to that wheeled-platform, and pushed hard. With a creaking rumble the contrivance jerked off eastwards from under the crucifix – and five tartan-clad bodies dropped swinging into eternity.

The drummer resumed his beat.

Historical Note

The hunting down of the MacGregors continued for some considerable time. As long as thirty years later commissions were issued to enforce the laws against the race, and bounties were still being paid for Gregorach heads. Nameless, the survivors had to call themselves Greig, Gregory, Grier, Grierson, Carse, Cass and numerous other surnames, particularly Murray. Some even adopted the hated name of Campbell; and the famous Rob Roy, whose mother was a Campbell of Glenlyon, had to subscribe himself Robert Roy Campbell on legal documents sixty years later. It was not until the end of the eighteenth century that the proscription of the name was eventually lifted, and those of the Children of the Mist who knew their ancestry could call themselves MacGregor again – although many, of course, the majority perhaps, retained their family's adopted names for convenience. The author's own mother was a Cass.

In 1774, John Murray, who had made a fortune in London, was successful in getting an Act of Parliament passed repealing the proscription, and was thereafter created a baronet, as Sir John Murray MacGregor. The Lyon Court then awarded him the arms and style of the chiefship. The present chief is Colonel Sir Gregor MacGregor of MacGregor, sixth Baronet, suitably a distinguished soldier.

As for the Campbells, on the whole they retained their ability to prosper, although not always so. Argyll's son, the eighth earl, espoused the cause of the Covenant against Charles the First, after being created first Marquis of Argyll. He managed to bring to execution in 1650 the great James Graham, Marquis of Montrose, his enemy; but he himself was executed at the Restoration of Charles the Second. His descendant, however, was created first Duke of Argyll and was another noted soldier, commanding the government forces against the Old Pretender at the fatal Battle of Sheriffmuir in the Rising of 1715; but curiously, he kept quiet links with the Jacobites, and was a friend of Rob Roy's. The present esteemed MacCailean Mhor, the twelfth duke, still lives at Inveraray Castle, is Hereditary Lord Justice General of Scotland and Admiral of the Western Seas.

As for the Glenorchy Campbells, their story is also dramatic. They achieved Black Duncan's dream of being able to ride on their own land from Atlantic salt water to that of the North Sea. He was made a baronet in 1625. Sir John Campbell, eleventh of Glenorchy was created, first, Earl of Caithness in 1677. But one of the original Sinclair family establishing the right to that title, the earldom was changed to that of Breadalbane four years later. The fourth earl was created Marquis of Breadalbane in 1831, but the marquisate became extinct in 1922 and the earldom came to a kinsman. Since then there has been a great diminution of the line's wealth and power, and the present Earl of Breadalbane and Viscount Glenorchy is no longer a great Highland landowner.

Sic transit gloria mundi! Or should it be *Fata viam invenient*?

NIGEL TRANTER

CRUSADER

Alexander the Third of Scotland was just seven when he inherited the throne. South of the border, England's King Henry the Third saw this as his chance to assert his paramountcy over the kingdom. At the age of ten, the boy was married to Henry's daughter.

But, through the hazards of power politics and dynastic marriage – as well as the more natural hazards of lively adolescence – one man stood by the young monarch.

Whether it was shooting the wild geese, helping him escape from the prisonlike confines of Edinburgh Castle or teaching him to stand up both to his ever-threatening English father-in-law and the unending feuds of his own countrymen, David de Lindsay, of Luffness in East Lothian, was his one true and constant friend.

The rolling Lothian and Border country and its compelling history are both brought marvellously to life in Nigel Tranter's magnificent account of a young boy and his destiny.

'Tranter's style is compelling and his research scrupulous. He reaches down the ages to breathe life into his characters.'

Frank Peters, *Daily Telegraph*

Royal Mail service in association with the Book Marketing Council & The Booksellers Association.
Post-A-Book is a Post Office trademark.

MORE NIGEL TRANTER TITLES AVAILABLE
FROM HODDER AND STOUGHTON PAPERBACKS